LORI WILDE

CHARMED AND DANGEROUS

"With a deft hand, Wilde blends humor and suspense, passion and mystery into a story both charming and dangerous." —BookLoons.com

"Quite the exciting romp. Fans will be charmed." —*RT Book Reviews*

"Witty...the chemistry between David and Maddie is hot enough to satisfy those looking for light summer reading." —*Publishers Weekly*

"Sexy, fun...Had me laughing out loud and sitting on the edge of my seat...If you're looking for the perfect summer read, look no further. Lori Wilde has already written it." —TheBestReviews.com

MISSION: IRRESISTIBLE

"Wilde is back with another wild and offbeat tale that combines curses, soul mates, and zany adventure. This novel has a nice balance of humor, sexy romance, and a large splash of danger—all fun stuff." —*RT Book Reviews*

"A funny, sexy romance."

—FreshFiction.net

"Ms. Wilde has penned another winner...I honestly do not remember the last time I was so immersed in a story...[The] combination of the legend, the modern day mystery and the romance was simply irresistible."

—FallenAngelReviews.com

DOUBLE
Trouble

DOUBLE
Trouble

LORI WILDE

FOREVER

NEW YORK   BOSTON

Forever
Hachette Book Group
1290 Avenue of the Americas
New York, NY 10104

www.HachetteBookGroup.com

Printed in the United States of America

First Edition: December 2014
10 9 8 7 6 5 4 3 2 1

OPM

Forever is an imprint of Grand Central Publishing.
The Forever name and logo are trademarks of Hachette Book Group, Inc.

The Hachette Speakers Bureau provides a wide range of authors for speaking events. To find out more, go to www.hachettespeakersbureau.com or call (866) 376-6591.

The publisher is not responsible for websites (or their content) that are not owned by the publisher.

Charmed and Dangerous

To my father, Fred Blalock, who nurtured my love of reading and mentored my budding writing talent. And to my mother, Francis Maxine Reid Blalock, who gave me the iron-will to succeed. Thank you. I love you both more than words can say.

Acknowledgments

Many thanks are in order for my wonderful editor Michele Bidelspach for sending me back to the drawing board after the first draft wasn't quite as good as it could have been. Thank you, Michele, for challenging me to dig deeper.

Prologue

North Central Texas
Christmas Day, eighteen years ago

It was turning out to be the worst day of Maddie Cooper's nine-year-old life.

For one thing she hadn't gotten the super cool purple-and-white Nikes she'd wanted for Christmas. Instead she wound up with a stupid half-a-heart necklace that matched the one her identical twin sister wore. Why was Mama always trying to turn her into a prissy girly-girl like Cassie?

For another thing, she'd wanted to go running in Granddad's cow pasture so she could pout by herself, but oh, no, Mama said she had to let Cassie come along.

As if her lazybones twin could even run. How was a girl supposed to become a famous track and field Olympic athlete if she couldn't practice in peace?

And then came the icing on the cupcake.

"Maddie, make sure you take good care of Cassie," Mama called from the back porch. She stood shivering in her see-through lace blouse, black leather mini-skirt and spike-heeled boots because she and Daddy were going to a party.

"How come I always gotta look after Cassie and she don't ever have to look after me?"

"You know why," her mother chided.

Yeah. She knew why. Because if left on her own, Cassie did dumb stuff like taping peacock feathers to her arms and jumping off the roof to see if she could fly.

Maddie marched through the pasture, her breath coming out in frosty white puffs. Cassie trailed along behind her, humming some goofy *Sesame Street* song. Gramma had bundled them up like marshmallows in their matching goose down coats and knit scarves. The only difference between them was Cassie wore rubber boots while Maddie had on her well-worn Pumas.

"Look," Cassie said. "The stock pond's frozen."

"Stay away from there." Maddie stopped beside an oak tree, took off her coat and then placed a palm flat against the trunk to keep her balance while she stretched. "Gramma says there's nothing more dangerous than an iced-over stock pond in Texas. It never freezes solid enough to hold your weight."

"Aw, pah." Cassie waved a hand and toddled out onto the slick surface. "Look at me! I'm skating."

Maddie rolled her eyes and refused to glance over. She was too busy limbering up her hamstrings and being mad. "Get off the pond, Cassie."

"You're not the boss of me."

"Mama told me to take care of you. That makes me the boss of you."

"Pfftt." Cassie gave her the raspberry.

"Get off the ice."

"Stop telling me what to do. Look, look, I'm in the Ice Capades."

"I'm not watching." Maddie folded her arms over her chest and turned to face the opposite direction.

"Good. Fine. Don't watch."

"I won't."

"You're boring anyway. I wish you weren't my sister."

"Me too!"

Maddie took off running, her sneakers slapping against the ground. Anger poked her hard in the ribs and that stupid necklace bounced off her chest and smacked her in the chin. She fisted her hand around the chain, snapped it from her neck and flung the heart into a clump of prickly yucca.

She ran until she got a stitch in her side. By then she was on the opposite side of the pasture. She heard a scary cracking noise. Loud as Granddad's rifle when he shot doves.

"Maddie!" Cassie screamed. And then she heard a splash.

"Cassie?" Maddie whirled around, scanning the distant pond. Her heart went boom-boom-boom in her ears.

No sign of her sister.

"Cassie!" Her frantic shout echoed back to her.

She didn't remember much about what happened next. She hurtled toward the pond, spying the gaping hole in the middle of the ice, but no Cassie. Not knowing what else to do, she sprinted to the house for Granddad and Gramma.

Granddad fished Cassie from the water. Her lips were blue and her skin was the color of snow and she wasn't breathing. Granddad blew air in Cassie's mouth until the ambulance came.

The next time Maddie saw her twin she was lying oh-so-still in a hospital bed. A machine was helping her breathe and other awful-looking tubes poked out of her.

Mama sat in a chair by Cassie's bed, holding her hand and crying. Daddy smelled like beer and his eyes were red. He kept walking back and forth and running his hands through his hair. Neither of her parents spoke to her. Maddie knew this was all her fault.

Why wouldn't Cassie wake up?

A doctor came into the room. He said Cassie might never wake up. Mama and Daddy stayed at the hospital. Granddad and Gramma took Maddie back to their house.

They put her to bed with hugs and kisses. They told her she wasn't to blame, but she didn't believe them. It was all her fault. Mama told her to take good care of her sister and she hadn't. She should have made Cassie get off the ice. She shouldn't have yelled at her. She shouldn't have run away.

What if Cassie never woke up? What if her sister died?

She sobbed low in her throat and reached up to touch the half-a-heart necklace to remind her she was one part of a twin set and realized the necklace was gone. She'd thrown it away.

Terror grabbed her stomach and Maddie thought she was going to throw up. Desperate to find the necklace, she crawled out of bed. She put on her coat, took her granddad's flashlight from its place by the back door and sneaked out into the pitch-black, ice-cold night.

She searched the pasture for what seemed like hours, digging through every clump of yucca she could find, getting poked through her gloves by the sharp leaves. Her teeth chattered from the cold. Her toes were numb. But she didn't care. When at last she found the necklace, Maddie let out a gasp of relief and burst into tears.

Dropping to her knees on the frozen earth, she tilted her face upward, beseeching the midnight sky.

"Dear God," she prayed and clutched the necklace to her heart. "I didn't mean those ugly things I said to Cassie. I love her. If you please just let her wake up, I swear I won't never ever let her get hurt again!"

Chapter 1

FBI special agent David Marshall loved a good fight and he played to win.

Always.

His personal credo: *He who hesitates is lost*. And David hated losing more than anything.

Whenever a situation called for action, he immediately seized control and bluffed his way through the consequences. Usually victoriously. He'd learned at an early age you had to battle hard against life or die. He had also discovered, that for the good of the cause, you occasionally had to bend a few rules.

But once in a while, one of his less prudent rule bending episodes came back to bite him viciously in the ass.

Like now.

Where in the hell was Cassie Cooper?

For the tenth time in as many minutes, David checked his wristwatch.

With an impatient snort, he sank his fists on his hips and scanned the rendezvous spot. Forest Park on the Trinity River, fourth picnic bench at the seven-mile marker of the jogging trail, eight A.M. sharp.

It was now eight-thirteen.

Had Cassie gotten mixed up about their meeting place? It was highly possible. The woman personified dumb blonde jokes.

Which was why the art theft task force had rejected using her as an informant. Even though Cassie was a public relations specialist at the Kimbell Art Museum and they knew Peyton Shriver had marked her as his next sweetheart victim.

Realizing that Cassie was the best lead he'd had on Shriver in years, David had taken matters into his own hands. He'd gone behind his boss's back and recruited her. No one except he and Cassie knew about her involvement in the case. Not even the men he had shadowing her. His men believed they were simply tailing her because she was Peyton's new girlfriend. Because of this, all their previous contact except for the initial meeting had been via phone or e-mail. He would deal with the fallout of his unorthodox police methods once he had Shriver securely in handcuffs. It was always easier to get Jim Barnes's forgiveness than his permission.

For ten years he'd been doggedly pursuing Shriver. The time had come to end this battle of wills. With Cassie's help, he'd known he was going to win it.

Come hell or high water he was determined to see justice served.

But last night his surveillance team had delivered bad news. They'd observed Shriver meeting with a world-class scumbag by the name of Jocko Blanco. The creep was a tattooed, pock-faced skinhead with a rap sheet as thick as a telephone book and a history of violent behavior.

Shriver might be a heartbreaking cad and an unrepentant thief, but he'd never physically harmed any of his victims. In fact, his courtly behavior was legendary. Blanco on the other hand was as dangerous as dynamite near an open flame.

Upon hearing the news about Blanco and Shriver hooking up, his first thought had been totally selfish. Yes! Two criminals for the price of one. That would show his boss he'd been right to make an end run around authority by involving Cassie Cooper.

But then his irritating conscience had voiced its opinion: *You can't keep her on the case.*

As eager as she might be to help him bring down Shriver, frivolous Cassie was no match for the likes of Jocko Blanco.

Regretfully, he had to terminate Cassie's mission. No matter how much he lusted to see Shriver cooling his heels in the slammer, he couldn't justify jeopardizing her life.

David shoved a hand through his hair and paced to the edge of the embankment on the opposite side of the jogging trail. He stared down at the thin ribbon of river several hundred feet below and then he swung his gaze through the rest of the vacant park.

Not too many people out and about this early on a damp, blustery February day. A couple of joggers off in the distance, an elderly man letting his dog take a leak on the trashcan near the park entrance, but no one else.

A heart-stopping thought occurred to him. What if Shriver had discovered Cassie was spying on him for the FBI? What if he had actually hired Blanco to bump her off?

Icy chills shot up his spine.

"Dammit, Cassie." He glowered, royally pissed off at himself.

He shouldn't have arranged a meeting. Instead of setting up the rendezvous, he should have just told her over the phone he was pulling her off the case. But he'd needed the tape she'd recorded of Shriver bragging about his exploits. Besides, David thought it only fair he break the news to her in person.

Where in the hell *was* Cassie?

He glanced at his watch again. Eight-fifteen.

Mindlessly, he reached to pat the breast pocket of his London Fog trench coat in search of the cigarettes that were no longer there.

It had been almost a year since he'd kicked the butts but in times of stress the old nicotine hankering still lingered. He'd given up the cigs not long after his ex- fiancée Keeley dumped him. Not because he still had a thing for her and was trying to win her back. No, that ship had sailed. In fact, she married an orthodontist not two months after they had broken up. Nope, he'd quit smoking simply to prove her wrong.

"Face it, David," Keeley told him the day she'd dramatically yanked off her engagement ring and tossed it in his face. "Your obsessive need to tempt fate and win at all costs is going to be the death of you. And I refuse to hang around and watch it happen."

"I don't have an obsessive need to tempt fate," he'd protested.

"Ha! Look, you can't even stop smoking long enough to have this conversation with me," she'd crowed. "What's puffing on a cancer stick, if not tempting fate?"

So he had quit smoking. He was at least going to win that argument.

But although he was loath to admit it, maybe Keeley had a point. If Cassie's subversive involvement ended up botching the investigation, his boss would have his head.

And his job.

Shriver would get away and David would lose.

Shit.

At that moment, a woman jogger appeared from under the train trestle. She was too far away for David to see her facial features, but his baser male instincts homed in on the luscious body striding rhythmically toward him.

Boobs bouncing in spite of the sports bra, blond ponytail swishing, hips rolling forward.

Mama mia, come to Papa.

And then she drew close enough for him to recognize.

Cassie. Thank God. Relief rolled over him.

He stared at her.

And she ran right by him without a second glance.

Dumbfounded, David's jaw dropped as he gazed after her retreating figure.

What in hell...?

He quickly looked in the direction from which she'd come to see if anyone was following her. Nobody. Hadn't she seen him standing there?

Perplexed, David trotted after her. "Hold up," he called.

She swiveled her head, saw he was following and started running faster.

Dammit. What game was the woman playing?

"Stop," he commanded, even as he sped up to cover the increasing distance between them. Damn, but she was in some kind of shape. Who knew?

He was running flat out by the time he caught her. He grabbed her by the elbow and spun her around to face him. They were standing on the edge of the embankment, both panting hard, their gazes locked.

Before David could suck in his breath long enough to speak, she whipped a can of mace from the pocket of her sweat top.

She was quick, but David was quicker.

"Oh no you don't," he said and clamped his hand over her pepper-spray-clutching fist before she had time to depress the nozzle. He wrenched the can away from her. "What's the matter with you?"

"Hands off, buddy," she commanded and jerked backward.

The force of her momentum was so strong she teetered unbalanced on the edge, a look of shock passing over her face.

"Oh," she cried, her arms windmilling wildly. "Oh."

Reaching for her, David grabbed at the first thing he could get his hands on. He ended up snatching the front of her workout pants, attempting to reel her in like an unruly tarpon.

She flailed. The material of her pants stretched out, exposing her naked skin, and David swiftly learned that not only was she wearing pink satin G-string undies, but that she was also a natural blond.

He blinked, his mind momentarily numbed with the breathtaking view.

"Hi-ya!" she yelled and aimed a foot at his crotch.

He dodged her kick but the movement sent him reeling off balance too.

Gravity took over and plunged them both headlong toward the river.

"Oh, crap," David muttered, finally realizing she wasn't Cassie. This spunky woman could be none other than her identical twin sister, Maddie.

The big man had an even bigger gun.

Maddie felt the hard delineation under his coat as they rolled down the wet, rocky knoll together. Her heart practically hammered out of her chest. He was going to rape her, shoot her and throw her in the river for fish bait. She just knew it.

For years, she'd been running in Forest Park unscathed, but as the cautious type who believed in always being prepared, she had an ongoing contingency plan.

Mace 'em in the face, kick 'em in the nuts, haul ass.

What had gone wrong?

Well, for starters the guy outweighed her by a good eighty pounds, but even so he was quicker than a cobra.

Do something now. Fight back. You can't die and leave Cassie alone.

As they rolled downhill, Maddie made a feral sound low in her throat and clawed at his face. Too bad she kept her fingernails clipped short. As soon as she had a chance, she'd go for the car keys in her pants pocket and gouge his eyes out.

"Ouch, damn, hell," he cursed. "Quit that."

They came to a stop just short of the water, his big body crushing hers into the muddy riverbank.

"Get off me you rapist pervert." She slapped at his chest and tried not to panic when her hand smacked against his shoulder holster.

Lungs heaving with the effort of drawing in air, he grabbed her wrists and pinned her hands above her head while straddling her. Uselessly, she tried to buck him off, but his weight held her prisoner.

"Maddie," he roared. "That's enough!"

She froze and stared into his potent dark eyes. A spark of sexual awareness, so intense it left her stunned, surged between them.

"How...how," she stammered. "Do you know my name?"

"I thought you were Cassie," he said.

"Oh." She blinked at him, letting this information sink in. "Let me guess, you two were playing some kind of kinky sex game in the park and it got out of hand?"

"What?" He frowned.

"Cassie's into all that red hot pursuit stuff. You must be her new boyfriend."

"No, I'm not."

They were pressed chest to chest, their lips almost touching. He had an unusually complicated mouth. The outer shape was angular and uncompromising, like some sort of hardware store tool, but at the same time the actual flesh of his lips appeared smooth, soft and inviting. His mouth, she decided, had a personality all its own.

"Then who are you?" Maddie snapped, almost as mad at herself as she was at him.

"David Marshall. FBI."

FBI? At least that explained the gun. What kind of trouble was her twin in now?

Cassie had told Maddie to meet her in the park at eight-fifteen because she had big news to share. Maddie had scheduled her morning run to coincide with the rendezvous. But her twin wasn't at the appointed spot and this bearish man claiming to be with the FBI was. The whole thing smelled fishier than the Trinity River.

"Let me see some identification," she said.

"Only if you promise not to knee me in the groin when I turn you loose."

"All right," she agreed warily, even though she had no intention of keeping her promise if she felt threatened in the slightest.

He released her hands and pushed up on his knees. Maddie lay on her back, head cocked, watching his every move and making sure he didn't go for his gun. Just because he said he was FBI, didn't mean he *was* FBI.

As she studied his face, she realized he was rather good-looking in a rugged, unkempt sort of way. He was tall and muscular with a granite jaw and chiseled cheekbones that, oddly enough, lent him a sensitive air. He wore his sandy brown hair clipped short and spiked up. She kind of liked the kingfisher thing he had going on, not that she was really noticing. His nose was neither too big nor too small for his face, but it crooked slightly to the left at the bridge as if he'd used it once or twice to stop an irate fist.

He got to his feet and held out his hand to help her up.

She hesitated.

He just kept standing there, hand outstretched.

Reluctantly, she accepted his offer of assistance and he hauled her to a standing position. Once on her feet, she immediately turned away from him.

"Hold on," he said, his skin still branding hers.

"What is it?" she snapped.

"You've got mud on your clothing."

And then, before she knew what he was doing, he reached out and briskly brushed off her bottom.

The touch of his palm against the smooth stretchy Lycra of her workout pants sent a shower of sexual sparks scorching up her backside. Maddie swallowed hard against the storm of sensation flooding her body.

Seriously dangerous stuff.

"There you go." He released her arm. "All dusted clean."

She gulped and her stomach lurched because her butt kept tingling long after his hand was gone. "Your badge?" she said, determined not to let him distract her.

"I'm getting to it." He removed his badge from his coat pocket and flashed it in front of her face.

She held out her palm.

"You wanna hold it?"

"Yes."

He rolled his eyes, but handed it to her. She traced a finger across the emblem. The badge winked goldly at her in the shaft of hopeful sunlight struggling through the cloud covering. It looked real enough, but she wasn't taking any chances. She'd heard about psychos who posed as law enforcement authorities and committed crimes.

"You won't mind if I call the local FBI division and check you out?"

"For crying out loud, woman." He snatched his badge from her hand. "I am who I say I am."

"Don't get testy, bub. You were the one who attacked me."

"Excuse me?" he raised his voice and glared. "Who pulled out the pepper spray and who tried to kick me in the family jewels?"

"You chased me down," she protested.

"After I asked you nicely to stop and you ignored me."

"Because you were a weird guy alone in the park."

"Weird? *You're* calling *me* weird?" He jerked a thumb at himself.

"Ya-huh."

He was studying her as intently as she was studying him, his gaze practically burning a hole through her bottom lip. What did he think of her mouth? Did he find it as interesting as she found his? Her heart was tripping a gazillion beats a minute and a bizarre sensation twisted her stomach.

Good grief! What had come over her?

He moistened his lips and swallowed. "You're nuttier than your sister, you know that?"

"My sister is not nutty," Maddie declared defensively. Impulsive, yes. Irresponsible, well at times. Impractical, that was a given. But he had no right to call Cassie nutty.

"She's a frickin' sack of cashews and tardy to boot. She was supposed to meet me here at eight o'clock and it is now..." He paused to glance at his watch. "Eight-twenty-five."

"Why were you meeting her?"

He hesitated.

She could see that he didn't want to tell her any more than he had to. "Well?" she demanded.

"Your twin was working for me. We were attempting to get the goods on an international art thief named Peyton Shriver."

"Get outta here."

"I am deadly serious."

"Cassie? Working for the FBI?"

An uneasy expression that she could not decipher crossed his face. "In an unofficial capacity."

"What exactly does that mean?" Maddie narrowed her eyes. She didn't like the sound of this. Not one bit.

"Look," he said, changing the subject and confirming her suspicion that something wasn't on the up and up. "Have you heard from your sister this morning? I've tried repeatedly to call her. Do you have any idea where she's at?"

"How was Cassie helping you catch this art thief?" Maddie asked, switching the subject right back again. He'd have to be slicker than that if he wanted to pull the wool over her eyes.

"Shriver had pegged Cassie as his next mark and he was courting her hot and heavy."

Maddie shook her head. "I'm not totally following you. If you know who and where the guy is, why don't you just arrest him?"

"Lack of concrete evidence. We need to catch him in the act. Plus, we suspect an influential art broker is backing his little forays and we want to nail that guy too. Your sister is helping me tighten the noose. Now where is she?"

"Exactly how is she doing this?"

He sighed. "You're not going to tell me where Cassie might be until I disclose everything, are you?"

"You got that right."

He growled softly and the sound was so electric it seemed to push right under her skin. Maddie forced herself not to shudder with perverse delight. What was it about this guy that simultaneously repelled yet attracted her?

"Okay, here's the deal."

Maddie could tell he begrudged having to fill her in. Well, too bad. If he wanted information from her, he'd have to pony up with some of his own.

The wind gusted cold and she felt her nipples bead beneath her sweat top. David was staring at her chest but trying to pretend he wasn't.

"You wanna go sit in my car?" He gestured up the hill toward the parking lot. The breeze tousled his already spiky hair, giving him a roguish look.

She shook her head and crossed her arms over her chest.

"I promise I won't bite."

Her natural cautiousness outweighed her desire for warmth. "I'm fine. Your story?"

"I've been tracking Shriver for years, but he's pretty damned slick."

"Slicker than you obviously." Maddie knew she was

aggravating him, but she couldn't seem to help herself. Call it retribution for the way his rugged good looks provoked her heretic hormones.

David glared. "Do you want to hear this or not?"

"Go on."

"Peyton Shriver is thirty-eight, a native of Liverpool, England," he said. "His father was a petty criminal who fell in with a dangerous crowd, got involved in armed robbery and ended up a lifer. His mother was an alcoholic who was run down by a truck on her way home from the liquor store when Shriver was ten."

"Poor kid."

"Save your sympathy. Shriver's aunt Josephine took him in. She lived in New York City and she'd married into money. She didn't have any kids of her own and she doted on her charming nephew. When Josephine died, her husband cut Shriver off without a cent. Desperate for a way to support the lifestyle he'd come to enjoy, he launched a series of sweetheart scams, focusing mainly on older women."

"What's that got to do with my sister?"

"Hold on. I'm getting to that. There was one victim in particular. Her family once had a great deal of money, but the fortune had been squandered over the years. She had planned on funding her retirement with the last remaining family heirloom, a Rembrandt worth close to a million dollars. Shriver romanced her, then waltzed away with the painting."

Something in his expression, something in the way his body tensed told Maddie this case meant more to him than just business. He'd flattened out his lips, fisted his hands and broadened his stance, as if secretly readying himself for a fight.

Had he known the woman with the Rembrandt? Was his pursuit of Shriver as much about revenge as duty?

"After that theft, Shriver dropped out of sight for several years," David said.

"Living off the money from the Rembrandt," Maddie guessed.

He nodded. "A few months ago a new spate of art thefts bearing Shriver's unique pretty boy signature—but focusing mainly on museum employees rather than rich women with private collections as before—began cropping up all over Europe. The FBI has been working closely with Interpol and we've tracked Shriver to Fort Worth. He's been casing the Kimbell and he started a relationship with Cassie."

"He's using her," Maddie said flatly.

"Yes."

"But you're using her too."

"Okay," he admitted. "But I only approached her because Shriver is completely nonviolent. He's never hurt any of the women he's charmed."

"What about those other women? Why didn't you recruit them? Why single out my sister?"

"None of the other victims would testify against him and Cassie was not only willing, but eager to help."

"Why am I not surprised," Maddie muttered under her breath.

"With Cassie's assistance, I had a good chance of foiling the robbery and finally putting Shriver away for a very long time."

"Had?" His tone made her nervous.

David cleared his throat. "Yesterday I discovered an old friend of Shriver's had blown into town."

"Yeah?"

"The guy's name is Jocko Blanco. He's also a thief, among other things."

"What sort of other things?" she asked, even though she was afraid to hear the answer.

"Armed robbery, gun running, drug smuggling. You name it, he's done it."

"Even physical violence?" Maddie croaked.

He paused. "I'm afraid so."

She felt the blood drain from her face and her head spun dizzily.

"Don't panic," David said. "I was meeting Cassie to pull her off the case and offer her police protection."

"But she hasn't shown up." Maddie swept a hand at the empty park, the old familiar dread flooding through her body.

"No, she hasn't."

She gulped. This wasn't good news. Not good at all.

David's cell phone drolly played the theme from *Dragnet*.

"Do you think it could be Cassie?" Maddie asked. "Does she have your cell phone number?"

"She does." He yanked the phone from his coat pocket and glanced at the small display screen. "But it's not her." He flipped the phone open. "Marshall here."

She studied him while he listened to the voice on the other end of the conversation. His countenance changed from dangerous rebel slouch to full-on badass cop posture. He pressed his mouth into a hard, uncompromising line. His gray eyes turned as moody as the heavy clouds brooding overhead. He swore viciously and kicked at a rock.

Alarmed, Maddie backed up, distancing herself.

"I'll be right there," he barked into the receiver and

then switched off the phone before jamming it back into his pocket.

"What is it?" she asked, knowing in her heart of hearts something was terribly wrong. She imagined a dozen what if scenarios, each more grisly than the last and all of them involving Cassie's safety. She sank her fingers into David's forearm and squeezed tight. "Tell me the truth. What's happened?"

He met her gaze with an uncompromising stare. "Some time during the early morning hours, Peyton Shriver used your sister's security clearance to break into the Kimbell Art Museum, override the alarm system and steal a Cézanne worth four million dollars."

Chapter 2

With single-minded purpose, David spun on his heel and scrambled up the embankment toward his car. That bastard Shriver had trumped him again.

"But the game's not over yet, you sonofabitch," David muttered under his breath. "Not by a long shot."

His neck flamed hot with anger. He had to get to the museum and find out exactly what had gone wrong. Cassie was supposed to give him a heads up if she suspected Shriver was about to make his move. But she hadn't.

Why not?

He didn't like the answers his gut flung at him. There were two obvious choices. Either Cassie was in deep danger or she'd thrown her lot in with Shriver. He could easily see flamboyant Cassie entertaining some *Thomas Crown Affair* fantasy about the guy. After all, Shriver was quite the rakish charmer.

Either scenario spelled mucho trouble.

"Hey wait, where you goin'?" Maddie scurried along beside him.

"To the Kimbell," he said, without looking over at her. The stubborn woman possessed the potential to become a royal pain-in-the-ass and he wasn't going to encourage her.

"What about my sister?"

"What about her?" he asked, slapping back the guilt digging into his conscience. He had no use for regrets. He made a decision, committed to a course of action and accepted the drawbacks. Only weak men second-guessed themselves.

"Where is she?"

"How should I know?"

"I'm coming with you."

"Don't you have to go to work or something?"

"I own my own gym. I'll call my manager and have her arrange for someone else to teach my exercise classes."

"You can't come."

"Why not?"

"I'm too busy to mess around with you."

"You owe me," she said, puffing up the hill beside him, matching his stride step for step.

"How do you figure?"

He hesitated just long enough to glare at her and wished he hadn't. The determined set of her jaw caused him to think wickedly inappropriate thoughts. Like what would she do if he hooked a finger under that tenacious little chin, tilted her face up to meet his and kissed her hard?

She'd probably sock you in the breadbasket.

Probably.

"You shoved me off a cliff."

"That was an accident."

"You involved Cassie with a criminal."

"What's that got to do with you?"

"We're twins."

"And...?"

Maddie tossed her head and her ponytail flicked provocatively from shoulder to shoulder. "Obviously, you don't understand the bond. We're exceedingly close."

"If you two are so chummy, how come Cassie didn't tell you she was working for me?"

She blinked. "I suppose you swore her to secrecy."

"Nope." This time she frowned. David could see it was bugging the hell out of her that her twin hadn't confided in her. "I do know one thing about Cassie."

"And what is that?" Maddie asked suspiciously.

"She was raring to prove herself to somebody and after making your acquaintance, I'm guessing that somebody is you."

"What's that supposed to mean?" Her emerald green eyes flared a warning.

"I don't have time for this." He stalked toward the Impala. "She's your sister, you figure it out."

"Wait, wait, wait." She placed a restraining hand on his shoulder.

"What?" He wanted to brush her off but he was afraid of what might happen to his libido if he touched her. Disconcerted, he stepped back and she voluntarily removed her hand.

"I've been abrupt," she said. "I'm just worried about my sister. Please forgive me."

"You're forgiven." He punched the alarm control on his keypad and his car chirped twice indicating the doors were unlocked.

"Great." She hurried around to the passenger side.

"Oh, no, no, no." He quickly reactivated the locks just as she reached for the handle.

"You're still not taking me with you?"

"That's right." He unlocked the driver's side the old-fashioned way and slid behind the wheel, but before he could get the door shut and the car started, Maddie flew over to jam her body between him and the door. She wrapped her fingers around the steering wheel, anchoring herself to his vehicle.

"You're fast," he said.

"And don't you forget it."

"Physical talents aside, you're staying here." He keyed the ignition and the engine rumbled to life.

"You're a rude, rude man."

"Bingo. Now get out of the way if you don't want me to back over you."

"Okay, you asked for it. I didn't want to have to resort to dirty tactics, but you've forced my hand."

"Are you threatening me?" He narrowed his eyes and met her gaze. Damn if a thrill of sexual excitement didn't blast straight through his groin. Nothing tickled him more than a worthy opponent.

"Yes I am."

"Bring it on."

"I will."

"I think you're bluffing."

"I never bluff."

He eyed her for a long moment. "What do you have up your sleeve?"

"I'll got to the media. Tell them that you involved a private citizen in your cops-and-robbers game and now she's missing."

"She's not missing."

Maddie waved a hand at the empty park. "You see her anywhere?"

"She's a flake. Maybe she just forgot."

"You know better than that," she chided. "Admit it, you screwed up, David Marshall. You placed my sister's life in peril when you recruited her to spy on your art thief."

She was right. And he loathed her rightness. He couldn't allow her to go to the media. They would be all over this story like hot on chili peppers.

And then his boss would be all over him.

He couldn't let Shriver win. No way, no how. Better to tolerate this smart-mouthed pop tart than ruin years of detective work.

"Take me with you or I go to the news stations," she reiterated.

"You wouldn't dare." He felt obligated to call her bluff one more time, test her commitment before giving her the green light.

"When it comes to my twin sister, I'll dare anything." The look on her face told him that she was dead serious. He admired her devotion to her sibling while at the same time he cursed it.

"This is not the optimal way to get in good with me." He glowered, doing his best to quell her with a withering glance.

"I could care less about getting in good with you." She defiantly thrust out her chest, which just happened to be at his eye level.

Trying hard not to notice what a truly exceptional pair of ta-tas she possessed and fantasizing about how they would look out of that sports bra and in a low cut va-va-va-voom dress, David clenched his jaw and unlocked the passenger door.

"Get in."

"Thank you." Tossing her head, she pranced around the car and climbed inside. David slammed the Impala into reverse and plowed out of the parking space, tires squealing as he burned rubber.

Fuck! He hated this. Bested twice in one morning.

David made Maddie wait in the employee lounge of the Kimbell Art Museum while he and his team assessed the crime scene. She was none too happy about it.

Before they got out of the car, he'd threatened to handcuff her to the steering wheel if she didn't agree to obey his orders. The 'I've-reached-the-limits-of-my-patience-don't-push-me-one-more-millimeter' expression on his face told her that he meant every word.

And then, just to rub his power in her face, he'd positioned one of the museum security guards in the doorway to keep her from wandering off and doing a little investigating of her own. Jeez. You'd think he didn't trust her.

Stuck with the situation, she had called her assistant and asked her to find a replacement instructor for the remainder of the week. She had no idea how long it was going to take to resolve this thing with Cassie, but it was better to be prepared for the worst.

She spent the remainder of the time calling all of Cassie's friends to see if they knew where she was, pacing the lounge and imagining the most terrible things when no one had heard from her. What if Shriver had taken Cassie hostage? What if this Blanco person had hurt her sister and she was lying helpless somewhere calling Maddie's name?

She reached up to finger the half-a-heart necklace she never took off. *Hang on, Cassie. Never fear. I'll find you.*

"Maddie."

She glanced over to see David standing in the doorway looking grim. Immediately, she was at his side. "What is it?"

"I sent a man over to Cassie's apartment."

"Was she there?" Maddie bit down hard on her bottom lip. Don't worry, don't panic, until there's something to panic about.

He shook his head. "The place was turned upside down."

"Ransacked?"

"No. It looked more like she had packed in a hurry."

"What are you saying?"

"You might want to prepare yourself for the possibility that Cassie has switched sides and become Shriver's accomplice."

Maddie shook her head. "No way."

"I'm going to search her locker. I thought you might want to be present," he said quietly.

For the first time since she'd met him, Maddie saw a look of compassion in his eyes. His sympathy scared her more than his aggressiveness. He was being way too nice. Why?

"Let's go," she said.

They stepped into the corridor together and that's when she saw the extent of his entourage. A half-dozen Fort Worth cops, a couple of plainclothes detectives, the mayor, the police chief, the museum curator and two other FBI agents.

Oh boy.

The curator gave her a pink plastic shopping bag decorated with black-and-white Picassos. "For Cassie's things," he said as if she were already dead.

The dull throbbing in Maddie's heart ratcheted into a sharp, steady hammering as they waited for a security guard to break into Cassie's locker. When the officer got it open and her locker had been dusted for prints, he stepped aside and let David at it.

Maddie held the bag outstretched while David removed items from Cassie's locker. He studied each object intently and then dropped them one by one into the open bag.

Hairspray, extra hold. Eyelash curlers. A wand of mascara. Lancôme Firecracker Red nail polish. Curling iron. Cinnamon flavored Altoids. A blue cashmere cardigan. A package of shrimp-flavored ramen noodles and an empty box of Godiva chocolates.

Maddie pressed Cassie's sweater to her nose, inhaling the scent of her twin before reluctantly dropping the cardigan into the bag. Her sister was in trouble. Really deep trouble. Wherever she was, Cassie desperately needed her.

David passed Maddie a photograph. It was a picture of Cassie and a very handsome dark-haired man of about forty at Billy Bob's in the Stockyards. Cassie's arm was draped over the guy's shoulder. They were standing in front of a mechanical bull, longneck beers in hand and mugging tipsily for the camera.

Maddie caught her breath, raised her head and met David's gaze. "Peyton Shriver?"

He nodded. "They certainly look like a couple."

"Appearances can be deceiving and besides, didn't you encourage her to fan a romance with him?"

"I didn't mean for her to fall in love."

"She didn't." Maddie glared. "You got her into this, I can't believe you're going against her."

"I'm not going against her, I'm simply following the evidence."

"If by some wild, ridiculous stretch of the imagination Cassie did fall for Shriver, then it's all your fault," she accused. "You've got to assume responsibility for getting her involved."

David turned away, leaving her with the frustrating

urge to kick him in the seat of his obstinate pants. He kept digging through the locker.

A copy of *Vogue*. Two hair clips. Four ballpoint pens.

"Ah-ha."

Maddie jerked her head around to peer over his shoulder to see what he was ah-ha-ing about. It was a travel brochure for Grand Cayman Island.

"What?" she snapped. She didn't like his self-satisfied expression. Men. They were so predictable. Gloating when they were certain they were right.

"The smoking gun."

"Since when is a travel brochure considered a smoking gun?"

"Since the world's biggest dealer in stolen art lives in Grand Cayman and he just happens to be very friendly with Peyton Shriver."

"Oh come on, that's quite a stretch, don't you think?" she said, even as fear tightened her gut. "I bet a lot of people have travel brochures to Grand Cayman in their locker."

"But those people don't work in a museum where a Cézanne just got heisted, nor are they dating art thieves," David said.

He was right and she knew it, but Maddie still couldn't accept the fact that Cassie might be a willing participant in a crime.

He touched her arm. "I know it's difficult sometimes, to accept the truth."

She gritted her teeth. She didn't want or need his pity. What did he know about the truth? All he cared about was bringing Shriver in.

"You're a cop. You should know a travel brochure proves nothing."

"It's a step in a treacherous direction."

The people behind them were murmuring, discussing the significance of David's find, but Maddie paid them no mind. Her attention was on the man standing to her left. The man with the penetrating dark gray eyes.

Eyes, that if he were on your side, could comfort you. Eyes that said, *You can always rely on me.* But if he wasn't on your side, if you were his enemy, those mercurial gray eyes issued an entirely different message: *Do wrong and I'll make sure you pay.*

Maddie shivered. She had no doubt that he could back up either message. He wasn't a guy you'd want to tangle with in a dark alley.

Or even a well lit one for that matter.

She shifted her weight, her anxiety escalating with each passing moment.

David's cell phone did the *Dragnet* thing. He answered with a terse, "Marshall."

She tensed and leaned forward, straining to hear the voice on the other end. She couldn't make out much of what he was saying but she did hear Cassie's name bandied about.

"Good work," he said and switched off the phone.

She raised her head. His eyes glowed with the thrill of his job. The man was a bloodhound through and through. Pick up a scent and he was off on the chase.

"What is it?"

He took a deep breath and she saw him trying to curb his excitement for her benefit. "Shriver and your sister caught the six-oh-five to Atlanta on Delta Air Lines. From there, they took a connecting flight to Grand Cayman."

Her heart slipped into her Nikes. "That still doesn't mean Cassie went willingly."

David steepled his fingertips. "I know this is hard for you to deal with, but you've got to accept the possibility your sister is a fugitive from the law. I know it's an ugly thought. I know you don't want to believe it. But Shriver has a Svengali effect on women. He can make them do almost anything for him."

"If you knew that about him, then why did you ask Cassie to work for you?"

"Shriver had already marked her as his next victim. She'd started dating him before I ever asked for her help."

"You could have warned her. Given her a chance to break things off with him." Maddie studied his uncompromising grimace. "But you weren't about to do that. Admit it. Nailing Shriver is an obsession with you. You don't care about the cost."

He shrugged but didn't deny her accusation. The jackass.

"Cassie did not fall in love with him," she said adamantly. "You don't know my sister."

Flighty though her twin might be, Cassie was honest to a fault, had never stolen so much as a gumball in her life and no man, no matter how charming, could cause her to commit a crime.

"Like it or not, here's something else you're going to have to be prepared to deal with," David said. "So just brace yourself."

She notched her chin up and met his challenging stare. "What's that?"

"If Cassie is involved with the theft of the Cézanne in any way, shape or form, when I catch her, I'm going to bring her to justice right along with Shriver. No excuses. No exceptions. Got it?"

Chapter 3

What was it with women?

David lined up behind a handful of business travelers at the ticket kiosk outside the Delta Air Lines counter at DFW airport. Why did they invariably fall for charming bad boys? Did they honestly think they could rehabilitate such men with their undying love? Or did they just get off on the thrill of danger? What had caused Cassie to throw her life away over the likes of Peyton Shriver?

He pondered these questions because he wasn't too keen on examining his role in Cassie's turncoat behavior. David rejected guilt as a useless emotion.

"David!"

He raised his head, saw Maddie barreling across the terminal toward him. He had the distinct impression she wasn't here to see him off.

She was dressed in a short denim skirt, a Hawaiian floral print blouse, a floppy, red straw hat and matching strappy, high-heeled sandals. The flirty ensemble looked like something Cassie would wear. She pulled a wheeled carry-on bag behind her and, over her arm, a denim jacket.

She was dolled up like Miss Hawaiian Tropics. Why? It was fifty degrees outside.

Helplessly, he found his gaze drawn down the length of her long, lean muscular legs to the tips of her toes painted a cheeky pink.

Uh-oh. This didn't look good. Not good at all.

"Wait up," she called to him.

He moved to one side to let the other travelers go ahead through the checkpoint. He needed to get rid of her. Now. His flight left in twenty minutes and he was determined to be on it.

"Thank heavens," she said, not even breathing hard although she'd sprinted to reach him. "I was afraid I was going to miss our plane."

"Our plane?"

"I'm going to Grand Cayman with you," she said brightly. "Do you like my outfit? I thought if I looked like a tourist I'd blend in better."

David stared, unable to believe she'd just invited herself along on his investigation. This was one pushy dame. He peered into her eyes and spied a determination so staunch he'd seen it in only one other place.

The mirror.

"You're not coming with me."

"I have to. You're convinced my sister is in league with Shriver but I know better. Cassie might be a ditz and I'll grant you, at times she's impulsive and misguided and easily distracted, but she's got a heart of gold and you simply cannot put her in jail. I won't allow it."

"You won't allow it?" He smirked, amused. Her vehemence was almost cute.

"I don't mean to be aggressive, but I've already figured out you don't do subtle. One way or the other, I have to get your attention. Cassie is not in on this heist with Shriver."

"And you're not the least bit prejudiced."

"I know my sister."

"Your loyalty is commendable, but it's clear you have a huge blind spot where your twin is concerned. Look at the evidence. Cassie has romanticized Shriver and she's picturing herself living some kind of outlaw, movie star lifestyle."

Okay, so he *was* sorry he'd ever recruited Cassie. But he wasn't going to let Maddie dream up some fanciful scenario that ignored the truth in favor of exonerating her sister. If he expressed regret, she might seize upon that as a loophole she could exploit.

Maddie shook her head. "You're wrong. Shriver has kidnapped her. I feel it in my bones."

"All I want is to see justice done. If Shriver kidnapped your sister, then you'll be the first to receive an apology. In the meantime, you're delaying me from my flight. If you'll excuse me." He turned back toward the security scanners.

She marched right along behind him. He stopped and she plowed into his back. He took her by the wrist and pulled her around to face him.

"You cannot come to Grand Cayman with me. Got it? The matter is not open for discussion."

"It's a free country, bub, I can go anywhere I want."

"And I could have you arrested for interfering with an officer of the law."

"You wouldn't dare." She jerked her wrist away from him and sank her hands on her hips. Her steely-eyed gaze challenged him to make good on his threat.

Dammit. Why did he have to admire her spunk and the open way she defied him? No covert sneaking around for this woman. If she was half this feisty in the bedroom, look out.

Ah, but then a slight quiver of her lower lip gave her away. She wasn't nearly as self-confident as she wanted him to believe, but she was sure giving it hell.

"Look," he relented. "I understand your concern for your sister. I promise I'll give Cassie the benefit of the doubt."

"I'm coming with you," she repeated, enunciating each word clearly as if speaking to a particularly slow child.

"You're not."

"I am."

"Please don't make me go over there and ask those security guards to detain you. Neither one of us needs the hassle."

She didn't say anything for a long moment. Finally she sucked in a deep breath and whispered, "Okay, fine, have it your way."

Maddie spun around, but her heel must have caught on something. She teetered precariously, then stumbled against him, reaching out with both hands to grab his jacket lapel to keep from falling.

The brim of her hat smashed him in the chin. Her firm, high breasts grazed his arm.

At the feel of her palms against his chest, instant heat pricked his groin. His body's inappropriate response to their physical contact irritated him. He battled against his lust.

It was so weird that she turned him on when her identical twin sister did not. What was that all about?

"Sorry," she mumbled, quickly righting herself, and then without another word turned and sashayed off.

Watching her go, he was unsettled to discover he felt

disappointed and it took him a minute or two to figure out why. It was because she'd given up so easily. He'd been looking forward to more of a fight.

Flustered, he shouldered his carry-on and moved once again toward the scanners. The line had grown longer since his encounter with Maddie. Impatiently, he glanced at his watch. He had less than ten minutes to board the plane.

He shifted his weight from foot to foot and rolled his eyes when a lady with tons of gold jewelry kept setting off the alarm. Finally, his turn came.

Just as he went to remove his duty weapon from his shoulder holster and check it in, an armed security guard tapped him on the collarbone. "Excuse me, sir, if you could just step over here."

What now?

He followed the guard to a small, enclosed area where two uniformed Dallas police officers stood, guns drawn.

What in hell...?

"Hands on your head," one of the policemen said.

"I'm FBI." David raised his arms. He knew they were only doing their job and he tried hard not to lose his temper. "I'm on the trail of a suspect and it's imperative I make my flight."

"The lady who reported you carrying a concealed weapon said you would claim that." The second officer moved around David and relieved him of his gun.

"Lady? What lady?"

"The one you've been harassing."

"What!"

"No sudden movements," the first officer said.

"I've got my ID right here." David made a motion to go for his badge. "I can prove I'm FBI."

"I said don't move!" the first officer trilled and pointed his weapon right at David's head.

"Where's your ID?" the second officer asked.

"Right breast pocket."

The man patted him down. "Nothing here."

"Try the other pocket." David felt like an idiot standing with his palms pressed against the back of his head, his elbows sticking out, getting frisked by Officer Overzealous.

Where was his badge? Had he left it in his car? But he couldn't have done that. The badge was as much of an extension of himself as his arm or his leg. He didn't forget it and he didn't lose it.

"Not here."

"It's there somewhere," he said through clenched teeth. "Look again."

"Last call for flight 234 to Atlanta," came the announcement over the speaker system.

Shit. He was going to miss the plane.

Then, all at once, David realized what had happened.

Maddie Cooper.

If he hadn't been so distracted by his body's very physical reaction to her, he would have caught on sooner. Her clumsy stumble against him had been no accident.

The unprincipled wench had picked his pocket and stolen his badge.

Cassie Cooper sprawled in a lounge chair outside the Hyatt Regency on Seven Mile Beach in Grand Cayman. She was sipping a piña colada and enjoying the afternoon sun and the salty ocean breeze blowing over her bikinied body. This sure was a great change of pace from damp, dreary Fort Worth in February.

Not three feet away, Peyton lay on a massage table beneath a cabana getting a Swedish massage from a tanned island girl.

Taking a long pull on her straw, Cassie twirled the pink paper parasol in her drink and marveled at her opulent surroundings. She still couldn't believe she'd convinced Peyton to bring her with him.

Mentally, she patted herself on the back. She was quite the little actress.

When David Marshall called her last night to set up a rendezvous she'd sensed something was up, even though he'd acted nonchalant.

For one thing, he'd asked her to bring all the evidence she'd gathered over the past few weeks to the meeting.

For another thing, ever since her accident as a kid when she had spent three months in a coma, she occasionally experienced a weird sort of hotness at the very base of her brain. The sensation almost always preceded an unexpected turn of events. While she'd been talking to David, her brain had started its familiar sizzle.

And she had just known, for whatever reason, David was going to pull the plug on her role as his informant.

She couldn't allow him to dump her. Not now. Not when she'd worked so hard. As they'd talked, a spontaneous plan spun in her head. A plan destined to make her the toast of the art world and the darling of the FBI.

A plan to prove to Maddie that she could not only take care of herself, but thrive in the process. A plan to show everyone that she was as tough and strong and smart as her twin.

And Cassie had come up with the perfect obstacle to keep David preoccupied while she carried out her strategy. That was when she had phoned Maddie and asked her to meet her in Forest Park at eight-fifteen. She knew

David would mistake Maddie for her. She also knew Maddie would give him hell. Especially if he told her that he had recruited Cassie to work for the FBI.

She grinned and rubbed her palms together just thinking about those two at each other's throats. What would be really nice was if for once Maddie got into trouble and had to turn to David for help. That way the tension between them just might turn into something delectable.

Once she had that problem solved, Cassie had jumped in with both feet, simply trusting that everything would work out the way she wanted.

Boldly, she had gone to Peyton and told him everything. How she had been working with the FBI to catch him, how she knew of his scheme to use her security clearance to get into the Kimbell and steal paintings.

At first, Peyton tried to deny it, but then she'd smoothly lied and told him she didn't care if he was an art thief or that he'd been using her.

She professed her love for him regardless of his past. She wanted to be his girlfriend and if he would take her with him, she would use her friendship with the curator at the Museo del Prado in Madrid to help him make off with a fortune. She had detailed a robbery so daring he'd quickly grown excited at the possibilities.

Greed had him agreeing to include her in his escapades. He'd fallen for her lie, hook, line and sinker. And here she was, an FBI operative, about to catch one of the world's most elusive art thieves.

Okay, so technically she was no longer working for the FBI since David had been about to pull her off the case, but Cassie was certain once he realized the lengths she'd gone to in order to stay in good with Shriver, he would apologize for not having more faith in her.

"Happy, luv?" Peyton called to her from the massage table.

"Terribly."

God, she was a sucker for a British accent. Cassie grinned and ignored the twinge of guilt.

She had to keep reminding herself Peyton was a notorious criminal who had conned over a dozen hapless women with his suave bullshit. If she didn't keep that bit of information at the front of her mind, she would end up thinking about how gorgeous his blue eyes were and how cute he looked with his thick ebony hair tousled so boyishly by the tropical breeze.

She sighed and took a caviar canapé off the silver tray presented to her by a tuxedoed waiter. If it weren't for Peyton's nasty habit of taking expensive things that didn't belong to him, he would be the perfect man. He certainly knew how to live the good life.

Don't forget your real goal. This is about proving you can stand on your own two feet. This is about showing Maddie you don't need her hovering over you.

Still, it was a shame about Peyton.

Cassie stretched and wriggled her toes. She'd just painted them a lovely shade of Wanton Sunset.

However, there was one teeny little flaw with her plan. How was she going to let David know what she was up to without arousing Peyton's suspicions?

She couldn't just pick up a phone and blurt it out. She had packed in such a hurry she'd forgotten her wallet. She only had her clothes and her passport. She was living it up on the grace of Peyton's largess. She couldn't even call from the hotel phone. They'd charge it to his account.

But Cassie didn't want the hunky FBI man thinking she had fallen under Peyton's spell and become his cohort in crime. One way or the other, she would find a way to send David clues.

"So," she said, sliding her sunglasses back up on her nose and trying her best to act cool and nonchalant, as if she didn't really care about his answer. "What do you have planned for the Cézanne, darling?"

Peyton smirked. "Don't worry your pretty little head over it. The details are in the bag."

"My, you are efficient." She managed to control her curiosity, knowing if she pushed too hard, too quickly, Peyton would kite her like a hot check. Being a spy was a tricky proposition.

"I've got a present for you," Peyton said, and then grimaced as the masseuse plowed her knuckles over his shoulder blade.

"Oh?" Cassie grinned. She loved unexpected gifts.

Peyton shooed the masseuse away, sat up and swung his legs over the edge of the massage table. He slid to the sand, slipped his feet into black rubber flip-flops and held out his hand to her.

"Let's take a walk."

Parking her piña colada on the small table beside her lounge chair, Cassie squinted up at him. He was backlit by the sun and the cabana cast a dark shadow over his face, giving him an ominous appearance. The breeze picked up, raising the hairs on her forearm and illogically her heart stuttered.

"Cassie?" His hand was still extended.

"Uh-huh?" She felt dizzy, from either the sun or his presence. Maybe both. Suddenly, she was very nervous.

Peyton inclined his head toward the beach. "Let's take a walk."

"Okay." She forced herself to smile brightly.

She sank her palm, still damp and cool from the condensation of her glass, into his hard, hot hand. His grip seemed unnecessarily firm. She gulped.

Did he suspect something? Was he on to her?

You're imagining things. Don't start assuming the worst. That's Maddie's job.

If Maddie could only see her now! Her sister would have a shit fit.

Eventually, she was going to have to get a message to her too.

Cassie ignored the annoying thought. She curled her bare toes into the warm sand as they walked, allowing Peyton to guide her closer to the ocean.

Watch out! He could try something funny. Pull you into the water and take you under. Maddie's ultra-cautious voice echoed in her head.

Pooh. Cassie shoved the irritating noise aside.

After they'd traveled several yards up the beach away from the other sun worshipers, Peyton stopped walking. He took both of her hands in his and gazed deeply into her eyes.

"I've never met a woman quite like you," Peyton murmured.

Cassie felt herself blush. "Why, thank you."

"And I want to trust you."

"You can," she lied glibly.

And the Oscar goes to Cassie Cooper. For her mesmerizing role as art museum public relations gal turned special agent for the FBI.

"How far would you go to prove your devotion to me?" he asked, his eyes growing deeper, darker.

Gulp.

She swallowed the lump in her throat. What had

seemed like a fool-proof plot last night in Forth Worth, Texas, was starting to look like a not-so-brilliant plan on the clean white sand of Seven Mile Beach.

"What do you mean?"

"I have to know that I can trust you with my life."

"You can trust me."

"I'm afraid I need more reassurance than just your word."

"What's it gonna take?"

"I was hoping you would ask me that question." He let go of her left hand and fumbled in the pocket of his swim trunks.

When he produced a small black velvet box, Cassie thought she might swoon or throw up or start laughing maniacally. This wasn't her first proposal and all three reactions were within the realm of possibility.

He cracked the box open, revealing a dramatic two-carat marquis-cut diamond engagement ring.

Her knees quivered and she had to hold on to his arm to keep from toppling over.

"Marry me, Cassie."

"Marry you?" her voice wobbled, as tremulous as her legs.

"I know it's sudden, but I'm as crazy for you as you are for me," Peyton purred. "Together, we'll make an awesome team, traveling the world, stealing our treasures, living the high life."

"Uh-huh." She breathed.

"And besides . . ." His grin was wicked. "A wife can't be forced to testify against her husband."

Oh, ho. Here was the real reason for his impromptu proposal. The diamond winked, beckoning her to gamble everything for her ultimate goal.

What the hell? Why not say yes? Before she had to actually prove herself by marrying him, she intended on seeing his handsome butt locked up behind bars.

Mores the pity.

"Yes, Peyton," she said and met his gaze head on. "I'll marry you."

He slipped the ring on her left hand, then pulled her into his arms and kissed her hard and long. When he released her at last, he pressed his mouth against her ear.

"But it has to happen tonight," he whispered. "I've made all the arrangements. If you are truly on my side, then you must marry me at dusk at my friend's estate on Dead Man's Bay."

Chapter 4

Miss," the flight attendant glowered at Maddie. "I'm going to have to ask you to stop pacing and take your seat. You're making the other passengers nervous."

"Sorry," Maddie mumbled and returned to her cramped seat at the back of the pláne. Her hefty, ruddy-faced seatmate shot his eyes heavenward and polished off his third bloody Mary before lumbering to his feet and letting her squeeze in next to the window.

She hated flying. For that matter, she hated traveling. She was a creature of comfort and missed her habits. Her short-lived Olympic career had been a royal pain in the keister, shuttling from tournament to tournament on buses, in planes, taking the train.

The only reason she had stuck with it as long as she had was because being an Olympian made her feel strong and in control of her life at a time when she'd desperately needed all the strength she could muster to look after her calamity-courting twin.

She needed double that strength now.

Her gut told her David Marshall wasn't going to relent in his position against Cassie. It was her gut that had instigated the backup plan to filch his FBI badge and then sic security on him as a gun-toting loony.

That was why she had worn Cassie's ridiculous high heels and her outlandish straw hat. The heels had been an excuse to lose her balance. The hat had been to camouflage his view of her larcenous hands.

And it had worked.

Her intention had been to get David detained long enough for her to make the flight and for him to miss it. Once she'd turned him in to security, she had slipped over to a different terminal to check in and had gone on to board the plane.

She knew David could unsnarl the tangle she'd wrapped him in pretty quickly, but all she'd needed was a head start. If she could get to Grand Cayman before he did, she would have a few precious hours in which to find Cassie. She intended on rescuing her sister from Shriver and bringing her home before the hard-assed Officer Marshall got his hands on her.

By the time David caught up with them, Maddie would have hired the best lawyer she could afford. She would even take out a second mortgage on her condo if she had to. Anything for her sister.

The brightness of the sun reflecting off the field of white clouds floating below the plane's wing hurt her eyes. And the weary, dogged sound of the engines made her feel oddly alone. She burrowed in her handbag for her drugstore sunglasses, slipped them on and wondered if David was already on another flight.

David Marshall. Mister My-Way-or-the-Highway.

Hmmph. Imagine. That irritating man telling her she couldn't go search for her own sister. Like he and what army were going to stop her?

She would have given a month's pay to be a fly on the wall when he had tried to flash his badge for airport security and found it gone. She grinned at the idea, but then she immediately felt contrite for taking pleasure in his misfortune.

She wasn't a malicious person. She'd only absconded with his ID badge because there had been no other way around him. She'd given him a legitimate chance to take her along and he had refused.

Idly, she wondered about him. Was he married? He didn't wear a ring. But who cared? It wasn't as if she was interested in him. He was far too annoying and bossy and pigheaded. The guy had the personality of a steamroller. Plus, he actually seemed to enjoy locking horns with her.

Who needed that kind of aggravation? Certainly not she. Cassie created enough commotion in her life.

"Ladies and gentlemen, we're making our approach to George Town and the pilot has switched on the seat belt sign. Please remain seated for the duration of the flight," the flight attendant announced over the intercom.

Fifteen minutes later they were on the ground. Relieved to be out of the sky, Maddie retrieved her carry-on from the overhead bin, thankful she didn't have to go through baggage claim.

She had packed lightly on the outside hope she would be bringing Cassie home in record time and also because she had an innate distrust of baggage handlers. She'd once seen one of those hidden camera investigative news programs where they had secretly videotaped sticky-fingered ramp workers rummaging through suitcases. One tasteless employee had even stolen a female passenger's panties. Creepy.

Once inside the terminal however, she paused in

confusion, not knowing what to do next. She was uncomfortable at not having hotel reservations or an itinerary to follow. She never traveled without detailing every eventuality.

She spied a sign directing her to ground transportation and followed the arrows out of the concourse. So far so good, but where did she go from here?

Argh.

She was miserable at this spur-of-the-moment stuff. Where was Cassie when you really needed her?

A balmy breeze licked her skin and the air lay heavy with the provocative scent of ocean and coconut and sugarcane. She stood waiting for inspiration to strike.

And then there he was.

David Marshall hailing a cab not twenty feet away.

Impossible! How had he gotten to Grand Cayman ahead of her?

Apparently, her sneak attack hadn't worked. Well, never mind, she had a new plan. Stick to him like glue.

"David!" She hollered and waved, but the slamming of the car door must have drowned her out. Either that or he was purposefully ignoring her.

Not that she could blame him for being angry, but she'd be damned if she'd let him out of her sight.

His cab pulled away from the curb.

Maddie rushed to the taxi stand and flung herself into the back seat of the next vehicle in line. The dark-skinned, dimple-chinned driver turned to beam at her over his shoulder.

"Where to Miss?" the man asked in an odd accent that was both British and island lyrical.

She gestured frantically at David's taxi careening through traffic. "Follow that car!"

*   *   *

David checked into a low budget motel several streets back from Seven Mile Beach. The FBI frowned on agents squandering their expense accounts on high-end beach resorts.

Then again, they also frowned on their agents recruiting citizens as informants when they'd specifically been told not to. Especially when those informants went renegade and turned into suspects. They also weren't thrilled with agents who got pickpocketed by a suspect's identical twin sister.

At the thought of Maddie, David blew out his breath. He was still steamed over her stunt at the airport. It was damned unsettling having his badge stolen by a beguiling woman so distracting he hadn't even noticed she had pinched his identity.

For about the ninety-ninth time since it happened, he ground his teeth at his own stupidity.

Luckily for him a federal air marshal, who'd once worked with David, had been transporting a prisoner through the terminal. The marshal had spied him getting frisked by the Dallas PD and he'd intervened, vouching for him.

Contrite over detaining an FBI agent, security had gotten David on an American Airlines flight leaving for Grand Cayman thirty minutes after the Delta flight. Actually, it turned out to be a better deal. The Delta flight stopped in Atlanta, whereas the American flight went straight through.

But dwelling on his glaring *faux pas* wasn't going to help him catch Shriver. And thinking about Maddie would only agitate him. He had to focus on the task at hand and forget about her.

David had no sooner accepted his key from the desk

clerk, returned his credit card to his wallet and bent to pick up his carry-on when he caught sight of a very familiar pair of jaunty red sandals.

Oh no.

He groaned inwardly. He wasn't in the mood for this.

His gaze roved from cute feet to shapely ankles and on up divinely curved calves. He appreciated the tanned knees, the firm thighs and those rounded hips. He visually traversed her flat belly, narrow waist and nicely rounded chest before reluctantly finding himself face-to-face with Maddie Cooper.

"Get an eyeful?" She sank her hands on her hips and glared.

Audacious woman.

He was the one who should be glaring. David shrugged. Hell, he was only human and she was some tall, cool drink of water. Nothing wrong with looking. If she didn't want him to stare, she should wear a snow parka.

"I should have known," he said.

"Known what?"

"That you weren't the type of woman to give up without a fight."

In spite of himself, David found his respect inching up a rung or two. She'd followed him, tracked him down and he'd never once suspected she was behind him. He made a mental note never to underestimate her again.

"This is where you're staying?" She scanned the lobby of the bare-bones accommodations.

He shrugged. "I'm a government employee."

"I'm not exactly flush with cash myself," she said. "I'll stay here too."

"You know Peyton and your sister are probably living it up at the Hyatt."

That pissed her off. He could tell by the way her eyes flashed a brilliant emerald green and how she drew herself up tall and squared her shoulders. She could have been a swimsuit model with her height and that amazing figure.

"Think what you will, Agent Marshall, but I know my sister. Which is why I'm here. To make sure you don't falsely imprison her."

Man, but she sure had an unerring talent for ticking a guy off.

She turned her attention to the desk clerk who'd been openly eavesdropping. "I'll take a room for the night, please."

The thin young man flashed her a row of white teeth and held out his palm for her credit card. David had seen enough. He had to leave before he said something he would regret. He picked up his suitcase and headed for his room.

"Wait," she called. "Wait for me."

He ignored her.

Five minutes later an angry rapping sounded at his door. He'd just taken off his coat and tie and was unbuttoning his shirt.

"What?" he demanded, flinging open the door, his fingers twisting at the second button.

"That was rude of you," Maddie said. "Running off and leaving me when I asked you to wait."

"I thought we'd already established the fact that I'm a rude guy."

She forced a smile. "Call me optimistic, but I had high hopes for your rehabilitation."

"Don't you get it, lady?" he snapped. "I don't want you along."

"It's not about what you want." She blithely trailed over the threshold. "It's about what's going to happen."

"Excuse me?" he bellowed.

She couldn't have picked a more inflammatory tactic, waltzing into *his* room, trying to take control of *his* investigation. She must be a glutton for punishment. What was the matter with her? Was she one of those women who liked to be spanked?

Well, it was time to turn the tables. He took an intimidating step toward her and undid another button. He wanted to see how long it would take her to run from the room.

He undid another button and then another.

His ploy failed.

She pretended not to notice what he was up to and instead sauntered over to the sliding glass door. She opened the curtain, freeing bright late afternoon sunlight into the room.

Then she spun on her heels to face him. "You're going to make me your partner on this investigation."

He snorted.

"What's so funny?"

"I don't know what schoolgirl fantasies you've got bouncing around in your head, but this isn't a James Bond movie, kiddo." He undid the next to the last button and took another step closer. "And I can't make you an honorary member of the FBI."

"You recruited Cassie to work for you. Why not me?"

"That was different."

"How was it different?"

"I get it," he said. "Severe case of sibling rivalry. You're jealous."

"I'm not jealous," she denied and her voice went up just enough to let him know he'd nailed her insecurity dead on. "Why would I be jealous of my twin sister?"

"Because she's not afraid to grab life by the throat and live and you are." He undid the last button and now he was standing just a hand's breadth away.

Anxiously, she sucked her bottom lip between her teeth.

Something about that nervous yet unintentionally sexy gesture gave him a funny feeling in the pit of his stomach.

"Who says I'm scared of life? I'm not scared. I hopped on a plane and flew to Grand Cayman without a day's notice, didn't I?"

"Yes, and it's making you a nervous wreck."

"I'm not a nervous wreck."

"Then how come your thumbnail is gnawed to the quick and you've got a Rolaids wrapper dangling out of your purse?"

Frowning, she tucked the errant wrapper back inside her shoulder bag and then jerked her ravaged thumb behind her.

"Well, it doesn't matter. You're following Shriver and I'm following my sister so we're always going to end up in the same place. Wouldn't it just be easier for you to let me in on what's going on?"

He could tell she was trying not to look at his chest but every so often she would sneak a peek at the expanse of skin revealed beneath his open shirt. She raised a hand to her cheek and he saw she was blushing pink.

Gotcha.

"Are you trying to blackmail me?" he asked, stripping off his shirt and tossing it onto the bed.

"No more than you're trying to intimidate me."

"Am I?"

"Aren't you?"

"Question is, do you like it?" he asked.

The air in the room seemed miserably hot even though he'd twisted up the controls on the air conditioner when he'd walked in. Or maybe it was the heat of his blood rushing through his veins.

"Nobody likes being intimidated."

"Don't be so sure of that. Ever heard of a submissive?"

"I'm not a submissive," she denied. "Far from it."

"You sure? You entered a man's room while he was getting undressed."

"That doesn't make me submissive. If anything, I'd say I was dominant."

"You dominating me?" The notion was so foreign, so utterly ridiculous that David burst out laughing.

His derision incensed her. She stabbed an index finger in his direction. "Maybe you're the one who's longing to be submissive."

"Oh yeah?" Swiftly he covered the remaining distance between them.

She backpedaled until she ran smack dab into the wall. David grabbed both her wrists, pinned her hands above her head and swiftly shoved one knee between her legs, completely hemming her in with no way out.

"This look like submissive to you, darlin'?" he growled.

They were both breathing hard, their lips almost touching.

"For your information I'm a third degree black belt in karate," she said.

"Bring it on. I'm fifth degree."

"You don't threaten me." She gulped, belying her own bravado.

He saw the column of her throat muscles pump hard and he knew he'd succeeded in intimidating her, but still she held her ground. She might be scared, but she was too damned proud to run away.

Dammit. Why did her bravery in the face of her fear turn him on so frickin' much? He was one sick puppy.

His gaze locked onto hers.

She raised her chin. She was so close her body heat set him on fire.

They stood there a long moment, neither of them blinking, neither wanting to be the first to back down. He forced himself not to think about how nice she smelled or how her chest rose and fell in cadence with his own raspy breathing or how much he wanted to kiss her at that very moment.

If he kept thinking like this, he'd be rock hard in a matter of seconds. He was halfway there already.

"Yep," she said, "I'll be out there on my own, no protection, no gun, a woman traveling alone. You know I'm gonna be pretty well defenseless."

"You're about as defenseless as a porcupine."

But even as he denied her vulnerability, he felt his guardian instincts charge to the forefront of his emotions. He'd always possessed this need to defend the underdog. It was one of the reasons he'd become a cop. Unbelievable how this irksome woman had figured that out about him.

How had she known the one thing he simply could not refuse was a damsel in distress? She didn't seem the type to take advantage of her femininity but here she was suddenly giving him a wide-eyed, helpless look. He knew he shouldn't fall for it, but damn his hide, he did.

"You're going to plague the living crap out of me until I agree to take you along."

"Pretty much." She nodded.

Sighing, he let her go and stepped back. "I can't trust you."

"Why not?"

"I can't have you trying to one up me again like you did at the airport. And speaking of that, give me my badge back." He held out his hand.

She fished in her purse, found his badge and passed it over to him. "I won't try to one up you again. I promise."

"Oh, that makes all the difference in the world," he said sarcastically.

"I'll swear on a bible." She raised her left hand while splaying her right hand over her heart. "Got a bible? Betcha the Gideons left one in the bedside table, they're reliable that way."

"No need to be a smart-ass. This isn't a court of law, you don't have to swear on a bible."

"Then how are you going to know you can trust me?"

"Swearing on a bible won't make me trust you."

"I never break a solemn vow."

The expression in her eyes told him that she meant every word. He decided to surrender, mainly because he knew if he didn't he would end up spending more time fighting her than chasing after Shriver and Cassie. But he also gave in because she seemed so earnest and a little desperate.

Besides, if she was with him, he could control her. Out there on her own she was a wild card and he couldn't afford to let her run amok and screw up his investigation.

"All right," he said after a long moment. "You can come."

Her shoulders sagged visibly at her hard-won victory. She blew out her breath with an adorable sound that made him feel warm and protective inside. Ah hell, he liked her.

"Thank you," she said, and headed for an overstuffed chair in the corner. He noticed her hand quivered ever so slightly as she lowered herself down. A cloud of dust motes drifted up. "Now let's establish some ground rules."

"Ground rules?" he echoed.

How cute. She still had the illusion that she had some measure of power in this crazy relationship. Mind- boggling. Give the woman an inch and she took the entire freeway.

"I promised not to one up you, but now you've got to promise me something."

"Like what?"

"No more using sex as a weapon." She nodded from his shirt to his bare chest. The heat of her gaze scorched his flesh.

"Excuse me?"

"You heard what I said."

"Wait a minute. Simply because I took my shirt off you think I was using sex as a weapon?"

"Don't forget calling me submissive and then pinning me to the wall with your knee to try and prove your point."

"How could I forget that?" He wriggled his eyebrows suggestively.

"Ah, ah." She pointed a finger. "See there, you're doing it again."

"You call eyebrow wriggling a sexual weapon?"

"It's innuendo."

"No, it's not."

"Oh, give it up. You know what you're doing and I know what you're doing and as long as we're working together I won't stand for any more of your masculine intimidation tactics. Got it?"

She was like an impudent kid, trespassing on a farmer's land, cockily waving a red flag at the bull in the pasture.

He could have replied in a thousand different ways, each and every response designed to put her firmly in her place, but somehow David managed to restrain his tongue.

Maddie was worried about her sister and even though he fought against the guilt, he felt responsible for what had happened. He had known Shriver had a spellbinding effect on women. He had also recognized Cassie was gullible and yet he'd enlisted her anyway. He'd used her hunger for excitement to fulfill his own needs.

Man, it hurt when your selfish decisions came back to bite your butt.

"No more using sex as a weapon," he agreed.

Maddie looked surprised at his capitulation. "Thank you. Now could you, um, cover up?" She waved a hand at his naked chest.

Grinning, he slowly leaned over, making sure she got an extra good view of his muscles and plucked his shirt off the bed.

"Any other rules I should be aware of?" He might as well know what her rules were so he could systematically set about breaking them.

"That's all for now, but you should prepare yourself for future rules as they arise."

He slipped on the shirt but didn't move to do up the buttons. He could tell she was still struggling hard against her desire to look at him. You couldn't deny it. They had sexual chemistry, no matter how unwanted it might be on both their parts.

"I can't promise you anything. I'll be fair with you, but that's all I can offer. Take it or leave it."

"I suppose I'll have to take it." She hopped up from the chair and edged toward the door, giving him a wide berth.

Good. He'd rattled her at last.

"Wait just a minute." He reached out and touched her elbow. She sucked in an audible breath.

"Yes?" her voice was soft, but her skin was softer.

"I have a few ground rules of my own."

"Oh?"

"When it comes to this investigation, you have to obey me without question."

"I can't agree to that."

"Then I can't take you along."

"But what if you tell me to do something detrimental to either Cassie or myself?"

"I'm afraid you're just going to have to trust me," he said, feeling her muscles tense beneath his touch.

"Trusting a stranger isn't my strong suit."

"Mine either, kiddo." He thrust his hands deep in the pockets of his trousers. "But for the foreseeable future, I'd say we're stuck with each other."

Chapter 5

Where are we going?" Maddie shouted an hour later as she sat in the passenger seat of the no-frills subcompact car David had rented.

The bargain basement vehicle didn't have air conditioning so they had all four windows rolled down. Her hair lashed her face like a hundred tiny whips. Her skin stung and she felt as if she was sitting in a NASA wind tunnel.

"To see Shriver's fence," David answered.

"Who is that?" she asked, battling valiantly to smooth her hair down.

"Name's Cory Philpot. He was raised in New York high society. He and Shriver have known each other for years," David hollered.

Maddie was still feeling unnerved from their encounter in his motel room. She thought about the way David had used his bare chest as a weapon of intimidation. How he'd speared his knee to the wall between her spread legs. How he'd pinned her arms over her head.

Her stomach went quivery all over again.

He seemed much larger than he actually was. Even

though his body wasn't the least bit bulky, he had a bearish quality about him. Maybe it was the wide shoulders or the broad chest. Maybe it was the way he managed to come off gruff and cuddly all at the same time.

Or maybe it was his uncommon combination of brute strength, cocky self-confidence, dogged determination and pure animal magnetism. He was deeply intense at times, while at other moments he seemed cynical and flippant. She liked the contrast but she did not know why.

Usually, she went for quiet, brainy guys who analyzed everything to death just as she did. She'd only been in love once and that had been during her senior year in high school.

Lance was a wild, reckless guy who ditched her for being too cautious. He'd even had the audacity to ask her why she couldn't be more like Cassie. Imagine! She'd told herself never again. She made it a habit to stay away from dangerous guys like the one sitting beside her.

The sun hunkered on the horizon, a big orange smoldering ball. The mingled smells of pungent fish, aromatic frangipani and sweet tropical fruits defined the aroma of Grand Cayman. They drove down the waterfront road passing quaint restaurants, souvenir shops and financial institution after financial institution after financial institution.

"What's with all the banks?" she asked, abandoning the struggle to tame her hair.

"Offshore accounts, laundered mob money, tax evaders. The Caymans are a great place to stash cash you don't want other people knowing about."

"I see."

David leaned back in the seat in a casual but oddly alert posture, like a male lion guarding his pride. One arm lay draped over the steering wheel, his other elbow rested against the window. Maddie tilted her head and surreptitiously studied his profile.

The wind tousled his short, golden brown hair. It gave him a relaxed, simple look and stirred a surprising appetite inside her. An appetite she tried to pass off as hunger. She hadn't eaten anything all day except two handfuls of roasted almonds on the plane.

Without meaning to, Maddie found herself wondering what it would feel like to run her fingers through that thick, unruly hair. What would his heated skin taste like against her tongue?

Her errant thoughts spun dizzily, wildly as she pondered how his warm body would feel straddling hers, moving over her, supplying them both with stark physical pleasure.

Beneath her skin, a strange hotness extended, throbbing outward. Something about him, something mysterious yet fundamentally masculine, called to her. But Maddie was determined to ignore the summons.

Her hormones did not easily influence her. Unlike her earthy twin, she had never been a slave to either her libido or her impulses. So why now was her brain sending her body a dozen frantic messages all centered on sating her sexual desires?

The uncharacteristic bent of her thoughts alarmed her and she quickly jerked her gaze away from his face, but not before he caught her giving him the once over.

Jeez, she'd practically been drooling.

His eyes narrowed, his thick lashes lowered as he swept a glance at her lap. Maddie looked down. Her denim skirt had ridden up, revealing a yard of thigh.

One eyebrow quirked on his forehead and he grinned like a man with a dirty secret. The faint laugh lines at the corners of his eyes deepened, making him somehow—impossibly—even more good-looking.

Damn him.

Maddie tugged her skirt down as far as it would go, which unfortunately wasn't far enough to extinguish the heat burning her cheeks.

Both sets of 'em.

"Eyes on the road, Mister."

"I could say the same thing to you." David chuckled. "I caught you checking me out."

Disgruntled with her unruly hormones, Maddie snapped her head around, stared purposefully out the passenger window and wondered why she was having such a hard time breathing normally.

The sun slipped below the horizon. All along the waterfront festive lights flicked on. Bonfires blazed on the beach. Yachts on dinner cruises bobbed in the harbor. People strolled the sidewalks in brightly colored casual wear. Grand Cayman was a nice island. Too bad she wasn't here to have a nice time.

"Where is this place?" she asked.

"Dead Man's Cove, tip of the North Shore."

"Quaint name," she said dryly.

"The Caymans have a bit of a pirate past."

"So I've gathered. What are we going to do when we get there?"

"I'm not sure."

"What does that mean?"

"We'll play it by ear."

"Do you think Shriver is there? With Cassie? Fencing the Cézanne?"

Was her sister okay? Was Shriver treating her right? Was she getting enough to eat?

David shrugged. "Your guess is as good as mine."

"Wow, you're a real fount of information."

"Detective work isn't an exact science."

"So tell me, is there anything you do know?"

"I know you're a nosy pain-in-the-ass," he said and glared at her.

"Watch the road," she said and automatically braced the flat of both hands against the dashboard.

She hated it when drivers took their attention off the road. Her sister was the world's worst. Cassie could talk on the cell phone, eat a bagel and apply mascara all the while hurtling down the freeway at seventy miles an hour. Maddie shuddered just thinking about it.

David might have muttered "bossy wench" but she could have misunderstood him. In actuality, he probably said something far less complimentary. You never knew about men.

Silence descended, broken only by the sound of Maddie's rumbling stomach.

"You hungry?" he asked.

"Yes."

"We don't have time for a restaurant. Fast food in the car suit you?"

"Anything." She nodded. As any athlete, she wasn't much for greasy fries and burgers but under the circumstances she'd take what she could get.

"Ah, the ubiquitous burger franchise," he said, wheeling the car through the drive-through. "What'll you have?"

"A salad. Fat-free Italian dressing. Hold the croutons."

"It'll be kinda hard to eat a salad in the car. I'll get you a burger." He pulled up to the order box. "Two cheeseburgers, a couple of orders of fries, two chocolate shakes and an apple pie," he said into the intercom. To Maddie he asked, "You want an apple pie?"

"I want a salad."

"Just one apple pie," he cheerfully told the anonymous female voice taking his order.

"That'll be twelve fifty-eight, sir. Please drive around."

Maddie plucked a twenty from her purse and held it out to him.

He waved her off. "My treat."

"If you planned on telling me what to eat, why did you ask what I wanted?"

"Because I've figured something out about you," he said, paying for their order and handing her the sack of burgers.

The food smelled so good Maddie feared she might start salivating. He took their chocolate shakes from the cashier and slipped them into the console cup holders.

"Oh, yeah?"

"Yeah."

"What's that?"

"You're the type of woman who does what's good for her whether she likes it or not. You toe the line so you can take care of everyone else. But secretly, you're just waiting for an excuse to let down your guard and do something wild like your adventurous sister."

"Ooooh, you've got my number, all right." She waved both hands in the air. "I've just been dreaming of a man who would come along and force-feed me junk food. Yeah, buddy, it doesn't get any wilder than that."

"Rome wasn't built in a day."

He chuckled and the deep sound wrapped around her like a comfortable hug. He was teasing her and damn, if she wasn't enjoying it. Why did she feel charmed by him?

She should be irritated, aggravated, annoyed. Instead her insides went all whooshy.

This wouldn't do. Not at all.

"What's that crack supposed to mean?" she asked in a quarrelsome tone. She would pick a fight with him if she had to. Anything to eradicate this warm, soft fuzzy sensation arrowing through her heart every time he glanced her way.

"You gotta start small."

"I get it. Today it's hamburgers, tomorrow the world."

"Something like that."

"You're so full of bullshit. Obviously, you've confused me with my sister if you're thinking I'm just waiting for some big strong man to come along and tell me what to do."

"Now, now. Don't disparage your sister. She might be in trouble, but she's a good woman. She just falls for the wrong kind of guys. You're lucky you have a sibling."

He smiled and his teeth flashed white in the illumination of the neon lights. The lighting softened his rugged features and the tender look in his eyes took her by surprise. Maybe he wasn't such a hard-ass after all. Could this tough guy be like the delightfully delicious sabras cactus? Prickly on the outside but sweet and soft on the inside. Her pulse skittered off kilter.

So why the armor-plated exterior? What was he so afraid of? He gestured toward the sack. "Pass me one of the burgers, will you?"

She moved the sack out of his reach, tucking it against the right side of her body. "Nope."

"No?"

"I've got your number too, mister."

His grin widened. "Let's hear it."

"You're one of those guys who's so focused on winning that you try to shut down your tender feelings by channeling your energy into blasting your way through any given situation."

"Now why would I do that?"

"Because if you're winning that means you're in control. Because if—horrors—you're not busy telling other people what to do, that means someone could be taking advantage of you. You view soft emotions as a weakness and nothing terrifies you more than being seen as weak."

"You think?" David asked lightly, but Maddie noticed he'd lost his teasing smile. Ah-ha! Apparently it was quite a different story when the pop psychology was on the other ego.

"I think."

"Well, I think you're one of those women who doesn't appreciate having their shortcomings pointed out to them, so in order not to have to face said shortcomings, they grasp at very thin straws and lash out at the person who observed their flaw in the first place."

"You think that was lashing out?"

"Uh-huh."

"Buddy, you don't wanna see me lashing out."

"I guess it would depend on what kind of lashing we're talking about. A physical tongue lashing is quite a different animal from a verbal tongue lashing."

"There you go with the sexual innuendo again."

"But you're so fun to tease."

"Maybe we should examine the reason you feel compelled to tease me, if indeed it is, as you claim, teasing."

"Maybe we should leave the psychoanalysis to the professionals," he said.

"I'll go for that."

"Could I have my supper now, please?"

She relented. He had asked nicely. She unwrapped his burger and handed it over.

The next few minutes passed quietly as they concentrated on fueling their bodies. The farther north they traveled, the more rugged the terrain grew. Smooth sandy beaches gave way to dense scrub, rocky thickets and sedge swamps. Just when Maddie was beginning to think that David had no earthly idea where he was going, the beaches reappeared.

After finishing her food, Maddie wiped her hands on a napkin and stuffed it, along with the greasy wrapper, back into the paper bag.

Well-kept bungalows graduated to pricier digs until they found themselves in Cayman Kai where the manor houses were lavish and the condos exclusive. David followed a string of cars down the road to Dead Man's Cove.

"Looks like someone is having one heck of a chichi party," she said, impressed with the assortment of Jaguars, Porsches and Mercedes-Benzes.

The line of cars slowed as they turned into the private drive of a very swanky plantation-style house surrounded by coconut groves. The cars were stopping at a checkpoint manned by a uniformed security guard.

David backed the car up and narrowly missed running into a Viper. He slipped their outclassed rental into drive and eased past the party house.

"What's going on?" Maddie asked.

"Change in plans."

"You mean we're not just going to walk up to the front door, ring the bell and say, Hey dude, you fencing Shriver's stolen Cézanne?"

"That was never my plan." He sounded irritated.

"What was your plan?"

"I agreed to bring you along, basically to keep you from screwing up my investigation. I did not agree to play twenty questions. Now hush," he said, scanning the waterfront.

"What are you looking for?"

"What did I just say about asking nosy questions? Weren't you listening? Or are you just bad at taking instructions?"

"That last part. Now what is it that you're looking for?"

"A secluded place to stash the car. Satisfied?"

"See? How hard was that."

"Woman, you try a man's patience," he growled under his breath and ran his fingers through his hair, as agitated as an air traffic controller on the heaviest travel day of the year.

She realized then that he saw her as nothing more than an annoyance he'd been forced to tolerate. She felt at once snubbed and defiant.

Who cares what he thinks about you? The only thing that matters is finding Cassie and bringing her home in one piece.

David switched off the headlights and edged down a narrow dirt lane leading to a public beach not far from Philpot's house. He pulled the car off the road and cut the engine.

"Stay put," he said, and got out of the car.

"No way. I'm coming with you."

She popped from the passenger seat and found herself ankle deep in fine white sand. It sucked at her high-heeled sandals, dragging her down with each step. The damned shoes were ridiculously useless. How did Cassie walk in the things?

"Why am I not the least bit surprised," he muttered.

Maddie slipped off the shoes, looped the straps over her fingers and hurried after him. They trudged through the sand, headed toward Philpot's mansion. Music filtered through the air. She identified it as some schmaltzy tune by The Carpenters frequently played at weddings.

"Not much of a party song," she commented.

But David wasn't paying any attention to her. He was like a bloodhound tracking a raccoon. His eyes were narrowed, his posture tense, his attention focused on Philpot's place. They couldn't see much of that section of the beach from where they walked, cloaked as it was by the coconut grove.

But as they crept nearer, Maddie spotted a makeshift altar set up on the beach, along with dozens of folding chairs and flaming tiki torches.

"I think it's a wedding," Maddie whispered.

"We're in luck," David said. "They'll be so busy with the wedding, no one will notice us. Now if fate is really smiling, Peyton Shriver will be among the guests."

"And Cassie," Maddie supplied, anxious for this single-minded FBI agent not to forget her sister.

"Get down," David said roughly and dropped to a crouch. He tugged on the hem of her skirt.

The brush of his knuckles against her thigh was slight, but it was enough contact to send her pulse staggering against her throat. Deliberately struggling to ignore the sizzle of awareness he'd generated, she squatted beside him in the sand.

"Now what?" she asked.

Through the trunks of the trees they could see a robed minister standing at the altar and two other guys, presumably the groom and the best man, positioned in front of him, but from this distance, Maddie couldn't make out their features.

"We go closer."

"Through the coconut grove?" Anxiously, she glanced up at the trees with their thick, heavy fruit looming above them in the deepening twilight.

"Sure, why not." David moved forward.

"Wait, wait." She grabbed on to his belt loop.

"What is it?" He turned and glared at her.

"Are you always this testy?"

"Only when being pestered by some pesky female. What is it?" he repeated.

"I read a guidebook about Grand Cayman on the flight over."

"And...?"

"The article warned to watch out for falling coconuts."

"For crying out loud. What are the odds of getting beaned by a coconut in the next five minutes?"

"Good enough that they bothered to mention it in a guidebook."

"Well, I guarantee you'll get beaned if you keep visualizing it. Fret about something enough and it'll eventually happen."

"See there, you prove my point. That's a perfectly good reason to keep out."

"It's a perfectly good reason not to visualize falling coconuts."

"I can't help but visualize them." She worried her necklace with her fingers.

"Fine, stay here if you want." David dived into the grove, wasting no time in ditching her.

Maddie hesitated, alternating between eyeing the coconuts dangling above and the FBI agent sneaking through the trees. Her innate sense of caution warred with her allegiance to her sister.

Stay or go?

Hang back and wait? Or take your chances and plunge ahead?

Risk your noggin or Cassie's life?

Tick-tock.

David was halfway through the grove when she realized loyalty trumped safety.

"Okay, all right, wait up, I'm coming," she whispered loudly.

"Shhh. I think I hear the wedding march." He stopped and cocked his head to listen.

She clamped her lips shut and nervously duck-walked behind him as quickly as she could. It wasn't easy, navigating the moist sand and the coconut trees in that position.

When Maddie heard the deadly whoosh-thunk of a descending coconut to the left of her, she almost peed in her pants.

Yikes!

The second whoosh-thunk, closer even than the first sent her stomach into spasms and her heart rate into hyperdrive. She felt like she was in the video game Frogger she and Cassie used to play as kids.

She scuttled faster and by the time she reached David, she felt edgy, overheated and even a bit faint. She cowered beside him, arms wrapped over her head, eyes squeezed closed. Her pulse stepped up its shallow, flighty beat.

David reached out and laid a hand across her shoulder. "I want you to prepare yourself," he murmured.

"Prepare myself to die by coconut?" Maddie asked, peering over her shoulder and praying she wouldn't see any angry island gods hurling ripe fruit at her.

He took her chin between his fingers and thumb and turned her head toward the beach. "Look at the bride."

"Yeah, okay, I see her."

She squinted at the woman in white walking rather stiffly down the green Astroturf laid out as an aisle. Maddie was a tad nearsighted, but glasses got in the way of sports and she'd never gotten the hang of poking plastic contact lenses into her eyes.

"You don't recognize her?"

"Should I?"

"It's your twin sister and unless I'm mistaken the groom is Peyton Shriver."

Before she could shriek, "What?" David clamped one hand over her mouth and snaked his other hand around her waist, pulling her down flush against his warm body.

"I told you she ran off with him voluntarily," he whispered.

Maddie tensed and she struggled to break free from his overbearing grasp. She had to get to Cassie and stop that wedding now, but David wasn't about to turn her loose. She aimed an elbow at his ribs and jabbed hard.

"Ouch, that hurt. Stop fighting me."

"Turn me loose," she mumbled around the salty taste of his skin.

"Only if you promise not to go ballistic."

Yeah okay, she would promise anything in order to get David to let her go, but that didn't mean she would sit here idly by and allow her sister to marry that sleazebag art thief.

Slowly he released her and then slipped his gun from its shoulder holster.

"Stay well behind me, or I'll handcuff you to a tree," he threatened.

"I think you're bluffing."

"Just try me."

Something in his tone of voice, told her he meant every word. The last thing she wanted was to be handcuffed to one of those coconut trees.

They both looked toward the beach. Her sister—if indeed the bride was Cassie—reached the altar and the music stopped.

"Dearly beloved," she heard the minister say.

She couldn't heed David's warning; she had to speak out. She didn't care if he got mad and handcuffed her to a coconut tree, she'd take her chances. She had to stop her twin from making a horrible mistake.

"Cassie, no!" she screamed. "Don't do it!"

David was on his feet, staying low, gun held at his side. Maddie was on his heels. They were at the edge of the grove when she glanced up and saw it, a coconut dangling precariously from the tree right above them.

Don't visualize it falling.

But she couldn't help herself. She was a worst-case scenario gal ever since that ill-fated Christmas day eighteen years ago. The harder she tried not to see the coconut cracking into David's skull, the more vividly she pictured it.

The coconut was going to fall.

She knew it as surely as she knew the sun would rise. In order to prevent David from getting assassinated by one badass milk fruit, she had to act now.

Without hesitation, Maddie lunged for his feet and knocked him on his back.

"What in the hell are you doing?" he yelled, just as the coconut dropped.

The hard green shell missed David, but lightly clipped the back of Maddie's skull.

Thwack!

Sharp waves of pain mulched her brain. She saw a million shimmering stars—yellow, white, blue—and smelled a dozen strange odors. She tried to stand but her knees were noodles and she wobbled precariously, grateful she'd taken off those deadly sandals.

"You saved my life," David murmured, staring from Maddie to the coconut and back again, obviously not realizing she'd been bushwhacked.

She blinked repeatedly and bit down hard on her bottom lip to keep from passing out. The pain was pretty intense, but she couldn't black out, she had to stop Cassie from getting married. She pushed her palm against the back of her head and willed the earth to stop spinning so fast.

"Maddie?" David knelt beside her. "Did you get hit?"

She tried to nod but it hurt too much.

"Can you hear me?"

"Uh-huh."

"Are you all right?"

Squinting she peered at David. How come there were two of him? He wasn't a twin. "Stop moving."

"I'm not moving."

There was something she was supposed to be thinking about. What was it?

Oh yeah. Cassie.

She swung her gaze toward the beach, saw Cassie and some guy holding hands and running through the tide toward a dune buggy parked on the sand.

"They're getting away." She gestured.

David jumped up and started to run to the beach but he hesitated and glanced back over his shoulder at her. She saw the internal conflict play across his face.

Stay and make sure she was okay, or go after his quarry?

She was afraid to trust him, but she had no real choice. "Go. Stop them. Save my sister."

"You're sure you're okay?"

"Yes. I'm fine. Go!"

He nodded, turned and sprinted off.

And that's when Maddie passed out cold.

Chapter 6

David ran up the beach, his heart thumping with adrenaline, his brain pounding out a single message. Stop Shriver. Stop Shriver. Stop Shriver.

But he was too late. The flasher lights of the dune buggy winked on and off as it disappeared over a faraway sand dune.

The well-dressed wedding guests gasped and scattered, knocking over folding chairs and shoving each other. The minister ducked behind the altar. One woman screamed. That's when David realized he was running with his gun drawn.

"Don't be alarmed, ladies and gentlemen," he said and held up his badge. "FBI." He pointed at the nearest man. "You, call an ambulance. My partner's been hurt."

His partner? Why had he said that?

He hurried to the grove, his gut knotting tighter with each step. He realized he was giving Cory Philpot plenty of time to hide the Cézanne if he did indeed possess it, but David couldn't afford to care about that right now. Maddie needed him.

It was dark in the grove and it took him a moment to see her body stretched out on the sand.

"Maddie?" he said softly. Anxiety grabbed his gut and squeezed hard.

He holstered his gun and knelt beside her. She looked so peaceful that at first he thought she was sleeping. He reached out to brush a lock of hair from her face and was startled to find her skin cool to the touch. He scooped her into his arms. She lay limp, not moving. Her breathing was shallow, but steady.

When she didn't respond, fear jammed his heart tight against his Adam's apple.

Please God, let her be okay.

"Maddie, can you hear me?"

Nothing.

Where in hell was that ambulance?

He cradled her in the crook of his arm and stared down into her face. In repose, she was especially beautiful, no worry lines furrowing her brow, no tension about her lips. A wisp of blonde hair curled against her cheekbone. He studied the curve of her chin, the sweet shape of her mouth, the slope of her cheek.

He had no idea what possessed him. Perhaps it was the fairy tale myth of the sleeping damsel brought to life by a kiss. Perhaps it was a desperate maneuver spurred by the guilt and fear he was determined to deny. Perhaps it was simply gut instinct.

He lowered his head and kissed her.

The minute his lips touched hers, she responded. Her mouth softened, grew warmer and her eyelashes fluttered lightly.

He felt her tongue gently probe his lips and she murmured a soft sound that turned him inside out.

Now that she had responded, he knew he should break the kiss, pull away, but she shifted into him and wrapped her arms around his neck, drawing him closer.

Ah, hell, he was just a man.

She tasted of heat and honey and heaven. She moved her lips against his, drinking him in. He heard his own heartbeat in his ears thumping loud and solid.

Stop this. Now.

But somehow the tables had turned and she was the one doing the kissing, giving him a momentous taste of her femininity. Her scent made him dizzy with desire.

This was so wrong on so many levels. He tried to pull back, but she held on like a cockleburr.

"Maddie," he mumbled around her kisses, "are you awake?"

She didn't answer; she just kept kissing him.

He gently shook her shoulders.

She continued pressing her lips against his chin, his cheek, his nose, wherever her mouth landed. Her eyes were closed, her response totally automatic. Even though she was technically conscious, she was still wandering in a foggy, mental never-never land.

"Sweetheart, can you hear me?"

She nuzzled his neck. She smelled like Christmas morning, full of wonder and surprise.

Stop thinking like this, he commanded himself.

"Mmm," she murmured.

"Wake up."

She licked his throat, her hot, wicked tongue scaring the living daylights out of him. How much damage had that coconut done to the pleasure center of her brain. Had it somehow flipped on her sexual switch?

He gulped and cautiously ran his fingers over her head in

search of a bump. She purred like a kitten and arched her back into him. He found a small knot just above her left ear.

Ho boy. What now?

He tried to disentangle himself and ease away. It was difficult, considering he wanted nothing more than to kiss her right back, but he wasn't the kind of guy who would exploit the situation, no matter how tempting. He liked his women to know exactly what they were doing when he made love to them.

"Come on," he coaxed. "That's enough of that. No more kissing. Wake up now." Gently he slapped her cheeks, hoping to rouse her to full waking consciousness.

Without warning, Maddie sat bolt upright, doubled her fists and punched him squarely in the solar plexus.

Peyton didn't stop until they were several miles away from Dead Man's Cove. He parked the dune buggy not far from the Rum Point ferry landing, and then he turned to clamp a hand over Cassie's wrist.

"What in bloody hell just happened back there?" he yelled.

"I don't know." Cassie wasn't lying. When she'd heard Maddie cry out her name she had been as surprised and confused as Peyton. How on earth had her sister managed to track her to Grand Cayman?

And when David had come running from the coconut grove with his gun drawn, well, her heart had just about stopped.

Undoubtedly, David and Maddie would have misinterpreted the wedding. They probably thought she loved Shriver and had decided to become Bonnie to his Clyde. Not that she could blame them from drawing those conclusions. The evidence was pretty damning.

As unsettling as their appearance was, she was really glad they'd shown up when they did, otherwise, she would be Mrs. Peyton Shriver right now.

Peyton grabbed her chin and forced her to look at him. "Look me in the face, Cassie, and tell me the truth. Are you still working for David Marshall?"

"N...n...no," she stammered, her gaze locked with his. She'd never seen Peyton act so macho and forceful. It was more of a turn-on than scary.

Easy, Cassie, no matter how sexy, he's still a thief.

His grip twisted like a vise against her wrist.

"Ow," she cried out. "You're hurting me."

Okay, she was officially not turned on anymore.

"The truth." Peyton didn't release her.

"I'm not working for him. I promise." She grimaced, her hand throbbing from the pressure of his clench.

"Then how did he find us here? How come he shows up just in the nick of time to prevent us from getting married?"

"I don't know. I swear on my mother's life. Please, Peyton, you're really hurting me."

He let her go and sat back in the dune buggy. "Maybe it was Philpot," he mused. "Double-crossing me. Trying to collect the reward the Kimbell is putting up."

"Or Jocko Blanco," she pointed out. "You just double-crossed him and he's bound to be looking for revenge."

Peyton shook his head. "Blanco would never rat me out to the feds. He'd just hunt me down and snap off my digits."

Cassie didn't ask him to elaborate on which digits.

"If it wasn't you who betrayed me, it has to be Philpot." Peyton nodded.

"It wasn't me, but maybe it wasn't Philpot either. Maybe David is just a good detective."

"Not bloody likely." Peyton laughed. "He's been trying to catch me for ten years. Ever since I scammed his dear old auntie. The man couldn't find his arse with both hands in a house of mirrors. No, someone ratted me out."

"It wasn't me," she insisted.

"I guess I have a decision to make." Peyton gave her a hard speculative stare.

"A decision?" she echoed.

"Whether to trust you and take you with me or leave you here for David Marshall to find. If you're telling me the truth, then he'll arrest you. The man is a bulldog. He won't care that you fell in love with me. To him you're as guilty as I am."

Cassie gulped. She was just starting to realize the trouble she was in. If she went with Shriver, David would be convinced she was in on the theft of the Cézanne. She would lose her job, and very likely go to prison when he caught up with them. If she stayed behind, Peyton would get away with the painting. She would probably still lose her job and she would not get what she wanted most in the world, to prove to Maddie that she was competent and capable and could stand on her own two feet.

What to do?

She wasn't one to vacillate. She had to convince Peyton to take her with him. The only way this whole scenario was going to have a happy resolution was if she set a trap for both Peyton and Jerome Levy, the art broker who had commissioned the theft of the Cézanne.

What she needed was a plan. A big, bold plan so foolhardy it just might work. She also needed a way to let Maddie and David know that she was still working the case from the inside.

But what and how?

She had to be very careful. She could not arouse Peyton's suspicions.

The ferry docked.

"There's my ride," he said.

"Don't you mean *our* ride?" she dared.

Peyton studied her. Cassie did her best to look sad and vulnerable and sexy all at the same time.

"Don't make this goodbye," she said, wracking her brain for a clue to leave behind that Maddie would understand. If her twin was convinced of her innocence, Cassie knew she would move heaven and earth to prove it to David.

"Give me one good reason why I shouldn't leave you."

"Because I know something you don't."

"And that is?" Peyton crossed his arms over his chest in a go-ahead-prove-yourself pose.

"The Prado is in the process of installing a new state-of-the-art security system. Even if my friendship with the curator can get us in the door, we might not be able to bypass the alarm like you planned. It depends on how far along they are in implementing the new method."

"So your convincing argument is that you're basically useless to me?"

"Not exactly."

"What exactly?"

"I happen to know whose system they copied right down to the same security code."

"Whose?"

She shook her head. "How stupid do I look? You take me with you, then I'll let you in on my little secret."

He cocked his head and eyed her speculatively. "Why didn't you tell me this before?"

"Because I wasn't sure I could trust you not to dump me once I'd served my purpose."

"The ace up your sleeve, ay?"

"Something like that."

Peyton laughed. "Cassie luv, you're some piece of work."

"So you'll take me with you?" She caught her breath and waited. He took so long answering she thought she might black out from breathlessness.

"I hope I don't end up regretting this," he said, "but come on."

He hopped from the dune buggy and held his hand out to her. She grabbed the train of her wedding gown so she wouldn't trip over it and gave him her other hand.

Leave a clue for Maddie. Think, think, think.

All at once the answer hit and Cassie knew exactly the right thing to leave behind for her sister to find.

"David, speak to me." Maddie hovered over him, clenching and unclenching her fists.

David lay on the ground, doubled over and gasping for air.

"I'm so sorry. I didn't mean to punch you. I don't know why I punched you. Autonomic reflex I'm guessing. You were kissing me and in my dazed state I thought you were a stranger trying to accost me. By the way, why were you kissing me?"

Unable to draw in air, he simply shook his head.

"Could you step out of the way, miss?"

Maddie glanced up to see two burly paramedics coming through the trees with a stretcher. She rose to her feet. The men hustled over, unceremoniously picked David up and dumped him onto the stretcher.

"Not . . . me," he wheezed.

"What did you say?" asked the paramedic, tilting his head toward David's mouth.

"Her." David waved a hand at Maddie.

Both paramedics turned to look at her. She shrugged. Yes, she'd taken a knock to the head, but she wasn't about to go to the hospital. Not when Cassie was still AWOL.

With her index finger she drew a circle in the air near her temple. "Coconut must have knocked him loopy," she said. "Don't listen to him. He doesn't know what he's saying."

The paramedics nodded and started hauling him away.

"Dammit, Maddie," David said, coming up from the stretcher in one lumbering movement. Apparently he'd gotten his breath back. "You get on this stretcher right now." He pointed at the gurney, looking like a disgruntled father chastising his child.

That attitude wasn't going to wash with her. "No."

"You got hit on the head."

"It's nothing. I don't even have a headache."

"Liar."

How did he know she was lying? Her head hurt like the dickens but she was not going to the hospital. She couldn't show weakness. Especially not now. Not when her twin sister had disappeared again. Not in front of this strength-is-everything FBI agent.

"I'm fine," she insisted.

"So no one goes to the hospital?" one paramedic asked.

"She does." David jerked a thumb at Maddie at the same time she said, "He goes."

"You both look fine to me," said the second paramedic.

"She got hit on the head by a coconut and she was unconscious for several minutes," David said.

"I thought you said he got hit by the coconut." The first paramedic raised his eyebrows at Maddie.

"Okay, so I lied, but I'm not going to the hospital." She shifted her gaze to David. "And you can't make me."

"Fine, great, go ahead, suffer the consequences of a concussion." He threw his hands up in the air, pivoted on his heel and stormed away.

"Hey, wait, where are you going?" Maddie took off after him, leaving the paramedics standing there perplexed.

"To do my job," he called over his shoulder.

"I'm coming with you." She scurried to catch up.

"Of course you are," he said, his voice heavy with sarcasm. "Heaven forbid you trust me to perform my duties. You would rather risk your health than have a little faith in me."

"It's nothing personal."

They were walking abreast down the beach toward Philpot's house. The guests had scattered but the altar remained and the tiki torches still burned. It looked romantic in a rather wistful sort of way.

"Sure as hell feels personal," he grumbled.

Maddie put a hand on his arm to stop him. She tried not to notice how strong his biceps were or how her fingers seemed to sizzle against his arm. "Where do we go from here?"

"I'm going to call the local police for help searching Philpot's house and locating the dune buggy."

"Because of the wedding you're more convinced than ever that Cassie is a part of this, aren't you?"

His eyes met hers. His gaze was not unkind. "How can you continue to deny her obvious involvement?"

"She's my sister. I just know."

"Tell me, Maddie, what would it take for me to earn such blind loyalty from you?"

The question knocked her off guard. "Don't ever let me down," she blurted.

He stared at her and their gazes fused. An invisible, high-energy current passed between them. Something unspoken but so real Maddie felt the pressure in the very center of her body.

"Good to know," he said at last. "Good to know."

Two hours later after David and the Grand Cayman police had thoroughly searched Philpot's mansion and found not even a hint of the Cézanne, David received a call from another contingency of police officers who had been searching the island for Shriver and Cassie.

They were standing in Philpot's living room, Maddie struggling to pretend her head wasn't still throbbing from the coconut. David hung up the phone and turned to her. "They found the dune buggy at Rum Point Landing."

Maddie plastered a palm against her throat. "And Cassie?"

He shook his head. "No sign of her."

"What now?"

"We're going to head on over to the dune buggy, see if we can find some clues."

Maddie noticed he said *we*. For some crazy reason her heart did a somersault.

"I'm ready," she said. "Let's go."

It took them only ten minutes to reach Rum Point Landing. David met with the police officer who'd found the dune buggy while Maddie gazed out at the ocean. *Cassie, where are you? Are you okay?* She sent her questions into the ether, hoping her twin would pick up the telepathy.

David touched her shoulder lightly. "Beautiful night."

"Yes."

"You want to help me go over the dune buggy?"

"Wouldn't that be breaking protocol? What if I found incriminating evidence and destroyed it?"

"Would you do that?" he asked.

"I might," she admitted.

He looked more than disappointed in her answer. He shook his head. "Then you better just sit on the dock and wait for me."

She'd just banished herself and she couldn't say why she'd done it. With a lump in her throat, she plunked down on the dock while David pulled on a pair of latex gloves. He took the flashlight one of the officers had given him and began processing the dune buggy for evidence.

Hugging her knees to her chest, she watched him work in the limited illumination from his flashlight. He looked so stern, so serious. He studiously pored over the vehicle, plodding, methodical, not missing a thing. She could tell he was damned good at his job and that didn't bode well for her sister.

"Maddie," he said.

"Yes?"

He held something in the palm of his hand. "Could you come here a minute?"

She rose to her feet, dusting off her bottom with both hands and half-heartedly ambled over. Maybe if she walked slowly enough his discovery would evaporate into thin air.

No such luck.

"What is it?" she asked once she'd reached him. She sounded quarrelsome and she knew it.

"Does this belong to your sister?" He shone the light on his palm and a small cross earring with a ruby in the center glistened up at her.

She caught her breath. She had bought those earrings for Cassie on their twenty-second birthday the year they had lived in Madrid.

With the uncanny intuition of a twin, she knew the earring was a clue Cassie had intentionally left behind for her to find. She also understood that if her sister had left a clue, it meant she was under Shriver's control and not free to get away or call her for help.

Or, she could have just lost the earring.

But Maddie didn't believe that, not for a second.

"Well?" David asked.

"It's hers." Should she tell him the rest? Maddie mulled over her choices. Should she mention her suspicions to David or should she keep quiet and go after Cassie on her own?

"And ...?" He cocked his head, looked at her expectantly. He seemed to know she was holding out on him.

"There is no and."

"I can read it on your face, Maddie. What aren't you telling me?"

Her gaze met his and she knew he wasn't going to let her get away with not talking. She might as well tell him.

That's right, his eyes coaxed. Give it up.

Knowing she really didn't have much of a choice, Maddie confessed. "Shriver's taking her to Madrid."

Chapter 7

With the help of the Grand Cayman police, David gained access to Shriver's hotel room at the Hyatt Regency on Seven Mile Beach. It was a quarter past eleven when he and Maddie stepped into the room.

David had one thing on his mind—find out where Shriver had gone. He felt like he was rapidly losing control of the investigation and he hated feeling stymied. The fiasco at Dead Man's Bay had dinged his ego. Shriver had been within his grasp and he'd let him get away. He had to do something, anything, to regain his sense of power.

The room was a wreck with the bedcovers strewn across the floor, dresser drawers pulled out and the closet door wide open. Someone had left in a big rush.

Maddie took one look at the room, slumped into a nearby chair and dropped her head in her hands.

Poor woman. She was exhausted. Dark circles ringed her eyes and she kept rubbing her temple. He knew she had a pounding headache from the coconut, but he also knew there was no way she would admit it.

She was tough. He'd grant her that.

Concern for her softened his heart. He had an unchar-

acteristically sentimental urge to draw her into his arms
and promise her that everything would be all right.

Knock it off, Marshall. No getting sloppy over a sus-
pect's sister.

"Why do you believe Cassie and Shriver might have
gone to Madrid?" he asked more to distract himself than
anything else and sauntered into the bathroom.

The shower curtain was half-in, half-out of the tub,
and there was water on the floor. Shriver hadn't been gone
long. Two hours. Three, tops. He and Cassie might even
still be on the island. The local authorities were checking
departing flights for him.

"Cassie loves Madrid." Maddie's voice sounded heavy,
defeated. "We lived there for a year when we were in college. She worked at the Museo del Prado."

"What?" David poked his head out of the bathroom.
"What was that last part?"

"Cassie worked at the Prado."

"She knows the museum inside out?"

"Yes."

David exhaled loudly. Ho boy, this tidbit of information
had all the earmarks of big trouble.

"I know what you're thinking." Maddie stood and
marched over to square off with him. The pulse in her
neck thumped. Like an ace poker player he was beginning
to recognize her tell. Whenever she was gearing up to give
him a hard time that pulse point danced.

"Reading minds now, are we?"

She sank her hands on her hips. "You're thinking she
and Shriver are going to rob the Prado."

"I never said that." Her feistiness amused him. Too bad
their timing was off. If they'd met under different circumstances he would be chasing her hot and heavy.

"My sister is not a thief."

"Much as I like a good fight, we've been over this ground before. Besides, I've got work to do. If you'll excuse me." He moved past her, his arm barely brushing hers.

That light touch should have been nothing.

Instead, it was everything.

Flesh against flesh. Heat against heat. Scent against scent. He'd never been more aware of anything in his entire life than the brief whisper of her skin scorching his. Holy cow, he had it bad and that wasn't good.

Mentally, he shook himself and stalked over to the bed-side table looking for anything to divert his attention from his damnable attraction to the woman staring after him.

Did she feel it too?

He didn't trust himself to look at her. If he saw the same desire written across her face, he would want her even more.

And he couldn't have her.

At least not yet. Not as long as her sister was a robbery suspect.

He tried to concentrate on searching for clues but his ears were highly attuned to the sound of her breathing. Was it his imagination or was she raspy with desire?

David glanced down at the notepad resting on the table and noticed there were indentations in the paper from where someone had written on the top sheet and then ripped it off.

"Do you have a pencil?" he asked.

"Yes, I think so. Hang on." She dug in her shoulder bag, extracted a mechanical pencil and rolled down the lead for him. "Here."

Their fingers connected when she passed the pencil over and he tried to ignore the inferno blasting up his arm but the blistering sensation was like ignoring the sun.

Never mind. Do your job.

He took the pencil and rubbed the lead across the indentations.

"Let me see." Maddie stood next to him, trying to peer over his shoulder. Her warm breath stirred the hairs on the nape of his neck and he felt himself stiffen like a starched shirt at a Chinese laundry.

"Jeez, woman," he barked. "Give me some breathing room."

"Okay, sorry." She held her palms up in a gesture of surrender and thankfully, stepped away.

David glanced at the paper in his hand. The pencil rubbing revealed not only the address of the Louvre museum, but also flight information to Paris.

"Well? What does it say?"

"I'm afraid this blows your Madrid theory all to hell."

"How's that?"

He passed her the paper.

"They're headed for Paris?" Maddie frowned. She seemed confused and for once David wasn't excited about being right.

"It looks like the earring your sister left behind wasn't a clue at all, but a red herring. If that's the case, it means unequivocally that Cassie is working with Shriver. And I think I know why they're going to Paris. We messed up Shriver's connection with Philpot. He's desperate to find a way to unload the Cézanne and Jerome Levy, the one man who can help him out of his pickle, lives in Paris."

"That's not what it means at all. I think the Paris info is the red herring. Shriver wanted you to fall for it and take off to Paris."

"Now why would he do that?"

"Because he's going to force Cassie to help him rob

the Prado. The curator, Isabella Vasquez, is a friend of Cassie's and I'm certain that's why Shriver took her hostage," she said, valiantly trying to support her own desperate theory.

Her chin was notched in the air, her hands fisted at her sides, her eyes glistening in defiance.

"I'm sorry, Maddie, but as far as I'm concerned this evidence points to Cassie's direct involvement. You're more than welcome to go to Madrid, but I'm booking the next flight to Paris."

"And while you're mucking around in Paris, Shriver will be using my sister's connections to rob the Prado."

"You're wrong."

The pulse point in her throat was beating triple time. "Now I'm beginning to understand why you've been chasing Shriver for all these years but haven't caught him."

"What's that supposed to mean?" David glared. She'd gone straight for the jugular. The woman knew how to slice a man deep.

Maddie shoved her face closer to his. He tried not to stare at her luscious lips and failed miserably. She was so incredibly sexy when she was steamed. It was all he could do not to kiss her.

"It means, Hot Shot, that if you would think things through and act more cautiously you might not waste so much time running up blind alleys."

"Not everyone needs to be as plodding and methodical as you," he retorted.

"This half-cocked loose cannon shtick is going to come back and bite you in the ass."

"This isn't the wrong move," he insisted stubbornly.

But even as he clung to his position, David knew if he made the wrong choice by traveling to Paris, not only was his FBI career in jeopardy, but his mistake could cost Cassie her life.

David Marshall was the most infuriating, arrogant man she'd ever met in her life and the fact that she was inordinately attracted to him only made things worse.

What was wrong with her? Why did she find his high-handed masculinity so exciting? Why couldn't she stop thinking about the irritating man and what had happened in the coconut grove? Why couldn't she stop wishing she'd been more awake for their kiss?

She'd given in to him. Not because she thought he was right about Paris, but because Cassie would need her protection if it turned out he was correct. She was the only thing standing between her twin and the hardheaded FBI agent determined to see her behind bars.

They chartered a plane from Grand Cayman to Miami and caught the next available flight to Paris at two A.M. Maddie took her assigned seat next to the window. She did her best to ignore David, but denying him was akin to denying the sun in the desert. Physically, he was so present. Big and prominent and...*there*.

Two little girls in matching dresses moved down the aisle of the airplane. The oldest one was eight or nine, the youngest barely six. They were carrying matching tote bags and the oldest one was holding the youngest one's hand. They took the two seats in front of Maddie and David.

Watching them caused Maddie's chest to knot up. How many times had she and Cassie boarded a similar plane, shuttling from their mother and stepfather's home in Belize or Panama or South Africa bound for their father's home in San Antonio? She knew exactly how the oldest one felt.

Responsible.

The flight attendant helped the girls get situated, but she'd no more than walked away when the youngest one undid her seat belt, turned around and peered at David over the back of her seat.

"Hi." The girl grinned at him. Six years old and already an incorrigible flirt.

"Hi, yourself." He grinned back. His smile was so genuine, Maddie forgot she was mad at him.

"I'm Katy."

David winked at her and she giggled coyly. "Nice to meet you, Katy. I'm David and this is Maddie."

"Sit back down," her older sister hissed. "And leave those people alone."

"That's Rebecca," Katy said with a dismissive flip of her hand. "She's my sister. She's bor-r-ring."

Maddie felt a special kinship with Rebecca. She knew what the girl went through trying to corral her ebullient sibling.

"You know what Mom said about talking to strangers." Rebecca tugged on her sister's sleeve. "Turn around."

"They're not strange, Becca."

"We don't know them, that makes them strangers." Rebecca was trying to keep her voice low, but her perky sister was having none of the subterfuge.

"We don't know the airplane lady either and you talked to her."

"She works for the airline. It's okay if you talk to her."

"But they're very nice, Becca," Katy coaxed. "Look at 'em."

Rebecca peeked around the seat. She arrowed David and Maddie a suspicious glance. "Sorry about her," she apologized. "This is her first time traveling without our mom."

"I like how your hair sticks up," Katy said boldly to David. She tugged at her own hair, trying to make it spike like his.

"Sit down," Rebecca repeated. "Or I'm gonna tell Dad on you when we get to Paris."

Katy wrinkled her nose. "Do you think that stupid Trixie will be there?"

"Probably, she's his girlfriend now."

Katy blew a raspberry.

"Come on, sit down," Rebecca begged.

"You're not the boss of me." Katy tossed her head.

Gosh, Maddie thought, if she had a dollar for every time she'd heard that line she'd own Bill Gates.

David leaned forward and spoke softly to the little girl. "The plane's about to take off, Katy, and you don't want to get thrown out of your seat. I'd hate to see you skin your knee. Why don't you sit down and put on the seat belt until we're airborne?"

"Okay," Katy said easily, turned around and plunked down. Rebecca shot him a grateful glance.

David looked over at Maddie. He was still grinning. She realized she had never seen him looking relaxed.

"Cute kid," he said.

"You're good with her."

"She likes male attention. Sounds like she doesn't get enough of daddy's time."

"That sounds familiar," Maddie muttered and it came out harsher than she intended.

"Strike a nerve?"

She shrugged. She wasn't about to tell him about her daddy issues. It was none of his damned business.

David let it go and nodded at the back of the girls' seats. "I'm guessing their names could just as easily be Maddie and Cassie."

"They're not twins."

"You two don't act like twins anyway."

"I know. Cassie is fun and sexy and charming and I'm stodgy and anxious and overly cautious."

"I never said that."

"I'm sure, like everyone else, you prefer her company to mine." Maddie knew she sounded like she was feeling sorry for herself, and maybe she was a little. Her life had been spent not only in her sister's shadow but being there to catch Cassie when her escapades went awry. Just once, she would like to have her own limelight, her own adventures.

"No," David said. "I don't think that. I think Cassie is flighty and irresponsible and self-centered."

"Hey, no bad-mouthing my twin. She's not self-centered. She just doesn't stop and think how her actions affect others."

"Isn't that what it means to be self-centered?"

"You don't understand her."

"So help me to understand."

Maddie told him then, about Cassie's accident and how it had shaped both of their lives. She told him about her vow to God.

"Cassie was in a coma for three months and in a rehab hospital for six months after that. She had to learn how to walk all over again."

"The accident on the pond wasn't your fault," he said.

"Yes it was. My mother told me to watch her."

"How come your mother always put you in charge? How come she wasn't the one watching Cassie?"

Maddie shrugged. "Mama is as scatterbrained as my sister. They're two peas in a pod. They're so caught up in having fun and being creative they forget about the mundane but essential things in life."

"Like?"

"For instance, Mom was famous for her odd-ball breakfasts, especially after Dad left. Cold pizza. A can of beans. Whatever was in the cupboard. If we were lucky, she would throw eggs in a plastic bowl, nuke them and call them scrambled. Of course, they exploded and guess who had to clean egg gunk off the inside of the microwave."

"Yuck."

"Could have been worse. At least she took the eggs out of the shells first."

"I can just see an industrious young Maddie scrubbing off egg plaster. I bet you wore rubber gloves and an apron."

"How did you know?"

"It fits." He smiled and she felt herself relenting toward him. Okay the guy could be a hard-ass, but sometimes he made her feel really special in a way no one else ever had.

"See. Boring even when I was ten."

"Not boring. Tough. You said your Dad left. What caused your parents to split up?"

"Cassie's illness ripped them apart. I love my Dad but he's something of a good-time Charlie. When the going got tough, Dad got going. Don't get me wrong. He stayed in our lives. We saw him every other weekend and a month in the summer but he couldn't handle serious stuff. He's still that way at fifty. I don't think he's ever going to grow up."

"You kept everyone grounded."

"Somebody had to."

"You're pretty amazing, Maddie Cooper. You know that?"

His words warmed her to the very back of her heart and she felt her throat tighten. She glanced out the window into the darkness so he couldn't see the mist of a tear in her eye. It had been a rough day and she was feeling a little emotional.

"Know what else I like about you?" he whispered.

"What?" She smiled faintly. Her cheeks tingled. God, she was actually blushing.

"You're strong and smart and thoughtful. You can be a little hardheaded at times, but so can I. You have a really sly sense of humor that slaps my funny bone. You're honest, trustworthy and dependable."

"You make me sound like a Boy Scout."

"Believe me, babe," he drawled and raked an appreciative gaze over her body. "There's nothing boyish about you."

Babe. He'd called her babe. She went all whooshy inside. Don't smile for gosh sakes, Maddie. He'll think you like his flattery.

Trouble was, she *did* like it. A lot.

"Are you flirting with me, Agent Marshall?" She slanted him a coy glance that was pure Cassie.

Their gazes locked. Wow-o-wow-o-wow. The heat from his intelligent dark gray eyes toasted her from the inside out. She stared into him, he stared right back.

Everything faded from her mind. Cassie, Shriver, the stolen art. Her past, their future.

Nothing mattered except the breathtaking electricity of the moment. The emotion on his face was intense and knocked her off balance. She saw so many things reflected in those eyes. Desire, confusion, curiosity.

David took her hand.

She wanted to draw back. She should have drawn back, but she was so tired and his hand felt so good that she just sat there, staring at his fingers. He had very nice fingers. Long and strong and comforting.

Watch out! You know better than to trust him. He's a cop and your sister is a suspect.

He angled his head toward her. "Would you be upset if I was flirting with you?"

"I don't know."

"It's not professional of me."

"No."

He leaned closer. "I shouldn't be doing this."

"Not at all," she murmured, moving in his direction.

"We really can't depend on this attraction," he said, inching his mouth ever closer to hers.

"Absolutely not," she agreed, her gaze trained on his lips.

"The timing, the situation, it's all wrong." He was barely whispering.

"Couldn't be worse." She shifted her gaze from his lips to his eyes and her heart almost jumped right out of her chest.

"How's your headache?" he asked, reaching over to gingerly rub the spot where the coconut had struck.

What was the protocol in a situation like this? Her dating skills were rusty. Not that this was dating, but it most certainly was a sexual attraction man-woman thing.

His fingers, firm but gentle, probed the tender area. She inhaled his warm masculine scent. Using the pad of his thumb, he massaged her temple in a circular motion with light, steady pressure. It felt so good she almost moaned out loud.

"Relax," he murmured. "Just relax."

Yeah, right. How was she supposed to relax when her head was practically nestled on his shoulder and those devastating lips were oh so close?

"That's right, Maddie, let go."

And the next thing she knew, they were kissing.

She couldn't say who made the first move. Maybe it was him, maybe it was her. Bottom line? It didn't matter. They were swept away like flotsam on the sea.

Closing her eyes, she savored the warmth of his mouth, oblivious to their surroundings. Her head reeled from the intoxicating power. His kiss was a thousand times more wonderful than the fantasies she'd been spinning.

He kissed her as if he couldn't get enough, drinking her in, teasing her with his tongue. He used just the right amount of pressure. The kiss wasn't too demanding, nor was it too plain. Not too wet, but moist and hot and perfect.

Then again, what else would she have expected from a man with such raw animal magnetism. She'd bet her last dollar that sex with him would be phenomenal.

The pilot turned off the seat belt sign, the faint dinging hardly registering in the back of her mind. She didn't notice that some passengers were moving up and down the aisles, that the flight attendants were serving drinks. She wrapped her arms around his neck and he threaded his fingers through her hair.

They were welded together, singed by the kiss to beat all kisses.

And if it hadn't been for little Katy popping her head over the top of her seat to giggle at them, Maddie feared they would not have stopped kissing until they reached Paris.

Chapter 8

David needed java. Pronto. A double espresso would be ideal but any variety of caffeine would do the trick. Something strong to wire his system, kick his butt into high gear and buzz his brain so fast he would forget all about the taste of Maddie's lips.

Before they'd left Grand Cayman for Miami, he had contacted Henri Gault, his counterpart at Interpol and asked him to put a surveillance team on Shriver and Cassie when they arrived in Paris. He was itching to get his feet on the ground and his head back into the investigation.

Henri, a reedy man with a thick head of dark hair, an oblong face and sad-sack eyes met them at the arrival gate.

"Why don't you go on through customs?" David nodded at the checkpoint.

He wanted Maddie out of earshot so he could discuss the case privately with Henri. He also hoped to minimize the risk of her spilling his secret. He didn't want anyone else knowing he'd recruited Cassie. As far as Henri knew, Cassie was simply Shriver's doxy, not an unofficial FBI informant turned art thief accomplice.

"You're not coming through customs with me?" Maddie asked.

He pulled his badge from his pocket. "I get to circumvent."

"Can't you circumvent me?"

"Nope," he said at the same time Henri said, *"Oui."*

Henri looked at David and he shook his head.

Maddie narrowed her eyes. "This is retribution for me swiping your badge back in Dallas, isn't it?"

"Payback's a bitch." He wiggled his fingers. "Bye, bye."

She glared, shouldered her bag and headed for the long customs line.

Henri glanced from David to Maddie and smirked. David knew what the Frenchman was thinking. "She's not my mistress."

"Then she's fair game, *non*?" Henri wriggled his eyebrows suggestively.

"No. Stay away from her if you prize your neck."

"Ooh-la-la." Henri laughed. "It must be *amour."*

"No it's not," he denied hotly. "She's Cassie Cooper's sister."

"And you let her come along with you?"

"It was either that or have her running around on her own getting into trouble. This way I can keep her under my thumb."

"As long as your thumb is the only thing you keep her under."

"Shut up."

Henri laughed and escorted him around customs. On the other side of the barricade crowds of travelers streamed past them. They moved to one side of the walkway, waiting for Maddie to clear the inspection.

"So what's the scoop on Shriver?" David asked, resting his shoulder against the wall.

"We followed him from the airport. He's staying at the Hotel de Louvre."

"Pricey digs."

"Shriver is poetic, not subtle."

"And Cassie Cooper?"

"She's not with him."

"Huh?" David squared his posture. "What do you mean she's not with him?"

"He was alone, *mon ami*." Henri shrugged. "Cassie Cooper went to Madrid."

David ran a hand over his jaw. It was scratchy with beard stubble. He hadn't shaved in two days. "You're sure?"

"Positive."

"Do we have anyone tracking her?"

Henri nodded. "Yes, we have a man on it."

"Good work." David took a deep breath and relaxed. This was an encouraging sign. Cassie's absence in Paris meant she probably was just Shriver's girlfriend and not his partner-in-crime as David had feared.

That tidbit of information should make Maddie happy.

And then a thought occurred to him. What if he could find a way to take advantage of this identical twin stuff? He had mistaken Maddie for Cassie on the jogging path. Under the right circumstances, Shriver might easily make the same mistake. Maybe David could find a way to use Maddie to entrap the art thief. Instinctively, he knew she would never go for it. The minute Maddie found out Cassie was in Madrid, she would hop the next plane to Spain and to hell with him.

You just can't tell her yet, the pitchfork-toting devil on his left shoulder announced.

David, chided the halo-sporting angel on his right shoulder. *You can't do that to Maddie. She's placed her trust in you.*

Trust, schmust. You wanna catch Shriver, don'tcha? Ignore goody-two-shoes and keep your trap shut, the devil urged.

Angel be damned. The devil made a lot more sense.

"Do me a favor, Henri, and don't tell Maddie her sister went to Madrid."

"Ah, I understand. You're trying to protect her."

"Uh . . . yeah . . . sure. That's it."

"Whatever you want," Henri murmured. "So we're assuming Shriver came to Paris to make amends with Jerome Levy. I've got a team on both Shriver and Levy by the way."

At the mention of Levy's name, David grit his teeth. For years he'd suspected Levy was the one who'd brokered the theft of Aunt Caroline's Rembrandt, but he'd never been able to prove it. He would love to bust Levy almost as much as he would enjoy busting Shriver.

"How else is Shriver going to unload the Cézanne if not through his old pal Levy? I cut off his connection with Philpot. There aren't too many brokers willing to fence a painting that hot."

"Shriver is taking a big chance showing up here," Henri continued. "He knows we're watching him. Why not lie low, sell the painting later?"

"I'm breathing down his neck hot and heavy, making things pretty uncomfortable. He doesn't want to get caught with the Cézanne in his possession. Circumstances are forcing him to take chances he wouldn't ordinarily take."

"Or maybe," Henri mused, "he's fallen in love with Cassie Cooper and this was his last big score before giving up a life of crime for his lady love."

"You French with the romance. Is that all you think about?" David snorted.

"One day, *mon ami,* love will hit you too," Henri predicted slyly.

"Hit who with what?" Maddie asked, arriving on the tail end of their conversation.

"Nothing," David lied, but he couldn't deny the intense awareness that smacked him in the gut whenever he looked into her eyes.

It's just lust. Nothing else, he told himself.

"I know what you're up to, Marshall," she said.

"I'm not up to anything." For one strange moment David had thought she was talking about the sexual fantasies wreaking havoc with his imagination.

"What have you been saying behind my back?" Maddie poked him in the chest with her index finger. "I know that's why you made me go through customs. You're hiding something from me about Cassie. What is it?"

The woman loved busting his chops. And the bizarre thing was, he respected her for it. Most people didn't have the courage to call him on the carpet. They bought into his bluster and let him have his way.

But that insistent index finger tapping his chest and the determined expression on her face stopped him in his tracks.

And damn if Henri wasn't snickering.

"The truth," Maddie demanded.

How in the hell did she know he was lying? Her perceptiveness knocked him off balance.

Turn the tables on her. Quick. Anything to wrestle back control and keep from feeling guilty.

"I'm offended," he said.

"Offended?"

"That you would impugn my character."

"Ha! It would be easier to offend a polecat, Agent Marshall."

Was she calling him a skunk? Man, but the woman was sharp with those zingers.

Henri guffawed. David glared at his friend.

Maddie eyed him speculatively. "You swear you're not keeping anything from me."

"Scouts honor." He raised two fingers, held her gaze and tried his best to look guileless.

"Were you ever a Boy Scout?"

"No. It's a symbolic gesture."

"You wouldn't betray my trust, would you David?" She sank her hands on her hips.

"Who me?"

That's it, the devil egged. *Lay it on thick.*

For shame. The angel clucked his tongue.

Hey, David justified himself. An FBI agent occasionally had to make a few moral judgment calls in order to score an arrest. And if catching Shriver meant delaying the truth from Maddie for a little while longer, he'd take his lumps like a man.

Because nothing, absolutely nothing, meant more to him than arresting the art thief. Bringing Shriver in meant far more than seeing justice done or evening the score for his aunt. It meant he was a winner.

At that moment, the two-way radio clamped at Henri's belt loop squawked. Henri answered in rapid-fire French. David had trouble keeping up with the conversation.

"What is it?" Maddie asked when Henri finished speaking and turned to look at them.

"Both Shriver and Levy are on the move," Henri explained. "Shriver left his hotel carrying something large and flat and wrapped in brown paper."

"The Cézanne," David guessed.

"It looks as if they are about to make the exchange."

"What about my sister?" Maddie asked. "Is she with Shriver?"

"No," Henri answered. "He is alone."

David rubbed his hands together. "Let's hit 'em."

They crowded into Henri's Mini Cooper—Henri and David up front, Maddie crammed into the back seat—and careened through the cobblestone streets, siren blaring. Henri's chase team gave him frequent updates over the two-way radio, as they played fox and hound with Levy.

Maddie was frustrated with her inability to speak French. She was desperate to know what was happening. And where was Cassie anyway?

After the last update, David glanced at Maddie in the rearview mirror. She met his gaze. "What?"

"Levy's headed up the Eiffel Tower."

"Shriver is going to hand off a valuable Cézanne at a crowded tourist spot? Seems pretty risky to me," she said.

David shrugged. "Maybe he's thinking it's better to hide in plain sight."

"Or maybe he's afraid to meet Levy in private," Henri suggested. "He did double-cross the man."

She curled her fingers into the seat cushion and managed to restrain herself from telling Henri to drive faster. She wanted Shriver in custody and her sister found.

"Cassie's okay," David said.

He was still studying her in the rearview mirror and that, along with the fact he'd just read her mind, unnerved Maddie.

"You don't know that. Shriver could have killed her."

"If he was going to kill her he would have done it in Grand Cayman, not paid for her ticket to Europe."

He was right, but Maddie couldn't stop imagining the worst.

Henri turned off the siren as they neared the Eiffel Tower. He made radio contact with his crew who told him Levy was headed for the top but they were holding off, waiting for Henri.

They parked, jumped out of the car and jogged toward the base of the Eiffel Tower. A swish of tires and the rumble of engines arose as vehicles passed them on the street. Henri was on the radio, contacting the team tailing Shriver.

"Where is our target now?" Henri asked. The radio crackled an answer.

Maddie moved closer to David. "What did Henri's man say?"

"Shriver's headed east on the Champs-Elysées. Coming straight toward us."

Her heart skipped. Startled she realized the irregular rhythm wasn't from fear, but from excitement. The same sort of excitement that had suffused her when she'd trained for the Olympics.

"Omigosh," she said. "We're about to catch him."

"Feels good, doesn't it?" David's eyes glowed, his excitement clearly matching her own.

The look they shared was magnetic, drawing Maddie deeper into David's world. She gulped, both invigorated and unnerved by the sensation.

Henri flashed his badge at the ticket booth and they scooted on through.

"The stairs will be quicker," Henri called over his shoulder and skirted around the huddle of tourists waiting for the elevator.

They took the stairs two at a time. The weather was a damp gray drizzle and the brisk breeze chapped Maddie's cheeks. But she didn't care. They were about to nab

Shriver and this Levy person. Once Shriver was in custody, she would find out what he'd done with Cassie.

She caressed the half-a-heart necklace hanging against her chest. *Hang in there, Cassie. I'm coming to save you.*

Without meaning to give in to her fears, Maddie found herself visualizing her sister bound and gagged in a dark closet somewhere. Her heart thumped. She clenched her fists, bit on her bottom lip.

"Stop imagining the worst," David said as they topped the stairs and exited to the second floor platform. "Cassie is fine."

How in the world did he know that's what she'd been thinking? The man was uncanny.

Henri was on the radio again. "They've got Levy in sight," he repeated for Maddie's benefit. "He's waiting at the top."

"And Shriver?"

"Heading this way."

From the second floor they were forced to take the elevator to the top. Luckily, in late February, the tourist crowd was fairly sparse. Henri displayed his badge and moved them to the head of the line but Maddie couldn't help feeling frustrated as they waited for the elevator to arrive. Any other day she would love to visit the Eiffel Tower, but today all she wanted was to get this over with. By the time they reached the top of the tower she was breathless from anxiety.

"Do you see him?" she whispered to David.

"Don't look now but Levy is standing about a hundred feet to the left. He's wearing a red beret and a black leather jacket." David slipped his arm around Maddie and pressed his lips against her ear.

She tensed.

"Pretend we're honeymooning tourists taking in the sights," he whispered.

"What for?" she whispered back, disconcerted by his nearness.

"It's our cover story."

"Like someone is going to ask?"

"Let's just stand over here in the corner, with our backs to the elevator. I don't want Shriver to recognize us and blow the whole sting. I might even have to kiss you if he comes our way."

"Kiss me?" Her voice sounded as shaky as her insides felt.

"Yeah, you know. As a dodge."

"Oh yeah." Was that all?

"Look honey," he said loudly as he guided her to the corner. "You can see the Arc de Triomphe from here."

David used his tall body to shield her from the brunt of the wind blowing up the tower. "You're cold," he murmured where only she could hear.

She *was* cold but that wasn't why she was trembling.

David took off his trench coat and draped it over her shoulders. Then, he put his arm around her again and drew her close to his side, his body heat merging with hers.

She shouldn't have enjoyed the hard feel of his arm against her waist. She shouldn't have noticed how nice he smelled or how his beard stubble scratched lightly at her earlobe. She shouldn't have been stunned by the considerate loan of his coat.

But damn her, she was.

"Do you think it's safe for me to try and get a look at this Levy character?" she asked.

Maddie needed to do something, anything to get her

mind off David's proximity and back on the situation at hand.

"Just don't be too obvious about it."

"Where did Henri go?"

"He and his men are taking cover on the other side of that group of Japanese tourists."

Cautiously, Maddie glanced around, pretending she was taking in the sights. To her left, she spotted Henri smoking a cigarette beside two other men. When she turned her head to look over her shoulder, she spied the man in the beret and leather jacket. He was glancing at his watch and frowning.

Where was Shriver?

The elevator door dinged open.

David took her into his arms. Her pulse quickened.

Their eyes met.

And then he was kissing her.

For one breathtaking moment she couldn't even remember what they were doing on the Eiffel Tower. All she could think about was the pressure of his mouth on hers.

Her knees went weak. Even through the layers of his clothing, she could feel the heavy beating of his heart. In spite of the cold, he felt blisteringly hot and wonderfully solid against her body.

David pulled his lips away but crushed her in his embrace. "Watch the people getting off the elevator," he whispered, yanking her back to reality.

"Okay."

"Do you see Shriver?"

She scanned the group stepping off. All she had to identify Shriver by was the photograph they'd found in Cassie's locker. If he'd changed his look, she wouldn't recognize him. But he was supposedly carrying the Cézanne in brown paper wrapping. That should make him much easier to spot.

But no one in this crowd was carrying anything that remotely resembled a priceless work of art.

"No," she whispered back. "But there's a bald, pock-marked man of about thirty going over to talk to Levy. He's wearing a leather jacket and skull and cross bone tattoos, numerous body piercings and wearing hobnailed boots."

David inhaled audibly.

She looked into his face, saw a grim expression furrowing his forehead. What? She telegraphed him the question with her eyes.

He shook his head and then covertly, they both peeked at the dude deep in conversation with Levy.

"Shit," David hissed.

"What is it? What's happening?" Maddie asked just as Henri appeared at David's elbow. She splayed a hand against her throat, felt her pulse flutter frantically.

"That's Jocko Blanco," David muttered.

At the very same moment Henri said, "My crew tells me Shriver went into the Louvre. He's opened the package he was carrying. It's not the Cézanne, but a sketchpad."

"Shit," David repeated himself. "Shit, shit, shit."

"What's happening?" Maddie asked, fear a rock in her throat.

"I was wrong. Shriver didn't come here to fence the Cézanne to Levy," David said grimly. "He's come to rob the Louvre!"

Chapter 9

How do you know he's going to rob the Louvre?" Maddie whispered.

"It's part of Shriver's MO. He goes to a targeted museum ostensibly to sketch paintings, but what he's really doing is casing the security system," David explained. "The painting he sketches is the one he eventually steals. Then he always leaves the sketch behind at the scene."

"So he enjoys taunting you."

"Yeah." David grit his teeth. To Henri he said, "Are your men able to see what painting Shriver is sketching?"

Henri passed the question on to his team over the two-way radio and waited for the answer. He made a sour face. "You're not going to believe it."

"Let me take a wild guess. The Mona Lisa."

Henri nodded. "Surely even Shriver isn't that daring."

"Who knows what that crazy sonofabitch is capable of? All I know is that he's *not* going to get away with it this time."

After ten years of having his failure flaunted in his face, David was past the point of no return. It was now or never. Shriver was going down. Already a plan was hatching in his head. A plan to exploit Maddie's resemblance to her absent twin.

"What about Levy and Blanco?" Henri asked, inclining his head in their direction. The two men were still absorbed in conversation, apparently unaware that just a few feet away they were being observed by Interpol and the FBI.

"Let's step back and regroup for now. But keep the surveillance team on Levy and add a man to watch Blanco."

"It's done," Henri said. "Do you suppose they are in on this heist with Shriver?"

"Either that or they're plotting revenge for the double-cross on the Cézanne. Engrossed as they are, it very well could be the latter."

"What about Cassie?" Maddie interrupted, nibbling her bottom lip and fidgeting in her handbag for some Rolaids.

"Yeah, well..." David scratched his beard-roughened chin. "There's something I need to discuss with you."

She folded her arms over her chest and narrowed her eyes at him. "So talk."

"Not here. Let's go grab some lunch and we'll discuss it over a beer."

"It's four-thirty in the afternoon."

"Okay, so it's an early dinner." He cupped his hand under her elbow and headed for the elevator, but she balked.

"I don't care about food. I want to find my sister."

"We'll get to that. I promise. In the meantime, you need to keep up your strength or you won't be any good to anyone."

That convinced her.

"Nothing fancy," she said. "Let's just eat and get on with it."

"There's an English style pub that serves fish and chips a couple of blocks from here."

"Sounds perfect."

The pub was dim and smoky. The smell of nicotine had David itching for a cigarette. He asked for a table in the back. They selected the fish and chips over the steak and kidney pie and David ordered a pint of Guinness.

"Want a beer?"

Maddie shook her head. "I don't drink much."

"Well if ever there was a time to imbibe, it's now. We're tired, frustrated and road weary. A drink might just take the edge off."

"You've got a point." To the waitress she said, "Crown Royal, neat."

"Whoa." No wonder the woman ate antacids like candy.

"I figure if I'm going to drink I might as well go for the gusto," she said.

"Gusto is one thing. A coma is something else."

"One shot of whisky isn't going to put me in a coma."

What the hell? Why not join her? It had been a long time since he'd sipped whisky. "I'll have a Crown Royal too."

"Now," Maddie said, once the waitress had departed. "Where do we stand?"

David studied her across the table. In the darkly lit room her hair was a richer blonde. Her lips glistened moistly from where she'd wet them with the tip of her tongue. Watching her gave him a shiver clear to the bottom of his spine.

She tucked a strand of hair behind her right ear and he caught a glimpse of an opal earring nestled in her lobe. He wondered if she had any idea how beautiful she was.

The waitress returned with their drinks. David took a sip of whisky and grimaced as the velvety smooth burn traveled down his throat. Maddie circled the rim of her glass with her index finger.

Around and around.

Mesmerized, David watched her fingers stroke the glass and he couldn't keep himself from imagining what it would feel like to have her drawing those same luxurious circles on his bare skin.

"So what happens next?" she asked.

"Um, that's exactly what I wanted to talk to you about." How was he going to get this topic started?

"I'm listening," she said.

He held up his palms. "What I'm about to tell you is going to piss you off, but I want you to hear me out before you go ballistic. Can you do that?"

Maddie picked up her glass and in one long swallow chugged the whiskey without even blinking.

David winced, amazed. Not one to be bested by anyone, much less a woman in a drinking competition, he gulped the rest of his whisky too.

"All right. Lay it on me," she said at the same time the waitress brought their fish and chips. "Oh and could I have another Crown Royal, please."

"Yes, miss. What about you, sir?"

"Make mine a double," he said, deliberately holding Maddie's gaze.

"Me too." She did not look away.

"Two doubles. I'll just pop round to the bar and fetch it for you," the waitress said.

Maddie dug into her fish with gusto, sprinkling the fried pollock with malt vinegar. He liked watching her eat. There was something incredibly sensual in the way her pink tongue darted out to whisk away crumbs from her lips.

David got so caught up in her process he forgot what he was supposed to be doing. He felt nice and warm from the whisky and he was enjoying the buzz.

"Go ahead," she said. "I'm listening. Piss me off."

This wasn't going to be fun, but he wasn't one to beat around the bush. "Cassie's not in Paris."

She stopped with a French fry half way to her mouth. "What?"

"Cassie's not in Paris," he repeated.

"Where is she?"

He cleared his throat. "Madrid."

"What?" Maddie asked so low and controlled he knew she was way more than pissed off. If looks could kill, he would have had forty stab wounds and a gunshot hole or ten.

"Shriver came to Paris. Cassie went to Madrid."

"How long have you known this?" She put the French fry down on her plate and fisted her hand.

She wants to punch me something awful.

Why that thought should charge his sexual engines, David had no clue, but it did.

"Since we landed."

"I see." She clenched her jaw. "I promised to hear you out before losing my temper. Go ahead. Tell me why you deceived me."

"I thought we were about to nab Shriver passing off the Cézanne to Levy and I knew you would demand to go to Madrid immediately if I told you."

"Darn straight."

He steepled his fingertips. "Here's the deal. I'm working out a plan to entrap Shriver and I need your help. In exchange, I promise to see that all charges against Cassie are dropped."

"There wouldn't be any charges in the first place if you hadn't recruited her. You're responsible for this." She was struggling to control her anger. He could see it in the jumpy pulse fluttering at her throat and the way she carefully enunciated each word.

"I didn't force her to run off with Shriver."

"She was an unwilling victim."

"If that's the case, why is she in Madrid while Shriver is here?"

He had her on that one. Maddie glared and folded her arms over her chest. "Cassie did not steal the Cézanne."

"The folks at the Kimbell don't see it that way."

"And neither do you."

"I'm offering you a chance to get your sister off the hook, scot free. Help me catch Shriver and we'll forget all about Cassie." David leaned back in his chair, watching her face and praying she would agree to his scheme.

The waitress set their drinks in front of them and Maddie polished off the double whisky as if it was Kool-Aid. She set her glass down and ordered another double.

"Don't you think you better slow down?"

She looked pointedly at his glass. "I think if you want to convince me to go along with your scheme you better keep up with me drink for drink."

"Is this a challenge?"

She shrugged.

Damn but the woman was dynamite. He didn't appreciate being goaded into drinking too much but he hated looking like a lightweight. He tossed the whisky down his throat and forced himself not to make a face at the acrid curl of heat spiraling down his throat. Or at the way his brain bobbled.

"He'll have another double, too," Maddie said to the agog waitress.

David's vision swam momentarily, but he shook it off. Maddie was watching him like the proverbial canary-eating cat. She thought he was a wuss. Well, he was beginning to think she was the queen of boozers. Who'd have thought a cautious, worrywart possessed such a high tolerance for hooch?

Never mind. He could handle this. Focus, concentrate. He blinked at her and smiled.

She smiled back and coyly lowered her eyelids. Was she feeling as sexy as he was? His heart thumped. He couldn't help but notice how well she filled out that print shirt. He chided himself for noticing but he couldn't stop sneaking covert peeks.

"Okay," he said, struggling to get his tongue in gear without slurring his words. "Here's the plan. I want you to impersonate Cassie. That shouldn't be too hard for you. We'll just get you sexier clothes."

At the thought of Maddie prancing around in the skimpy outfits Cassie preferred, David's temperature soared. But if his plot was going to work, Shriver had to believe Maddie was her twin sister. And Cassie wore tight skirts, super high heels and belly baring blouses.

"What else?" She cocked her head and eyed him speculatively.

Funny, she didn't seem the least bit impaired from downing three double shots of whisky in less than fifteen minutes.

"Shriver is staying at the Hotel de Louvre. Henri's team still has him under strict surveillance. We want you to go to his hotel room, pretending to be Cassie, and tell him you found out the digital signature code that will shut down the alarm system at the Louvre from your friend who works at the Prado. The Prado and the Louvre now have the same security system so he'll believe you."

"Then what?"

"You and Shriver will break into the Louvre and steal the Mona Lisa together."

"You're asking me to commit a crime?"

"Under the auspices of Interpol and the FBI. We'll let you get away and then swoop down when Shriver passes the art off to Levy."

"How do you know he'll pass the art off to Levy?"

"Because," David said, "before you go see Shriver, you'll call Levy, pretending to be this fabulously wealthy countess referred to him by a mutual collector who wants a bargain for a very special work of art for her daughter's birthday. Levy knows exactly where to go for such a unique gift."

"Shriver."

"You got it."

"Don't you think Levy will be suspicious after we tailed him to the Eiffel Tower? He's got to know he's under surveillance."

"Levy's always under surveillance. He's the biggest art fence in Europe. He expects it. All part of his usual routine."

"I dunno." She shook her head.

"About what?"

"I can't trust you. You turned against my sister, how do I know you won't do it again?"

"Your sister was the one who turned, not me."

"Who knows, maybe I'll fall madly in love with Shriver too."

She enjoyed yanking his chain. If he hadn't been on the verge of drunkenness, he would have realized it sooner. He decided to ignore that last remark.

"Here's the bottom line. Help us catch Shriver and your sister goes free. Don't help and she's right back to being an accomplice."

"There's one other option," Maddie said as the waitress set down the fresh round of drinks. She lifted her glass to his. "Bottoms up."

If it took getting plastered to seal this deal with her, then he would do it. David raised his whisky. "Cheers."

They toasted and swallowed their drinks in unison.

He had trouble getting it down. His gut was asking him what in hell he was doing as his brain went wee-hee! He was dizzy and hot. He needed to go to the bathroom but he was afraid to stand up.

Maddie sat across from him, a calm smile on her face. His vision blurred. He wanted to tell her how pretty she was but it came out like, "Youm a berry bootipul wooman."

"One more." She leaned forward and pressed her lips against his ear and whispered. "You drink one more double shot with me and I'll go along with your plan to impersonate Cassie and rob the Louvre with Shriver."

"Okey-dokey." He felt sloppy happy. Maybe she was planning on taking him back to their hotel and having her way with him. He certainly wasn't opposed.

Maddie motioned for the waitress to bring them another set of drinks and a few minutes later, she brought over the double shots.

"Down the hatch," Maddie murmured.

Hell, he didn't know if he could even get the glass to his lips. Where were his lips by the way? They were tingly numb.

He watched the column of Maddie's throat move as she dispatched the final shot.

Are you a man or a mouse? That irritating devil voice that got him in so much trouble whispered.

With considerable effort, David raised the glass to his lips, closed his eyes and knocked the whisky back. "Ahh."

Maddie's mouth twitched and he realized she was trying not to laugh.

"Whassso funny?" he slurred.

"Remember I said there was one more option?"

He nodded. Or at least he thought he nodded. "Whazzat?"

"Drink you under the table, go to Madrid, retrieve my sister and head home to the States."

"You can't drink me unner the table." He wobbled in his chair.

"I think I already have."

"Uh-huh." He pushed back his chair and staggered to his feet. "See. I perrrfetly fine."

"Yeah, you're fine." She got up and picked up her shoulder bag.

"Hey," he said, trying to point a finger at her but his frickin' finger wouldn't hold still. "Where ya goin'?"

She waved and headed for the door.

"Wait." He charged after her, only to have the floor rise up to meet his face.

He hit the wood with a resounding thunk. If he hadn't stuck out a hand to break his fall he probably would have fractured his skull. He ended up staring at a French fry squashed on the floor next to his nose.

Maddie squatted down beside him.

"Oh," she said. "Maybe I forgot to tell you. The reason I don't often drink alcohol is because I have a mutant metabolic disorder of the liver enzymes. I can drink all the liquor I want and I never even get buzzed, so what's the point? Well, unless you're trying to drink some smart-assed guy under the table."

He groaned.

"And remember what you told me at the airport? Payback really *is* a bitch."

She rose to her feet and swished away before David could reach out and grab her ankle.

And just before he passed out he heard her tell the waitress, "He'll be paying the bill."

If David hadn't lied to her, Maddie would have felt bad about drinking him under the table. He wasn't the first man she'd bested in a tippling contest, but he was the only one she hadn't told about her metabolic condition beforehand.

Of course, if he hadn't lied to her, she would have had no reason to drink him under the table.

She'd discovered her dubious gift quite by accident. In college, Cassie got buzzed on one shot of tequila, but Maddie could down the whole bottle, including the worm, and not get the least bit soused. The handy talent had earned her a few dare bucks when she was twenty-one, but since then, she'd never exploited her talent.

Until now.

Maddie marched to their hotel, head held high. Once in her room, she checked the transportation schedule and ended up booking the next supersonic train to Madrid. She had a little less than an hour to pack and get to the station. By the time David roused himself from his Crown Royal stupor, Maddie would already be in Spain.

For the sake of time, she eschewed the elevator and hurried down the stairs. She had a map of Paris in one hand, her carry-on in the other.

Imagine! David Marshall actually thinking she'd go along with his crazy scheme to nail Shriver by pretending to be her sister.

At least he has a lot of confidence in you.

Bullshit. The man had just been desperate.

She hurried through the cobblestone square, past a

gorgeous fountain. It was already dark and the lights had come on, bathing the city in a festive glow.

On the steps of the Louvre, a group of sightseers in mittens and parkas stood in a semicircle, observing something. Maddie cut around them and discovered they were watching a mime.

She shuddered. She hated mimes. She found their silent gesturing menacing.

This mime wore a top hat with red wig springing out from underneath. His face was made-up with the traditional white grease paint and he wore black trousers with wide suspenders. His black shirt was slashed with white horizontal stripes. A CD player spinning Parisian cabaret torch songs sat at his feet. He had a blanket spread out to collect the coins people tossed.

Pathetic way to make a living. To avoid walking in front of him, Maddie veered to the left.

And the mime shuffled in front of her, blocking her path.

Maddie gave him a quick, tolerant smile that said, *Hey, dude. Even though I have no respect for what you do, that doesn't mean we can't both coexist. Now get the hell out of my way.*

She sidestepped.

He followed. The serious expression on his face never changed.

Maddie ducked her head, feinted left but zipped right.

He wasn't faked out.

She cleared her throat and spoke one of the few phrases in French that she knew. *"Excusez moi."*

He didn't budge. In fact, he cocked his head as if she was from another planet and he was an anthropologist studying her alien behavior.

She stepped to the left again.

And damn if he didn't match her movements exactly.

Why was the freak mocking her? Maddie planted a hand against his sternum and shoved.

He pushed back with his chest.

The stupid crowd loved it. They were clapping and cheering him on.

"Get out of my way," she insisted.

Silently, he aped her words, all the while creating dramatic sweeping gestures with his arms.

She jumped right and darted forward but he ran backward, staying directly in front of her. Somewhere, a clock chimed the hour. Six elongated chimes. The train left at six-twenty and the station was over a mile away. She'd have to hail a taxi in order to make it.

Hurry, hurry, you don't have time for this.

The mime sank his hands on his hips and flounced prissily, wagging his head back and forth and shaking his behind.

Angered, she dropped her suitcase and took a kickboxing stance. "Come on dude, I've taken down one arrogant man today, I have no trouble making it two."

He mimed her. Fisting his hands and raising them in mirror image of hers. He gave a taunting smile.

The crowd roared with laughter.

Maddie's cheeks flamed with shame. Oh this was too much. Being humiliated by an annoying mime.

Maybe there was a policeman nearby. She glanced around but didn't see one. Typical.

The mime stared at her chest and narrowed his eyes. Pervert.

And then he made the grandest *faux pas* of all. He reached out, ran his hand over Maddie's half-a-heart necklace and tugged on it.

The delicate chain snapped.

Now his behavior made sense. It was just a ploy to steal her necklace.

Rage suffused her. Nobody messed with her necklace. Growling, hands in attack position, Maddie launched herself at the mime.

She tackled him like a defensive end sacking a quarterback. They fell to the ground together. She sat on his chest and wrapped her hands around his neck. With each word, she pounded his head against the stone steps.

"Give." Pound.

"Me." Pound.

"Back." Pound.

"My." Pound.

"Necklace." Pound.

The crowd gasped.

Maddie felt a fist at the nape of her neck. Someone grasped her by her collar and yanked her off the dazed mime. "Stop it right now, before you murder Marcel Marceau."

"He stole my necklace," she howled, arms flailing. She was prepared to fight anyone and everyone for that necklace.

"Maddie," David's voice broke through her bloodlust and she realized he was the someone who'd pulled her off the mime. "Is this what you're battling for?"

She spun around to look at him. His knees were wobbling like a top, his eyes were bloodshot and he reeked of whisky, but in his hand he was clutching her necklace.

"Yeah. He ripped it off my neck," she said breathlessly and turned back to point an accusing finger at the mime.

But the guy was already gone. All they could see was the top hat and red wig dashing away through street traffic.

Chapter 10

Something about the mime niggled at him, but David was too drunk to recognize what it was and too late to confront the guy head on. He was long gone.

But Maddie was right here. In his grasp. He wasn't about to let her escape again.

David pulled handcuffs from his pocket. Before his intent had time to register, he quickly clamped one end around Maddie's right wrist and the other end around his left. He had to manacle her to him. If she decided to bolt and run, he was in no condition to pursue her.

"Hey!" Maddie protested, alarm in her eyes. "Hey!"

The crowd applauded.

She stuck out her tongue at them.

They jeered.

"Come on." David jerked her in the direction of the hotel where Henri had reserved rooms for them. "Before you start an international incident."

She dug her heels in.

"Don't give me a hard time," he growled, "or I'll let the crowd at you. You'd be mincemeat in a matter of minutes. The French take their mimes very seriously."

"I'm not going with you."

"Yes you are." It required every bit of strength he could muster to bend down, scoop up her carry-on and drag her in the direction he wanted her to go.

"Nazi."

"Let's not get into the name calling." He was slurring his words, his gut roiled precariously and his head was pounding like a bass drum, but he wasn't about to let her know that. He still couldn't get over the way she'd outsmarted him.

Again.

"Where are you taking me?"

He gritted his teeth. "Thanks to your ruthless cunning, I'm not in any shape to plot a *coup* against Shriver tonight. We're going to the hotel so I can sleep off the whisky. But here's how it's gonna go down. In the morning, you're going to Shriver's room, impersonating Cassie, and convincing him to let you help him rob the Louvre. Got it?"

"You think I'm cunning?" She cast him a sideways glance.

"Yes I do," he said and damned if she didn't look inordinately pleased.

He noticed she was no longer resisting him as they walked wrist in wrist up the Champs-Elysées. People were staring at them curiously. He paused a moment to slip his raincoat off his shoulders and slide it down his left arm to hide the handcuffs.

"But," he reminded her, "I also said you were ruthless."

"I'm not ruthless."

"Oh, yeah? What do you call taking advantage of your peculiar metabolism in order to drink a man under the table and then leaving him passed out in a bar? That's not a particularly nice thing to do."

"Neither is lying." She glared.

He might have enjoyed their verbal sparring if he hadn't felt so utterly wretched. As it was, with each word he spoke it seemed as if someone was driving a pickaxe clean through the base of his skull. Each step was a slog through half-set cement. And when he tried to think, his brain shrieked.

All he wanted was to get to the hotel, flop down on the bed and sink into oblivion. He'd worry about Shriver when his drunken toot subsided.

Maddie, however, had totally opposite goals.

"I think we should go to Madrid and get Cassie," she wheedled.

"No."

"Why not?"

"Because you're damned lucky I'm even standing and it's all your fault. You owe me. Big time."

By the grace of God, they arrived at the hotel. David hurried for the door and stumbled over the curb. He would have taken a header for the second time that day if Maddie hadn't tugged him back with the handcuff.

"I see your point," she said.

The trip upstairs was a blur. They reached his room and David set her bag down in the corridor and weaved as he tried to insert the card key.

"What are you doing?" she asked.

"Trying to get into my damned room."

"Aren't you going to uncuff me so I can go to my own room?"

"Hell no." His knees buckled and he fell against the door. He was sinking fast. Only sheer effort of will had carried him this far from the floor of the pub. "You're spending the night with me."

"Alone? In your bed?"

"Don't sound so panicky. Even if I was inclined to molest you, which I'm not, Herman is in a whisky induced coma."

"Herman?"

He glanced at his crotch, then looked at her and arched an eyebrow. Or at least he thought he arched an eyebrow. He really didn't know for sure. He couldn't feel his facial muscles.

"Oh. You named your penis Herman? Wait, don't confirm that, I really don't want to know."

He grinned. "Are you charmed?"

"Hardly."

Again, he reached out to swipe it through the sensor pad but damned if there weren't two of them blending and blurring together. He closed one eye.

Ah, that was better. He leaned forward and almost toppled over again.

"Jeez, you're a menace to society, Marshall. Give me that." Maddie snatched the key card from him and easily opened the door.

He still couldn't believe she was unaffected by the alcohol she'd consumed. The woman was amazing.

Charging over the threshold with Maddie in tow, he made a beeline for the bed and collapsed face down. He was asleep before his head hit the pillow.

Maddie stood at the side of the bed staring down at her heavy tether. David was snoring softly, his face plowed into the bedspread, his left arm raised in the air. His raincoat stretched across the handcuffs linking them.

Great. She was chained to the sexiest man to ever irritate the bejeezus out of her.

She supposed she deserved this. Her plan had backfired. Thanks to that stupid mime.

But at least she had the necklace back. Maddie stuck

her free hand into her pocket and fisted her fingers around the gold half-heart. The cool feel of it reassured her.

Cassie was okay. At least that's what she kept telling herself.

In the meantime what was she going to do about David?

She couldn't stand here all night, and from the amount of whisky singing through his system, he wasn't likely to move for hours. Then again, he had managed to rouse himself off the floor of the bar and show up just in the nick of time to prevent her from committing first-degree mime-a-cide.

The man had an indomitable will. She'd grant him that.

And he was very cute in a brute force sort of way.

Cocking her head, Maddie studied the logistics of positioning herself on the bed beside him. Why couldn't he have passed out on his back instead of his stomach?

Gingerly, she crawled onto the bed and stretched out on her belly. Cheek pressed into the bedspread, she forced herself to forget those unsavory stories she'd read about hotel bedspreads.

Don't be so persnickety for once, Maddie. Just go with the flow. Cassie's voice popped into her head. *You can't regulate everything in life.*

Ah, but going with the flow was Cassie's forte, not hers. To distract herself, she studied the back of David's head.

He had a nice hairline and she loved the spiky cut. His neck was strong, but not too thick. And he had free-hanging earlobes. She preferred unattached earlobes. They were much nicer for nibbling on than the attached kind.

In that moment, it was all she could do not to prop herself up on her elbow, lean over and take that delectable lobe between her teeth and lightly bite him.

A treacherous heat started in the pit of her stomach and spread outward.

Good grief!

What was the matter with her? She was better off thinking about bedspread stains instead of this push-pull of attraction that made her want to kick him off the bed at the same time she yearned to cuddle him.

This was whacky. She was going to stop thinking all together. She was just going to close her eyes and go to sleep.

Yeah. Right.

How come her eyes were still open?

She toed off her Nikes and they fell, plop, plop, to the floor, all the while her gaze tracked from David's neck to his broad shoulders to the slope of his ribcage.

Even through the material of his shirt, she could detect the honed ridges of his muscles.

Ach! Go to sleep.

She eased his coat up the handcuff and used it to drape her shoulder, as much to put a barrier between them as to keep warm. She wasn't afraid he was going to try and jump her bones in the night. He was out. No, what she really feared was that her own fingers would betray her and go exploring in places they had no business exploring.

The scent of him teased her nostrils and stormed her imagination. His smell resurrected the memory of last night on the plane and the unexpected kisses they'd shared. No kisses had ever moved her the way his did.

Or left her wanting so much more.

Why was she so turned on by him? Why now? This was the totally wrong time in her life. Plus, he was arrogant and high-handed and overly competitive.

And brave and protective and generous.

Face it. You're enjoying this.

Damn her hide, she was. But David must never know.

It had been a very long time since she'd shared a bed

with a man and she had forgotten how nice it felt. That's all this sensation was about. David wasn't any more special than any other guy.

Ummm-huh. Sure. Go ahead. Lie to yourself.

Suddenly, the cell phone in David's jacket pocket played the *Dragnet* tune.

"Pssttt, David," she said.

He didn't move.

"Joe Friday's callin'." She raked her fingers lightly over his ribs. "Wake up. It might be Henri with news about Shriver."

He didn't so much as groan.

She bumped his butt with her knees. "Hey, wake up."

What if the phone call was from Cassie?

The second the thought occurred to her, Maddie was fumbling for the phone with her free hand, desperately searching for the pocket.

Don't hang up, don't hang up, don't hang up, she prayed.

At last she found the phone and managed to flip it open one-handedly. "Hello."

"*Bonsoir,* Mademoiselle Cooper," Henri's voice greeted her and Maddie's hopes fell.

"Hello, Henri."

"May I speak to David, please?"

Maddie propped herself on her elbow and stared down at David. Dead to the world. "I'm afraid he's…um…" She didn't want to rat him out and tell Henri he was drunk. "Indisposed."

"I see."

It sounded as if Henri was struggling not to laugh. What was so funny?

"May I take a message?"

"I just wanted to see if David had convinced you to go along with his plan to entrap Monsieurs Shriver and Levy.

Since you're answering his phone, I assume you have agreed. *Mais non?*"

Maddie sighed. It seemed she really didn't have much of a choice. "I haven't decided."

"I understand. Pulling off this deception would take a great deal of courage. Even if David is too stubborn to tell you so himself, I know he would appreciate your assistance. He's been chasing Shriver a very long time but David never gives up. He refuses to accept defeat."

"He's got a lot invested in the outcome of this case, doesn't he?"

"He didn't tell you about his Aunt Caroline?" Henri asked and Maddie realized he was trying to determine the exact nature of her relationship with David.

"No," she admitted.

Henri hesitated. "I'm not sure I should tell you. Most of it I know only through office gossip. David doesn't talk about himself much."

"If I'm going to do this thing, then I need to know why."

"Good enough," Henri said after a long moment. "Just don't tell David I told you."

"Done."

"David was in college when it happened. He was about to start his junior year as an art history major."

"David majored in art history?"

"Initially, *oui*. But what happened with his Aunt Caroline caused him to go into law enforcement instead."

Maddie had to strain to hear what he was saying. Between Henri's soft French accent and the crackly cell phone static, she didn't want to miss any of the conversation. It sounded as if Henri was about to give her the key to David's vulnerability. And when it came to dealing with the uncompromising David Marshall, the more she understood him, the better.

"That was a big leap," she said, ears pricked, body tensed. "From art history to police work."

"Not really. David was always pulled in two directions. His mother and his aunt came from high society, but over the years the family fortune dwindled to the value of one Rembrandt. David's father was an army intelligence officer. He wanted David to become a soldier, but his mother was dead set against it. His parents were killed when he was twelve or thirteen and he went to live with his Aunt Caroline. She urged him to follow his mother's wishes and become an art dealer."

"I don't see that refined side of him at all," Maddie murmured, her gaze roving over David's sleeping form. "He looks like a bloodthirsty soldier through and through."

"Ah, don't let his toughness fool you. It takes a long time for him to let down his guard, but he's got a very soft heart."

Henri's words caused Maddie's own heart to go all mushy. The idea that David wasn't all brute strength and arrogant bluster stirred her in a weird way.

"While David was away at college, his aunt met a much younger man through her volunteer association with the Metropolitan Museum of Art. The man romanced her and then stole the Rembrandt right out from under her nose. The painting was meant to fund her retirement and David's inheritance."

"I think I understand. The much younger man was Peyton Shriver."

"*Oui.* Jerome Levy was the broker who commissioned the theft and we're convinced Levy still has the Rembrandt in his vaulted collection."

"All this time David's been trying to catch those two."

No wonder he'd been desperate enough to recruit

Cassie as an informant. Maddie already knew David hated to lose and Shriver had given him the slip for almost a decade. That had to burn.

"While Shriver went underground for several years, living off the spoils of the Rembrandt, David became an FBI agent and specialized in art theft detection."

"He wants revenge," Maddie said.

"Justice would be a fairer word. His loyalty to his aunt runs deep. She took him in when he had no one. The poor woman would be penniless if it weren't for the money David sends her every month."

Maddie's heart did another smooshy, whooshy dive. She wondered how David would react if he knew Henri had spilled his most tender secret.

"Thank you for telling me all this," she said. "It makes a difference."

"No matter how gruff he might seem at times, he is a good man," Henri said.

"I'm beginning to see that."

"So tomorrow you will help us trap Shriver?"

Maddie swallowed hard and moistened her lips. She felt a jolt of adrenaline—part fear and part excitement—surge through her. Could she do it? Could she convince Shriver that she was Cassie and then rob the Louvre with him?

The thought grated against every cautious bone in her body, and yet, she wanted to do this. For her twin sister.

And for David?

"Yes," she told Henri, committing herself to something that scared the wits out of her. "I'll do it."

In the middle of the night, David's brain flung off the Crown Royal-induced fog and started poking at him with a vengeance.

Wake up, screamed his conscience. *You've missed something important.*

Haltingly, his synapses backfired as he tried to recollect what he couldn't quite recall.

He remembered the third double whisky he'd downed at the pub—but just barely. He remembered Maddie stepping over his prostrate body and waltzing out of the pub. He vaguely remembered staggering through the streets of Paris looking for her and finding her attacking a mime.

The mime.

His brain niggled and his gut clenched. Yes. There was something about the mime.

Wake up. Sit up. Get up. This is urgent.

What was it about the damned mime?

The mime had tried to steal Maddie's necklace. The necklace that was the mate to the one Cassie always wore.

No, no, that wasn't it. David struggled to force his eyelids open.

Something about the mime had seemed very familiar but he'd been too busy with Maddie and too drunk to notice it at the time.

David tried to turn over in bed. Maddie groaned beside him.

He froze. What was she doing in his bed?

Had he . . . had they . . . um, done it? He had wanted to make love to Maddie, that was for sure. But he didn't remember doing the deed. If he'd made love to the woman of his dreams, surely he would have remembered that, no matter how much whisky he'd consumed.

He raised his left hand and discovered Maddie's slender wrist was handcuffed to his thick one.

Holy shit, what *had* happened?

Oh yeah.

He'd forgotten he'd handcuffed himself to her to keep her from running off to Madrid without him while he slept off his accidental bender.

They hadn't had wild, kinky, handcuff sex after all. Bummer.

But that was a good thing.

Right?

Forget about sex. Get your mind back on the mime.

Yeah, yeah. What was it about the mime that had dragged him out of his slumber with a bastard of a headache and a mouth so dry he feared two gallons of water wouldn't quench his thirst?

Think. Think.

He blinked.

Maddie mumbled and moved against him. The touch of her against him sent a thrust of blood to his groin.

"What is it? What's wrong?" she asked. Her hair was tousled, making her look impossibly sexy.

"Where were you standing when you run afoul of that mime?"

"On the steps outside the Louvre. Why?"

"Sonofabitch," he cursed as his mind exploded with the answer he'd been scrambling for. "I had it all wrong."

"Had what all wrong?"

"He didn't come here to rob the Louvre but to case the security system so he could rob the Prado."

"What are you talking about?" Maddie frowned. "I'm not following."

"Don't you see? That was no ordinary mime. That was Peyton Shriver!"

Chapter 11

Maddie fidgeted in the dining car of the high-speed train at seven A.M. on Thursday morning while the Spanish countryside zipped past the window. They'd taken the train because the airport was in chaos with delayed flights following a bomb threat. She wore a practical traveling ensemble of loose fitting blue jeans, a long-sleeved red V-neck pullover sweater, her denim jacket and her favorite sneakers. She always felt more in control when she had her Nikes on.

David sat across from her, glowering intently. Between massaging his temple repeatedly and snarling at her over his coffee, she'd figured out his hangover must be pretty damned intense.

Following his three A.M. revelation that had whipped Maddie from a dead sleep, he had called Henri and the three of them had rushed to Shriver's hotel.

Henri's surveillance team had sworn it was impossible for Shriver to have left his hotel room, but when the manager opened the door, they had found a forlorn room service waiter trussed up on the floor in his underwear. Shriver had ordered a Monte Cristo and tea around five o'clock the previous afternoon. When the waiter had arrived with his order, Shriver had bonked the guy on the head with a lamp, stolen his clothes and taken off.

Henri's men checked all out-of-town transportation and discovered Shriver had bought a ticket for the ten P.M. super-speed train to Madrid the night before. David immediately booked seats for himself and Maddie on the next train out.

And now here they were, barreling toward their destiny.

Maddie crossed her legs and then uncrossed them again. She rolled her linen napkin up and then unrolled it. She tapped her foot and drummed her fingers and cleared her throat several times but never said anything. She squeezed and released her abdominal muscles in a series of isometric exercises. She fingered the necklace she'd repaired just before the trip, checking to make sure the clasp Shriver had broken would hold. She mentally prepared herself for any eventuality, but nothing alleviated her escalating trepidation.

A cheese omelet and buttered toast sat in front of her but she was so wound up she couldn't force food into her mouth.

"Eat," David growled and pointed at her plate with his fork. The expression in his eyes was dangerous, edgy, as if he knew what she looked like without her clothes on.

Heat rose to her cheeks and she hopped up from the table, her legs restless to pace the miles ticking down the track and release the nervous sexual energy clogging her brain. "I've got to walk. Clear my head."

"I'll come with you."

"I'll be all right on my own," she said firmly.

"My legs need stretching too."

She wished he would leave her alone. She felt irritable, out of sorts, short-tempered.

Maddie was accustomed to being in control but

whenever she got around David, he tried to take the reins. She didn't like his high-handedness. Nor did she care for her occasional odd longing to simply allow him to take over so she didn't have to worry anymore.

"So," David said after they'd traversed the train twice, weaving in and out of the cars packed with people speaking French and Spanish, Portuguese and Italian. "What was your event in the Olympics?"

"You knew I was an Olympian?"

"I ran a background check on you before we left the States," he said.

"Then don't play coy, if you ran a check on me you already know the answer to your question."

"Hundred meter dash. You were very fast."

She raised her chin. "I still am."

"What happened in Atlanta? Why didn't you take home a medal? You were favored to win. How come you never raced again?"

They had come to a stop in the last car. Maddie ducked her head, ostensibly to look at the scenery whizzing by, but she was actually struggling to put on a cool impassive face. She could tell him it was none of his business, but then he would know her failure still bothered her.

He was leaning against the only empty seat at the back of the car, trying to get a peek at her face. They were sandwiched between the lavatory and the exit door and he was scrutinizing her like a quality control examiner giving a pair of panties the thrice-over before tagging an 'inspected by #32' sticker in the waistband.

That irreverent thought stirred a complicated visual of David slipping his rough, masculine fingers inside the waistband of her red cotton bikini briefs.

"Pardon," apologized an elderly Spanish woman with a

very generous caboose. The woman tried to squeeze past them on her way to the lavatory. Maddie stepped to one side, David to the other, but the woman's ample bottom got wedged between them.

Maddie inched back, but she ended up stepping on a little boy's foot. He screamed and his mother scolded her in Spanish. Maddie apologized profusely in the same language.

David plunked down in the empty seat. The elderly woman popped free. He reached out, grabbed Maddie by the wrist and pulled her onto his lap. He offered the disgruntled mother a disarming smile, then pulled a package of airplane pretzels from his pocket and gave them to the little boy.

"There," he said. "Now everyone's happy."

"Such a little problem solver," Maddie said from her perch on his lap.

"Sarcasm becomes you."

"Just my luck."

"Are you trying to get my goat?"

"Who me?" She wanted to get up, but there was nowhere else to go and continuing to block the aisle seemed perilous.

On the seat beside them sat a blade thin young man in his late teens. He kept eyeing Maddie. David bared his teeth at the kid and wrapped a possessive arm around her waist.

"What are you doing?" she asked.

"Staking my claim."

"What?"

"Relax. It's just for appearances. To keep the locals from getting any funny ideas about feeling you up."

"Thanks for watching after my virtue," she said. "But I'm perfectly capable of slapping grabby hands. I lived in Madrid for a year, remember?"

"Yep, the year you flubbed up in the Olympics," he

said. "Speaking of the Olympics, you never did tell me why you quit running."

"I didn't quit running. You met me on the jogging trail, remember?"

"I meant how come you stopped competing?"

She could ignore him, she could tell him to shut up, or she could just tell him the truth and get the man off her back.

The elderly woman meandered back up the aisle. She looked at Maddie sitting on David's lap, winked and murmured the Spanish word for kismet before moving on her way.

Europeans. What a romantic bunch. Good thing Maddie didn't believe in any of that soulmate rot.

"Why not?" David repeated. God, but this guy had a one-track mind.

"I blew it, okay? I choked. I collapsed under pressure. I hesitated and I was lost."

"Funny," he said.

"Funny ha-ha or funny odd?"

"Funny, in I never figured you for a quitter."

"My coach dumped me. He said I didn't have star quality. How do you deal with something like that?"

"You prove him wrong."

Maddie shook her head. "Water under the bridge. I'm too old to compete now. My gym is very successful, I don't need to prove myself to anyone."

"Is that all there is to it?"

"Yes."

"Bullshit. You're kidding yourself."

"How do you mean?" His breath was tickling the back of her neck. She squirmed and tilted her head away from him.

"What about Cassie?"

"What about her?"

"Subconsciously I think you lost the race on purpose. I think you were afraid to win."

"Excuse me, that doesn't make any sense. What does me winning a race have to do with Cassie?" But as non-sensical as his theory was, her pulse quickened.

"Because if you won the gold, you would grow as an athlete and as a person. And if your world expanded and you changed then you might outgrow your role as Cassie's protector." David hooked a finger under her chin and forced her to look him in the eyes. "And you can't handle the thought of losing the role you've clung to since childhood. You've filtered your life through Cassie's experiences. That way, you don't have to get out there and mix it up on your own."

"You are so full of it."

She felt hot and slightly sick to her stomach. She didn't have to sit here and listen to his amateur psychoanalysis. But something inside her resonated with the truth.

Maybe? Yes? Could he be right?

Had she intentionally bungled the race? Did she live vicariously through Cassie while keeping her own life steady and low-key to accommodate her twin? It was a stunning and uncomfortable prospect.

Without any warning, without rhyme or reason, the stress of the past three days took control. She hated the tears welling up behind her eyelids. She was tough and in control and she would not cry in front of him.

It was PMS. That's why she was so emotional. Not because David had just seen straight into her soul.

Leaping from his lap, she turned and barreled into the lavatory behind them.

She should have known he would follow. Before she could get the door slammed, he'd jammed his foot in the opening fast as a smarmy door-to-door salesman.

"Talk to me, Maddie. I want to help."

"Get your foot out of the door, please. I gotta pee," she said.

"You're lying."

"Leave me alone. I'm fine." She sniffled. She caught a glimpse of her face in the mirror mounted over the sink.

The tears had already started to fall. She wiped at her cheeks, desperate to get rid of him and collect herself, but the man was a friggin' bulldozer.

"Nope. I'm staying right here until I know you're all right."

"I don't want or need your sympathy. Don't you get it?"

"I'm thickheaded, so sue me." He shouldered his way into the tiny lavatory with her and slammed the door locked behind him.

They glared, both breathing hard. The train jostled and they careened into each other.

Maddie gulped. She was trapped. There was no room to turn around, nowhere to run.

"Talk to me," he demanded.

She shook her head.

"Okay then, don't talk." He wrapped his arms around her waist and pulled her against him. "Go ahead and cry. Just let it out."

"No," she said stubbornly. "I'm not crying. I don't cry. I'm not a crier."

"Of course you're not."

He gently stroked her hair. She could feel the steady strumming of his heart. In spite of her best intentions, Maddie found herself weeping helplessly on his shoulder.

Dammit!

Why was she so susceptible to this man? How did he seem to know exactly when she was at her most vulnerable? What was it about him that pried her from her defenses in a way no one else ever had?

Pull back. Get away. For heaven's sake, Maddie, stop with the waterworks.

But she did none of those things.

"Look at me."

Reluctantly, she met his gaze.

His eyes locked onto hers and she couldn't look away. No, that wasn't right, she didn't *want* to look away.

She wanted to contradict their reality. She wanted to forget that he was a determined FBI agent and her sister was a robbery suspect. She wanted to ignore the fact they were in a cramped lavatory on a speeding train in a foreign country with every passing mile thrusting them closer to an uncertain and unpleasant destination.

What she wanted was to pretend they were a normal couple in a normal place under normal circumstances, quietly, sweetly, tenderly seducing each other.

But when his mouth came down to capture hers, his kiss was anything but quiet or sweet or tender.

"What are you doing?" she whispered.

"What does it feel like to you?"

"Like you're taking your frustrations out on me."

"You might have something there," he concurred. The hum of his words caused her lips to vibrate in a tingly, pleasant way.

"Since your motives are suspect you should probably stop kissing me."

"And you should probably stop talking."

Her lips were cool, but his were fiery hot. They came together like fresh-from-the-oven apple pie and two scoops of premium vanilla ice cream.

Tangy. Melting. Sinfully delicious.

She kissed him back, her tongue tentatively exploring his mouth.

He nibbled and sucked.

She followed his dance, not fighting him. In fact, she was kissing him back with an uncontrollable urgency that stole her breath.

He threaded his fingers through her hair, tugging out the hairclip that held her ponytail. He bathed his hand in the silky cascade.

"David," she moaned softly and then reached up to undo the top button on his shirt. She meant to scare some sense into him. To get him to stop kissing her. Or at least that's what she told herself.

"Yes?"

"You're right. I have been living my life through Cassie, not branching out on my own. Never doing anything impulsive. I want to do something crazy and impulsive right now."

"Oh yeah?"

Her heart thumped. Was this really part of a plan to chase him off or did she actually want him to make love to her? She did not know her own motives. How unsettling.

"Make love to me," she blurted. "Right here, right now, right this very minute."

"Huh?" He looked nervous.

"They have the mile high club for people who do it on a plane. What do they call it when you hook up on a train? The all aboard club?"

"Whoa!" He took one step back but there was nowhere else to go. "Maddie, let's not rush into something we'll both regret."

"I spent too much time worrying about tomorrow and not enough time living in the moment," she bluffed. "I want to live, David. I want to experience everything life has to offer."

She undid another button on his shirt and wriggled her pelvis against his hip. "Come on, kiss me again."

His erection burgeoned. He blushed. "I'm sorry about that."

"No reason to apologize. I'm flattered." She smiled and cupped him through his trousers. What in the hell was she going to do if he didn't retreat?

At that moment she knew she didn't want him to retreat. She wanted to make love to him. This wasn't a bid to chase him off. This was what she really needed. His hard masculine body shattering to completion inside hers.

"I think we should forget about the all aboard club," he whispered shakily. She loved that she'd reduced him to quivering jelly.

"Why?" she asked and nibbled at his chin.

"It's...um....I have a headache."

"And I've got just the cure for what ails you, big man."

Hungrily, she jerked his shirt from his waistband and shoved her palms up the bare planes of his abdomen. She shivered with delight as her hands skimmed his heated flesh.

He groaned. "Please Maddie, don't do this unless you mean it. Do you have any idea what you're doing to me?"

"I think I can guess."

"Vixen."

"Stud."

"I want nothing more than to nail you against this wall with your legs wrapped around my waist."

"Do it then." She met his gaze, challenging him to make good on his threat.

His eyes glistened with passion. He was hot for her and his desire stoked her higher, egging her on.

She'd never behaved so imprudently. Had never done anything so daring. But she was tired of Cassie having all the fun. It was her turn to do something crazy and downright stupid for once.

David's fingers were at her jeans, working the snaps. For the first time in her life she wished she was wearing a short, flirty accessible skirt instead of comfortable jeans.

Egad! What was happening to her? She was turning into her twin.

But it was too late for regrets or second thoughts. David had her zipper down and his hand inside her panties.

Maddie groaned and his fingers went exploring. He found her sweet spot. She clutched the muscles of his upper arms to hold herself steady but the rock hard feel of him only served to further unbalance her precarious equilibrium.

Her heart churned and her head spun. His thumb moved over her feminine button of arousal with the sure, gentle strokes of a man who'd done this many times before. Her eyes rolled back in her head. It felt that exquisite and she exhaled his name on a sigh.

David.

His name seemed to echo in the small confines but maybe the sound was only reverberating in her head.

David, David, David.

"Don't stop, don't stop, don't stop," she begged as his hand rhythmically worked magic.

"Never, babe, never." His head was bent to her ear and he ran his hot, wet tongue over the outer edge.

Such bliss!

She was so very close to coming.

Then the train jerked to a stop sending them tumbling atop the closed toilet lid together in a tangle of arms and legs.

Well hell.

David scrambled off her. "Are you okay?" he asked tenderly.

No! Of course she wasn't okay. She'd just been robbed of an orgasm.

What was wrong with her? She should be thanking her lucky stars he hadn't tripped her trigger. The fact no man had ever given her an orgasm would place him in a class all by himself.

And that would make him special.

And if he was special that meant she was starting to care about him.

And if she was starting to care about him that would mean... well, what *did* it mean?

"Maddie?"

"I'm fine." She reached down and hastily did up her pants.

She stared at the lavatory floor unable to look him in the eyes. Her gaze landed on his black leather shoes. Oh Jeez, she was in trouble here.

Don't overanalyze. Just breathe.

But she couldn't seem to draw in air through her constricted lungs.

Calm down. You didn't completely lose your head and almost practically rape an FBI agent. You really didn't.

No?

No.

Yeah? Then who was that ripping the shirt off his back and sticking her tongue down his throat? You trying to tell me that wasn't you?

But he had started it.

And she had taken things to a whole new level. Maddie wrung her hands. She was going to be sick.

Breathe. Just breathe.

How did Cassie manage being so impulsive? It felt terrible and out of control and ... very exciting.

She clamped her lips together to keep from moaning out loud. Her mouth still sizzled from the imprint of his.

He reached out to her.

Don't touch me. Please don't touch me.

He touched her.

And she melted as his fingers lightly skimmed over her forearm.

"It's okay. Don't be embarrassed. I'm honored. Flattered."

Ah damn. He was still trying to comfort her. How sweet. How obnoxious.

"I'm not embarrassed."

He must think she was Looney Toons. One minute crying on his shoulder, the next minute begging him for sex. She closed her eyes and swallowed back the lump of shame lodged in her throat.

Maybe she could blame it on hormones. Was it hormones? God, she was Looney Toons. She needed to get away from him. She needed to pace.

Before she ended up throwing herself at him again.

She wasn't accustomed to these wild, crazy emotions, didn't understand how to exorcise them. She'd never made out with a near stranger in a lavatory before. She had no idea why she'd done so now.

Looney Toons. It was the only explanation.

Someone knocked on the door. A masculine voice asked in Spanish if they were through with the lavatory.

"I think we're in Madrid," David murmured.

"Yeah."

"You wanna..." He made a circular gesture at her eyes. "Wash your face?"

The man outside knocked again.

"Un momento," Maddie called.

"I'll just wait outside," David said.

"Good idea."

But he didn't leave. He just kept standing there. Looking at her.

"And you uh…" She waved a hand. "You better button up your shirt and wash your hands. I'm sure you smell of me."

"I do." He grinned wickedly. "And your scent is intoxicating."

Oh God. This was more awkward than the morning after drunken-one-night-stand-sex. Not that she knew what that felt like from personal experience, but she could imagine it would go something like this.

Great, she had all the guilt of a one-night stand and none of the fun. Wasn't that just her luck?

David's cell phone picked that moment to do the *Dragnet* thing. He listened for a moment, the expression on his face impassive, but the muscle at his jaw twitched and she knew immediately something bad had happened.

"What is it?" she asked after he rang off.

His eyes looked both solemn and sorrowful. The way you looked at someone when the news was very bad indeed.

She raised a hand to her throat. "Tell me."

"That was Henri."

She swallowed and braced herself against the sink. "Yes?"

"Early this morning, about the same time we were boarding the train in Paris, a blonde woman matching Cassie's description and a masked man robbed the Prado at gunpoint."

Chapter 12

The steps of the Prado were thick with uniformed officers. Curious tourists ringed the area cordoned off by the *policía*. A flash of his badge got David and Maddie escorted to the front office. David introduced himself to the officer in charge.

"*Buenos dias,* Señor Marshall. I am Antonio Banderas," the man said in heavily accented English.

"Antonio Banderas?" David repeated.

"*Si,* like the actor. We are distant cousins." Antonio presented them with his profile. "You can see the family resemblance."

David pressed his lips together to keep from chuckling. *This* Antonio Banderas looked nothing like the actor. He was short and bald with a paunch, thin lips and a nose shaped like a button mushroom.

He caught Maddie's gaze. Her eyes twinkled and she had slapped a hand over her mouth. Her sides shook with suppressed mirth. The harder she tried to stop, the more noises she made. If she didn't knock it off, he was going to start laughing too.

Antonio stared intently at Maddie, his brows pulled down in a frown.

At first David thought Antonio was mad at her for mocking his name. But when the stocky policeman wouldn't quit ogling her even after David spoke to him, he got offended.

"Señor Banderas," he said sharply.

Europeans might have a different outlook on the whole sexual thing but it was just damned rude to undress another man's woman with your eyes when he was standing right beside you.

There you go. Letting your feelings for Maddie get in the way of business. You gotta stop wanting to punch his lights out.

"You!" Antonio pointed an accusing finger at Maddie. "You are the one who stole the El Greco."

Oops. His mistake. Antonio hadn't been staring at Maddie because he was mad or because he thought she was sexy, but because he'd mistaken her for Cassie.

"No." Maddie shook her head and raised her hand.

"Arrest her!" Antonio commanded his armed men.

"Wait, wait, wait." David stepped between Maddie and the approaching officers. "This is Maddie Cooper, the suspect's identical twin sister."

Antonio looked suspicious. "Twins?"

"Yes, Señor Banderas." A tall, lithe Castilian woman spoke from the doorway in flawless English. She was dressed impeccably in a cream colored pantsuit and her thick black hair hung in a single braid down her back. "That's her twin. You must be quite concerned, Maddie."

"Hello, Izzy," Maddie greeted the woman.

"Izzy?" David asked.

The woman clasped his palm in a firm handshake. "Isabella Vasquez. The curator."

"Special agent David Marshall, FBI, art theft division."

"I know who you are, Mr. Marshall. Your reputation precedes you."

"I'm so sorry about the mixup," Maddie apologized. "I don't know why they think Cassie was involved in the robbery."

"Mixup?" Isabella laughed humorlessly. "I'm afraid there is no mixup. Your sister used our friendship to lure me to the delivery entrance before the museum opened. That's when she and her lover, dressed like delivery personnel, attacked me at gunpoint and held me hostage while they stole El Greco's *Knight with His Hand on Chest*."

"But how did they just waltz out of here? Why didn't someone try to stop them?" David asked.

"They used a dolly to smuggle the painting out of the museum in a shipping crate. Because I had let them in and they had arrived in a delivery truck, the security officer thought they were just picking up a special package for me."

"That was always Cassie's favorite El Greco," Maddie murmured.

"I know," Isabella said. "I'm very angry with her. I feel betrayed."

"There must be some mistake. Cassie, wielding a gun and holding you hostage?" Maddie shook her head, denying reality.

"There is no mistake." Isabella narrowed her dark eyes.

David hated the desperate tone in Maddie's voice. He felt her pain low in his gut. It was the same, helpless sensation he'd felt when Aunt Caroline had told him that Shriver had swindled her out of the Rembrandt.

"We have proof," Antonio Banderas interjected. "Would you like to see the security tape?"

"Absolutely," David said.

"This way."

Antonio led them into a room filled with television monitors and spy cameras. Isabella Vasquez followed at their heels. In Spanish, Antonio instructed the technician to play the tape of the robbery, while Isabella remained standing in the doorway, arms crossed.

"I can't bear to watch," Isabella shuddered. "I'll wait in my office."

The screen filled with Isabella's image. They watched while she walked down an empty corridor toward a heavy metal door. Isabella punched a series of numbers into the electronic keypad on the wall and the door opened.

Cassie appeared first. She wore the uniform of an international delivery service. She was smiling and although there was no audio, you could tell she had greeted Isabella with a friendly, *"Buenos dias,* Izzy."

David slid a side glance over at Maddie, saw her hands were fisted in her lap and her breathing had grown both rapid and shallow. He leaned close to her ear and whispered, "Breathe deeply. Don't hyperventilate."

She glared at him. He knew she hated being told what to do, but she did obey, forcing in a deep but jerky breath.

On the screen Cassie stepped over the threshold and into the museum. Immediately a man wearing a uniform that matched Cassie's but with a ski mask pulled down over his face and a deadly .45 magnum clutched in his left hand, barged in behind her.

The man clamped his fingers around Cassie's upper arm and pointed the gun at Isabella's heart.

"Freeze it there a moment," David said.

Antonio repeated David's instruction to the technician who stopped the tape. David narrowed his eyes and studied the frame.

Cassie looked almost as panicked as Isabella. Her eyes were wide, her face pale and she was gnawing her bottom lip. He leaned in closer to the monitor. The gunman's fingers dug so deeply into Cassie's arm that her sleeve bunched around his sausage-sized digits.

David shifted his attention to the man's left hand. The hand that clutched the .45.

What he saw sent a river of chills coursing down his spine.

A skull and crossbones tattoo.

Deep in his heart he instantly knew two things. One, Cassie Cooper had not willingly robbed the Prado; she was as much a victim as Isabella Vasquez.

And two, the gunman was not Peyton Shriver.

The thug in the ski mask was none other than Jocko Blanco.

Maddie couldn't believe what she was seeing. She rubbed her eyes, blinked twice and looked again.

No denying it. The woman caught on camera was her sister.

David had been right all along. Her twin had gone renegade. How could she tell her mother that Cassie was headed for prison?

Nausea ambushed her, slick and hot.

"I'm going to be sick," she moaned, and clamped a hand over her mouth.

David grabbed a nearby trashcan and shoved it under her face. It smelled of pencil shavings, coffee grounds and orange peel.

Maddie gagged.

A lock of her hair broke free from her ponytail clip, and David gently swept back the errant strand while at the same time pressed a cool palm to her heated forehead.

He rubbed her back and murmured sweet nothings the way her mother had when she was ill. Her father had never been there when she got sick. She remembered one time, before the divorce and after a trip to Six Flags where she'd wolfed down too much junk food, and she told her dad she was going to throw up, he'd thrust her toward her mother, said "You deal with her." Then he'd taken off to the local bar.

"It's okay," David murmured. "It's perfectly all right. Throw up if you need to."

She closed her eyes, took a deep breath and managed to hold on to what little breakfast she'd eaten on the train. "I think I'm okay now."

She lifted her head. David passed her the glass of water Antonio had fetched.

"I still can't believe, Cassie would…" Overcome with emotion, Maddie broke off and closed her eyes against the image frozen on the monitor.

"Is there someplace where Maddie can lie down?" he asked Antonio.

"In Isabella's office," Antonio replied.

"I'm okay," Maddie insisted. "I want to keep watching the tape."

"I don't think that's such a good idea," David said.

"I'm not moving until I know exactly what we're up against."

"All right," he conceded and nodded at the technician. "Roll it."

They watched as Cassie and the gunman forced Isabella down the corridor and into the main gallery. Walking stiffly but with her head held high, Isabella led them to the room housing the El Greco.

The masked man kept the gun trained on Isabella while Cassie tied her up and left her on the floor. Then together,

Cassie and the man boxed up the El Greco in the crate they'd brought with them and left the room. They disappeared off camera for several minutes.

"Where did they go?" David asked Antonio.

The policeman shrugged. "There are a few areas of the museum out of camera range."

Cassie and the gunman reappeared on the hallway camera wheeling the crate on the dolly.

David blew air through his teeth with a prolonged hissing sound but Maddie didn't dare glance over at him. She couldn't stand to see the pity on his face. Nausea swept over her again and she felt dizzy.

"I think I'll lie down now," she said.

"Good choice," David said. "Come on."

Antonio led the way to Isabella's office. David kept his hand braced against the small of Maddie's back, guiding her along, offering support. They passed the ladies room on the way and Maddie made note of it in case she felt the urge to puke again.

"Hang in there," he whispered.

God, he was being too nice to her. She wished he would stop being so nice so she could hate him for being right about Cassie.

She was still having trouble absorbing everything she'd just seen. Disoriented, she eased down on the black leather couch in Isabella's office and didn't resist when David told her to tuck her head between her knees.

This wasn't like her. She didn't come unglued. She was the strong one. If she wasn't cool and calm and thoroughly in control, then who in the hell was she? She'd always been so certain of herself. She was Cassie's twin sister. Her loyal protector, her staunchest defender.

Isabella voiced her internal fears. "You must be very

shocked, Maddie. I've never seen you fall apart. It is frightening, though, to think that Cassie has become a common criminal. I can hardly believe it myself."

"Could you give us a moment in private, Señora Vasquez?" David asked.

Isabella nodded and departed, pulling the door closed behind her.

David threaded a hand through his hair and plunked down on the couch beside Maddie. "It looks bad for Cassie," he said and she had a feeling he was choosing his words very carefully.

"I can't believe she did it." Maddie shook her head repeatedly. "But it's right there, caught on tape. My twin sister is a thief."

David said nothing.

"Why?" Maddie asked. "Why would she do this?"

"Maybe it's a case of Stockholm Syndrome. Where the kidnapped victim identifies with her captor. Like Patty Hearst."

"Patty Hearst went to jail," Maddie said gloomily, but she clung to his explanation.

"Yes, but she got a light sentence."

"That's supposed to comfort me?"

He shrugged. "I'm trying my best."

"I thought you didn't believe Cassie had been kidnapped."

"Maybe I was wrong."

She looked at him. "I know you're just trying to make me feel better, but it's not working."

"Then how about this?" David slipped an arm around her.

"How about what?"

"This."

He kissed her. Lightly, slowly, tenderly. The exact opposite of the way he'd kissed her on the train.

His lips tasted like cool peppermint and total calamity, but she didn't even care. His arms were strong around her waist and his tongue was welcoming against hers. She accepted what he offered and heaven help her, she kissed him back.

In past relationships, she'd had trouble letting go. Kissing was often awkward and fraught with expectation. She usually thought about her performance too much, worried what the guy was thinking about.

But with David, she just melted.

His thumb slid along her jaw, stopped at the pulse point in her neck. Her heartbeat jumped against the pad of his thumb and something primordial in her throbbed in response.

David picked up on her mood and deepened the kiss while his hands got busy elsewhere. He spread his fingers against the base of her skull, threading through her hair while his other hand inched up inside her sweater.

She could feel the urgent need in the eager yet hesitant way his hand skimmed over her bra, touching her breasts with an excited caress. His eagerness told her he hadn't been with a woman in a long time.

She tasted his yearning, smelled his impatience.

It matched her own.

She sank into him. Instinct, nature and her body crowded out the protests telling her this was the wrong time, the wrong place, the wrong man.

But she could think of nothing except how good his tongue tasted in her mouth, how sweetly her breasts tingled against the brush of his knuckles, how wonderfully numb her mind was.

He swept her away and she allowed herself to be tossed by uncertain waters, clinging with her arms around his neck, her eyes closed, her body immersed in sensation.

His breath was warm. The room was warm. Her feminine core warmer still.

Warm and moist and willing.

Dear God, what was she doing?

Her body's wet reaction to his kisses yanked her back to reality. How could she have let herself go so irresponsibly?

For two breathtaking minutes she had been absorbed in her own selfish needs and had completely forgotten about Cassie's predicament.

What kind of sister was she?

To assuage her guilt and remind herself of her mission, she reached up to touch the half-a-heart necklace. But it was gone.

Vanished.

And she had no idea when or where she'd lost it.

"Oh no," Maddie moaned. "I really am going to throw up."

Bewildered, David watched Maddie dash into the hallway in hot pursuit of the ladies room. Well, that was a first. His kisses had never made a woman toss her cookies before.

Yeah, Marshall, you're a real lady-killer.

Problem was, he felt woozy himself and it had nothing to do with the kiss and everything to do with the fact he'd just violated every one of his ethical standards.

What was it about Maddie that shattered his best intentions? How come his instincts to comfort and protect her always seemed to end up with him getting touchy-feely?

Because this attraction wasn't purely physical.

And that's what scared the living hell out of him. This stupid, inexplicable need to be her knight in shining armor.

He'd crossed some bizarre threshold into a funhouse mirror of distorted emotions that he could not trust.

Hadn't he learned the hard way you couldn't depend on love to be there when you needed it?

He couldn't be in love with her. He wasn't in love with her.

And yet, why did it feel like magic every time he kissed her?

David shook off his mental confusion. Forget the kiss. Forget your feelings. Forget trying to make sense of your relationship with Maddie. You've got bigger troubles.

Like, where was Cassie? And how had Jocko Blanco gotten his hands on her? And what had happened to Shriver?

He hadn't been able to bring himself to tell Maddie his suspicions that Blanco had kidnapped Cassie, used her to break into the Prado and then spirited her away along with the El Greco. He would need to study the tape again, but every bone in his body was telling him Cassie had not been a willing participant in the crime.

When he thought about Blanco's ruthless reputation, his own stomach churned.

So what to do? Tell Maddie about his fears concerning Blanco or let her go on believing it was Cassie and Shriver on the tape?

He didn't like either alternative, but he knew one thing for sure, the longer Cassie was with Blanco, the more dire her situation. He had to take action and the sooner the better.

Before he could make a decision, Maddie came staggering back into the room.

"David," she cried. "Come quick. I know where Cassie's gone and I have proof Shriver forced her to help him steal the El Greco!"

When they heard Maddie shout, Antonio and Isabella

came running from the security office and spilled into the corridor to join David and Maddie on their mad trot into the ladies room.

Maddie had David by the hand and she was dragging him through the door.

"What is it?" he said. "What did you find?"

She screeched to a halt in front of the bathroom mirror so suddenly he almost smacked into her.

"Look, look!" she cried triumphantly and gestured at what was written in flaming scarlet lipstick across the mirror.

Midnight Rendezvous.

"What in the hell is that supposed to mean?" David asked, not getting what she was babbling about.

"When we lived in Madrid Cassie had a hush-hush affair with a notorious playboy from Monaco. He would send his private plane—*Midnight Rendezvous*—to pick her up."

"You've got to be kidding."

"I'm afraid not. My sister is very flamboyant. She even partied with members of the royal family. Of course, I was a nervous wreck during the fling. Those small planes go down all the time and who knew if the pilot shared the playboy's party-hearty philosophy."

"So what's that got to do with anything?"

Maddie clutched his sleeve and tugged like an impatient child trying to capture her father's attention. "This proves Cassie's not guilty. This is her favorite lipstick. She had to write the message in code in case Shriver came into the restroom and caught her. She's sending me a clue, David. This clue says she's been forced to help steal the painting and Shriver's taken her to Monaco."

Chapter 13

Cassie huddled in the passenger seat of the rented Peugeot with Jocko Blanco behind the wheel. They'd flown from Madrid to Nice, rented a car there and were driving to Monaco where Jocko had a buyer for the El Greco—which was now locked in the trunk—all lined up.

He was taking the curves like Lucifer, snarling and honking at slower moving vehicles. Whenever Cassie so much as gasped, Blanco would fling her a threatening glance and fondle the ugly looking gun in his lap.

Oh God, where was Maddie when you needed her?

Cassie clutched the dashboard until her knuckles were white and prayed for a miraculous deliverance.

Jocko Blanco had entered her bedroom through the open balcony window the night before and taken her hostage. The Interpol guy who'd been tailing her ever since she'd arrived in Madrid had attempted to come to her rescue when Blanco dragged her out the side entrance of the hotel, but Blanco had shot him in the shoulder and left him for dead in the alley.

Blanco had then stolen a delivery service van. Just before dawn, he'd forced her to call Isabella Vasquez and ask the curator to meet her at the delivery entrance.

He'd spoiled all her intricate plans.

Cassie had tried to resist, but he'd twisted her arm so it brought tears to her eyes. She wasn't physically tough like Maddie. Between the threat of more pain and the cold handgun shoved hard against her side, she'd had little choice but to play along. She kept hoping she would think of a way out of this.

She wondered where Peyton was and what he would do when he showed up in Madrid and found her gone. Would he assume the worst and think she'd thrown in her lot with Jocko?

And what about Isabella? Was her friend still trussed in the museum? Cassie chewed the inside of her cheek. Had anyone found her yet? She prayed that Izzy was okay. She'd made sure to tie the ropes as loosely as she dared and she'd apologized for having to gag her.

How badly she had wanted to give her friend some clue that Blanco was holding her hostage. But she'd been terrified that if Blanco knew what she was up to, he would simply shoot Izzy, the way he'd shot the Interpol guy. She refused to risk Izzy's life in order to save her own skin, so she'd kept quiet.

Cassie knew the heist had been recorded on security cameras. She knew the authorities would assume that the masked, gloved Blanco was Peyton. She had realized she would have to do something to prove her innocence while keeping Izzy safe. She had to let Maddie know she'd been taken prisoner to Monaco.

Seized with inspiration, she had begged Blanco to let her go to the bathroom before they left the museum. At first, she thought he was going to say no. She hopped around like a four year old on the playground until he finally relented and told her to make it snappy.

She dashed into the bathroom and scrawled *Midnight Rendezvous* in the only thing she had handy—her favorite tube of Lancôme. Never mind that the lipstick cost twenty-eight dollars a pop, once on, the stuff did not come off without a high quality make-up remover.

She was certain her sister would know what *Midnight Rendezvous* meant. Maddie had certainly been pissed off enough about her madcap affair with the flashy playboy.

What if Maddie doesn't come after you?

When has she *not* come after you? No need to worry on that score. Her sister was as predictable as Big Ben.

Blanco whipped the car around a puttering truck loaded with crates of live chickens and snarled a fresh batch of expletives. Feathers flew across the windshield as the startled driver swerved onto the narrow shoulder.

Cassie caught her breath. Okay, okay, okay. Calm down. What would Maddie do in this particular situation?

Um, well, Maddie probably would never be in this situation.

Of course that was a given, never mind that part. Think rational. Think reasonable. Think common sense.

She could grab the steering wheel. Hmm, yeah, right. Blanco weighed a good two fifty. She was a hundred pounds lighter. He'd probably just elbow her in the mouth and bye-bye dental work.

Think, think.

Gosh, this thinking before you acted stuff was really hard work. No wonder Maddie was perpetually crabby.

If she was quick, she could just lean over and bite the blazing thunder out of his hand.

And then he would probably just knock her head into his lap.

Yikes! She didn't want to go there.

So what? You're just going to sit here like a helpless ninny? This is not going to help you prove you're as smart as Maddie.

Yeah, well, maybe she was over that.

Cassie sneaked a glance at Blanco. Maybe she could stab him in the neck with her stiletto?

Now there was an idea whose time had come.

Slowly, she leaned forward and reached down to slip off her sharp-heeled sling back.

Blanco glowered and stroked his gun. "Don't even think about it."

"What?" She rounded her eyes and tried to look totally ingenuous.

"Sonofabitch, motherf—" he exploded.

Cassie jammed her fingers in her ears so she wouldn't have to hear the rest of Blanco's cursing. He was glaring intently into the rearview mirror and swerving like a drunk on New Year's Eve.

Tremulously, Cassie peeked into the side mirror and her heart lurched into her throat. There was a boxy ice cream truck behind them, coming up fast.

Too fast.

Sweet tea and almond cookies! Blanco was already doing eighty, how fast was this other driver going?

Then her heart leaped with hope. Maybe it was Maddie or David or both. Maybe they'd already found her message, pieced together what had happened and were on their way to save her.

In an ice cream truck?

Sure, why not?

Blanco goosed the car faster just as they rounded the side of an imposing hill.

The ice cream truck dogged them, gaining ground. Over the loudspeaker attached on the roof, the truck was playing what sounded like *Pop Goes the Weasel*.

Blanco cornered the next curve, the car almost tipping on two wheels.

All around the cobbler's bench.

Cassie yelped.

"Shuddup."

She gulped and hung on tight.

The monkey chased the weasel.

The ice cream truck was getting closer. Blanco had his foot jammed to the floor. Their car had reached its top speed.

And then the ice cream truck smashed into their bumper. Hard.

This time Cassie did more than yelp, she shrieked. Omigod, who was ramming them and why?

She tried to see who was behind the wheel of the ice cream truck, but the windshield was tinted, obstructing her view, and things were moving way too fast.

Blanco lost control of both the car and his gun. The handgun slid across the seat and landed on the floor at Cassie's feet.

"Leave it," Blanco shouted as if to an obedient dog and trod the brakes.

Cassie's head jerked at the unexpected change in tempo, but she didn't take her eyes off that gun. She unbuckled her seatbelt and dived for the .45 at the same time the ice cream truck rammed them again.

The passenger door flew open and Cassie tumbled out—along with the .45—onto the graveled shoulder of the road. She landed on her butt and bounced a couple of times. The impact hurt like hell. Forget about that. You're free, you're free.

Pebbles bit into her palms and her knees were skinned but she was okay.

Which was more than she could say for Blanco. Dumbfounded, she watched open-mouthed as the car went smashing down over the side of the cliff.

Pop goes the weasel.

The ice cream truck stopped just short of the edge. Terrified, Cassie shifted her gaze to the driver.

The door swung open.

And Peyton Shriver got out, concern knitting his brow. "Cassie, luv, are you all right?"

My antihero!

Cassie dusted herself off and ran into his open arms.

"What aren't you telling me?" David grilled Isabella Vasquez. He'd managed to talk Maddie into staying with Antonio Banderas while he questioned Isabella alone. He'd had a sneaking suspicion the woman wasn't telling everything she knew about the robbery.

Isabella nervously clasped and unclasped her hands. "I don't know what you're talking about, Señor Marshall."

"Oh, I think you do. Why did you so willingly let Cassie Cooper in the private entrance? How come the robbery went off so smoothly?"

"Are you accusing me of something?"

"Are you guilty of something?"

She kneaded her brow and began to pace. "It's not what you think. Or at least it wasn't."

"So why don't you tell me what happened?"

"If this gets out to the press, I'll lose my job."

"Or perhaps go to jail?"

"It wasn't supposed to happen this way. Cassie lied to me. She betrayed me."

"Talk to me Isabella. I'm on your side."

She stared at him long and hard.

"All right," she relented at last. "Two days ago Cassie came to see me. She told me about this plan she had to catch Peyton Shriver. She told me she was working with the FBI and she needed my help."

"You agreed, just like that?"

"Cassie is very persuasive, but the reason I agreed to help her is because of the political infighting; my job at the Prado is in jeopardy. If I could be instrumental in helping catch one of the world's most infamous art thieves my position here would be solidified."

"So exactly what were you supposed to do for Cassie?"

"She wanted to copy the El Greco. She's very talented at re-creations."

"You mean forgeries."

"It's only forgery if you try to pass it off as the real thing."

"Go on."

"I was supposed to place the real El Greco in the vault and replace it with the copy so she and her art thief accomplice could steal it. Her accomplice of course wouldn't know it was a copy. I was to let them in the side entrance, give them the digital signature code and let them rob the Prado. They would be taking a fake. I didn't see how the plan could go wrong. But instead of showing up on Friday night as we'd planned, she and the masked gunman held me up at daybreak this morning. Cassie never brought me the reproduction, so it was the real El Greco that they stole."

David stared at Isabella, stunned, his mind whirling with what she had just told him. He and Maddie had both been wrong. Cassie had not fallen for Shriver. Nor had she been kidnapped. She had gone willingly with him, yes. But not because she'd become enamored with Shriver and his lifestyle as David had initially suspected but because she'd gotten off on playing spy girl and was trying to trap Shriver on her own.

Holy shit, what an airhead plan.

The thing was, Cassie's scheme just might have worked. Except for the unexpected interference of Jocko Blanco.

Dammit. Recruiting Cassie Cooper was turning out to be the stupidest thing he'd ever done in his entire life.

Maddie paced the terrazzo floor of Antonio Banderas's office, tensing and relaxing her abdominal muscles. The isometric exercises were designed to help her deal constructively with tension.

The security officer watched her from behind his desk with somnolent eyes. He was smoking a stogie and the pungent scent of cigar tobacco filled the room.

She glanced at her watch. It was almost lunchtime. Which explained Antonio's laziness, but didn't tell her why David was taking his sweet time wrapping things up with Isabella. They needed to get on the road to Monaco ASAP. Each passing moment put them farther away from her sister.

After seeing Cassie's message scrawled on the bathroom mirror, David had asked her to hang out with Antonio for a few minutes while he took Isabella aside for more detailed questioning. She hadn't wanted to let him question Isabella on his own, but David told her that he thought she might be more forthcoming if Maddie wasn't in the room.

But that was over an hour ago.

"I think I'm just going to go check on David." Maddie

motioned with her thumb toward the corridor. "See if there's some kind of problem."

Antonio waved a hand at the sofa. "Please Señorita Cooper, sit down, relax. Have a snooze."

"A snooze?"

"Did I say it wrong?" He seemed concerned that he might have made a language *faux pas*.

"No. I just don't understand how you can expect me to snooze when my sister is in such trouble. I need to be out there looking for her, doing something."

"You Americans." Antonio took a puff of his cigar. "Always with the hurry."

It had been five years since she had lived in Spain and she'd forgotten how irritatingly leisurely the natives could be. What they perceived as relaxed, spontaneous and flexible Maddie saw as indolent, disorganized and unreliable. Cassie, of course, had fit right in, while Maddie, with her need for order, structure and discipline had stood out like a prison warden in kindergarten.

"You are very stressed," Antonio said.

"No kidding."

"Would you like some coffee?"

"Like caffeine is going to help me relax?"

"You're right, bad idea. Please sit." He gestured at the sofa again.

"No thanks. I really do have to find Agent Marshall." She made a move for the door.

And a policeman stepped forward from the corridor to block her way.

"Excuse me." She moved to the left.

He waltzed with her.

Alarm knotted her chest. She turned and looked back at Antonio. "Am I being detained?"

Antonio gestured at the sofa a third time. "Please, no trouble."

"Are you arresting me?"

He shook his head. "Not arresting. No."

"But I'm not allowed to leave."

"Not until Agent Marshall gets back."

"And where has he gone?" Maddie's voice went up an octave and she realized she was within inches of losing her composure.

"I'm not sure." His smile was apologetic but unwavering.

"When will he be back?"

Antonio shrugged.

"What's going on here?" she asked in a careful, modulated tone, when she wanted to yell at the top of her lungs.

"Señor Marshall said you were getting in his way. He asked me to keep you here until he returns."

What? What! David had ditched her?

Bastard. She couldn't believe she'd trusted him. Why had she trusted him? She'd known better.

Maddie started pacing again. Wasn't that just like a man? When the going gets tough, the men take off.

Bastards. The lot of them.

"Señorita Cooper?" Antonio got up from his desk and tentatively approached her.

"What?" she snapped.

Quickly, he backpedaled, raising his palms in a defensive gesture. "Calm down."

"I'm calm. I'm completely calm." She glared and gnawed her thumbnail. "Why would you think I'm not calm? I'm always calm. It's what I do. I'm the calm one. Ask anybody."

"Calm as a time bomb," Antonio muttered under his breath.

"What? What did you say?"

Antonio looked terror stricken. "If you will just calm...
er...sit down, I can phone Agent Marshall and discover
when he intends to return. Is that acceptable?"

"How about this? How about I call him instead?" Maddie reached for the phone and then realized she didn't
know David's cell phone number. "What's his number?"

"I'm afraid I cannot give you that information."

"Why not?"

"Please." With the cautious movements of a man trying to soothe a wild tiger with a toothache, Antonio eased
around his desk.

"You wait with Paulo." He nodded toward his man
blocking the doorway. "And soon I will return with news
from Agent Marshall."

Yeah, right, okay, bucko.

Maddie faked a smile and forced herself to sit. "See?
I'm sitting like a good girl. Now go call Marshall."

Antonio slipped past her as if he thought she might spon-
taneously combust at any moment. She savored her anger
while her mind churned. She didn't know where David had
gone or what he was up to but she knew what she had to do.
Get the hell out of here and find a ride to Monaco.

David probably didn't believe her about Cassie. In fact,
that whole time he was being nice to her, telling her he
thought maybe her sister had a case of Stockholm Syndrome was nothing but a big fat lie.

And, she recognized the kiss he'd given for what it
undoubtedly was, a ruse to get her to let her guard down
with him so he could ditch her.

Grrr.

*David Marshall, you are so going to pay for this stunt
when I catch up with you.*

She had to get out of here. Now.

Maddie glanced at the guard in the doorway. "Paulo," she said in Spanish. "I'm feeling overheated." She fanned herself. "Could you get me a drink of water, please?"

"When Officer Banderas returns."

"I think I might faint. Please."

Taking a cue from her sister, she fluttered her eyelashes, undid a button on her blouse and slowly ran her tongue over her lips.

Paulo shook his head.

Terrific, first time she ever tried to flirt her way out of a bad situation and the guy turns out to be gay. Just her luck.

She sat a moment, scanning the room and thinking.

Her gaze fell on Antonio's desk. His still lit cigar smoldered in the ashtray. Beside the desk sat a trashcan full of discarded paper.

Hmm.

"You don't mind if I pace, do you?" she asked Paulo. "I pace when I get nervous."

He shrugged.

"Thank you." Maddie rose to her feet.

Nonchalantly, she paced. La-di-dah.

She cast a sidelong glance at Paulo, he was leaning one shoulder against the doorjamb, not paying her too much attention.

Good.

She paced closer to Antonio's desk. She spied a picture of an attractive woman and two smiling girls by the window.

Eureka.

"Oh," she squealed in Spanish. "Is this Antonio's family?" She made a beeline for the photograph and held it up for Paulo to see.

Paulo nodded. "*Si,* it's his family. But he doesn't like anyone touching his stuff. Put it down and come back over here." He waved at the sofa.

"Oh, okay."

Then oh so casually, she leaned over to set the picture frame back on the window ledge. Wiggling her fanny to hide what she was doing, Maddie bumped the cigar into the trashcan.

Paulo never saw it and Maddie sauntered back to the sofa.

One minute passed. Then two.

Crap. Had the cigar gone out?

Three minutes. Four.

Just when she was about to despair over her foiled attempt to start a fire, the acrid smell of smoldering paper filled the air.

Paulo sniffed. "Do you smell something burning?"

Maddie shook her head. "I think it's just Antonio's cigar."

Paulo nodded, her explanation appeasing him. Until bright orange flames began licking above the trashcan.

"Oooh, oooh," Maddie gasped, playing her part to the hilt. "Fire! Fire! *Fuego! Fuego!*"

The minute Paulo ran for the fire extinguisher, Maddie darted out the door.

Chapter 14

The road from Nice to Monaco was breathtakingly picturesque, but David barely noticed. His focus was on Cassie and the disturbing realization that she had some-how fallen into Blanco's clutches.

Was she even still with Blanco? The man was ruthless. Once she'd served her purpose, he was just as likely to kill her as he was to keep her. Unless he had an even uglier, more nefarious plan in store.

That thought shoved ice cubes up his spine.

What was Blanco up to? Was Levy behind Cassie's kidnapping? Were they going to ransom her to Shriver in exchange for the Cézanne? Or was Blanco still in cahoots with Shriver and they were making some kind of an end-run around Levy?

Remorse gigged him unmercifully. Guilt over ditching Maddie at the Prado joined the party. He shouldn't have left her, but he'd had no real choice. He'd already got-ten one sister mixed up with Jocko Blanco; he certainly wasn't placing both of them in danger. He had grabbed the next flight from Madrid to Nice, and then rented a car to drive the rest of the way into Monaco.

By now, Maddie had probably realized he wasn't coming back. Which might explain the inexplicable burning sensation around his ears. No doubt, at this very moment, she was cussing him up a blue streak.

Oh well, he would live.

But would Antonio? David had left the poor policeman to deal with the fallout of Maddie's obsessive devotion to her sister. He definitely owed the guy for keeping Maddie safe and off his hands.

The sky darkened the closer he drew to Monaco. It was early afternoon and a wicked rainstorm was on the way. He rounded a sharp curve and noticed the roadside barrier at the edge of the cliff looked as if it had recently been broken through.

He followed the curve, casually glancing in his rear-view mirror and saw the glint of metal in a swatch of sun that managed to break free from the cloud covering.

Squinting, he took a second look. Could that be an automobile bumper?

Yes. It was definitely a car bumper.

Shades of Princess Grace. Had someone taken a header off the bluff?

Dammit.

He was already too far behind Blanco. He really couldn't spare another moment, but how could he not stop and render aid if there had been a car accident?

Tick-tock. Cassie was in trouble.

But the people in the car might be seriously injured and he was the only one in sight.

He who hesitates is lost, the phrase his father had drilled into his head from the time he was a tiny tot sprang into his brain. *You must win at all costs.*

Yet how could he ignore someone in need? And how

could he overlook the lesson he'd just learned? His hunger to win at all costs had unnecessarily put Cassie in danger. Stopping to help would be a form of making amends.

David's gut tightened, telling him what he must do. No matter how much stopping might go against his instincts to plunge after Blanco. He simply had to detour.

He braked and did a U-turn. He slowed and pulled over at the smashed barrier. He killed the engine, got out and walked to the edge of the cliff, gravel crunching beneath his shoes.

Cautiously, he peered over and caught his breath at what he saw.

It was a car wreck all right.

The reflective taillight of a nondescript tan rental car winked at him. The trunk flapped open. The hood was solidly embedded in the body of a cypress tree. If it hadn't been for the tree, the car would be resting at the bottom of the ravine and whoever was inside would have no chance of survival at all.

Urgency shot a lance of fear through him. As far as he knew, he was the first on the scene. There could be a family down there. A mom. A dad. Kids. They needed him.

Worry shoved him down the cliff. Moving as quickly as he dared, David picked his way over the uneven terrain, his pulse pounding hard, sweat beading his brow and upper lip.

By the time he reached the driver's seat, his body was at a ninety-degree slant and he had to grab on to roots and foliage in order to maintain his balance.

He could see a man slumped over the wheel but there was no one else in the vehicle. His heart rate kicked up another notch. He wrenched open the door.

The man groaned.

David spoke to him first in English, then in French, telling him to hang on, that help was on the way.

Dammit. Why hadn't he called for an ambulance before climbing down the hill? He had been trained better than that. Why was he so scattered, so muddled these days?

Maddie.

No. He wasn't going to blame her for his recent rash of bad decisions. This was his responsibility, no one else. David reached into his jacket pocket for his cell phone. He peered at the numbers.

Funny, the back light wasn't coming on. He punched the power button again.

And felt two heavy, hammy fists circle his neck and squeeze tight.

Startled, David jerked his head up to find himself nose-to-nose with a bruised and bloodied but very much alive, Jocko Blanco.

"You came after me, you saved me." Cassie snuggled next to Peyton on the front seat of the ice cream truck after they'd climbed down the hill and taken the El Greco out of the trunk while Blanco was still unconscious. She nestled her head against his shoulder and savored his masculine aroma.

"Don't read too much into it. I also rescued the El Greco."

"But you could have left me with Blanco and you didn't. That means you like me."

Would he have done the same thing if the El Greco had been alone in the car with Blanco or if the painting hadn't been there at all? She knew the answer. The painting was primary; she was the afterthought.

"You came awful close to getting left in the car along with Blanco," he said.

"Oh?" She ignored the uncomfortable ping in the pit of her stomach. Maddie was the worrier, not she. "Why's that?"

"I thought you had betrayed me."

"Why would you think that?" *Don't let him see you sweat.*

"When I saw you in Paris, I thought you'd gone to Levy behind my back."

"But I was never in Paris."

"I realize that now, but it took me a while. Until I remembered you had a twin sister. I had no idea you two looked so much alike."

"You saw Maddie?"

Peyton rubbed the back of his head and winced. "Yeah, I met her. And is she ever a bitch."

"Hey, that's my sister you're talking about."

"If it hadn't been for that necklace I would have thought for sure you were still working with David Marshall. Actually, he's the one who showed up to rescue me from your twin."

"I don't understand."

"I was dressed as a mime, casing the Louvre. When I came out of the museum, I spied you in the crowd. Except it wasn't you, but I didn't know that at the time."

"Maddie hates mimes."

"Tell me about it. I started mimicking you...I mean her...because I was mad that you'd come to Paris when you were supposed to be currying favor with your curator friend in Madrid. Then I saw the necklace. It was the right half of the heart. Your necklace is the left side." Peyton reached over and fingered the gold charm at her throat. "That's when I knew she wasn't you. That's also when she attacked me and Marshall had to pull her off."

"Maddie attacked you?" Wow. She knew her sister hated mimes but this was beyond the pale.

"Like a lioness. The necklace chain broke off in my hand and she thought I was stealing it."

Ah, that made sense. Maddie had been rabid about their necklaces ever since the frozen pond incident. "It means a lot to her."

"So I gathered."

"David Marshall didn't recognize you?"

"I was disguised as a mime, remember, and I ran off quickly." Peyton paused. "Plus, I think Marshall was drunk."

"Weird. That doesn't sound like David."

"Do you know him that well?"

"Are you jealous?" She teased, doing her best to charm him.

"Not jealous. Just worried about your loyalties."

Peyton eyed her speculatively and Cassie knew she had to do something to reassure him that she was on his side. Which meant now was as good a time as any to let him in on a small segment of her plan.

"Peyton," she whispered in a singsong voice, leaning in closer and blowing softly into his ear. "Just to show you how committed I am to making this relationship work, I'm going to tell you an idea I have for doubling your take on the Cézanne and the El Greco."

"Doubling my take?" That perked him right up. "Now you're speaking my language."

Cassie nibbled his earlobe. "It's dead simple."

"I'm listening."

"We hold a silent auction."

"I don't understand."

"We get Jerome Levy and Cory Philpot to invite all the wealthy collectors they know to bring their...ahem...ill-gotten works of art that they'd like to sell or trade to our underground equivalent of an afternoon at Sotheby's. We charge a broker fee and let Philpot and Levy split the take."

"That makes no sense."

Cassie raised a finger. "Hear me out. This would put you back in good graces with both Philpot and Levy. We could hold it at one of those elegant five star hotels in Venice. Since it's Carnevale, a lot of their clients are likely to be in the city already."

"But what about me? How do I get my money?"

"You tell Levy and Philpot that the impetus for the auction is to unload the red hot Cézanne and El Greco. Get them to tell their collectors that since there is so much heat on us, we're willing to let the paintings go for bargain basement prices."

Cassie's heart quickened as she waited for him to take the bait. Do it. Go on. Say yes.

"But if we let the paintings go at a bargain basement price how am I going to double my money?"

"Simple. We make copies of the paintings. We show the real paintings to the authenticators, and then pull a switcheroo, keeping the originals to ransom back to the museums for a hefty sum."

"But where do we get someone we can trust to make forgeries so quickly?"

"You're looking at her."

"You?"

"Me."

"No kidding?"

"Hey, I spent months in bed as a kid with nothing to do but draw and paint. I loved working with watercolor and started imitating artwork I saw in picture books. I was quick and accurate. But, I was mightily disappointed to discover I had zero talent for creating anything original. However, I can copy like a Xerox."

"How long would it take to replicate the paintings?" Peyton asked.

"Give me lots of chocolate and coffee, canvas and paint and then get out of my way. I can have them done in twenty-four hours."

"Really? You're that fast?"

"And that good," she bragged shamelessly.

"You're brilliant, luv." Peyton kissed her on the cheek.

"Aren't you glad you saved me?"

"Completely. We'll go to Venice. You concentrate on making the copies and I'll set up the auction."

"Deal," Cassie said and they shook on it.

She settled back against the seat and inwardly sighed with relief. Thank heavens he'd gone for her plan. Everything was falling into place. She would replicate the Cézanne twice and the El Greco again, thereby ending up with two sets of forgeries. She would keep the second set a secret from Peyton. It would be her ace in the hole.

Shriver would get Levy and Philpot to lure in the collectors and art dealers interested in picking up cheap masterpieces to Venice. Then in the meantime, she would call David Marshall and tell him exactly when and where to arrest Peyton, Levy, Philpot and the greedy collectors.

What could possibly go wrong?

David lay battered and bruised on the side of the hill, the steep canyon looming below him, the road stretching far above his grasp. With one eye, he stared up at the blanket of clouds crowding the Mediterranean sky and knew he was truly screwed.

He'd lost all track of time. It seemed he had lain here for days. His throat was parched from hollering for help, his lips were dried. His right wrist was broken and his left eye was swollen shut and he couldn't seem to muster the energy to crawl up the hill.

Blanco had pistol-whipped the crap out of him.

"You're the world's biggest schmuck, Marshall," he growled under his breath, and then decided he needed to stop talking out loud. The vibrations made his head throb even harder.

Good God, he was no better than impulsive Cassie Cooper, shimmying down the hill, throwing open the wrecked car door without once stopping to think that Blanco might be behind the wheel.

And you call yourself an FBI agent. For shame.

He closed his eye and swallowed. And speaking of Cassie, he hated to even wonder about her whereabouts. She hadn't been with Blanco, that much was clear. But had she escaped? Or had the thug done away with her?

What would he tell Maddie when he saw her again?

Correction, *if* he ever saw her again.

An overwhelming sense of loss washed through him. He'd made such a mess of things. He'd fallen down on the job, disappointed himself and placed not one, but two women in jeopardy.

All his life, he had feared being a loser. Of not being able to measure up to his father's high standards and the lofty Marshall name. And now, his greatest fear had just come to pass.

He'd blown it. Big time.

Yep. He was screwed. His single-minded pursuit of Shriver, his blind determination to win at all costs, was to blame for his graceless downfall.

So now what? He had left Maddie at the Prado after giving Antonio strict instructions not to let her leave until he returned, so there was no hope of rescue from that resource.

After beating him senseless, Blanco had taken both his duty weapon and his car. He stood no chance of driving or shooting his way out of this situation.

And when he'd tried to call for help on his cell phone he'd realized he hadn't remembered to recharge the batteries since this whole thing began back at the Kimbell museum three days earlier.

Had it only been three days since Shriver had heisted the Cézanne?

So what now? Lie here and wallow in self-pity or do something about it? He opened his good eye again and studied the distance from his perilous perch on the steep hillside to the road above.

Two hundred yards minimum. Straight up.

He had one option. Scale the incline in the rain with a broken wrist, a black eye and a brain-stabbing headache. Not a particularly cheery thought.

Still, it was better than waiting for the buzzards to find him. Taking a deep breath to bolster his courage against the pain, David began to crawl.

"You've gotta drive faster," Maddie told herself. "I know you hate exceeding the speed limit but if you have any hopes of catching up with Cassie and Shriver you've got to jam the pedal to the metal."

Tentatively, she pressed harder upon the accelerator of the car she had rented in Nice after she'd flown there from Madrid. That project had been almost as big an undertaking as getting past Paulo. At least she hadn't had to start another fire. Now she was finally on the road and free of that infuriating David Marshall.

Thank God. She prayed Cassie and Shriver were still in Monaco. Of course, she had no idea how she was going to find them once she got there.

Try not to fret about that yet. Take it one step at a time.
Good advice, but could she take it?

She turned on the radio. Julio Iglesias was belting out a song. The music got on her nerves so she switched it off. She tried isometric exercises but found she couldn't concentrate. She turned on her headlights against the gloomy sprinkles of rain and flicked on the fan to bring fresh air into the car. Her clothes smelled like cigar smoke and charred paper and travel funk.

For the first time all day she realized she had no notion where her luggage was. When was the last time she had seen it? The train? Yes, that had to be it. But never mind. Her luggage was gone now. She could buy new clothes later. Hell, once she found Cassie, she would take her on a shopping spree.

"Cassie," she whispered. "Hang on. I'm coming. I know you were forced to rob the museum. I believe in your innocence."

The lights of Monaco twinkled in the distance and Maddie urged the car even faster.

There. She was going a full eight miles over the speed limit. Not so cautious now, huh?

See, I can take risks.

She rounded a curve on her way up a hill. There was something up ahead. Maddie slowed and squinted through the rain. Her headlights caught a man staggering into the middle of the road.

"Eeek!" Maddie screeched and trod the brakes, coming to a stop just in the nick of time to keep from plowing over David Marshall.

Chapter 15

"Maddie?" David blinked against the headlight glare at the ethereal form of the woman hurrying toward him in the rain.

Was she a mirage?

If she was a mirage, she was the most beautiful mirage ever to be conjured by a delusional brain.

But how did she get here? How did she get away from Antonio Banderas? Had she talked the policeman into letting her go? Or had she escaped? She was a pretty good escape artist. Maybe she'd challenged Antonio to a drinking contest. If that was the case, he felt sorry for Antonio.

Maybe you're dead and living out a sexual fantasy.

No, that couldn't be. His sex fantasies centered on his masculine prowess and pleasing Maddie within an inch of her life. In his current condition, he couldn't satisfy a sock puppet.

"David!" she cried and reached him just as his knees gave way.

His nose filled with the wonderful smell of her. It was Maddie. No mistaking her aroma. He had no idea how she'd found him, but she was here.

Thank God.

She caught him under his arms and he almost bit through his lip to keep from screaming in pain. He grunted and fell against her.

"Are you all right?"

"My arm," he managed to pant.

"Omigod, your wrist is broken."

"Yeah."

"And your face! Oh!" She hovered, just dying to mother him. He couldn't say he minded. "Your poor handsome face."

She thought he was handsome? He would have smiled if his lip didn't hurt so much.

"Oooooh." She touched his left eye that was swollen shut.

"Easy."

"Poor baby." Tenderly, she kissed his cheek.

In a million years David would never have suspected he would enjoy being made a fuss over. He'd lost his mother at a young age and he'd toughened up quick, eschewing mushy emotions, going so far as to make fun of boys who cried on the playground. But Maddie's concern made him want to wallow in his wounds. He wanted more touching and kissing and caressing.

"What happened?" she whispered.

"Can't talk now," he mumbled through gritted teeth. It was all he could do to stay conscious.

"Yes, yes, you're right. I'm sorry. Here. You grab on to me so I won't hurt you."

He wrapped his good hand around her upper arm. "Let's get to the car."

"Are you sure you can make it?"

"I'll be fine, woman, unless I end up catching pneumonia from standing here in the rain."

"I'm sorry," she apologized again. "I'm just so flustered at seeing you beat up. It hurts me here." She touched her heart with her fingers and David felt something inside his chest flip.

Shake it off.

Determinedly, he put one foot in front of the other and ignored the sappy feelings stirring inside him. At last, they made it and Maddie helped him ease slowly into the passenger seat.

He was soaked to the skin and the eye that was swollen shut throbbed like an ingrown toenail. His teeth chattered—tick-tick-tickety-tick—like loose rice in a tin cup. He was cold and dizzy and his body hurt like the blazes in a dozen different places.

Buck up. You can't look weak in front of her.

"Breathe deeply," she coached. "I'll get you to the hospital as quickly as I can."

He nodded, just barely. Her calm competency reassured him. He lay back against the seat and concentrated on dealing with the pain.

She didn't ask any more questions and he was glad for that. He wasn't ready to tell her about Blanco yet, or the stupidity that had landed him in the canyon.

"Maddie," he said. "I left you behind with Antonio for your own good. I shudder to think what would have happened if you'd been with me."

"Shh," she said. "No talking. We can talk later. You hang in there."

In that moment he knew she'd forgiven him for ditching her. She wasn't going to hold a grudge or pick a fight.

What a woman.

The car smelled of her. Nice. Womanly. Uniquely Maddie. They rumbled along in the rain.

"Move over, step on the gas, Grandma," Maddie grumbled to a slow moving vehicle in front of them. "We have an emergency here."

She was adorable in her urgency. David gazed at her with his one good eye. She drove with both hands on the wheel, eyes trained on the road, her chin set with serious intent. Right now, he loved her take-charge attitude. Sometimes, the way she tried to muscle in and take over infuriated him, but for the time being, he loved that she was in the driver's seat.

"Outta my way, sucker," she said and slammed her palm into the horn. "Hey, that jerk flipped me off. Well, up yours too, buddy."

He almost smiled. If his damned wrist didn't hurt so much he would have.

She was colorful. He had to grant her that.

"Here we go, here we are. It's the hospital."

Maddie left the car running and dashed inside the squat white building with a large red cross over the door of the emergency entrance. Sisters-of-something-or-other hospital. He couldn't read the lettering too clearly. Having just one eye played hell with a guy's visual acuity.

But his eye was still sharp enough to notice the sweet sway of Maddie's hips as she hurried inside. Watching her hips made him think of when he'd touched her on the train. And thinking of the train made him remember that after Henri's phone call, they'd forgotten to retrieve their luggage.

Too bad. He had condoms in his bag. Not because he'd been planning on getting lucky. The rubbers had been tucked in the side pocket ever since an unfruitful vacation to a singles resort last year.

Yeah, Mr. One-Armed Cyclops. As if you could even do anything if you had condoms.

But the lack of protection didn't stop him from thinking

about making love to Maddie. Damn if he wasn't working on a woody, in spite of his plentiful aches.

You've made enough mistakes this trip. Stop thinking about sex.

Still, it was better than thinking about the pain.

Maddie returned shortly with a nurse and an orderly. They helped him out of the car and into a wheelchair.

The orderly wheeled him into an exam room, while Maddie stayed at the reception area to answer the desk clerk's questions.

The nurse assisted him onto the gurney and asked him if he was allergic to anything. She started an IV in his good hand, and then left the room. Later, she returned with an injection.

He was grinning two minutes after the drug hit his veins. Ah, sweet freedom from pain. The nurse departed again, but left the door ajar.

"Payment?" He heard the desk clerk ask in French.

"No par-lay fran-say," Maddie replied. *"Habla español? Habla ingles?"*

Maddie and the clerk began a cobbled conversation of French, Spanish and English he couldn't really follow as he drifted in and out on a sea of morphine relief. What he did follow, was the soothing lilt of Maddie's voice. The sound of it grounded him, kept him from completely floating away.

"Pssssstt."

Huh?

"Pssssstt, David," Maddie whispered from the doorway.

Reluctantly, he pried open his eye. He thought he said, "what is it?" but it came out more like "mphmlottamut."

"You got insurance?"

He nodded.

"Can you give me the info? They were making a big

deal out of getting paid so I had to pretend to be your wife. Until I told them we were married they weren't even going to let me see you. But now they want this money situation taken care of."

"Wife?"

Now there was a pleasant thought. Maddie as his wife. He imagined coming home from work to find her cooking dinner. No, scratch that image. Maddie wasn't the domestic goddess type. Let's see. He envisioned them getting up at dawn every morning, running five miles together before coming home to make love in a sweaty heap on the floor. Ah, much better.

"Don't blow my cover, okay? I'll get freaky if they won't let me in to see you. I need to see you to know you're okay."

Aw, but that was sweet. "I'm okay."

"Just play along, please?"

"Sure. When did we get married?"

"I told them we were on our honeymoon after a whirlwind courtship."

She approached the gurney, her gaze sweeping over him. A look of concern worried her cute little face but when she caught him watching her, she forced a smile.

"Our honeymoon, huh?"

"It was the only thing I could think of to explain my ignorance of your medical history. The nurses think you're terribly romantic, proposing to me during a gondola ride in Venice with us both in Regency era dress."

"Great. You make me sound like a doofus."

"It's always been my fantasy marriage proposal from the time I was a kid, so sue me."

"I knew it." He smiled.

"Knew what?"

"You're much more romantic than you let on."

"It was a childhood fantasy. Luckily I had one, it made the lie more convincing."

"So how did I perform on the wedding night?" He tried to wink but being one-eyed, it didn't come off very debonair and his words were definitely slurred.

"David! You're drugged."

He gave her a thumbs up with his good hand.

"Terrific," she muttered. "Just what I need. A stoned FBI agent with a broken wrist."

"Wallet," he said.

"What?"

"My insurance card is in my wallet. Take my Mastercard too, just in case they won't take American insurance. I'm not sure how their health care system works. Maybe you have to pay and your insurance company reimburses you."

"Where's your wallet?"

"Right hip pocket."

She glanced around the room. "Where's your pants?"

"I'm still wearing them."

"Why haven't they taken your pants off yet?"

"I dunno." David felt as placid as a marshmallow riding around on a magic carpet. "Maybe they decided to leave the task for my young bride."

"You're a lot friendlier when you're looped. You know that?" Maddie complained. "I'm really starting to miss the old, grouchy Marshall."

"Why? He's an egotistical asshole. Stick with me, kiddo, and I'll make sure to always put you first."

"That's what I'm afraid of."

"Why are you afraid of a little TLC? You can dish it out but you can't take it?"

"Could you just lift your butt off the gurney?" She was running her hand underneath the back of his thigh.

He laughed. "That tickles."

"Raise your butt."

"You know, that's the nicest thing anyone has ever said to me."

"Poor you. Butt in the air."

He dug into the gurney with his heels and arched his back. "How's that?"

She was skimming her hands over his backside, grappling for his pocket. "Quit squirming."

"I can't."

"Are you purposely trying to make a fool of me?"

"No." David clamped his mouth shut to keep from laughing. Damn, but those were sure good drugs.

"Ahem!" From the doorway, the nurse cleared her throat. "May I help you?" she asked in French.

"My wife, she..." Simply saying the words made him chuckle. Or maybe it was because Maddie's long slender fingers were still tickling the hell out of his butt.

"This is your wife?"

"Oui." David said, cheerful.

The nurse marched over to the gurney and stuck a small plastic cup in Maddie's hand.

"What's this?" She gaped at the cup.

The nurse spit out instructions in French before breezing out the door.

"What did she say?" Maddie asked, still staring suspiciously at the cup.

"You still wanna be my pretend bride?"

"Yes, why?"

David grinned. "Because the nurse said you have to help me get naked so I can pee in that cup."

Chapter 16

Thank God, David had finally fallen asleep. If she had to hear him call her his sweetie pie or snooker doodles or make smooching noises one more time she could not be held responsible for her actions.

Who knew he was such a sentimental fool when he was loaded on painkillers?

They'd been at the hospital for over six hours and now it was just after eleven o'clock at night. After running tests, casting his wrist and giving him a dose of antibiotics, the doctor had dismissed him with a prescription of Vicodin and orders to get plenty of rest.

Plenty of rest. Ha.

She drove through the darkened streets of Monaco looking for a hotel. David snored softly in the back seat. She really didn't want to stop for the night. She wanted to keep searching for Cassie, but David was counting on her to take care of things and she wouldn't let him down.

Plus, she needed some sleep herself. And food and a bath.

The thought of a hot bath was what tipped her over the edge. Besides, Cassie and Shriver had to sleep too. She stopped at the first hotel she found.

Since she'd been masquerading as his wife all night, she went ahead and checked them in as Mr. and Mrs. Marshall because she was honestly afraid to leave David alone for the night. He was so snockered she feared he'd pitch face first into the pillow and smother himself. But she did request a room with two beds.

"David," she said, after she'd procured their room and went back to the car to roust him.

"Hmph."

"Come on, wake up. Time for bed."

"Huh?"

She repeated herself.

"You're waking me up to put me back to sleep?"

"In a bed."

"With you?" He gave her the same sly, sexy grin he'd been throwing her way ever since they'd gorked him at the hospital.

"No, not with me. I have my own bed."

"Rats." He reached up to finger a strand of her hair that had swung loose from her ponytail. "I love your hair. It's so soft and pretty."

"Come on, Lothario. Give me your good arm."

After several failed attempts, she finally got him out of the car, onto his feet and into the hotel. David leaned heavily against her and by the time they made it to their room, Maddie's entire left side tingled with radiant heat from his body.

She propped him against the wall while she opened the door and turned to find him sliding slowly to the floor.

"No, no, no, none of that. Stay on your feet." She caught him just before his legs gave way and got a shockingly good look at the depth of the bruising on his face. She cringed in sympathy.

"Hey there," he said brightly. "Where have you been all my life, beautiful?"

"Avoiding guys like you."

"How come?"

"How come what?" she said, getting her shoulder under his left arm and jacking him up.

"How come you've been avoiding me?"

"Shhh," she said.

"Why?" He glanced up and down the hall. "Is someone coming?"

If she hadn't been so tired and hungry and worried, this whole fiasco might have been comical. As it was, she couldn't wait to get him inside and into bed.

Once over the threshold, Maddie was unsettled to discover there was only one bed. The thought of having to complain and get switched to another room this late at night was so daunting, she simply blew it off. David would be passed out cold in no time flat and she could sleep on the covers in her clothes. No problem. Especially after being handcuffed to him last night.

But last night you were mad at him.

So?

Tonight you're feeling sorry for him. It's a whole other thing.

As if anything sexual was going to happen. The man was a walking—albeit barely—pharmacy.

After dumping David on the bed, she stepped over to the phone to call room service.

"We stopped serving at ten," the woman on the other end told her.

"Please," Maddie begged, lying through her teeth. "We're on our honeymoon and my husband broke his wrist and our luggage got lost and I'm just at my wits' end."

The woman murmured sympathetically. "I could send up something simple," she relented. "Soup, crackers, cheese, fruit."

"Perfect, thank you, you're a lifesaver." Maddie hung up and turned to find David eyeing her with a seductive gleam in his eyes.

"Hey babe."

"Room service is on the way. I'm going to hop into the shower."

"Can I come with you?" He was peering at her with cocky, Cary Grant charm.

"No."

"You're no fun." He pretended to pout.

"Do you think you can let room service in if they show up while I'm still in the shower?"

"Sure thing." His speech was still slurred. She wondered how long it would be before the shot wore off.

"How's your wrist?"

He stared down at the green Fiberglas cast. "Looks okay to me."

"Does it hurt?"

"Nope." He pulled open the drawer to the bedside table and leaned so far over to peer inside that Maddie feared he'd topple into it.

"What are you looking for?"

"A comb. My hair is mussed up."

"Your hair is always mussed up. I like it that way."

"Really?" He ran his good hand through his hair and grinned again.

"I love it. Now can you behave for five minutes?" God, it was like having a toddler.

"Uh-huh."

She went to the bathroom, leaned against the door and

let out a sigh before slipping off her sweater. That's when she caught a glimpse of herself in the mirror.

Egad! She looked horrible. More proof that David was out of his head if he could flirt with her when she looked like this. Her hair was lank and stringy, dark circles ringed her eyes and dots of David's blood were splattered on her cheek.

Idly, she wondered how he'd managed to drive his car off the cliff, but the time had never been right to ask. She undressed and stepped into the shower.

The hot water was pure heaven and while she yearned to luxuriate under the pulsing spray, she didn't dare leave him alone for too long. Her legs were hairy but her razor was in her bag and only God knew where that was. She'd just have to live with prickly legs.

Maddie got out of the shower, wrapped her hair in a towel, put on one of the two white terrycloth robes hanging on the bathroom door and stuffed her underwear in the sink to soak. After David fell asleep, she would wash her things out by hand and hang them over the towel rack to dry.

She returned to the bedroom to find David munching on bread and sipping champagne.

"What are you doing?" She marched across the room to snatch the glass from his hand.

"Drinking champagne and feeling no pain."

"Are you nuts? Mixing alcohol and barbiturates? You're not some sixties rock star."

"Ah, what's it gonna hurt?"

"For starters, it could put you into a coma." Maddie eyed the bottle. "How did you even get that opened?"

"Room service did it for me."

"How efficient of them."

"Wanna cracker?" David extended his plate of crackers and cheese toward her. "I'll share."

"Stop eating on the covers. You're getting crumbs all over," she said, but what she was thinking was, Honey, you can eat crackers in my bed anytime.

"You sound like my father."

"Your father? I'd have thought I sounded like your mother."

"Nope. Dad was the perfectionist. Military man. Toe the line or suffer the consequences. Do you have any idea how many push-ups I can do?"

She shot a glance at his broken wrist. "Right now?"

"Well, maybe not right this minute. But normally, I can do five hundred and seventeen."

"Why not five hundred and eighteen?"

"Dad's record was five hundred and sixteen."

"Ah. Right. Competition. I guess your Dad was impressed when you broke his record."

"He was dead by the time I broke his record."

"I'm sorry to hear that."

David shrugged and wobbled a little. "Aw, he was an s.o.b."

Something about the way he said those words tore at her heart. "Made your life difficult, did he?"

"He made me the man I am today." There was pride in his voice.

"What happened to him? If you don't mind me asking?" Henri had said David didn't like talking about himself but the pain medication had loosened his lips and Maddie was going to take full advantage.

David shrugged. "He and my mom were killed when I was twelve. They were gunned down in the streets of a Third World country. My father was a four star general in town for a peace treaty." He laughed harshly at the irony.

"That's awful." Maddie put a hand to her chest. A lump of sympathy crowded her throat and her heart ripped for the poor little boy he'd once been.

"The embassy was in chaos and I was in shock. I just walked out the back entrance and ended up wandering the streets for three days, living as best as I could before the authorities found me and sent me to New York to live with my mother's older sister."

"Your Aunt Caroline."

"Yeah." He looked surprised. "How did you know?"

"Henri blabbed."

David rolled his eyes. "That crazy Frenchman. He thinks if he tells you something personal about me you'll fall in love with me."

"Really?"

He waved a dismissive hand. "You know how the French are about romance. From the minute we stepped off the plane together he's been convinced you're my lover."

Maddie felt breathless. "Whatever gave him that idea?"

"He says it's the way I look at you."

Flustered, Maddie changed the subject. "Did they ever catch the people who murdered your parents?"

"Nope."

Well, that explained a lot about him. She understood now why he was so dogged, so determined. Why he had such a strong need to see justice done, to win at all costs.

She didn't know what to say. Any words she could dredge up sounded silly or misguided or patronizing. Instead, she ended up telling him how her mother had gone a bit crazy after their dad left. How she drank too much, forgot to pay the bills or buy groceries. How she hopped from one inappropriate guy to another, dragging her and Cassie along with her.

"I mean here I was fifteen and waiting up until three o'clock in the morning for my mom to come home from the nightclubs when it should have been the other way around. I never really got to be a kid, you know."

"Wow," David said. "That's pretty heavy duty."

"Not nearly as heavy duty as your story. And mine does have a happy ending. My mother met her current husband, Stanley, and he snapped her out of the funk she was in. Stanley's a rock solid guy. She's tried pretty hard to make up for those years she fumbled. I don't hold anything against her. She did the best she could."

"I appreciate you sharing that with me." He traced a finger over her cheek. "It took a lot of courage for you to open up."

She cleared her throat, eager to retreat from the intimacy of their shared confidences. "Do you need some help with the soup?"

"Normally I would say no. I'm an independent bastard." David raised his casted wrist. "But, considering that I have no depth perception with one eye swollen shut, I'm right handed and so hungry I could eat a mastodon raw, I'll take you up on the offer."

She sat beside him on the edge of the bed and her heart beat crazily.

He leaned over to sniff her neck. "You smell soapy clean."

"Thank you," she said primly, desperate to ignore the thrill of pleasure his warm breath generated as it raised the hairs on her nape.

"And you look really cute with your hair all twisted up in a towel. How do women do that?"

"Ancient feminine secret. If I told you I'd have to kill you." She dished up a bite of chicken soup and held her palm under the spoon so she wouldn't spill any on him. "Open up."

"I feel like a fool."

"Don't let that stop you. Come on."

Reluctantly, he opened his mouth and she touched the spoon to his lips.

Her gaze met his one good eye.

Feeding an invalid should not have been provocative or seductive or erotic.

But heaven help her, it was.

When he flicked out his tongue to accept the soup something hot and melty ran through her.

"Hmm," he moaned. "I didn't know soup could taste so good."

Hell, she never knew that the noise of a man appreciating his soup could sound so sexy. Even the slightest touch, the briefest glance, the smallest sound took on heightened significance.

A drop of wet liquid glistened on his lip and she had the most irresistible urge to kiss it off.

Help me! Help me! Help me! she prayed. She was rapidly losing control.

Maddie gulped and with a trembling hand, went back for the next spoonful. What was happening to her?

"Too bad I'm so busted up," he said.

"What?" she sounded panicky even to her own ears. Why did she have this overwhelming desire to get naked and rub herself all over him?

"If I weren't banged up, you wouldn't have to feed me. I notice you're having a little trouble."

"If you weren't banged up, I wouldn't be snuggled up next to you in bed."

"I was simply making an observation. Our little dinner *tête-à-tête* seemed to be turning you on."

"I am not turned on."

"Your nipples are poking through your robe."

Dammit! They were.

"Stop looking at my nipples."

"I didn't mean to make you mad."

"You didn't."

"You seem mad."

"I'm not." *Mad with desire for you is what I am and it has nothing to do with your sexual healing and everything to do with mine.* "Here's another bite." Hastily, she shoved the spoon toward his mouth.

"Whoa, slow down. Let's take this nice and easy."

The way he said *nice and easy* was clearly a come-on. He lowered his voice on those two words. Maddie refused to look at him. Refused to acknowledge the power of her own needs just aching to be sated.

This was too weird. Rattled, Maddie forgot to hold her palm under the spoon and ended up dumping soup on him.

"Oh damn." She snatched up the napkin from the tray and dabbed at his shirt. "I'm so clumsy."

"You're not clumsy. It's hard feeding someone else."

Especially when that someone else was rife with sexual innuendo.

"Here," she reached for the spoon once more. "Let's try again."

"I think we better just stick with the crackers and cheese and apple slices," he said huskily.

"Good idea."

They ate in silence, nibbling their snack, neither of them looking at the other. When they were finished, Maddie put the tray in the hallway. She turned back to find David standing beside the bed.

"I'm afraid I'm going to have to ask you to help me get undressed," he said.

"Sure. No problem."

Liar.

She reached up and began unbuttoning his shirt. Might as well start with the least threatening item.

"Hey," he said. "I just now noticed. There's only one bed in here."

"I know. I asked for two beds, but this is what we got."

"Is this going to be a problem? Sleeping in the same bed with me?"

"I slept with you last night."

"Yeah, but I was drunk."

"And tonight you're drugged."

"So we're cool?"

"It's not a problem for me if it's not a problem for you. Just as long as you don't try any funny business."

He inclined his hand toward his busted wrist. "I'm not exactly a threat."

"That's why it's not a problem." Maddie finished unbuttoning his shirt, revealing the broad expanse of his thick, muscular chest.

Talk about a six-pack! A dorm full of sorority girls could get falling down drunk off this guy's belly.

Swallowing hard against her rising desire to rake her fingers along the dense, compact ridges, Maddie reached instead for his belt buckle.

And she accidentally brushed her knuckles against his fly.

Immediately, he hardened.

Wow. Compliment accepted.

"I'm sorry, Maddie," David apologized and darned if, beneath all his black and blue marks, he wasn't blushing.

"It's all right," she lied. This was the last straw. She'd been barely holding it together from the moment she'd almost run over him on the highway.

"I don't mean any disrespect. Forgive me for the boner. It's just that you're so darned sexy and I've been dreaming of making love to you for days and you smell so good and I feel so damned rotten and..."

"Shhh." She laid a finger over his lips.

"No seriously, I'm really sorry. I'm embarrassed and ashamed over my lack of control. I have no excuse for my behavior. Absolutely none."

"Will you just shut up?" Maddie said and kissed him.

Chapter 17

As an athlete, Maddie listened to her body and right now, it was telling her to go with the flow. Her skin sizzled with heightened warmth, her muscles quivered fluidly, her breathing, though controlled, lifted her to a whole new level of experience.

David tasted like champagne and chicken noodle soup and Camembert cheese and sesame seed crackers. He ran his wicked tongue along her lips and down her chin. She tossed her head, exposing her neck and waiting for his heated kisses to find her pounding pulse point.

With unerring accuracy, he homed in on that erogenous region and nibbled like a Pharaoh at his wedding feast. He cupped the back of her head in his left palm, holding her still while he devoured her scorching flesh.

"Are you giving me a hickey?" she asked.

"Do you want one?"

"No. Yes. Oh, just keep doing what you're doing. It's making my toes curl."

"Good answer." He wrapped his good arm around her waist and drew her closer.

She knew he was still flying high on the drugs they'd

given him at the hospital. Knew she was skimming along on adrenaline and no sleep and the very real fear that David could have lost his life tonight. It seemed a sacrilege not to celebrate his survival. And while Maddie knew better than to trust this sweet freefall into the abyss of pleasure, she followed it anyway.

Where in the hell is your infamous common sense? Where's your caution?

Out the door, out the window, out of this world. Who knew? Who cared? Not she. Not at this moment. She had plenty of time for remorse and recrimination tomorrow. For once, she was going to do something impulsive, totally out of character and completely irresponsible.

He loosed the belt on her robe and it fell open. When the cool air hit her heated skin, she sucked in her breath. Glorious!

But not half as glorious as what David was doing to the hollow of her throat.

Flick, flick, flick, went his tongue.

Sizzle, sizzle, sizzle went her groin.

Had she ever felt so desperate, so achy, so out of control?

While her intense feelings scared her, they also liberated her. Here she was, in Monaco with a man she barely knew, taking a walk on the wild side.

Cassie would be proud.

Her mother would be proud.

Okay, she was even proud of herself. Never in a million years would she have guessed herself capable of such complete abandon. She nestled against David, absorbing his body heat, enjoying the pure physical sensation. They were alive. That's all that mattered.

He lowered his head and lightly kissed a trail down her cleavage. Maddie drew in a long, shuddery breath. Oh yes.

Dipping his head lower still, he took one beaded nipple in his mouth and she almost screamed, it felt that exquisite.

Her practical side was getting scared. She could almost hear her knees knocking.

Before she had time to reconsider her rash rush to intimacy, David was kissing her again with an urgency that French-fried her wary voice and short-circuited the last wire of her resistance.

They fell onto the bed together, careful of his broken wrist, but not much else. David pawed at her robe, roughly thrusting the lapel out of the way. Maddie grappled with his belt, tugging the smooth flat leather free from the loops and tossing it across the room.

He pushed her into the mattress, kissing her all over. Her lips, her eyes, her cheeks, her chin. He swept her away on wave after wave of erotic emotions.

Joy and fear. Lust and tenderness. Excitement and trepidation.

They were breathing hard, breathing in tandem, inhaling the same air, inhaling each other.

She fumbled with the hook and eye on his trousers. He ran his fingers across the fine blond hairs on her chest.

He groaned.

She moaned.

She slipped her hand past the waistband of his pants and into his underwear. She sucked in her breath, daunted by the heat of him, hovering on the verge of generous discovery.

At the same time she was investigating him, he was investigating her.

"You've got the flattest, tautest tummy I've ever seen," he marveled, strumming his hand over her abdomen.

"Two hundred sit-ups a day on an incline board," she bragged shamelessly, thrilled that he loved her body. Some men thought she was too muscular, but apparently not David.

He slid his fingers slowly between her thighs and Maddie thought, *I can't believe I'm here, doing this. Letting myself go without overanalyzing things.*

While his fingers explored below, he let his tongue do the walking above her waist, licking her like a lollipop.

Her nipples bloomed under his attention and her breasts grew heavy with need. If he was this good when he was chock full of painkillers, she shuddered to imagine what he was like when he was up to full speed.

He's vulnerable. You're taking advantage of him.

That thought brought her up short and she stopped rummaging in his underpants.

"What is it?" he gasped, raising his head to gaze into her face. At the sight of his swollen eye guilt kicked her in the gut. "What's wrong?"

"You're wounded and I'm acting like a sex fiend. I should be taking care of you, babying you."

"Hush." He laid an index finger over her lips. "I need sexual healing."

"But—"

"Not a word."

"You don't really want sex," she mouthed around his finger.

"Be quiet."

"What you really want is some good old fashioned TLC and I started..."

He clamped his hand over her mouth. "What part of stop talking don't you understand?"

"Daydid," was how his name sounded from behind his salty palm.

"What I really want is to make love to you, Maddie, so don't ruin it by over-thinking things, okay?"

"Okay."

"Now, where were we?" He lowered his head again.

Maddie tapped him on the shoulder. "We can't do this."

"Why not?"

"I don't have a condom. Do you have a condom?"

"In my bag."

"And where's that?"

"Probably on the supersonic train shuttling back and forth from Paris to Madrid."

"My point exactly."

"I'll go get a condom. Just hold that pose."

"You can barely walk and it's after midnight."

He sighed and rolled over onto his back. "So that's it?"

"This was a bad idea from the beginning."

"It was a fine idea."

"No it wasn't. I should never have kissed you. Why did I kiss you?"

David groaned and this time not with pleasure. "Do you have to analyze everything to death? We were both horny. Things got hot and heavy. Common sense prevailed. End of story. Now let's go to sleep."

"You're right. I should just let this go. We'll forget all about it. Yes. It's forgotten."

Apparently so. David was already snoring.

Great. He was cattywampus in the bed, crowding her out. Fine, she'd just go blow dry her hair and wash out her lingerie. Let him sleep. He needed the rest.

In the meantime, however, what was she supposed to do with the throbbing ache he'd created between her legs?

*   *   *

He couldn't forget all about it.

David listened to Maddie puttering around in the bathroom while he pretended to be asleep. The drugs were wearing off and his numerous pains were returning to needle him.

She was humming softly under her breath and he caught himself straining to recognize the tune and finally identified it as a song by Faith Hill about the rapture of a mind-blowing kiss.

He smiled at the ceiling. He had gotten to her whether she would admit it or not.

Trouble was, she'd gotten to him too.

In a way nobody had in a very long time. Maybe even never. He thought about Keeley, about how he'd felt when he was around her and he had to confess his feelings then were nowhere near as intense as these strange and inexplicable emotions he was having for Maddie now.

The delicious smell of her remained in his nostrils, a tantalizing ghost scent. The honeyed flavor of her lips lingered on his tongue, rich, full, promising. He shook his head, remembering how quickly he'd grown hard when she'd barely touched him.

He couldn't keep lying to himself. He wanted Maddie more desperately than he had ever wanted any woman. Keeley included. He found her, quite simply, irresistible.

Some men might think she was too muscular or that her chin was a little too pointed. But he appreciated the contrast of that determined chin in juxtaposition to her soft, bow-shaped mouth. He admired the richness of shadow in her cheekbones, the clarity of light in her emerald eyes. He loved studying the geometry of her form. Her lines and curves, the angles and circles that made up her womanly body.

But his feelings for her went far beyond her physical attractiveness.

He respected how she was warm, supportive and compassionate with those she loved. He admired her work ethic and her steady reliability. She enchanted him utterly and he had never expected to be so smitten, but here it was.

He loved her loyalty, her no-bullshit outlook on life and how she fought the good fight. He enjoyed being around her. She sparked his interest with her clever sense of humor and her pragmatic approach to problem solving.

He even found her worrywart tendencies endearing. It showed she truly cared. And while he sometimes found her cautiousness a challenge, she challenged him in a good way. After what she'd told him about her family, he understood why she had trouble trusting other people to be there for her the way she was there for them.

Which was kind of weird when you thought about it, because he'd never been big on offering his trust indiscriminately. But if he ever got Maddie to put aside her doubts and trust him completely—what a precious gift that would be.

Did he dare hope for such rewards? Was he expecting too much?

He also knew it was no coincidence she'd been the one to find him after he'd been beaten up by Blanco. Even though David wasn't a big proponent of destiny, he believed something had placed her on that road at just the right time. She had an instinct for being there whenever you needed her. He probably owed her his life.

And to think he'd ditched her at the Prado.

He felt guilty and misguided and ashamed of himself for not having more faith in her. He should have told her about his suspicions that Blanco had kidnapped Cassie away from Shriver. He should have told her what Isabella had told him about Cassie's plan. He should tell her now.

She would want to know.

Yes. Maddie was a tell-it-like-it-is kind of woman. She didn't play games and she liked being informed about what was going on around her. She didn't stick her head in the sand and ignore reality.

And man, how he wanted her.

David swung his legs off the bed, grabbed his discarded shirt and headed for the door. He was going after condoms and he wasn't coming back until he found them.

He returned twenty minutes later with a box of square foil packets in one hand and a grin on his achy face. He dry swallowed a pain pill to help him see this seduction through. He was going to make love to her tonight, broken wrist, blackened eye and all.

"Where have you been?" Maddie demanded, hands on her hips, worry pulling her brows into a frown. "When I came out of the bathroom and found you gone, I almost had a heart attack."

He held up the box of condoms.

"You didn't?" Her frown dissolved into a shy Mona Lisa smile.

"I did."

"David...I..."

"Getting cold feet?" He stalked across the room and wrapped his good arm around her waist.

"I've just been thinking..."

"Stop thinking, babe, and just feel," he murmured.

The thing was, he'd been thinking too. He had the notion they were standing on the verge of something truly monumental but he had no idea how to articulate his feelings, so he would just show her.

With fingers full of hungry, aching need, he peeled off her robe until Maddie stood completely naked before him.

He forgot to inhale. God, but she was gorgeous. He'd never seen anything sexier. He gazed into her eyes and his chest knotted. This was his Maddie, looking at him as if he'd created the sun and the moon and the stars.

Her nipples beaded taut and her disheveled hair curled provocatively about her slender shoulders. She was completely exposed to him, vulnerable, all her protection gone, but she did not shy away. She did not shrink back.

She was so brave to trust him.

David drank her in. Every dazzling inch of her. From the hollow of her throat, to her rounded breasts, to the flat smoothness of her belly to the sweet blond V at the juncture of her thighs.

Her cheeks flushed rosy at his perusal. Her eyes sparkled, reflecting his expanding excitement. She wet her lips and never took her gaze from his face.

He clenched his fists to keep himself from grabbing her and taking her right there on the floor. He wanted their first time to be nice and slow and easy. He wanted it to last. He wanted to please her beyond her wildest expectations.

His cock throbbed and his throat tightened as she reached out to unbutton his shirt for the second time that night. Her touch was soft, yet stimulating. It was incredible.

He was without a doubt the luckiest bastard on the face of the earth. To have this warm, strong, supple woman caressing him as if he were pure gold, when she was the find, the treasure, the glistening diamond. He was just an old chunk of coal.

Doubts suddenly flooded his mind. What did he have to offer a woman like her? The FBI was his life. He craved excitement, the thrill of the chase. It was the reason Keeley had left him. Secretly, he feared the quiet stability of a loving relationship. Feared it because he just knew he'd eventually screw it up. He had no idea how to be the kind of solid, rock-steady man someone like Maddie needed.

She leaned into him and softly brushed her lips against his. "Stop thinking," she whispered. "You're thinking too much. Enjoy the moment."

Here she was, turning the tables on him. Just when he thought he had her figured out she did the unexpected.

He kissed her, putting all his long-dormant emotions into it.

Several minutes later, she pulled back to take a breath.

"Wow," she said. "Wow."

"You ain't seen nothing yet," he teased.

Eagerly, she peeled the shirt off his shoulders, over his cast and then let it drop to the floor. Her fingers went to his zipper and he hissed in his breath. He wrapped his hand around hers.

"Let me."

David shucked his pants in record time, almost tripping as he kicked them into the corner. Maddie turned, displaying the creamy curve of her delectable fanny and walked toward the bed.

He followed.

Chapter 18

The pressure building inside Maddie's body was low, deep, and hot. It was a heavy liquid flame, denser than mercury, more flammable than gasoline.

She wanted him inside her, filling her up, easing this intense, throbbing ache. She wanted to fly into a million pieces and lay breathless forever. Her need was as desperate as a wild animal, thrashing to get free from its cage.

"I need you," she said. "I don't want to wait anymore."

"Oh babe," he groaned.

He pulled back the covers and eased her down onto the cool sheets. He hugged her close and she could hear the steady thumping of his heart.

"Close your eyes."

She did and he kissed her eyelids. First one, then the other and back again. No one had ever kissed her eyelids before and it felt amazingly erotic.

He ran his good hand through her hair and that was an erotic sensation too. He kneaded her scalp. Back and forth, soft and slow.

Then he planted kisses down the length of her nose until he got to her lips. He paused.

"Don't stop, you wicked man." She opened her eyes and found him staring at her.

"You ready for this?"

"I've been ready since the moment I first saw your naked chest in that motel room in Grand Cayman."

"No kidding?"

"Don't get egotistical on me now."

"I thought you didn't like me."

"I didn't like the feelings you stirred in me."

"You were turned-on that day?"

"You couldn't tell?"

"No."

She nudged him in the ribs. "I'm turned-on now. Or at least I was. Get to it, man."

"Yes, ma'am," he said and claimed her mouth.

He tasted wonderful.

Maddie moaned as his wicked tongue flicked across her palate, the sound of her pleasure humming against his mouth. She felt weak and dizzy, strong and steady all at the same time. A carousel of sensation, spinning her around and around.

He tightened his grip, his masculine hands reassuring her that she wasn't making a mistake. His excited touch sent a thousand minuscule infernos fanning out down her abdomen, scorching her, rousing her higher and higher until her body was nothing more than a trembling, molten core.

His mouth left hers, and he tracked his sinful tongue over her eager flesh, forging a channel of ripe heat to her throat where he sketched erotic triangles along the length of her collarbone.

He seemed to know her body more intimately than she knew it herself. With unerring accuracy, he found her every erogenous zone and used his discoveries to full advantage. Massaging the underside of her jaw, stroking the smooth area between her elbow and her armpit, nibbling the back of her knees, blowing lightly on the spot just below her navel after he'd licked it.

When he blew warm air gently into her ear, she giggled at the tickly sensation and felt younger than she had in years. She felt lighthearted. He made her want to play.

He used his tongue to maximize her pleasure, dispatching shuddering waves of chilly thrills throughout her body and when he stroked her inner ear with his tongue, she literally quaked.

His touch was magic, making her forget everything but this moment. She breathed him in, inhaling his masculinity, savoring the uniqueness of their joining.

Ah, the power of his fingertips. The mystery of his tongue.

He stretched his body over hers, lying atop her but propping his weight on his elbows. She worried about his broken wrist but it didn't seem to bother him. His erection throbbed hot and hard against her belly. He stroked her cheek with a hand and gazed into her eyes.

She hiccupped against the intensity of emotion written on his face. She telegraphed her own feelings to him, staring deeply into his soul.

You're special.

She knew him. The way she'd never known another. Not even the connection she had with her twin could rival this bond, this link, this nexus of meaning so intense there was no need to speak. In fact, words would have lessened the impact of what they were both feeling.

He dipped his head, breaking the visual bridge between them, but where his gaze left off, his lips took over. Gently, he sucked one of her pebble hard nipples into his red hot mouth.

Maddie hissed in her breath. Chills peppered her body like buckshot, searing the root of every single nerve ending she possessed.

Her breasts swelled and ached against his mouth and she whimpered. "Please, please."

"Please what?"

She was swept away by this mounting hurts-so-good pressure, she couldn't even speak.

"Do you want me to stop?" He pulled back leaving her damp nipple bereft.

"No, no, don't stop."

"You want more?"

She nodded.

"More of this?" He lightly flicked her nipple. "Or would you rather have some of this?" He made his penis bounce against her belly.

"I'm greedy," she admitted. "I want it all."

"And you deserve it all," he said.

He shifted, positioning himself with one hip pressed into the mattress.

And then he began to explore, trailing his fingers from her breastbone downward on a treasure hunt that soon had her quivering from her feet to her head.

"Wait," she said, fighting off the deliciousness of it all. "I have to tell you something."

"This isn't the part where you tell me you used to be a man?" he teased. "Because babe, I don't believe it for a minute."

"Don't be silly, I'm serious."

He propped himself on an elbow. "All right, Serious. I'm listening. So what's the big secret?"

"It's not that it's a secret, it's just something you don't tell a guy until things advance to a certain point."

"I take it we've reached that point."

"Passed it actually."

"I'm listening. You can tell me anything," he assured her. "I don't want any secrets between us."

"You really mean that?"

"Absolutely." He nodded, grinning impishly. "If you really did used to be a guy I'll just learn how to deal with it."

"David, stop teasing."

He forced away his frown and cleared his throat. "Do I look serious enough?"

"Oh you." She shook her head.

"Okay, I'll settle down." He took her hand and gazed into her eyes again. "What do you have to tell me?"

"I've never...um...I'm not sure how to say this."

He blinked at her. "Maddie, are you trying to tell me you're a virgin?"

"No, I'm sorry, I'm not a virgin. Are you terribly disappointed?"

"Don't be ridiculous. You're twenty-seven years old and damned attractive. I'm glad you haven't been waiting just for me to show up. The pressure would be intimidating."

"Oh."

"That didn't come out right." He pressed a palm to his forehead. "What I mean to say is, I'm certainly not a virgin. How could I expect you to be one?"

"Whew," she giggled. "That's a relief. And here I was worrying I'd have to teach you all about making love."

"I'm not saying I don't have a lot to learn. I want to memorize every inch of your body. Just tell me what feels good to you, babe."

"You've been doing a great job so far."

"We've gotten sidetracked. Let's go back to whatever it is you wanted to tell me." He rubbed his thumb against her palm.

"Well, it's along those lines. Of knowing my body I mean."

"Yes."

"I'm ... I've never ..."

He arched an eyebrow. "Had an orgasm?"

"Not with a partner."

"All right."

"I'm just telling you so you won't be disappointed or upset if I can't come with you inside me."

David touched her cheek. *Maybe you've just been with the wrong partner,* he thought but what he said was, "That's okay. Thanks for telling me."

"I'm so glad you understand."

"I'll tell you what," he said, rolling over onto his back. Now that she'd told him she'd never had an orgasm with a partner, he was more determined than ever to make sure she did. "From here on out you're in control."

"Really?"

He thrust his hands over his head. "I'm tied up. Can't move unless you tell me I can. I'm yours for the taking, do with me what you will."

And please don't make me come before you do.

She straddled his waist and leaned over him, her breasts rubbing provocatively against his chest. She kissed him with a passion that filched his breath and left him at her mercy.

Her tongue plunged deeply into his mouth. She saucily bit his lower lip. With a feral, pressing need, her hands clasped his body. His breath was coarse and jagged in his throat as he clutched her hips to his.

"No hands," she admonished and reluctantly, he raised his arms over his head again.

She sat up and he gloried in the sight of her above him, in the diffuse light from the bathroom, coupled with the moonlight shining through the bedroom window.

Damn! She was a goddess.

Her knees were flush against his flanks, her bottom pressed against the top of his penis. She was so close. His body cried for her to take him inside her warm moistness, but at the same time he wanted to wait.

"Show me," he said. "How you like it. How you pleasure yourself."

Maddie hesitated a moment, then she reached for his left hand. Totally mesmerized by her sensual movements, he gave her his hand and waited, trancelike for her to make good use of it.

She moved his hand downward, and placed his fingers against her velvet opening.

Oh yeah. Gently, he began to stroke her with his index finger.

"That's right," she cooed.

While his first finger stayed busy carefully strumming her straining hood, he slipped his second finger past her warm, milky lips and into her moist secret cave.

Excruciating excitement flashed through him and he groaned. "You're so wet and hot."

"For you," she murmured. "All for you."

Her words brought a sense of pride to his heart and he experienced love for her so strong it pushed at the back of his eyelids.

He clenched his jaw and swallowed hard.

Without warning, she pulled away from him.

"Whaaa?" He stared at her dumbstruck and pained. She wasn't turning back now. No.

She slid down the length of his body, gliding her hands

nimbly over his skin. She undulated with catlike grace, her motions supple, her hot probing tongue licking down his belly.

"No, if you go down there, I won't last a minute."

"What's your recovery time?" She winked and he came undone. Groaning, he shoved his hand through his hair and reminded himself to breathe.

She kissed his body with promises of unimaginable ecstasy. She rolled her tongue over his navel, teasing and cajoling.

Her breasts dangled provocatively above his penis. His gaze fixed on her jiggling, rosy-pink nipples. His penis stiffened, straining as if trying to reach up and touch those gorgeous nubs. Reaching down, she lightly tangled her fingertips in his hair.

"Please, I want to be inside you."

"All in good time."

"You're loving this. Torturing me."

"Uh-huh." She winked.

"Tease."

When she cupped his balls, he hissed in a scalded breath and when her hand traveled up to stroke his shaft he had to close his eyes and fight to keep from coming in her palm.

"You're so big and thick," she said, with awe in her voice. She made him feel like a million bucks.

Then she blew a stream of hot breath on the throbbing head. Involuntarily, he lifted his hips off the mattress, straining for her.

"Enough," he said.

He couldn't take the teasing one more minute. Grabbing her around the waist, he rolled her over, tumbling them both to the edge of the mattress. He dropped his feet to the floor, pulled her hips close to him.

"Wrap your legs around my waist," he growled.

She obeyed.

He liked this position. It was his turn to tease.

He caressed her tender, feminine flesh, inhaled her musky womanly scent and breathed in pure pride. She was with him!

She quivered and pulsed against his hand and he knew he could make her come with his fingers, but he wanted to see if he could take it higher. If he could be the one to give her an orgasm during intercourse.

Then he dropped to his knees and kissed her sweet inner lips, drinking up her warm, womanly flavor. No one on earth tasted like her and the essence that was Maddie branded into his brain. He would never forget this moment, this taste, this woman.

On and on they played the game, on and on. Touching and stroking, licking and nibbling, bringing each other to the brink of orgasm many times but never tumbling over the precipice, until they were breathless with need, their eyes shiny with feverish desperation.

"I can't..." Maddie whispered.

"I know," he answered.

"Condom, please, now, hurry."

"Okay." He tore into the box of condoms, grasped a corner of one foil packet in his teeth and ripped it open. He rolled the condom on with the speed of an Olympic athlete going for the gold.

"Take me," she said, the minute he positioned himself beside her on the bed.

He could no longer resist. David knelt between her thighs and spread them wide.

The core of her womanhood welcomed his throbbing tip with a tightening twinge. He eased in gently, not wanting to cause her any discomfort.

She arched her hips upward, wrapped her arms around his shoulders and pulled him down, forcing him in deeper, spearing herself with his body.

"Ooh." She sighed, her warm breath feathering his hair. "Aah."

His heart pounded in a wild, frenzied rhythm. Go slow, he told himself, but he could not. She felt too good, this felt too right.

She writhed against his movements, eyes closed, head thrown back, hair spilling over the pillow like golden sunshine.

You are my sunshine, he thought recklessly.

He reveled in her soft coos of pleasure. He could feel her body responding to every precise, sensual stroke he delivered. In the quivering of her buttocks, he felt her bliss. She was close, so very close. He grinned.

While he stroked her with his body, he also stroked her with his hand, tenderly tweaking her trigger spot. The small, hooded button surged against his attention, begging for more.

His lungs shredded with the effort of breathing past the intensity of his desire for her.

"I'm on fire," she moaned. "I'm on fire."

"I know, sweetheart, I know."

"David, David," she cried his name and he'd never heard a more precious sound cross a woman's lips. She clutched his shoulders with both hands and rocked her pelvis like a mad woman. "I'm close, I'm close."

Ah, he thought, for the *coup de grâce.*

He angled his head and took one burgeoning nipple into his mouth, never stopping his slow, steady stroking. His left hand stayed busy, gently caressing her hood. He suckled her. Cautiously at first and then picking up the tempo.

She writhed and thrashed, bucked and moaned. He never let up even though he was getting a cramp in his calf. To hell with his discomfort, this was about giving Maddie the pleasure she so justly deserved.

She raked her fingernails over his back, she tugged at his hair. He closed his eyes to fight off his own release, knowing that if he could just hold out for a few more minutes, he could take her with him.

He raised his head and peered into her face. Her eyes were closed, her face twisted into a mask of sexual anticipation. Her breathing was incredibly shallow, her face flushed.

"Look at me," he said. "Open your eyes and look at me."

Her eyes flew open and they tumbled into each other. The world fell away. Monaco did not exist. The hotel room did not exist. The bed did not exist.

It was as if they were floating in a separate universe. They were the only two people occupying this deep, vast space. Just he and Maddie and their beating hearts.

Lub-dub, lub-dub. Beating as one cosmic force.

She started to close her eyes.

"No, no, keep looking at me."

She stared into him.

He stared into her.

And then they were one being. One force. There was no separation.

They cried out in unison when their simultaneous climax hit. Their gaze never separated as they were mirrored back to each other.

He was she. She was he. Yin and Yang in perfect harmony. Two halves of the whole. One.

Wave after wave of sensation washed over them,

sending them hurtling together on the shores of sexual release. But with the deceleration of tension, came a quiet, soft, incredible peace.

This was right. This was perfect.

"David," she whispered his name on a reverential breath. "Thank you, David."

He smiled tenderly at her, his heart so full he could not speak. He did not move. He never wanted this moment to end.

Maddie. Maddie. Maddie. Had any name ever sounded so sweet?

She smiled back, reached up and lightly traced her fingers along his lips. "I love being joined to you like this."

He nodded, the emotions so thick in his throat he feared he might actually cry if he started talking. He had never known such connection with another human being was possible. Had never dreamed he'd find such a woman. He'd always viewed love as a dark mystery that struck others but had somehow left him unscathed. That was probably why he hadn't been heartbroken over his breakup with Keeley. The love had never really been there.

But now he knew the truth. Love was mysterious, oh yes. But he was not immune. He'd once thought he was too idealistic to fall for the earthy, helpless trap of love, but he'd been wrong.

He'd been wrong about so many things.

What he thought was a heedless swirl of foolishness was instead the pinnacle of life itself. He wasn't a poetic man, although he'd always admired beauty in art. But this feeling made him want to spout Wordsworth and Browning and Teasdale until he had no breath left.

His heart sang like a bird.

His heart bloomed like a cherry tree in spring.

His heart refracted like a rainbow, full, vibrant and unashamed.

He, David Marshall—the man who'd immersed himself in his work, the man who played to win at all costs, the man who was never quite sure where he belonged— was in love.

Maddie lay in the dark listening to David's soft snores, her body still quivering from the effects of their stupendous lovemaking.

She wanted to cry with joy but she was too overwhelmed for tears. She'd never had an orgasm with a partner. She figured she never would.

But David...ah David. She hugged her pillow to her chest and grinned in the darkness. Thank you, David, thank you.

Her body was sated and her heart was full. She felt peaceful, relaxed and wonderfully reckless. Maybe that's what it took for her to have an orgasm. To simply relax and let go of her fears. To turn loose and fall headlong into passion.

Careful. That old naysaying voice was back, ruffling the waters of her newfound serenity. *Don't jump to conclusions. Don't assume you have a relationship just because he pushed all the right buttons.*

So what should she assume? That they'd had one great night of unbridled passion and that was it?

Protect yourself. Hold back. This was just fabulous sex. You can't forget that David is ultimately your enemy. No matter how much you like him, he's out to jail your sister.

Right.

The last thing she needed was to go soft in the head over a man who was married to his job.

She had her sister to think about and the vow she'd taken on that cold December night oh so long ago. Cassie came first. Always.

So here was her plan. She'd play it cool. Act like nothing monumental had happened. If their joining had meant more to David than mere sex, then he was going to have to be the one to make the first move. He was going to have to open up and talk to her. She'd bravely taken the physical risk, opening her body to him. Only time would tell if he was brave enough to let down his steely guard and take an emotional gamble on her.

Until then, Maddie was making darned sure she kept her own heart well out of the fray.

Chapter 19

So where do we go from here?" Maddie asked David over an omelet the following morning.

She'd been unusually quiet, waking him not long after dawn with a gentle nudge and a nod at the bedside clock.

They'd avoided talking or even looking at each other as they got dressed and left the room. For his part, David was pretty fuzzy on the details of the night before. He remembered making love to her. Remembered her orgasm quaking around him. Who could forget that?

But he didn't remember what he'd said. Or what she'd said. Or if there had been any expectations for the future on her part. Hell, he didn't even remember how he felt about all this. Everything beyond their explosive physical connection was pretty much a blur.

How did she feel about what had happened? Should he ask?

But fear of learning more than he could handle held him back. He elected to go with the closed mouth policy Maddie seemed to have adopted. If she wanted the sex to be casual, he was cool with that. The fewer complications, the better.

Right?

Don't ask. Don't tell. Best policy.

She'd put up the wall, he wasn't inclined to scale it. Not now anyway. Not until the investigation was over and he knew where they stood.

"Pardon?" He pretended to be highly interested in his croissant, buttering it with elaborate intent.

"There are no more clues from Cassie," Maddie said. "We've run into a dead end. You're the detective. Where do we go from here? Do you suppose she and Shriver are still in Monaco? Why do you think they came here? Is there a famous art collector or something that lives nearby?"

"Maddie . . . I," he started.

"Yes?" She leaned forward, her gaze fixed on his face and she clucked her tongue. "Your eye looks awful."

"Don't worry about me. I'll live."

"We never discussed your accident last night. What happened? Did your car fishtail in the rain?"

David cleared his throat. "I didn't have a car accident."

"No?" She looked confused.

"I came upon an accident and went down the hill to see if I could help. I pulled the driver from behind the wheel. He turned out to be Jocko Blanco. He took me unaware, beat me up, stole my car and my gun."

"Oh, David." Concern swam in her eyes and she raised a hand to her throat. "Jocko Blanco is here? In Monaco?"

"I'm afraid it's worse than that."

"Worse?" Her bottom lip trembled. He tried to keep his face impassive, neutral but somehow she picked up on his body language. She already knew something was wrong.

Steeling his courage, he told her what he should have told her back at the Prado.

"No." Her face paled.

"I'm afraid so."

"So I was right. Cassie didn't willingly rob the Prado."

"She did not."

"You think Blanco kidnapped her away from Shriver and used her as a pawn to gain access to the museum?"

He nodded.

"So where is Cassie?" she whispered hoarsely.

"I don't know."

"Where do we go for answers?" She gazed at him intently, her bottom lip caught between her teeth.

She was depending on him to find her sister and he would not let her down. David had the oddest sense that helping her was the most important thing he'd ever done and at that moment he knew he had to make a choice. Stay on Shriver's trail or go look for Cassie.

Four days ago, he would have snorted in derision if anyone had told him that anything could get in the way of his single-minded focus on collaring the art thief. For ten years, ever since Shriver had cruelly robbed his beloved Aunt Caroline of both her dignity and the Rembrandt, he'd lusted to see the man behind bars.

He'd even changed his major to law enforcement and joined the FBI just so he could hunt Shriver down and make him pay. He'd lain awake at night, imagining just how satisfying it would feel to clamp handcuffs on the thief who'd glibly used dozens of women to make his ill-gotten fortune. He'd dreamed of recovering the Rembrandt and returning it to his aunt. He'd spent a decade envisioning the happy smile on her face when he broke the good news. He wanted so badly to repay her for everything she'd done for him.

He had yearned for justice, yes, but he'd also longed for revenge. No one treated his loved ones badly and got away with it. He'd been determined to win at all costs.

But that was four days ago. A lot had happened. Exactly when had his priorities shifted from bringing in Shriver to saving Maddie's sister?

When he'd realized Blanco was the masked man at the Prado.

Even now, a cold chill passed over him. Cassie's life hung in the balance and a life, anyone's life, would always be more important than stolen art.

But, maybe, if he was lucky, he could save Cassie *and* send Shriver to prison for a long, long time.

"I'll call Henri," he assured Maddie and then he made a vow he would spend his last breath trying to keep. "And I promise you, whatever it takes, I won't stop until I find your sister."

"I believe you," she whispered and he was gratified by her trust. "But will we find her alive? Or dead?"

They wandered around the streets of Monaco waiting for Henri to call David back, not knowing where else to go or what else to do. All Cassie's breadcrumb clues had dead-ended in this quaint little country. Maddie tried her best not to imagine the worst, but fighting her instincts was a losing battle.

David reached over and took her hand. "Stop visualizing disaster."

"How do you know that's what I'm doing?"

"Whenever you're thinking scary thoughts, you screw your forehead up tight."

"Do I really?" She reached up to smooth her forehead with two fingers.

"Yes, really."

Maddie inclined her head at him. In spite of the broken wrist and black eye and the cut along his jaw, he looked dashingly handsome in the early morning sunlight. Strong and reliable and there.

That was the most important part.

He was there. Holding her hand.

She remembered what he'd sworn to her in the restaurant and she held it close to her heart. *And I promise you, whatever it takes, I won't stop until I find your sister.*

She realized she was counting on him to keep his promise. Somewhere along the way, she'd started believing in him.

And that terrified her.

Be careful. Don't let him know how you really feel about him.

They stood on the sidewalk, studying each other, and Maddie was struck hard by the intensity of her feelings. *I could fall stone cold in love with him if I let myself.*

That notion scared her even more.

But you won't!

She'd never been in love, never wanted to be in love, had avoided anything that remotely looked like love.

Because she didn't trust it.

Her parents had once been wildly, madly, crazily in love and poof, a sick kid had ended it all. If you couldn't trust a wedding vow, what could you trust?

"Stop it." David rubbed her forehead with his thumb. "No more dark thoughts."

She had to admit this was pretty handy. Having someone monitor her inner negativity. He was good for her.

But was she good for him?

"No, no." he rubbed her forehead harder. "You're too young and pretty for frown lines."

The cell phone he'd just recharged in the cigarette lighter of Maddie's rental car blasted the *Dragnet* theme.

They both jumped.

David reached for the phone with his right hand but the bulky cast stopped him in mid-reach. The phone rang again.

"Hurry, hurry, before he hangs up," Maddie said.

He fumbled in his jacket pocket with his left hand and ended up dropping the phone.

"Let me do it." Maddie grabbed for it at the same time David bent down and they ended up cracking their heads together.

"Ouch!"

"Ow!"

Frowning, David answered it on the fifth ring. "Marshall here."

Nervously, Maddie gnawed a thumbnail. He listened intently, nodding occasionally but never once letting his expression give any clues about the information he was receiving.

"Okay, Henri, thanks." He rang off and shifted his gaze to Maddie.

"Well?"

"They found my rental car with Blanco's prints all over it."

"Where?"

"At the Piazzale Roma car park outside Venice."

"Any word on Cassie?" She clasped her hands. Please, please, please let her be okay.

"I'm sorry, sweetheart, no."

Venice was architectural poetry.

A floating fantasy. A dozy reverie of mist and sunshine. A winding labyrinth of walkways and waterways of complicated beauty.

All her life, Maddie had daydreamed of visiting Venice. She'd pictured herself strolling along the cobblestone streets, gliding through the canals in a graceful gondola, shopping in the Rialto district. She'd longed to watch artisans blowing exquisite glassware. She'd thirsted to drink Bellinis at an outdoor café.

And she'd blushed to think of kissing a handsome stranger under the Bridge of Sighs.

To think she was in the city of her dearest fantasies in the midst of Carnevale and she could not enjoy a minute of the experience. All she cared about was finding Cassie.

They arrived on a vaporetto sardined with tourists. By the time the waterbus arrived at their stop, Maddie was yoga breathing to ward off claustrophobia.

At least she told herself it was claustrophobia. What she really feared was that among the maddening throng, in the narrow pathways of this ancient city, she would never find her sister alive.

Venice in February was an overwhelming jumble of sights and sounds and scents. The weather was chilly but not uncomfortably cold. Maddie snuggled deeper into her denim jacket and eyed the throng of people—many dressed in colorful Carnevale garb—streaming through the streets.

Faces were hidden behind elaborate masks. Hair was secreted beneath decorative wigs. Excited shouts of pleasure and rich laughter filled the air.

A woman in a huge bustle waltzed with a man wearing a startling codpiece along the edge of a piazza. Roaming troubadours in Renaissance attire strummed mandolins or lutes. Young women wore feathers and lace and an abundance of jewelry.

Maddie stopped and stared, unable to absorb it all.

"This way," David said.

Getting a hotel at the last minute in Venice during Carnevale would have been impossible if it weren't for Interpol. Henri had pulled some influential strings, grabbing them a VIP suite at the exclusive Hotel International near the Piazza San Marco.

David took her hand and while she appreciated the comfort of his touch, she couldn't help bristling. She was still upset with him for not telling her his suspicions about Blanco back at the Prado. He claimed he hadn't told her because he'd wanted to protect her, but Maddie couldn't help wondering if he'd kept silent because he was too hardheaded to admit he'd been wrong about Cassie.

They edged their way to the middle of the bridge but once there, discovered they couldn't move any farther.

Up ahead, something had captured the crowd's attention and no one was budging. From above, the noonday sun cast a festive glow over the city. Below them, gondolas, waterbuses and barges cruised the canal.

"You know," she said to David, "if someone had a heart attack right here, right now, they'd die before help could get to them."

David shook his head and smiled wryly.

"What?"

"Do you always have to imagine the worst case scenario?"

"It helps prepare me for any eventuality," she said, defensively. "I like being prepared."

"Well, you can stop worrying so much. I'm here."

Maddie snorted. "As if I would rely on you."

"You still don't trust me?" He sounded hurt. "Not even after all we've been through together?"

"Don't take it personally, you're a little busted up." She waved at his broken wrist.

"Didn't get in my way last night."

She felt her cheeks color. She didn't want to talk about last night. She'd lost her head, lost her mind, lost every shred of common sense. She didn't want to be reminded of her mistake.

"You're a hard nut to crack, Maddie Cooper," he said, his unblackened eye snapping with an intelligent light.

She glanced away, not knowing how to deal with her feelings. Did he think it was good or bad that she was distrustful? Did he admire her prudence or believe she was just a nervous Nelly?

Maddie shifted her attention to the surrounding mob. It was an eclectic mix of old, young and in between. She heard several languages bandied about: French, German, Italian, Japanese.

David asked a Frenchman if he knew why everyone was stopped on the bridge.

"The Spectacle of Angelo," the man answered. "It starts in ten minutes."

If she'd been on vacation Maddie might have been able to relax and enjoy the pedestrian traffic jam but as it was, she felt as jittery as if she'd just downed ten cups of strong coffee.

Everyone was watching the Campanile several hundred yards ahead, waiting for the performance to begin. Everyone that is, except for Maddie. She was busy scoping out her environment, and searching the crowd for any signs of Cassie.

A young mother dressed in a T-shirt emblazoned with the British flag stood several feet behind them. She was scolding an older child who'd been misbehaving, not paying attention to her toddler trying to climb onto the bridge parapet. One slip and the boy would plunge into the canal.

Maddie's heart leaped into her throat and she could think of only one thing.

The day Cassie fell into the pond.

Maddie slipped free from David's grasp and wound her way through the crowd.

"Ma'am," she shouted. "Your baby!"

But apparently the woman couldn't hear her over the crowd noise.

"Maddie," David called her name. But she was utterly focused on what she was doing. All she could think about was getting to that little boy before he fell. She elbowed people aside, hurrying as best she could.

"Ma'am, ma'am," she kept hollering.

Dear Lord, don't let me be too late.

The toddler was marching along the top of the narrow ledge, wavering on his chubby little legs as he peered down at the water.

She was so close.

Desperately, Maddie lunged forward at the same time a woman with an oversize handbag turned sharply to see what was happening.

"Oops," the woman exclaimed in a British accent.

The swinging purse caught Maddie off guard, smacking her squarely in the back. She tripped over the cobblestones and fell awkwardly across the bridge railing right beside the toddler.

"Look!" the boy said and grinned at her.

"Oh my," gasped the mother, finally realizing what was happening.

Maddie shoved the boy toward his mother who safely caught him. But the motion knocked Maddie completely off balance.

The next thing she knew, she was falling over the edge.

Chapter 20

Maddie didn't tumble into the canal.

Just as she toppled over the bridge, a barge loaded with several large vats glided by. David reached the edge of the bridge where Maddie had been standing at the same time her feet ruptured through the plastic cover of one of the vats.

He jumped off the bridge after her, aiming for a flat empty spot on the barge near the vats. The crowd on the bridge hollered instructions. He landed with a hard splat and stumbled to his knees. Quickly, he swung around, and saw Maddie's head disappear under the rim of the vat.

What was in those containers? Toxic chemicals? Petroleum products? Battery acid?

Adrenaline had him sprinting for the vat. Fear had him praying she was all right. Worry had him ignoring the pain shooting through his right wrist.

He reached the vat, which was taller than he. He clambered atop a stack of wooden pallets beside the vats. With his heart in his throat, he peered inside, not knowing what he would find.

He saw Maddie slowly sinking into a thick tub of raw honey. Honey. Just plain old honey.

"I've gotcha, sweetheart." David grabbed a fistful of Maddie's hair just before her nose submerged.

She was thrashing around, apparently trying to swim, but there was no swimming in the thick, brown syrup.

"Help!" she sputtered.

"I'm here," he murmured and their eyes met. He saw relief on her face and felt his corresponding relief relax the tension knotting his gut. "I'm here."

"Get me out of this before I attract ants."

"Yes, ma'am." He tried his best not to laugh.

She tried to swipe honey off her face with a hand thick with the sticky stuff. "Oh bother."

"Now we know why Winnie the Pooh always says that," he said.

"Did you see that little boy on the bridge? Can you imagine what would have happened if he'd been the one to fall in here?"

"He would have been all right. You'd have jumped in after him," David said. "When it comes to protecting other people you're braver than a firefighter."

"You think so?"

"Nobody else in that crowd ran to rescue the boy."

"I don't think anyone else saw him."

"Trust you to notice someone in trouble, Miss Mother Hen."

The two-man barge crew picked that moment to stroll over and investigate the commotion. They helped him pull Maddie from the honey.

The men struggled not to laugh. They kept turning their backs to snigger and chortle, before turning around again and with straight faces offering clean-up suggestions in Italian.

David had to admit that she was a pretty comical sight.

Her clothes were plastered to her skin and with every step she took honey rolled off her.

"Don't you laugh at me, too!" She shook a finger at him and a big blob of sweet goo smacked him squarely in the chest. He had to slap a hand over his mouth to hold back his own laughter.

"It's not funny," she growled.

"Yeah, it is."

"You're a horrible man, you know that?"

He could tell from the tiny upward pull at the corners of her mouth that she was beginning to see the humor in the situation. "Insult me all you want, sweetheart, I'm the one who pulled your fanny out. Without me, you'd be breathing treacle."

"So what do you want? A merit badge?"

"A kiss would be nice."

"You're serious? You want to kiss me? Now?"

"Yep."

"You're taking a risk. I could wallow all over you, suck you down to my level."

"But you won't."

"How do you know?"

"Because I'm the one who can get you cleaned up."

"You're so smug."

He moved toward her, his mouth itching to capture hers. He was just so damned happy to discover she was all right that he had to kiss her, no matter how inopportune the moment.

Maddie tilted her head toward him, presenting her cheek.

"That's not going to cut it, babe. I want the lips."

She relinquished and puckered up.

David leaned in and pressed his mouth to hers. He'd

never tasted anything sweeter and he wasn't talking about the honey. His naughty libido wished they were somewhere private so he could lick her clean to the last drop.

David imagined that they resembled a very peculiar version of the Bavarian couple who emerged from Aunt Caroline's cuckoo clock at midnight to steal a quick kiss before popping back into their respective houses. Him with his blackened eye and busted wrist and Maddie dipped in bee spit.

The Venetians clapped and cheered.

"Our audience approves."

"That's all fine and dandy, but what am I supposed to do now? I don't have a change of clothes and I don't think the concierge is going to let some honey-glazed American go traipsing through their chichi hotel lobby."

In his rudimentary French, David asked the men if they had something onboard he could use to drape over Maddie. One man nodded, disappeared and returned with a newspaper. Not exactly what he had in mind, but it would do.

"What are you planning?" Maddie asked, eyeing the newspaper suspiciously.

"I'm arranging it so you can at least walk around without enticing the local wildlife." David opened the newspaper, separated the pages and then pasted them to Maddie. "What's black and white and read all over?"

"Hardy-har-har."

"I'm betting this is one worst case scenario you never anticipated."

"You got me there."

When he finished covering her clothes, he wrapped her feet with newspaper. In the end, he was almost as messy as she, with honey and bits of newspaper sticking to his cast and printer's ink decorating his skin. He started to shove his hand through his hair, but stopped himself just before he got a head full of honey.

The bargemen let them off at the nearest dock and they had to walk back to the Piazza San Marco. Poor Maddie was struggling valiantly to keep from sticking to the ground with every step.

"This is just fabulous," she muttered and glowered at the passersby staring openly in her direction. "As if I'm more interesting than Carnevale?"

"You are pretty eye-catching," he said.

"I don't want to talk about it anymore."

"You never let *me* get away with avoiding uncomfortable topics."

She bared her teeth and growled.

"I'm on to you, Maddie. You don't scare me."

"You forget. I'm covered in honey. I can wreak much sticky havoc on you." She shuffled forward, arms outstretched zombie-style.

He held up his tacky hands. "You already did."

"You think that's bad, you ain't seen nothing yet."

"Oh," he said. "Here we are. The Hotel International." He gave Maddie the once-over. She was the cutest darned newspaper mummy he'd ever seen.

"What should I do?"

"I'll go check us in, then I'll come around and let you in a side entrance."

"Hurry up. I'm starting to draw flies."

He checked them in and then slipped out a side door to find Maddie pacing and muttering to herself behind the hotel.

"Psst." He dangled their room key for her to see. "This way."

"I feel like I'm in a bit from *I Love Lucy*," Maddie grumbled.

"I guess that makes me Ricky."

"More like Ethel."

He chuckled. "Insult me all you want, sweetheart. I can take it."

They ascended the staircase to their room, Maddie leaving bits of honeyed newspaper sticking to everything she touched. David opened the door, stepped aside and bowed with a flourish.

She tramped over the threshold, then stopped and stared.

"Wow," she said. "Fancy shmancy."

David moved through the suite, opening doors and checking the premises. He didn't want any ugly surprises like Jocko Blanco hiding under the bed. Maddie trailed after him, taking it all in.

"This place is almost as big as my condominium in Fort Worth."

It was decorated in an elegant Old World style that combined vintage furniture with new pieces, but David hardly noticed. Instead, he was checking the security. There was a large sitting area, two separate bedrooms and a private bath.

He ambled over to open the drapes and revealed French doors. They were on the second floor with a balcony overlooking the Piazza San Marco.

While it might seem romantic, the balcony and the trellis of vines growing up the side of the hotel posed a security problem. Anyone with the desire could scale the trellis and break into their room.

He tested the locks. "Make sure you keep this door locked anytime you aren't on the balcony."

"Okay."

David stepped back and jerked a thumb toward the door. "I'm just going to go call Henri, let him know we've arrived."

"Hey!" She sounded panicky. "You're not leaving me like this!"

"I thought you'd want some privacy."

"Wait, wait, wait."

"Yes?"

"How do you expect me to get out of these clothes by myself?"

"Come on." He grinned. "Say it."

"Say what?"

"You need me."

"I'm not saying that."

"Okay." He knew he was cruel to tease, but he just couldn't resist. "I'll see you later."

"All right, come back. I need you," she said through clenched teeth. "Now get in this bathroom and help me out of my clothes."

"Oooh, I like it when you get all dominatrix on me."

She stuck out her tongue.

"Now that's an interesting thought, but let's wait until you're cleaned up."

"What lit your fire, Sparky?"

"I don't know. Maybe the excitement of you almost drowning in a vat of honey."

"Maybe it's that knock on the head Jocko Blanco gave you yesterday."

"Don't underestimate yourself, Maddie." David said. He didn't know why he was feeling so damned giddy.

"Well, don't just stand there looking all googly-eyed, help me get this sweater over my head."

He fished around between the layers of newspaper and

goo to find the hem of her sweater. Gently, he peeled the garment up over her head.

It got stuck halfway, giving him a perfect full-on view of her breasts.

"Ahem, David," she said in a muffled voice. "I can't breathe."

Snap out of it, Marshall.

What was happening to him? What kind of erotic spell had this woman woven? He finished tugging the sweater from her head, but it got caught in her hair.

"Ow, easy. You're pulling my hair."

"Sorry, sorry."

He worked to free her hair and several minutes later finally disentangled her from her sweater and dropped the soiled mess to the floor. That's when he realized his breathing was labored and sweat was pooling under his arms.

Their eyes met and the resulting jolt of electrical response had them both turning away. David reached for the porcelain knobs on the white claw-foot bathtub at the same time Maddie started peeling strips of newspaper off her blue jeans.

He added a squirt of bubble bath to the water, and then backed toward the door. "You should be able to take it from here."

"Wait." She pointed a finger at him.

Damn. If he didn't get out of here soon, something was going to pop up. Briefly, he closed his eyes and willed himself not to get aroused.

It didn't work.

He wanted her so much and that desire terrified him. No woman, not even Keeley, had ever been able to distract him from his work.

Until now.

Until Maddie.

Startled, David realized he hadn't thought about Cassie or Shriver or the stolen artwork since Maddie had tumbled off that bridge.

The realization disturbed him.

He was different around her, less competitive, more laid-back. He had changed. She was changing him.

Why and how it was happening, he had no idea, but he didn't like this feeling. Not at all. It was too close to losing control.

He inhaled sharply.

"David? You okay?"

Maddie's eyes were wide with concern. Steam from the hot bathwater curled around her face, dampening her hair. She looked like some nurturing yet naughty nymph just waiting for him to come play with her. He kept his eyes trained on her face and purposely avoided looking at her body.

But he knew that amazing figure was there, calling him with a powerful lure. Last night he'd made love to her, but he'd had an excuse for his behavior. He'd been drugged, out of his head, wounded and vulnerable.

Today was different. He was lucid and sober and impervious to his body's sexual response.

Yeah, right, his penis taunted, poking hard against the zipper of his pants.

He had to get out of here. Now.

"Um," he said, edging for the door. "Why don't I just go ahead and give you that privacy? Looks like the only way you're going to get the rest of that gunk off is to soak."

"Okay."

"I'll just go buy you some new clothes. What size do you wear?"

"A six. And I'll need new shoes. Those sneakers are beyond salvaging. Size nine. Don't say it. I know I've got big feet." She grinned.

"Gotcha, size nine clothes, size six shoes."

"No, no, the other way around. I'd have to chop off my toes to fit into a size six shoe."

"Right, right." He stared at the ceiling, at the floor, at anything but her. It was all he could do to keep from tossing her in the bath, jumping in beside her and doing incredibly sexy things to her.

"Are you sure you're all right? You're acting weird."

"Great. Terrific. Be right back."

And then he ran out the door as fast as his legs would carry him.

Chapter 21

David never made it into a dress shop for Maddie's new clothes. He'd no sooner left the hotel than his cell phone rang.

"Marshall here," he'd barked into the phone but he could barely hear over the noise of the Carnevale merrymakers. He was expecting Henri, but the voice on the other end was female.

"David?"

Jamming his index finger against his other ear, he said, "Hang on. I can't hear you. Let me get inside somewhere."

"Hurry, I don't have long to talk."

Someone chose that moment to blast a noisemaker behind him. He winced and ducked into a tobacco shop that looked relatively quiet.

"Who is this?" he asked.

"It's me, Cassie." She sounded exasperated that he hadn't recognized her voice.

"Cassie!" The hairs on the back of his neck lifted. "Good God, woman, where are you?"

"I'm in Venice."

"Me too. At the Hotel International."

"Wonderful, I was praying you'd tracked me here."

"You're in serious trouble, you know that?"

"Tell me about it. This undercover FBI stuff is a lot harder than it looks."

"Are you with Jocko Blanco?"

"Not anymore. Thank God. Peyton rescued me. And none too soon, let me tell you. I shudder to think what might have happened if . . ."

"Where is Shriver?" he interrupted.

"That's what I'm trying to tell you. He could come back any minute and he doesn't completely trust me. Which is good since I'm double-crossing him and to tell you the truth I'm starting to feel kind of bad about it. He's not really a rotten guy, David. He's just misguided."

"Where in Venice are you?"

"We'll get to that in a jiffy. Just hear me out."

"I'm listening." He forced himself not to sound cross.

The man behind the counter was giving him the once-over. "Pipe tobacco?" he asked in English.

David shook his head and turned his back on the guy. "Cassie?"

"You probably should give up smoking."

"What?"

"If you're thinking about romancing my sister. Maddie hates smoking."

"What? I don't smoke and I'm not romancing your sister!"

"Sure, uh-huh."

"Could you get to the point?" he snapped.

"Testy. Maddie must be giving you a run for your money. She can get on your nerves with that overly cautious stuff, can't she?"

"I thought you said you didn't have much time to talk."

"You're right. Here's the deal. Shriver is about to dispose of the paintings."

"Why the hell didn't you say so in the first place?"

"Don't yell at me."

"Okay. I'm sorry. I won't yell." David took a long, slow deep breath so he wouldn't yell at her again. "Tell me about the paintings."

"I set it up."

"Set what up? The fence?"

"No silly, the sting."

"What sting?" She was nuttier than a macadamia farm. No wonder Maddie watched over Cassie as if it was her life's mission. The woman needed a keeper.

"I made forgeries of the El Greco and the Cézanne."

"Why?"

"Here's the plan I talked Shriver into. We hold an underground auction. He gets Levy, Philpot and all the collectors he can find willing to bid on stolen art together in one room. We have the real paintings authenticated to everyone's satisfaction and then we do the old switcheroo with the forgeries. After we pull the scam, I told him that we would ransom the paintings back to the museum and double our haul."

Stunned by the level of her cleverness, David could only mutter a disbelieving "What?"

"Don't misunderstand," she said hurriedly. "I wasn't actually going through with this scheme."

"But you made forgeries?"

"Just for Shriver's benefit. But listen, at five o'clock this afternoon he's holding the auction at the Hotel Vivaldi in room 617. If you want to catch Shriver red-handed, along with the unscrupulous potential buyers, be there."

"All right." He nodded to himself. Maybe Cassie wasn't

so crazy after all. "I'll be there. Is there anything you want me to tell Maddie?"

"I've gotta go. I heard Peyton in the hall." She rang off.

David snapped his phone shut, adrenaline pumping through his body. He didn't know what to make of Cassie's call, but he did know one thing, his lust to bring Shriver to justice had returned with a vengeance. Grinning to himself, he turned to the shopkeeper behind the counter and asked him how to get to the nearest police station.

"Who's on the phone, luv?" Peyton asked Cassie. He was standing in the doorway, disappointment on his face, resignation in his voice.

"Um…" Cassie slipped the receiver into its cradle, her heart pumping fast. "Wrong number."

"You're going to have to do better than that." He stepped into the room, suddenly looking very menacing and kicked the door closed behind him. He pulled the gun she'd taken from Jocko Blanco out of his pocket.

Uh-oh. Trouble.

"What's with the gun?" she asked, giving him her best wide-eyed innocent expression. "You don't like guns."

"I decided I needed to learn to like them."

"How come?"

"I thought I could use this one for protection."

"Against what?"

"My enemies."

"I'm not your enemy, Peyton."

"You're certainly not my friend. I've been listening at the door for quite some time."

Gulp. "It's not what you think."

His smile was wistful but the look in his eyes was

deadly. Cassie took a step back and eyeballed the door. He stood squarely between her and freedom.

"Don't lie to a liar, luv."

"Peyton…I…I…" Cassie sputtered, at a loss for words.

"You called David Marshall," he said flatly.

Come on. Concoct a likely story. You're good at thinking on your feet.

Cassie wracked her brain but came up with zip in the good excuses department.

"And here I was thinking we might have a real future together." He clucked his tongue and stepped closer. Cassie drew a deep breath and forced herself not to back up. "Serves me right for getting these romantic ideas."

"The phone call was not what it seemed."

"It's exactly what it seemed. You planned to rat me out to Marshall all along, but only after you convinced me to set up this auction so you could take my connections down with me."

"Are you terribly mad?" she asked, wrinkling her forehead. "It really wasn't personal. I just wanted to prove to my irritating twin sister Maddie that I could do something useful."

"Like catching an art thief?"

"Not just any art thief," she flattered, "but the world's best."

"You've put me in a difficult position. I'm going to have to do things I wouldn't usually do."

"Hey, your problems are your own fault. If you hadn't targeted me as your next mark, none of this would have happened."

"My mistake," Peyton said. He came closer until they were nose to nose.

Cassie struggled to control her fear, forcing herself to breathe normally, to smile cheerfully. She had no idea what Peyton was capable of. "Do you forgive me?"

"If you forgive me for what I'm about to do to you."

"What's that?" Her voice rose an octave.

"Open my suitcase."

"What?" Was he going to chop her into little pieces and ship her home in his luggage?

Peyton nodded at his suitcase resting on the luggage rack at the end of the bed. "Open it."

Nervously, she obeyed because he was bigger and stronger and he had a gun and she was still hoping she could flirt her way out of this. She released the snaps and unzipped his suitcase. His clothes were carefully folded. She gave him extra credit for neatness.

She glanced at him. "Now what?"

"Under the clothes." He motioned with the gun. "I was hoping I wouldn't have to use it but you've left me no choice."

"Peyton..."

"Shh. Under my shirts."

She slipped her hand beneath his shirts, her fingers making contact with a coil of rope.

Oh boy.

"Let's have it."

Slowly, Cassie pulled out the rope.

"Good girl, now bring it here."

What was he going to do? Goosebumps lifted the hairs on her arms and her mouth went spitless.

He took the rope from her. "Take off your clothes."

What! Was he going to rape her? In spite of all her efforts to control her fear, Cassie felt her legs tremble.

"Take off your clothes."

"I won't." She notched her chin upward.

"I guess I'll have to do it for you." He reached for the buttons on her blouse.

She slapped his fingers. "Hands off. I can do it."

He smirked, watching her with half-lowered lids. "Too bad we never had a chance to make love. I can tell I missed something special."

"Yes you did," she said tartly, standing before him in her bra and panties.

"Those too."

"What?"

"Your knickers."

"Aw, come on."

He waved the gun, not pointing it at her, but threatening her with it. "Off with the underthings."

"Why?"

"Just do it."

"Peyton..."

This time he did point the gun at her. "Please don't make me hurt you."

"Okay. Okay. No shooting." She shimmied out of her panties and then unhooked her bra and let it drop to the floor. How friggin' humiliating.

"Hands behind your back," Peyton said.

She complied, waiting with bated breath to see what he would do next.

"Now turn around."

"Oooh, sounds kinky," she teased, desperate to lighten things up and get him to change his mind.

"I'm not playing. Turn around."

Cassie did as he asked; grateful at least that he couldn't see the expression on her face. She knew her eyes would give away her fear.

"You're lucky I'm just going to tie you up and leave you here," he said, wrapping the rope around her wrists.

She didn't know what he'd done with the gun while he was tying her up but she was too big of a wimp to fight him at that point. He would only win and she would end up getting hurt in the process. She wasn't strong and physically fit like Maddie.

"That's so terribly sporting of you, thanks," she said sarcastically.

"Could be worse. I could give Jocko a call and tell him where to find you."

"You wouldn't." Her heart thumped.

He traced a finger along her jaw. "I would."

"I thought you two were at war with each other."

"We negotiated a peace treaty."

"Hey," she said, narrowing her eyes in suspicion. "How come you packed rope? You intended on ditching me all along, didn't you?"

"It crossed my mind."

"Stop acting so betrayed. You're not any more honest than I am."

He sighed wistfully. "I had such high hopes that the rope wouldn't be necessary. But alas, we obviously weren't meant to be." He tightened the bindings. "Now, into the bathroom."

"The bathroom?"

"I'm going to tie you to the toilet."

"Oh, that's really rude. Taking my clothes and tying me to the john."

"Would you rather me lash you to the bed with no access to the water closet?"

She thought about it for a moment. "No."

He marched her into the bathroom, made her sit down and laced her hands around the back of the toilet bowl.

"By the way," he said, once he'd finished tying her up. "Just to let you know, I'm taking all your clothes with me. In case you get any crazy ideas about escaping."

"That's really low."

He shrugged. "All's fair in love and war."

"We were never in love."

"True enough. Oh, and by the way, your phone call to David Marshall isn't going to ruin the auction."

"What do you mean?" Cassie frowned, trying her best to look cool, calm and collected without any clothes on.

"I told you the wrong time on purpose. The auction isn't set for five o'clock."

"It's not?"

"No." Peyton grinned, leaned over and placed a kiss on her cheek. "It's in thirty minutes."

What was taking David so long?

The soap and water had dissolved the honey long ago and bits of newspaper floated around her. And even though she'd twice let out some cold water and refilled it with hot, the bath had gone cold and the bubbles dissipated.

She'd been in here at least an hour, her hands and feet shriveling into pale prunes. Leaning over the edge of the tub, she peered at her clothes plastered onto the bathroom tile. There would be no salvaging those garments without a heavy-duty washing machine and that was still an iffy proposition. Her luggage was lost in the wilds of Europe. Essentially, she was naked in a foreign country, dependent on a man she didn't even trust all that much.

Come on, Maddie, David is an FBI agent. He's not going to abandon you. He's probably just having trouble finding your size.

When the going gets tough, men take off. The old

refrain that had formed her belief system about the opposite sex circled in her brain.

That's utter nonsense. Why would David leave you stranded in a tub?

Same reason he'd given her the slip at the Prado, to find and arrest Cassie on his own. He had a perfect opportunity and he'd seized it.

No he didn't.

How about the way he ran out of here?

Don't jump to conclusions. Remain calm.

But even as she was giving herself a pep talk, Maddie was reaching for the towel. That's it. If he didn't come back within the next fifteen minutes she was never ever trusting another man again.

Briskly, she toweled herself off and marched into the bedroom. Too bad he didn't have any luggage either. She would have borrowed his clothes.

Maddie stood in the middle of the room, assessing her options. Hmm, perhaps she could fashion a toga for herself out of a bedsheet, pretend it was a Carnevale costume, slip down to the hotel gift shop and pray that they sold apparel.

Not the best plan in the world, but it was the only one she had.

She searched the bathroom, found a sewing kit and spent the next fifteen minutes fashioning a toga from a sheet. Once she was certain the makeshift garment would stay on, she opened the French doors and stepped out onto the balcony. She'd give David one last chance to appear before taking matters into her own hands.

Below her window Carnevale was in full swing. Loud riotous music played. Delicious aromas filled the air. Revelers danced in the streets, wearing all manner of costumes and masks. She would fit right in.

Part of her was angry with David, but another part of her was worried. Maybe he hadn't ditched her. Maybe something bad had happened.

Maybe he'd run across Blanco again.

Either way, she needed clothes. She turned to go back into the room to retrieve her Mastercard from her honey-coated shoulder bag when she saw something in her peripheral vision that rooted her to the spot.

Was that Peyton Shriver moving through the crowd on the other side of the square? Maddie stepped farther out onto the balcony and narrowed her eyes.

Come closer, she mentally willed him.

He must have picked up her vibes, because he did walk in her direction.

Yep. It was indeed Shriver. His plain beige coat amid the colorful Carnevale costumes was what had snagged her eye. She searched for Cassie in the crowd around him, but Shriver appeared to be alone.

She had to get down there, had to follow him.

What if he spots you? What if he and Blanco aren't at odds as David contends but working together? What if . . .

To hell with *what ifs*. Where had caution and prudence gotten her? Shriver was out there right now. She had a chance to do something about it. Was she going to stay here and cower in a hotel room hoping David would come back and take care of things? Or was she going to plunge ahead, take a chance and sally forth after Shriver.

Go, Maddie, go. She heard Cassie's voice, clear as if her sister was standing beside her.

She stared at the crowd, intimidated by the thought of waltzing around in a bedsheet. You can do it. She raised her chin. Yes. She would do it.

Glancing around, she realized she'd lost the beige

coat in the mass of humanity. Oops! Where had Shriver gone?

Panicking over the thought that her indecision might have lost her her only link to Cassie, Maddie desperately scanned the people for Shriver.

Ah, there he was, going into a church not far from the hotel.

She wasn't about to let him escape now. Resolutely, Maddie squared her shoulders, marched out the door, down the stairs, through the lobby and into the Piazza San Marco.

She moved through the costumed throng, her gaze beaded on the church where she'd seen Shriver disappear only minutes before. No one gave her a second glance in her makeshift toga, and for that she was grateful to Carnevale.

What she wasn't so thankful for was the wave of humanity keeping her from her target.

You can't let him get away.

She elbowed aside a drunken Marco Polo who was leering openly at her breasts and dodged a man on stilts juggling orange glowing balls. The air was ripe with enticing aromas—freshly baked pastries, roasted turkey legs, generously spiced pan-seared fish—but Maddie barely noticed.

She vaulted over a two-year-old sitting on the steps of a shop eating gelato. She zigged past strolling young lovers holding hands and zagged around slow-moving tourists gawking at the sights.

The trip across the Piazza San Marco seemed the longest trek of her life—much longer than any race she'd ever run—although it probably took less than three minutes. Finally, she pushed through the door of the church and blinked against the contrast from the bright sunshine outside and the dimly lit interior.

She stepped away from the door and stood there a moment getting her bearings and letting her eyes adjust. A few people sat in the pews praying. She swung her gaze up and down the aisles.

No sign of Shriver.

He was gone. She'd lost him.

Dejected, she sagged against a pillar.

What now?

And then she saw him pass by the window. He was outside the church. His head was down as if he was talking to someone either shorter than he or someone sitting down.

As quickly and quietly as she could, Maddie padded through the church in her bare feet to the door at the other end of the building, her pulse spiking in irregular blips.

She went through the exit to a narrow walkway between the church and the canal.

A shadow fell across her. She looked up and gasped.

An ominous figure in a long black robe stood before her in the most sinister costume she'd ever seen. He wore a breastplate of mosaic mirrors and he was carrying a large, evil-looking scythe. His head was a skull mask, covered in the same small reflective glass as the breastplate. She could see herself fractured into a hundred tiny, bedsheet-wearing Maddies.

His deep laugh was wicked and menacing.

The Grim Reaper.

She froze, trapped in the surreal moment, wondering if it was a nightmare.

Then the Grim Reaper simply shouldered his scythe and stepped around her, his knee-high black leather boots echoing sharply on the cobblestones as he headed for the Piazza.

Clutching a hand to her heart, she heaved in a shaky

breath. The man had scared her. More than she cared to admit.

Settle down. It's just Carnevale. Forget the guy in the Grim Reaper outfit. What about Shriver?

Still unnerved, she looked to the left where she'd last seen Shriver and spotted a gondola stand but no art thief.

She'd lost him.

Dammit.

But no, wait. There. Out on the canal. Shriver was in a gondola headed away from her. As she watched, the gondola disappeared around a corner.

What to do now? She had no money to hire a gondola to follow him, she was barefoot and in a makeshift toga.

She was defeated. Time for Plan B.

You have no Plan B.

Well, she'd better get one, pronto. Maddie gnawed a thumbnail. She really only had one option. Head back to the hotel and hope David had returned in her absence.

Unhappy with her plan, but not having a viable alternative, Maddie pivoted on her heel to return to the hotel but found herself staring down the barrel of a very wicked looking handgun.

Chapter 22

This was a fine mess.

Cassie sat perched on the toilet, her naked body covered in goose bumps, the rough rope gnawing nastily at her tender wrists as she listened to the echoes of the door slamming behind Peyton. When she got out of this predicament, boy, was she going to make him pay.

In the meantime, how was she going to get out of this?

Think, Cassie, think.

Bad idea. Thinking was not her strong suit. What would Maddie do?

Wrong question. Maddie would never get herself into such a snafu.

Okay, but what if by some wild stretch of the imagination, Maddie *had* gotten herself into this situation. What would she do then?

Knowing her Wonder Woman twin, Maddie would probably just bust through the ropes with her superpowers.

Ha, ha, this is serious. Concentrate.

She had less than thirty minutes to get free, call David and tell him what happened. Otherwise, when he showed up at the Hotel Vivaldi at five and found no one there, he would think she really *was* in cahoots with Peyton and had just set David up.

And she'd end up going to jail instead of getting on the cover of *Art World Today*.

Not good. She would look ghastly in prison stripes. If that wasn't an impetus to get on the ball, she didn't know what was.

Think, Cassie, think.

She scanned the bathroom. Her makeup and beauty supplies were strewn all over the counter but what good could an eyelash curler or a tube of lipstick do at this point?

And then she spied her trusty battery-powered travel curling iron peeking provocatively at her from behind a bottle of Opium perfume.

Aha!

Now for the hard part. Reaching it.

David was returning through the Piazza San Marco when his cell phone rang again. He'd just completed a long discussion with Henri and the chief of the Venice police. He had also gotten a new duty weapon issued to replace the one Blanco had stolen. Both the local authorities and Interpol were preparing to join him at five o'clock to raid the Hotel Vivaldi and catch Shriver in the act of auctioning off the paintings.

"I've gotcha now, Shriver," he murmured gleefully under his breath, just as the phone did the *Dragnet* thing.

He flipped it open. "Marshall."

"David, it's Cassie again." She sounded breathless, anxious.

"Hang on, I'm in the Piazza San Marco and I can barely hear you. Let me get someplace out of the way." He cornered a church and ducked onto the narrow side street running along the canal. "Go ahead."

"Shriver caught me on the phone and he heard me talking to you and he made me take off my clothes and he tied me to a toilet and..."

"Whoa, whoa, slow down."

"Can't. No time. Listen carefully."

"I'm listening."

"Shriver gave me the wrong time. The auction isn't at five o'clock but in ten minutes!"

"What!"

"I know. I'm sorry. Apparently he didn't trust me so much and fed me the wrong info."

"Is it still at the same hotel?" David asked, wondering if Cassie was jerking him around. Maybe she'd realized how much trouble she was in and she was trying to get herself out of hot water.

"Yes, yes. At least I think so. I hope so."

He had ten minutes to get to the Hotel Vivaldi on the opposite side of the city in the middle of Carnevale. Even a superhero couldn't have made it, but he had to try. He'd spent too many years and too much of himself in pursuing Shriver. He wasn't going down without one hell of a fight. If he didn't win this one, he'd become the laughingstock of the FBI.

David's face flushed with embarrassment. No dammit. He was going to win. He was going to catch Shriver and Philpot and Levy and get his Aunt Caroline's Rembrandt back.

A woman's sudden screams drew his attention. Was someone getting mugged?

He jerked his head in the direction of the sound. About a quarter of a mile farther down the narrow street, a bald man was trying to pull a struggling woman—who looked as if she was wearing a bedsheet—into a waiting motorboat.

"Take your hands off me if you value your testicles, bub!" the woman hollered.

There was no mistaking that voice. Or that nerve.

Maddie.

A chill of fear squeezed his spine when he realized the bald man was Jocko Blanco.

"David? David?" Cassie asked from the phone. "What's going on? You don't have time to waste. You've got to get to the Hotel Vavaldi or Shriver's going to get away!"

"To hell with Shriver, Blanco's got Maddie." He snapped the phone shut and took off at a dead run.

But he was far too late. Long before he could reach her, Blanco had successfully dragged Maddie into the motorboat and they were zipping off down the canal, headed toward the Venetian lagoon.

"I like the toga," Jocko Blanco said, keeping one hand on his gun and the other on the speedboat's steering wheel. "And the no-bra look. By the way, your headlights are on. Does that mean you enjoyed our tussle or are you just cold?"

"I'm cold," she said haughtily.

"Should have thought about that before you decided to go boating in a bedsheet."

"I didn't decide to go boating. You kidnapped me."

"Serves you right for escaping. How did you escape by the way? Shriver said he tied you buck naked to the toilet." Blanco wagged his tongue lasciviously. "I was looking forward to seeing that."

What? Maddie stared at him, not understanding one word of what this cretin was saying. She sized him up. Beefy, shaved head, skull and cross bones tattoos on his hand. She'd seen this guy before. At the top of the Eiffel Tower talking to Jerome Levy.

"You're Jocko Blanco."

"Ah, babe. Don't tell me you forgot me already. I thought I made a pretty strong impression on you back in Madrid." He pursed his lips in a pout. "Now here I find you barely even remember my name. And after all we shared together."

Oh!

Realization dawned. He thought she was Cassie. Shriver must have tied Cassie up to a toilet somewhere and told Blanco to go fetch her. But why?

He winked at her and clucked his tongue. "Don't worry, sweetcheeks. I'll make sure you won't forget me again. My name is going to be the last one to pass those luscious lips of yours." He ran the nose of his gun along her jaw and laughed when she flinched. "Put your hands out in front of you."

"What?"

"Don't give me no crap, just do it."

Rolling her eyes, Maddie extended her hands.

He grabbed a roll of silver duct tape sitting on top of a shovel in the bottom of the boat and then wrapped it around her wrists, binding them together.

"Ow, not so tight."

"Quit whining."

I've got a third degree black belt in karate. I'm not taking this crap.

A week ago fear would have frozen her to the seat, but a lot had changed in seven days. She'd gone without adequate food and sleep. She'd been knocked off a bridge and dunked into a vat of honey. She'd been forced to run nearly naked through the streets of Venice. Frankly, she had reached the end of her tether.

You've picked a bad day to mess with me, pox-face. With a well-aimed kick, Maddie planted her foot in Blanco's crotch.

And made contact with something toe-crunchingly hard.

Yeow! Startled, she glanced at Blanco's face.

"Specially made jock strap with an aluminum alloy cup." His grin was wicked.

"I take it women kick you there a lot."

"Provides one hundred percent protection. Don't believe me?" he bragged. "Go ahead. Kick me again."

"That's okay. I'll pass."

"Good, then just sit back and behave."

Yeah, right. Desperate to escape, she searched the lagoon. "Help!" she cried out to a passing vaporetto. "Help!"

"Save your breath. It's unlikely they understand English."

"Help! He's trying to kill me!"

"Lover's spat," Blanco sang out to the passengers, smiled, waved and goosed the speedboat faster.

Once they were out of sight of the waterbus, Blanco cocked the gun and pressed it against her temple.

"I could just kill you now," he said. "Think about it. The only reason you're still alive is because I don't want to have to scrub your blood off the boat. I'm lazy that way."

Maddie tried to swallow, but she was scared spitless. All right, racking him hadn't worked. What now?

Maybe she could reason with the guy. Find a way to buy some time.

"So one way or the other, you intend on killing me?" she said.

"That's pretty much the plan."

"But why?"

"You're an inconvenience to Shriver."

"How much is he paying you? I'll pay more."

Blanco snorted. "On a museum employee's salary? I don't think so."

Think of a good lie. Come on, come on. Bluff. Be outrageous. What would Cassie say?

"What if I told you the Cézanne and El Greco are fakes," Maddie babbled, saying the first thing that popped into her head. Cassie was extremely gifted at copying great works of art quickly. It was within the realm of possibility that she could have made forgeries. Cassie loved showing off her talent.

"I'd say you were lying in order to save your hide."

"But what if I wasn't?"

He studied her a moment. "I'm listening."

"It's all part of a sneaky plot I concocted to outwit Shriver." Maddie was grasping at straws, embellishing as she went along and praying like hell Blanco's greed was greater than his knowledge of artwork masterpieces. She was probably okay on that score. He looked like a velvet-Elvis-dogs-playing-poker aficionado. "And he's setting you up as the fall guy."

"What do you mean?"

"Shriver's been planning these robberies a long time. He hooked up with me because he knew I could create identical replicas of the Cézanne and El Greco." Please don't let him ask me why, Maddie prayed. She really hadn't thought this thing through.

"Why?"

So much for thinking on her feet.

"Well?" Blanco raised both eyebrows.

"Er...umm...because Shriver loves the paintings so much he wanted to keep them for himself but he also wanted the big bucks." Maddie held her breath and tried not to visibly wince at the lameness of her *faux* explanation.

To her amazement, Blanco nodded. "He does love those

damn paintings. Me, I never got the attraction: What's the big deal about some old dead guys slapping paint on canvas and everyone calling it great art? Personally, I prefer photographs. Much more real."

"Ansel Adams," Maddie said.

"Yeah." Blanco nodded. "He's pretty good. I like Richard Avedon too, although they have completely different styles."

"What about Annie Leibowitz?"

"Naw. She's the one who does all the babies in pumpkins and shit like that, right? Too schmaltzy for me."

"No, that's Anne Geddes. Annie Leibowitz photographs celebrities. A lot of her work has appeared in *Rolling Stone*."

"Oh yeah. She's cool." Blanco snapped his fingers. "Hey, have you ever seen that guy who takes photos of naked people lying down in city streets and bizarre places like that? Now that's compelling."

Gee, they were actually bonding. Maddie decided to push it. "You know, Jocko, Shriver's just using you. Getting you to do his dirty work. You kill me, and then he calls the cops on you. Next thing you know, you're in the big house marking time."

The hoodlum chortled, but he looked unsure of himself. "Big house? Marking time? You've been watching too many old gangster movies."

Maddie shrugged, trying her best to appear nonchalant. Her bid to turn Blanco on Shriver had better pay off or else she and Cassie were in deep swamp water.

And she would never see David again.

No more sneaking through coconut groves together. No more cutting up in hospital emergency rooms. No more rescuing each other from their misadventures.

She would miss the taste of his intoxicating mouth, the sound of his deep, sometimes stern, but always caring, voice and the smell of his manly scent.

Why her first thought was of David and not her twin she could not say. What she did know was that the idea of never seeing David again tore at her heart with razor-sharp tiger claws.

And where was her sister? Without Maddie to look after her, track her down and save her, what would happen to her? Maybe she could trust David to take care of Cassie when she was gone?

No. She couldn't depend on that. She'd never been able to depend on anyone except herself. She had to get out of this mess. Had to save her sister.

But she was in serious trouble. No one knew where she was. When David returned to the hotel to find her gone, he would have no idea what had happened to her. No clue where to look for her body.

Cassie had to do something. David had gone to save Maddie. She paused a second to savor that image. For once in her life Maddie was the rescuee instead of the rescuer. But with David in hot pursuit of Blanco, there was no one to stop Shriver. No one except herself.

But how?

She was at least thirty minutes away from the Hotel Vivaldi and what was she going to do when she got there anyway? Shriver had hired security guards and he wasn't dumb enough to let her fool him again. If she went to the police, they would probably arrest her as a fugitive.

She'd exhausted her charm and her luck.

The jig was up.

That is, unless she invented something completely creative.

Lori Wilde

Think. How could she marshal a squadron of police to the Vivaldi pronto?

Think, think, think. Quick, quick, quick.

Then inspiration struck.

She hurried to the phone and called the police. The dispatcher answered in Italian. Cassie asked for someone who spoke English. After a wait that seemed agonizingly long but was probably only about three minutes, a man with a sexy sounding voice came on the line.

"This is Dominic Salveto. I speak English."

Cassie swallowed hard and forced herself not to flirt. This was serious business. She couldn't let herself get side-tracked by sex appeal.

"Dominic," she said sternly and then lied through her teeth. "There's a bomb in the Rialto room of the Hotel Vivaldi and it's set to go off in fifteen minutes!"

David zipped through the Grand Canal in a borrowed police boat. Blanco had a good ten-minute lead on him and he could only pray his suspicion that the thug was headed out to sea was a correct one.

If the bastard so much as breathed germs on Maddie and gave her a cold, David would hunt him down and squash him like the cockroach he was. The vivid intensity of his bloodlust took him aback, but he couldn't help his feelings. His gut squeezed, his head churned, his heart thundered with fear and concern and something much, much more.

At this point, right and wrong didn't exist. All that mattered was Maddie.

You should never have left her alone in the hotel room. If you'd stayed you would have made love to her and you know it.

And she would be safe in your arms at this very moment.

But he hadn't stayed. He'd let both his fear of emotional intimacy and his almost maniacal need to capture Shriver, drive him away from her.

Just when she needed him most.

He picked up a pair of police issue binoculars, brought them to his eyes and scanned the horizon. Straight ahead of him several boats bobbed together in the distance, most of them in a cluster.

Blanco would shy away from witnesses or potential rescuers. David swung the glasses to the right, saw two or three boats motoring along in that direction. He looked left. Only one boat over there.

Knowing he was taking a calculated risk by changing his course, knowing Maddie's very life lay in his hands, David headed north, following his gut.

"Hang on, Maddie, I'm coming," he said aloud, refusing to believe he was on a wild goose chase. This was the right direction. It had to be. He was going to rescue her.

Unless she was already dead.

Chapter 23

Blanco wasn't buying her art forgery story, even though Maddie kept bargaining, elaborately embellishing the lie.

"What kind of idiot do you take me for?" he snapped.

A big one, she hoped. Maddie batted her eyelashes at him. "I don't think you're an idiot."

"Then you must be as big an airhead as Shriver says you are."

"He called me an airhead?"

"He said killing you would be easy because you're too much of an airhead to even see it coming."

Maddie was insulted on Cassie's behalf. "Like you and Shriver are nuclear scientists. For your information, you don't even have the right woman."

Blanco narrowed his eyes. "What do you mean?"

"Weren't you supposed to go to a hotel and find me chained to a toilet?"

"Yeah."

"Then why do you suppose you captured me out on the street?"

"Because you got loose. Peyton's notoriously terrible at

tying people up. He's not too good at anything that messes up his manicure."

"No. That's not the reason. It's because I'm not Cassie." She shifted uncomfortably. The only thing between her bottom and the hard wooden bench was one thin layer of bedsheet.

"Okay, I'll play along. Who are you?"

"I'm her identical twin, Maddie. Kill me, you kill the wrong sister and Shriver will be highly ticked off at you."

"Your forged painting story was more plausible," he said. "I'd stick with that one if I were you."

"You don't believe me?"

"Not for a minute."

"Okay, it's your funeral. Don't say I didn't warn you. When you get back to Venice and find Cassie got free and called the cops, you're going to feel really stupid."

"Blah, blah, blah."

"You were with my sister when you forced her to rob the Prado. Can't you tell she's twenty pounds heavier and soft as a marshmallow?" Maddie flexed a bicep. "You're saying you can't tell a difference?"

Blanco glanced at her muscle. "Well, Miss Smarty Pants, if you're not Cassie, then how do you know I was the one who robbed the Prado? The news media is blaming Shriver. And you. Nobody's even mentioned my name."

"What was that all about, anyway?" Maddie asked. "What's going on with you and Shriver? How come sometimes you're working together and sometimes you're fighting each other?"

"It's complicated. Besides, you already know the answer."

"No I don't."

"Hmph."

"What's so complicated about your relationship with Shriver? You guys gay or something?"

"No!" Blanco scowled. "He's my half-brother. We got the same old man. Except he was married to Peyton's mama but not mine."

Ah. Sibling rivalry. That explained a lot. She could tell Blanco resented his brother's legitimacy. "So what happened between you two?"

"Jerome Levy paid Peyton and me to heist the Cézanne from the Kimbell for a high-powered collector. Except Peyton got a better offer from Cory Philpot. He had the hots for you and was thinking of quitting the business, so he double-crossed me."

"That was rude."

"Thank you."

"Hey, I understand completely about thoughtless siblings," she said, still frantically trying to figure a way out of her predicament.

"To get even with him, I horned in on his deal with you at the Prado. I figured I'd steal the El Greco out from under him and we'd be even."

"When did you guys kiss and make up?"

"When Peyton found out you were still working with the Feds and he knew he was going to have to get rid of you." Blanco's lip curled in a snarl. "Pretty Boy doesn't have the guts to do his own dirty work so he calls me and says he'll cut me in for half on this auction deal if I do away with you."

"What auction deal?"

"Stop playing ignorant. You're getting on my nerves with that." Blanco waved the gun in her face. "Shut up."

He stared out over the bow of the boat. Maddie turned in her seat to see what he was looking at. Up ahead loomed a small island with what appeared to be a crumbling, abandoned monastery.

Uh-oh. This looked like the place where he planned to put a bullet between her eyes and stash her in a shallow grave.

Over my dead body.

Well, yeah, Maddie, that's sort of the general idea.

Blanco killed the motor and slowly beached the boat on a pebbly shoal. The gravel grated against the hull and the air hung thick with the odor of dead fish. Maddie tasted the coppery flavor of her own fear.

Don't panic. Stay calm. No worst case scenarios. She was living a worst case scenario. No need to obsess about one.

She wondered how much time had passed since Blanco had abducted her and if David had gotten back to the hotel yet. She imagined his ruggedly handsome face, drawn with concern, and her eyes misted with tears.

Would she ever see him again?

A deep longing filled her heart. The longing for all the things she'd missed out on. The feeling was so intense she lost her breath. She felt a monumental stirring inside her, a sharp shift, a cagey change. She wanted so badly to live, to see how things turned out between her and David.

Face facts. There's not much hope of that.

"Get out of the boat," Blanco commanded.

"Screw you," she said, not to Blanco, but to the nagging, worrisome voice that had dogged her for years. The doom and gloom voice that kept her from taking a chance on life, on intimacy, on love.

"Get out," he repeated, cocking the gun and for one dizzying moment she thought he meant to shoot her right then and there and leave her body floating in the sea.

But then he swung one leg over the edge of the boat and stepped out onto the wet rocks. She shivered, the damp chill invading her bones.

"Move it," Blanco said. "And no more smart-mouthed backtalk."

Stumbling a bit, she managed to climb onto shore in front of him, even though having her hands bound threw her off balance. She had to think of some way to stall him until she could come up with a plan to save her life.

"Walk."

"Which way?"

"Toward the monastery."

Nice. He was going to murder her in a church. Obviously, he wasn't Catholic. Neither was she, but there had to be some rule against killing someone in a place of worship.

Maddie decided to balk. She stood her ground, refusing to move.

"Get going," Blanco growled and pushed the gun against the back of her head. She smelled the ominous scent of gunpowder.

An odd serenity stole over her and Maddie realized Blanco could do whatever he wanted to her and it didn't matter. The sudden stilling of her fretful voice was liberating.

"I'm not moving," she said calmly and turned to face him.

The end of the gun was pointed straight at her nose but she didn't flinch. Blanco looked confused.

"I've got a gun," he said unnecessarily.

"So I see."

"I'll shoot you if you don't move."

"Go ahead. You're going to shoot me anyway. What difference does it make?"

"I want to keep you out of sight. In case a plane is flying over or sumthin'."

"Sorry. I'm not going to make it easy for you."

He growled. "Go!"

"No."

Blanco gritted his teeth. "I've met stubborn women before, but none as stubborn as you."

"I'll take that as a compliment."

"It was meant as criticism."

She shrugged.

"March!" He howled.

She shook her head.

Blanco cocked the gun.

Maddie stood her ground. She didn't even blink. She had no idea what weird mental Valium her body had defensively churned into her brain, but she was not afraid.

All these years she'd spent worrying and fretting and agonizing over every small hazard, every tiny danger, every minuscule risk. For what?

"You're not her, are you?" Amazed, Blanco stared open-mouthed. "You *are* the twin sister."

"I tried to tell you."

"Shit!" He stamped his foot. "Shit, shit, shit. Peyton is going to have a fit."

Just then, the sound of a speedboat tearing through the water at full throttle drew their attention to the water.

Maddie was already facing that direction, her bound hands clasped in front of her, but Blanco had to turn to see what was happening.

The sight of the blue and white police boat raised her spirits. Was that...? Could it be...? She squinted. David at the controls?

When the going gets tough, men take off.

But not David. There was her man bigger than life, coming to her rescue.

Maddie's heart soared.

But only for a fraction of a second. Blanco swung the gun around.

"David! Look out! He's got a gun!"

Blanco got off a shot at the same time David hit the deck. He ducked his head and rolled to the back of the boat.

Oh God! She thought Blanco had missed but she couldn't be sure. Please let David be okay.

Blanco fired again.

David jumped overboard, disappearing under the water's surface.

The water was ice cold. He would get hypothermia in a matter of minutes. She had to dispatch Blanco's gun. Now.

The time for calm passivity had passed. Blanco could shoot her if he wanted, but she'd be damned if she would let him hurt the man she loved.

Maddie whooped a loud war cry and with a well-aimed kick, sent Blanco's gun jettisoning to the bottom of the Lagoon.

David popped to the surface of the icy water, his lungs crying for air. Salt water burned his eyes. He blinked, trying to locate Maddie and Blanco on the beach.

The boat blocked his vision. He couldn't see them, but the shooting had stopped. Why? Where were they? He heard his own raspy breathing as harsh and loud as a ticking clock.

His feet touched bottom. He slogged ashore, crouching low, attempting to stay down in case Blanco was waiting in ambush.

He crept around the edge of the motorboat and cautiously raised his head. He spied Blanco dragging Maddie by the neck in a macabre dance, heading for the aged monastery. Beside the monastery, at the very edge of the water on the opposite side of the island loomed a crumbling campanile.

The minute he saw the bell tower, David knew what Blanco intended.

"Sonofabitch," he cursed, shook off the excess water weighing down his clothes and took off at a dead run.

By the time he reached the monastery, he was out of breath and shivering like a malaria victim. Blanco and Maddie had already disappeared inside.

He burst through the door into the empty church. A rat scuttled in front of him, rose up on its haunches and chattered angrily. David grit his teeth. He hated rats.

Shrugging off his revulsion, he plunged through the church, kicking up dust and pushing through the serpentine tendrils of cobwebs. From the direction of the bell tower, he heard the steady clump-whump, clump-whump of Blanco dragging a reluctant Maddie up the stairs. He also heard Maddie's muffled voice either bargaining or arguing with her captor.

Fear chilled him deeper than the cold water. White fingers of dread wrapped icily around his heart. He had to get to her before Blanco threw her off the tower.

No time to waste. Urgent. Urgent. Maddie needs you.

He took the steps to the bell tower two at a time, barely registering that the stairs shifted and swayed beneath his feet. He was busy fumbling for his gun even while knowing it probably would not fire in its waterlogged condition.

By the time he reached the top step, he was shaking so badly he could hardly stand. He'd never been so cold.

Ahead of him was the closed door leading into the bell tower.

Hurry, hurry, get to her.

He was desperate, but his policeman's instincts warned him not to charge ahead. He knew untold dangers lay behind closed doors. He hesitated, gun drawn, listening.

The silence echoed deep and disturbing.

Perhaps he'd been wrong. Perhaps Blanco had not taken her into the bell tower. He wet his dry lips, thinking what to do next.

Then someone screamed.

Chapter 24

Maddie bit down hard on the sweaty hand Blanco clamped over her mouth. He tasted like dirty feet smelled.

Ptui. She spit.

Biting him was risky. He was holding her with one hand around her waist, the other plastered over her mouth, at the very edge of a gaping hole where the floor of the bell tower used to be.

If he took one step forward, she would be dangling in empty space. The boards had rotted away years ago and it was one long drop to the jagged rocks poking from the water below.

She heard David charging up the stairs on the other side of the closed door and a terrible image flashed through her head. She could see him barreling through the door, propelled by his high-minded need to win at all costs and momentum shoving him through the open pit.

She had to warn him!

If she bit Blanco there was a good chance he would drop her. But she had no choice. She wasn't about to let David die.

When her teeth cut through his flesh, Blanco yelped like a girl.

Wimp.

He jerked his hand from her mouth and staggered backward, blessedly taking her with him. He landed heavily against the stone wall and Maddie fell onto his thick chest.

The entire tower quaked with the impact and a fine dusting of sand and mortar rained from the ceiling.

Maddie gasped.

The campanile was ready to collapse. Any sort of scuffle could do the trick and send the ancient structure crumbling into the water.

Blanco scrambled to his feet, never letting go of Maddie's waist.

The tower trembled again.

Her ribcage ached where his fingers dug in and her wrists burned from the chafe of the duct tape. But the pain was inconsequential considering they were on the verge of plunging to their deaths.

She and Blanco stood on the south side of the open hole, directly opposite the closed door.

The stone walkway on either side of the hole was less than two feet wide. No bell remained in the recess above them, but there was a ratty old rope dangling from the empty cavity. She eyed it speculatively, just in case she was driven to desperate measures.

Dream on. That decomposing rope wouldn't hold a rag doll's weight. Not that she could even grab for it with her hands bound.

Slowly, the door creaked open.

Maddie held her breath and waited for David to appear. He spoke before he stepped into view. "Let her go, Blanco."

"Let her go down the hole? Sure. No problem." Blanco waltzed her to the edge again. Briefly Maddie closed her eyes, fighting nausea.

"You drop her and I'll kill you."

There he was.

Her lover.

Filling the doorway with his reassuring broad-shouldered presence, his duty weapon clutched in his good hand. He was soaked to the skin, his hair plastered to his head, his cast dark with dirt, but he was still the most incredible sight she had ever seen.

David's gaze met hers. Are you all right? he telegraphed with his eyes.

She nodded.

Blanco used her as a shield, ducking his head behind hers in case David took a notion to play sharpshooter. "You wanna see your girly alive again, I suggest you go back down those stairs, get in your boat and cruise away. Give me breathing room and I'll leave her here on the island."

"No can do, Blanco."

"Why not?"

Yeah, why not? It sounded like a terrific plan to Maddie.

"For one thing," David continued, "there's a jail cell reserved in a United States federal prison with your name on it. You've got a nonrefundable one-way ticket to justice, pal, and I'm your travel agent."

Maddie rolled her eyes. Dandy. Just dandy. Was putting people behind bars the only thing David ever thought about?

Not that Blanco didn't deserve to get socked away for the rest of his life. Personally, she could really get into locking the cell door, incinerating the key and performing a celebratory clog dance. Yee-ha.

But she was all for letting the creep get away if his

escape spared their lives. Where did winning get you, if in the end, you were pushing up petunias?

"Looks like we've got ourselves a Venetian stand-off," Blanco said.

"Looks like," David replied tightly.

"I think I'm going to call your bluff."

"How's that?"

"I want you to toss your gun into the sea," Blanco said. "Or I'll throw her down the hole, I swear I will."

"You're not going to do that. Once your hostage is gone, you're mine for the taking. And while I prefer to arrest you, killing you wouldn't trouble me too much. I'll take justice any way I can get it."

His hostage? Well that wasn't a very romantic way to refer to her. She had a name for heaven's sake. Why not use it?

"And I don't believe for one second you would jeopardize her life in order to get me." Blanco sneered.

"Why not? She's been nothing but a royal pain-in-the-ass," David said evenly.

What? Now that wasn't nice. Not nice at all. Maddie glared at him but he didn't make eye contact. Why was he saying such things about her? She thought he liked her. She thought she liked him.

Oh, who was she kidding? She was in love with him. But now, he was acting as if he didn't care about her at all. She was going to have one helluva broken heart.

Unless she ended up with a broken skull first.

Blanco moved suddenly, yanking Maddie forward until her feet left the precarious perch and she was hovering directly over the abyss.

Gulp!

"No!" David shouted and lunged for Maddie as if to catch her.

Ah, maybe he really did care. Her heart leaped.

"Throw the gun away," Blanco repeated.

David's gaze met Maddie's. His jaw tightened. She saw the war of conflict in his eyes. This was a lose-lose situation and nothing could be worse for a guy who loved to win.

"She's getting awfully heavy lawman. Better make up your mind before I lose my grip."

"Put her feet back on solid ground."

"No."

David cocked the gun. The click of the hammer sent icicles through Maddie's veins. "By dangling her over the hole you've left your head exposed. I have a clear shot."

"You kill me, she dies."

"She's going to die anyway."

Blanco pondered this a moment. "Okay. I'll pull her back, but you throw the gun away at the same time."

"All right."

"Step over to the right and pitch the gun through that window arch."

David sidled right and Blanco danced left heading for the open door, all the while holding Maddie over the opening. He had to be getting tired. What if he dropped her accidentally? Her mind raced. How to get out of this?

"Keep going," Blanco said and David inched farther away from the only means of escape.

The tower shivered against their movements.

This was bad. Really bad.

"Now," Blanco said.

Simultaneously, David threw his gun over his shoulder while Blanco settled her feet onto the ground. The gun tumbled through the window arch and disappeared from view. A second later, they heard a distant splash.

Blanco shoved her at David and bolted for the door.

Maddie cried out as she fell, the yawning chasm waiting to gobble her up.

"Maddie!"

David grabbed for her and caught her by the ankle with his one good hand. Fear shoved his heart into his throat. She was dangling above a thirty-foot drop. He was the only thing between her and definite death. A nasty premonition of certain doom crawled over his scalp.

He could not drop her, but already his fingers were growing numb from the effort of holding her up.

"I've got you, sweetheart," he said, surprised to hear how calm he sounded. "Don't worry. I've got you."

But for how long?

The tower rumbled.

Chunks of the structure broke off. More rubble dusted them from above.

"The stairwell's pulling away from the tower!" she yelled. "We'll never get down."

At that moment, the stairway separated from the tower and fell in upon itself. In the clamor of collapsing stone, they heard Blanco scream. The sounds daggered into his brain.

He peered over the edge of the hole; saw that the bedsheet Maddie wore had peeled down over her head. Her hands, bound with duct tape, dangled below her head. She swung in the wind, trusting him. He was nauseous with fear. He could not let her go. He would not.

You've got to do something now.

His fingers cramped while his mind frantically searched for a solution. He reached into his back pocket with casted wrist and found his handcuffs. Grimly, he cuffed his left wrist to her ankle.

"David! What are you doing?"

"Sweetheart, I'm shackling myself to you. If you go down, I go down too."

"Don't be a fool, save yourself."

"I don't run away from trouble," he said and reached out with his casted wrist to grab her other leg when it swung past.

Now what?

The pressure of her weight caused the handcuff to gnaw into his wrist so tight it was all he could do to keep from groaning in pain. His casted wrist wasn't in much better shape. He gnashed his teeth.

"How many incline sit-ups did you tell me you could do?" he asked, willfully numbing his mind to the agonizing pain in his arms and hands.

"Two hundred."

"Well here's the good news, sweetheart, you've only got to do one. I've got your feet, I want you to sit up all the way. When you reach the level of the floor, I want you to slip your arms around my neck. Do you think you can do that?"

She *had* to do it. It was their only chance.

The pain in his wrists intensified as Maddie curled her elbows into her chest and rolled up. The fierce ache spread up his arms, through his shoulders and into his back until he was one throbbing mass of hurt.

David heard her grunt over the exertion and he knew she was hurting too.

"Come on, you can do it," he said as much to himself as to her.

He clenched his jaw, locked his legs around the stone pillar. She was close now. Almost through the opening. But the look of pain on her face matched the searing burn in his muscles.

"Almost there."

Her skin was flushed red from the effort, the veins on her neck and forehead bulging.

What if she couldn't do it?

Don't think like that. She'll make it.

"Come on baby. Two hundred sit-ups. That's it. You're almost here."

She was breathing as hard as he was when her head came back through the hole and their eyes met.

Instantly, they were one. One force, a team, lifting together.

"Arms around my neck," he whispered, scarcely able to breathe. He was hurting that badly.

She separated her elbows as far apart as she could with her hands bound. She dropped her wrists behind his head, encircling his neck with her awkward embrace.

Gathering the last bit of strength he possessed, David gave a mighty cry and rolled them both backward.

Maddie cleared the hole.

They lay on the stone floor, gasping for air. His hand was handcuffed to her ankle. Her arms were locked around his neck. Every muscle in their bodies twitched. They were covered in sweat and dust.

"I'm okay, I'm alive," Maddie keep repeating joyfully as he gently unlocked the handcuffs and then peeled off the duct tape. Her wrists were raw and bleeding and so were his. Their blood mingled.

"Yeah." He laughed, giddily. "Yeah."

"You saved me. You chained yourself to me." She gazed deeply into his eyes and then he was kissing her with the most soulful kiss in the world, branding her with his lips.

"You nearly died," he whispered, burying his face

in her hair and holding her close against him. "I almost lost you."

He was overwhelmed not only by what had just happened, but also by the intensity of emotion surging through him. Did she feel what he felt? Could he trust the power of their connection or was it merely a manifestation of surviving the worst together?

Was this love?

Boom, boom, boom went his heart.

Creak, creak, creak went the bell tower.

"We're not out of the woods yet," he murmured. "The stairwell collapsed. The tower is crumbling and we have no way down."

Maddie pulled back and stared at him, as if recognizing for the first time what a truly dangerous predicament they were in.

David shifted onto his knees, grasped the wall to pull himself up. As he did, more stones broke free and the tower bobbled like a rocking horse.

"Easy," Maddie cautioned.

He glanced over the edge of the window arch. "There's only one way down."

His eyes met hers. He looked grim.

"The water," she whispered.

He nodded. "We're going to have to jump. Can you do it?"

"I have a fear of drowning. Ever since Cassie's accident."

"It's our only chance," he said. "I wouldn't suggest it if we had a choice."

She rose to stand beside him, her body swaying along with the tower. On one side they could see the jagged rocks lying under the water. No jumping off there. She shifted her gaze to the other side.

"What if it's not deep enough?" She gulped.

"We'll be killed."

"Together."

"Yes."

"And what if we're not killed? What if I drown?"

"You won't drown. I won't let you," he said gruffly.

Maddie placed her right hand in his left. "I'm trusting you."

She couldn't have paid him a grander compliment.

"I swear I won't let you down."

"This is big for me."

"I know."

"I'm scared."

"So am I."

"You'll be there for me?"

"Have I ever let you down?" He kept his voice tender, his gaze steady.

She looked deep into his eyes, peered far deeper into him than anyone had ever peered.

More stones broke loose, smashing and bumping as they fell. The tower was going. If they waited much longer, the decision would be out of their hands.

"Ready?" David whispered.

Maddie took a deep breath and nodded.

Together, they moved as close to the ledge as they could.

"Arc your body outward," David said. "Then roll your legs up and tuck your head down. A cannon ball isn't the most graceful, but it's our best chance for survival."

"All right."

She stood beside him, poised to jump. She glanced down. "I can't."

"Don't look at the water. Look at me." He squeezed her hand tightly.

Maddie wrenched her gaze from the water and met his eyes again. She was so brave! His heart wrenched with the intensity of his feelings for this courageous woman.

"Atta girl. We're just going to step off. We're taking a stroll. That's all. No big deal. You can do this."

"Uh-huh."

Chapter 25

After calling in the bomb threat, Cassie called the front desk and talked the concierge into buying her an outfit from the gift shop and charging it to Peyton's account. The preppy black slacks and white wool sweater and sensible loafers were more like something Maddie would wear but she shrugged it off. Beggars couldn't be choosers.

Besides, she felt more responsible, more in control, more reliable these days. She might as well look the part. Once she'd acquired her new threads, she took the originals of the El Greco and the Cézanne that she'd hidden under her mattress after she'd made the double set of forgeries, rolled the canvases up in cardboard tubing and went to the Hotel International. Pretending to be Maddie, she claimed to have lost her room key. Once she had access to the room, she stashed the paintings in the open wall safe—good thing David hadn't found a reason to use it yet—assigned the lock a combination code and sashayed out again.

Mission accomplished. No one could accuse her of being in cahoots with Shriver now. Then she hurried over to the Vivaldi to find out what was happening over there.

And she arrived just in time to see Levy and Philpot being taken from the hotel in handcuffs.

Not wanting to be recognized, she dodged behind a statue and waited until the art brokers had been led away in handcuffs before slipping inside the building. Her heart hammered with excitement.

Had they nabbed Shriver? Was he already in custody? Or had the elusive thief managed to give them the slip?

The place was in chaos with cops and news media and hotel personnel running willy-nilly. To think she'd caused all this bedlam.

Cassie grinned and tried to look inconspicuous as she slinked down the corridor toward the Rialto room.

So far so good.

She was almost there. She quickly skirted past a janitor's closet that stood slightly ajar. She craned her neck, trying to get a peek around the burly door guard into the Rialto Room.

That's when a hand clamped over her mouth and an arm snaked around her waist and she was yanked backward into the janitor's closet.

Floating. Drifting dreamily. Maddie was aware of the cold water, but oddly enough the frigid temperature didn't register against her skin. Nor was she panicked about being face down in the water.

Her eyes were closed and she didn't try to open them. She didn't want to see. She simply wanted to embrace this light airy feeling where nothing seemed hurried or dangerous or even real.

Was she dead? Had she been killed by the fall from the disintegrating tower?

Hmm. Well, this wasn't so bad.

Only one thing bothered her. Just one tiny flaw marred her peaceful flow. She was dead and she'd never told David that she loved him.

Such a shame.

That's what you get for holding back. You had a chance for true love and you blew it.

Then she started thinking of all the times she'd held back, afraid to take a risk, afraid of getting hurt, afraid to trust.

And now here she was finally figuring out that dying was no big deal. Her biggest worst case scenario had come to pass and all she had were regrets for the opportunities she'd lost. The things she had never tried.

I should have given it my all at the Olympics. I should have stopped playing cleanup for Cassie years ago and concentrated on taking care of myself.

If she had her life to live over, knowing what she knew now, she would make some very different choices. She would dye her hair punk-rocker red just to see what it looked like. She would eat a doughnut now and again. She would strip off her clothes and dance naked in her back-yard during a summer rainstorm.

If only she had a second chance!

Then she thought of the things she was never going to get to do. She'd never be able to apologize to Cassie for not letting her stand on her own two feet. She wouldn't get to tell her father how much he'd hurt her when he'd abandoned the family. She wouldn't see her mother one last time or teach another aerobics class or walk in a garden with the sun on her face. She'd never sing lullabies to her babies. Never send them off on their first day of school with a hug and a wave. She would never worry when they didn't make curfew the day they got their driver's license.

Something inside her heart ripped. Babies made her think of being married and being married made her think of being in love and being in love made her think of David.

She would never be able to tell David she loved him.

This realization brought a raw, intricate pain, shredding her earlier peace. She didn't want to be dead. She couldn't be dead. She had so very much to live for.

"Maddie! Maddie!"

Who was calling her? Was that Cassie? She frowned. Or at least she thought she frowned. She couldn't really tell. Did dead people frown?

She felt herself being yanked around.

Ow! Who was pulling her hair?

So much for the quiet dignity of death.

She tried to struggle, to fight the water, to fight for her life but her hands seemed leaden and reluctant. Was she dead or not? She couldn't seem to move or open her eyes, but someone kept yelling her name. A rough, frightened masculine voice.

David. It had to be David.

Her heart gave a crazy little hop and she wondered when she would get to float out of her body so she could see him.

"Don't you dare leave me, Maddie Cooper," he raged. "Breathe, dammit, breathe."

It sounded like he was getting mad. She tried to obey, tried to breathe, but her lungs didn't want to expand. The languid ease of the water was gone and her back was pressed against something hard. The ground?

"I gave you my word I wouldn't let you drown," David was babbling. "And I never go back on a promise. Never. So you can't drown. Get it. You won't drown. Don't give up on me. Fight. Fight. Fight for your life."

He might have slipped a hand under her neck, but she was so numb she couldn't really tell.

"Breathe." She thought he might have been stroking her face. "Breathe."

She felt pressure against her lips. Heat against her cold flesh. Her lungs, which had been peaceful in the water, now ached and burned. She heard more sounds. A seagull's caw, a fish breaking the surface of the water, a helicopter rumbling overhead.

And she experienced the heavy rush of David's life-giving breath forcing its way into her narrowed airway. Her stomach churned. She was going to be sick.

With a sudden gasp, Maddie sat up. David rolled her onto her side and held her tenderly while she purged the seawater from her body.

"That's my girl," he soothed, gently running his fingers through her hair, stroking her forehead. "Cough it all up."

She opened her eyes and looked into his face.

Not dead. Not by half. David had given her the precious second chance she'd mourned so woefully. She was reborn.

"David," she croaked.

He clutched her to his chest, rocked her back and forth in his arms. The helicopter flew above them, blades whirling. The force of the air sent dirt and debris blowing over them. Luckily the bedsheet was so wet and tangled around her legs, that the breeze from the helicopter couldn't raise it.

Maddie tilted her head and saw it was a police chopper. Henri Gault was half hanging out the door. He waved to them.

"The cavalry is here," she whispered.

"Late as always," David murmured.

"Where's Blanco?"

"Don't know, don't care. All I care about is you." His eyes shone with the truth of his statement. His words and the concerned expression on his handsome face warmed her in the way nothing else could have.

The helicopter touched down. Henri and a Venice police officer hopped out and hurried toward them in a running crouch.

"You all right?" Henri shouted over the noisy chopper.

David nodded.

Henri pointed to the rubble of the campanile. For the first time since David hauled her from the sea, Maddie looked back at where they'd been. The sight of the demolished building struck her like a slap. If they hadn't jumped they would both be dead. No one could have survived. She gasped and David tightened his grip around her.

"From the air we could see a man crawling over the rocks," Henri said.

"It's got to be Blanco," David said.

Henri clamped a hand on his shoulder. "Relax, *mon ami*, we'll take care of this one for you."

"Thanks."

Henri and the policeman took off after Blanco and the helicopter pilot came over with blankets. David wrapped Maddie warm as a papoose and although she protested, he insisted on carrying her to the chopper, his casted wrist be damned. She wrapped her legs around his waist and allowed him to tote her like a toddler.

"There are clothes in the helicopter you could change into," the chopper pilot said in heavily accented English as he eyed their sopping wet garments. "They are costumes my wife and I wore for a Carnevale pageant this morning and I was supposed to take them back to the costume shop but didn't have time. You can wear them. I wait out here while you change inside."

"Thank you," David said.

They found the costumes, wriggled out of their wet things and into the new outfits.

"I look like Jane Austen," Maddie said.

"Lucky you. I look like Lord Dandy."

They blinked at each other. They were both wearing Regency era dress. Just like her fantasy. Maddie gulped. Stupid, stupid fantasies.

"I guess we're both lucky it's Carnevale. No one will take a second glance," she said.

"Yeah," he agreed huskily and she couldn't help but wonder if he was thinking what she was thinking. "It's better than being wet."

Henri and the policeman returned, supporting a hobbling Blanco. They loaded him onto the police boat David had shown up in and the policeman motored Blanco back to the mainland while Henri rejoined them in the chopper.

"Love the costume," Henri grinned at David as he climbed into the helicopter. "Shall we waltz?"

David shoved a hand through his hair and the shirt-sleeve brushed against his cheek. He was expected to believe manly men in the nineteenth century wore crap like this? And to think Maddie's dream proposal consisted of her beloved dressed up like a pompous ass. Women. Who could figure 'em?

"I'm grateful for your help," he growled at Henri. "So I'll ignore that comment."

"Better be nice to me. I have more news."

"News?" David tensed and leaned forward. "Good or bad?"

"Is it about my sister?" Maddie interjected.

David shot her a glance. If she didn't look so cute in that pageant dress, he would have been irritated with the interruption. Now on her, the Regency thing worked. Especially the way the cut of the dress emphasized her assets.

Henri nodded. "Your sister called in a bomb threat to the Vivaldi. At least we suspect that it was her. We traced the call and it came from Shriver's room at the Hotel Polo."

Maddie groaned and dropped her head in her hands. "Why would she call in a bomb threat?"

"To get the police to the Vivaldi in time to foil Shriver's art auction," David said.

"I don't understand. Is Cassie with Shriver or against him?" Henri asked.

"Neither do we," David muttered darkly. "Did they succeed in stopping the auction?"

"They stopped the auction," Henri confirmed.

"And they caught Shriver?" David fisted his hand and his gut clenched. Was this it then? The culmination of ten years' worth of police work. Was his dream about to come true? His hand trembled. He was that moved by the notion of finally, *finally* winning this thing.

Henri shook his head. "Shriver disappeared."

David cursed. Not again!

"But what about Cassie?" Maddie asked. "Where is she?"

"There is an all points alert out on her for calling in the bomb threat," Henri said. "No one knows where she is."

"Did the police at least nab Levy or Philpot?" David snarled.

Henri smiled. "They did even better."

"Oh, yeah?"

"They arrested both Levy and Philpot, almost a dozen collectors and they recovered seven stolen paintings including your aunt's Rembrandt."

"No kidding? They've got Aunt Caroline's Rembrandt?" David slumped against the back of his seat. Well, at least that was something. He imagined the joy on his aunt's face when he returned the painting to her and his spirits lifted. This wasn't over yet. He would get Shriver too.

"Levy brought the Rembrandt to the auction to dump it. Apparently the pressure we've been putting on him was too hot. He was desperate to ditch it."

"High five," David held up his left hand.

"You Americans with the victory celebrations." Henri grinned and smacked his palm.

"Hey, it's been a long time coming. I'm due a little victory dance."

"Not so fast, *mon ami*. I'm afraid there's more unpleasant news."

"What's that?"

"The Cézanne and the El Greco are still missing. The ones we found at the Vivaldi auction were forgeries."

David sucked in his breath. Cassie had been a busy girl. "Where are the originals?"

"That's what your supervisor wants to know," Henri said.

David swallowed. "You called Jim Barnes?"

"No, he came to Venice after receiving your telegram."

"I didn't send him a telegram."

Henri shrugged. "Someone did. And they signed your name. The telegram said you had the originals in safe-keeping."

"What? I don't have the originals!" Panic took hold of him. Calm down. Chill. You'll figure it out. You're so close to wrapping this up. Don't take a dive now. "Who could have sent Jim the telegram with my name on it? And why would... oh, shit."

His eyes met Maddie's and in unison they both exclaimed, "Cassie."

Henri went to the boat launch to meet the police and oversee Jocko Blanco's arrest. "Go on," he told David. "Find Shriver. This case belongs to you. After ten years, you deserve the win."

Leaving Henri behind, David and Maddie ran through the streets of Venice looking like a deranged Mr. Darcy and Elizabeth Bennet. If she hadn't been so worried about Cassie, Maddie might have seen the humor in the situation. As it was, she was desperately missing her half-a-heart necklace. Ever since she'd lost that necklace in Spain things had gone dramatically from bad to worse.

They zipped around the Carnevale crowd and clattered through the Piazza San Marco on the boards set out to provide a makeshift walkway for spanning the encroaching tidewater. They arrived at the Hotel Polo where Shriver and Cassie had been staying. An investigative team from Interpol was there, along with David's boss Jim Barnes, meticulously combing through Shriver's room for evidence.

"Marshall," Barnes barked, the minute he spotted David standing in the doorway.

Maddie saw David's shoulders tense and his jaw clench. "Yes, sir."

"You look like hell, man." The salt-and-pepper-haired Barnes was in his mid-fifties with a bulldog face, buzz cut and stocky build.

"Ran into a slight problem."

"I hope the other guy looks worse."

"He does, sir."

"And what's with the foppish outfit?" Barnes made a face at David's costume.

"Undercover at Carnevale," he said.

Maddie had never seen this side of David. All correct and by the book. It was a far cry from the usual loose cannon persona he wore in the field. He was a secret bad boy, she realized. Eager to please those in power, but deep down inside not really willing to let go of control for anyone.

Jim Barnes took the telegram from his pocket and handed it to David. "You want to explain this?"

Maddie hesitated in the hall behind him, her gaze trained on David's face. Would he tell his boss the truth? That he had recruited Cassie to spy on Shriver and she'd been the one to make forgeries of the paintings and hide the originals?

Would he assume responsibility for breaking all the rules and take his lumps? Or would he pretend that Cassie's accomplishments were his own and throw her sister to the wolves?

"Do you have the original Cézanne and El Greco?" Barnes asked.

Maddie closed her eyes briefly. Please, David, please, David, please say the right thing.

"Yes," David said and with that one word, he shattered all hope for their future.

Maddie opened her mouth to call him a liar, to defend her sister, but no words came out. She was too stunned to speak. Mind numb with the realization that David actually would do anything to win, no matter what the cost, she turned on her heel and stiffly walked away.

"Good job." Jim Barnes slapped him on the back. "Now bring in Shriver and Cassie Cooper and that promotion belongs to you."

"Maddie," David called out to her. "Wait a minute. I have to talk to you."

But she didn't want to hear rationalizations or excuses.

"Maddie!" David bellowed. "Stop right there."

To hell with that. She was one person he wasn't going to best. She ducked her head and ran. *I won't cry. I won't give him the satisfaction of breaking my heart.*

"Maddie, don't you dare take another step."

She flipped him the finger just before she dashed through the fire exit door and plunged down the stairs.

"Sir," David said to Jim Barnes. "I need to leave right this minute. I love that woman and I've got to straighten things out. She's misunderstood my intentions."

"Well isn't this just precious. Bullshit, Marshall. What you need to do is tell me where those paintings are."

"I don't have access to them at the moment."

"What do you mean you don't have access to them? Did you send me this telegram or not?"

"I did not."

"Then who did?" Barnes's face was a thundercloud.

"Cassie Cooper."

"Shriver's girlfriend? What's she got to do with all this?"

David blew out his breath. If Barnes got pissed, then Barnes got pissed. At this point, he didn't much care. He wasn't going to hang Cassie out to dry, no matter what Maddie believed him capable of. "She's not Shriver's girlfriend."

"What do you mean?"

"She's been working for me all along." Which was true. Cassie had been on his side whether he'd known it or not.

"You told her to call in a bomb threat?"

"I told her to do whatever she had to do to stop Shriver."

"So you went behind my back and recruited her. Just like I told you not to."

"Yes, I did. And it was a good solid plan." Until Blanco had fouled things up. "We've been working together to round up Levy and Philpot and Shriver and the stolen artwork."

"So where's the El Greco? Where's the Cézanne?"

"Cassie has placed them in a secure location."

"How do you know?" Barnes glared, his nostrils flaring.

"I just know."

"So if she's working for you, then where is she? Where's Shriver?"

"At the moment, I don't know."

"Are you sure she wasn't just scamming you, Marshall? Ever think that maybe you're the dupe?"

"I'm not a dupe."

"Bring me Shriver and those paintings, Marshall. Now. Or you're out."

"You're firing me?"

"If you go after that woman, yes. My patience with you is at an end. You've gone behind my back one time too many. Your call. Either the promotion or the boot."

David ground his teeth. He was jerked in two opposing directions. On the one hand there was his job, which was much more than just a job. It was a career. It was his identity. Once upon a time the promotion would have meant everything to him.

But now there was Maddie.

Fireworks were going off on the Grand Canal. A parade of lights on the water. A spectacle of flotillas. Maddie ran through the narrow streets along the canal not knowing where she was going, not really caring. All she wanted was to escape David and the aching pain in her heart.

She kept running until her side hurt and she couldn't

get her breath. She had trusted David and he'd betrayed her. With one bald-faced lie, he'd claimed to have the paintings and he'd taken credit for the work Cassie had done. He didn't care about her or her sister. All he cared about was winning.

Her stomach twisted in knots. A rocket exploded into ribbons of colorful light overhead. The crowd oohed and aahed.

Maddie skirted a clot of people lined along the bridge and turned down the cobblestone walkway. Glancing up, she was taken aback to see she was on the steps of the Hotel Vivaldi. The place where Shriver had held his illegal auction and Cassie had called in the bomb threat. She didn't see any policemen. Had they already cleared the robbery scene?

The crowd was on the move, trailing along the canal, following the water parade away from the Vivaldi. Within minutes, the immediate area was silent, deserted.

From her peripheral vision, Maddie caught movement in the shadows of the side street. A man and woman struggling over something.

It's none of your business, Maddie. Stay out of it.

Another rocket from the fireworks display exploded into the night sky.

The couple was silhouetted in the reflected glow and she could clearly see the man had a gun.

Maddie's heart leapfrogged into her throat.

It was Cassie and Shriver.

Years of honing her protective instincts toward her sister sent Maddie hurtling straight for them. She didn't stop to think things through. Only one thing pounded in her head—the same thought that for the past eighteen years had rarely left the forefront of her mind—save Cassie, save Cassie, save Cassie.

"Get away from my sister!" she yelled and with the intensity of a wrestler intent on full body smackdown, Maddie charged into Shriver.

And knocked him into the canal.

"What are you doing?" Cassie shrieked as Shriver disappeared into the black water.

Maddie spun around to face her sister. "Are you all right?"

"Dammit, Maddie. You've gone and screwed up everything."

"What?" Cassie was mad because she'd saved her life?

"When are you going to stop interfering?" Cassie's eyes flashed fire and she sank her hands onto her hips.

"I was just trying to help."

"Well stop it! I'm tired of you always running interference for me. You act as if I'm a child. We're not nine years old anymore and I'm not your responsibility, so leave me alone."

"But I came to Europe after you."

"No one asked you to. That's the problem. You've always just assumed it was your place to take care of me. Well, it's not."

"But you're always getting into trouble."

"Maybe that's because I've never had to suffer the consequences of my actions. You were always there to catch me if I fell, so why hold back? But guess what, Maddie? I'm tired of being the airhead sexpot. I wanted to be strong and competent and capable like you."

"But…but…" Maddie sputtered, completely taken aback. She'd had no idea Cassie felt this way. "I vowed I'd never let anything happen to you."

"Vow, vow, vow. I'm so sick of you waving that vow in my face. Know what I think about that vow, Maddie?

Here's what I think about that stupid vow of yours." Cassie ripped the half-a-heart necklace from around her throat and flung it into the canal.

"Cassie!" Maddie gasped and instantly her hand went to her own neck to finger the necklace that was no longer there.

"There! The necklace is gone. The vow is broken. You've been exonerated of all guilt. It was never your fault that I fell into that pond. It was my fault. All mine. Stop being a martyr and get a life."

"Is that what you think of me?" Maddie asked, aghast. All the times she'd resented Cassie for having to clean up her messes, Cassie had been resenting her for doing the cleanup.

"Ladies, ladies," Peyton Shriver interrupted, climbing up the side of the retaining wall with his gun pointed right at Maddie's head. "Let's not fight. Let's just go get the originals of the Cézanne and El Greco."

"I'm not afraid of you," Maddie said. "There's two of us and one of you. Your gun is wet. It probably won't fire."

"His gun might not fire," said a familiar voice from the darkness. "But mine will."

Chapter 26

David pushed upstream against the mass of costumed tourists following the fireworks water parade. He had no idea which direction Maddie had gone. Nor did he know where to start looking for Shriver, Cassie or the paintings.

He was almost back to square one. Maddie hated him. Shriver was on the lam along with the paintings and he hadn't a clue what Cassie was up to. If it weren't for Blanco, Levy and Philpot cooling their heels in jail and Aunt Caroline's Rembrandt sitting safely in the evidence room, he would feel like a total failure.

It's not over until it's over.

He wasn't out of options yet.

Pausing in the doorway of a closed shop to let the thick of the crowd pass him by, he called the police station to see if Henri was still there. The chief officer on duty told him Henri had gone to the Hotel Vivaldi. Not knowing where else to search, David decided to hook up with his Interpol counterpart and see if he had any thoughts on Shriver's possible whereabouts.

But no matter how hard he tried to concentrate on the job, he couldn't stop thinking about Maddie.

He'd known by her shocked reaction that she'd misunderstood when he'd told his boss he knew where the paintings were. He hadn't meant to usurp Cassie's victory but rather to include her as his partner.

Maddie had immediately jumped to the wrong conclusion and assumed he was taking credit for Cassie's *coup*. He didn't know why he'd phrased it the way he had unless deep down he'd been unconsciously testing her trust in him.

She'd failed miserably.

Or maybe you were the one who failed for testing her loyalty in the first place, whispered the angel on his shoulder.

David knew it was true. Maddie wasn't at fault. He was. He had to find her. He had to apologize. He couldn't lose her. He had to open up his heart and tell her how he felt. Because until he let her in, how could he expect her to trust him?

But where to look?

Muttering under his breath, he started for the Hotel Vivaldi.

Henri hadn't told him how Shriver had managed to escape when the police had busted the auction. Shriver was a slippery bastard. David couldn't count the number of times he'd almost had him and then somehow Shriver had eluded him. Ten years of chasing. Ten years of hard police work. No other art thief could rival Shriver's incredible longevity.

In fact, Shriver had only been arrested once and that was in Paris back at the beginning of his larcenous career, long before he'd scammed Aunt Caroline. Oddly enough, Henri had been the arresting officer.

Shriver had done a short stint in prison, but he must have learned a lot while he was there. He'd come out with a more sophisticated technique. He seemed to have a knack for getting into places other thieves only dreamed of. It was almost as if he had a second sense about such things. Or as if someone on the inside was feeding him security information.

How had Shriver done it? How had he, time and again, evaded capture? How had he repeatedly bested the most elaborate security systems in the world? Courting female museum employees got his foot in the door, yes, but that wasn't enough. He had to have had access to complicated codes and knowledge of tripwires and timing mechanisms and infrared sensors.

It was almost as if Shriver knew as much about the various museums as the art task divisions of the FBI or Interpol.

Then suddenly, with the shocking stab of a lightning jolt David realized something he should have realized a very long time ago.

"Henri?" Maddie stared open-mouthed at the man who stepped from the shadows with his duty weapon drawn.

"Oui." Henri gave a regretful half-smile. *"C'est moi."*

"You two are in on the heists together?" Maddie blinked as the truth slowly sank in.

"Not this time," Henri said sadly to her, then to Peyton he said, "You've been a very naughty boy. Not keeping me apprised of what you were up to. How can I help you if you don't talk to me?"

"Don't you get it? I don't want your help anymore," Shriver said hotly, his gaze locked on Henri. "I'm through. I've had enough. I want a different sort of life. The El Greco, the Cézanne, they're my ticket out of this relationship."

Henri's laugh was high-pitched, almost maniacal. "What? You leaving me for the likes of her?" He waved a hand at Cassie. "You think an airhead like her can take my place?"

"Hey!" Cassie protested.

"You always knew I liked women too," Shriver countered.

"But she's not the reason I'm leaving. I'm tired of doing all the work, living on the run while you get to sit back and play Interpol man. And I'm sick of your jealousy. It's annoying."

"Without me, you are nothing but a common criminal," Henri yelled. "I'm the one who gave you international acclaim. Alone, you couldn't break into hives."

"You two are lovers?" Cassie squealed.

"He loves me," Shriver said. "I was just in it for the art."

"You told me you loved me too!" Henri cried.

"So I lied." Shriver shrugged.

"Bitch," Henri said and shot him.

Shriver staggered backward into the canal, clutching his hand to his chest.

Maddie and Cassie shrieked and hugged each other.

Henri swung the gun around. "You two are next, but first take me to the paintings."

"It's over, Henri. Put the gun down," David's voice rang out from the bridge. Maddie swiveled her head, saw him crouched, ready to shoot.

"Not so fast, *mon ami*." Henri lunged forward, grabbed Maddie around the neck and pressed his gun against her temple.

Stunned, Maddie could only blink. This couldn't be happening. Not twice in one damned day.

"Why, Henri, why?" David asked. "You were such a good cop."

"You don't understand," Henri said and that's when Maddie realized he was crying. "I loved him. It was all for him. He craved the glamorous life. I had the power to make it happen."

"All these years, whenever I was close to catching Shriver, you were the one tipping him off."

"David, forgive me. But I loved him. Surely now that you have Maddie, you understand how that feels."

What did Henri mean? Was David in love with her? Maddie's heart thumped.

"We can work this out, Henri. Let her go. Put the gun down."

"And if I say no?"

"Then I'm going to have to kill you."

"Who cares? Without Peyton I have nothing to live for." He was sobbing so hard, he loosened his grip on Maddie.

Her mind raced. If she could shift her body just a little, get enough leverage, she could flip him over her head and into the canal.

Just as Maddie was about to make her move, there was a smashing noise behind her and Henri slumped against her, heavy as a sack of lead. The weight of him knocked her to the ground.

"Umph," she grunted as the air left her lungs and she whacked her head on the cobblestones.

When she finally stopped seeing stars, she looked up to discover Henri's prostrate body splayed across her. Above him stood Cassie triumphantly wielding a broken wine bottle left behind by some Carnevale revelers.

"That'll teach you to mess with my sister," she crowed.

"Cassie," Maddie exclaimed. "*You* saved *me*."

"I did, didn't I?" Cassie proudly puffed out her chest.

"I guess you can take care of yourself." Maddie grinned.

And then there was David, hovering over her, looking frantic and breathing hard.

"Maddie, sweetheart," he cried as he knelt to slap handcuffs on the dazed Henri and pull him off her. "Are you all right?"

"I'm fine. Thanks to Cassie."

David smiled at her sister. "Good work."

Cassie's face glowed.

"Um," Maddie said. "Shouldn't someone check on Shriver?"

Cassie peered over the edge of the canal. "He's not quite dead yet. In fact, I think he's made a miraculous recovery. If I'm not mistaken, that's him swimming off."

"Sonofabitch," David swore. "He's not getting away this time."

David ran after Shriver. When he drew abreast of him, he dived into the canal. Shriver tried to swim in the other direction but he was too exhausted.

David caught him.

He bit David's hand and tried repeatedly to kick him.

David sighed, drew back his fist and cold-cocked him. "That's for Aunt Caroline."

Shriver's head lolled back. He was out. David dragged him from the canal, handcuffed him and left him on the bank while he hurried back to check on Maddie.

Maddie and Cassie were huddled together talking sister stuff. Henri was lying where David had left him.

"Peyton is alive? Did I kill him?" he asked David.

"No."

"But how? I shot him point blank in the heart."

"Bulletproof vest. Apparently he anticipated that you would have a wicked jealous streak."

"Thank heaven, he's alive," Henri murmured.

David shook his head and crouched beside his colleague. "How did it come to this?"

"*Amour, mon ami.*" Henri sighed. "It makes you do crazy things."

Henri was right on one score. Love could make you do crazy things.

Except what David was about to do felt anything but

crazy. It might be impulsive and premature and ill-timed but nothing had ever felt so rational, so sane, so perfectly right.

It was just after midnight. He and Maddie were leaving the police station. Shriver and Henri were in jail. Cassie had retrieved the Cézanne and El Greco from the safe in his hotel room and turned them over to Jim Barnes. David still hadn't figured out how she'd managed that one. He'd gotten his promotion and he'd called his Aunt Caroline to tell her about the Rembrandt. Her tears of joy had sated the lust for justice he'd been chasing for the past ten years. He'd gotten everything he'd ever wanted.

Except for one thing.

The one thing he'd never even known he wanted, but had needed desperately.

Love.

They were still wearing the Regency costumes they'd borrowed from the helicopter pilot. They passed a gondola stand. David reached out and took Maddie's hand. "Would you like to take a gondola back to the hotel?"

She peered into his eyes and the look she gave him turned him inside out. "That would be nice," she said.

They settled into the gondola. The moon was huge. The gondolier sang a famous Italian love song. It was the most romantic damned thing he'd ever heard. A knot of emotion swelled in his chest.

Ah, crap, protested the devil on his left shoulder. *You're no good at this mushy stuff, Marshall.*

Well, advised the angel on his right, y*ou better just get used to it.*

Maddie trembled in the seat beside him.

"You're cold," he said.

"No," she denied. "Not cold."

He sucked in air.

"You're trembling too!" she exclaimed.

"Yeah."

"But you're wearing wet clothes. I'm sure you are cold."

"I am cold but that's not why I'm trembling."

"No?"

They were staring into each other's eyes, neither one daring to breathe.

And then he got down on one knee.

"What are you doing?"

"It might not be under the best of circumstances and my Mr. Darcy suit might be a bit soggy, but when else am I going to have the perfect opportunity to give you your fantasy proposal?"

"Oh, David!"

Maddie pressed a hand to her chest. If she didn't hold it down, she feared her heart might simply flutter away.

"I know we've only known each other a week. I know you're the cautious type. I know we've been through a lot of stuff and you're probably worried that the thrill of the chase is what's got me feeling this way about you."

She couldn't talk. She could only nod.

"I know we've both had a few problems with the trust issue but I think that just got resolved tonight."

"Uh-huh."

"I'm not suggesting we rush into anything. When I want something I have a tendency to just plunge right in and bluster my way through it. But I don't want to bluster my way through life with you."

"You don't?"

"You were right about me. I like to win because it means I'm in control and I mistakenly thought that if I wasn't controlling every situation that meant I was in a position of weakness. I can see now how wrong that belief is. And I've learned that there are a lot more important things than always having to win."

"You have?" she squeaked.

"Romantic sentiment doesn't come easy to me, Maddie, but dammit, I love you. And I want to marry you. We can take all the time you need. A year. Five years. Ten. Hell, if nothing else we both know I'm determined."

He was offering her the one thing she never thought she would have. For years, she'd avoided love and commitment, telling herself she could never really become involved with someone because she had to take care of her sister. But the reality was she had used Cassie as an excuse. She realized that now. She'd been hiding behind her childhood vow. Afraid of making a mistake. Afraid of getting hurt. Afraid of taking a chance on love.

"Oh, David! I love you too. So very much." Her throat clogged with happy tears. "And I don't want to wait a long time to marry you. I've waited twenty-seven years to start my life. I've been cautious and guarded and scared to trust. But I'm not afraid anymore. I might have misunderstood you at times, but you've never let me down."

Love and moonlight shone in his eyes. He looked at her as if she were the greatest prize ever to be won. "Is that a yes?" he whispered.

"Yes, yes, yes," she cried.

Then he took her into his arms and kissed her and it was as if she'd belonged there always.

Epilogue

It was turning out to be the best day of Maddie Cooper's twenty-eight-year-old life.

For one thing, she was about to be married to the sexiest, most self-confident FBI agent on earth. Her sassy twin sister Cassie, who'd become a media darling after helping mastermind the biggest art theft bust in history, was able to get off work from her new job as PR director at *Art World Today* magazine and serve as her maid of honor. Her mother and stepfather had flown in from Belize and her father had driven up from San Antonio. And David's Aunt Caroline had arrived from New York to share their special day with them.

For another thing, she and David were spending their honeymoon in Europe, seeing all the sights they'd been unable to visit on their first trip. And while they were there, David insisted she interview with a renowned track and field coach who specialized in helping retired athletes make a comeback. She was going to give the Olympics one more shot. And this time, she wasn't holding back.

She stood in front of the mirror at the church rectory in her Regency-inspired wedding dress. Her heart fluttered to think she was about to get everything she'd ever dreamed of.

"Psst."

Maddie turned her head and looked at the door. "David?"

"Yes."

"You can't see me in my dress. It's bad luck."

"I've got my eyes closed. Let me in."

"That's cheating."

"Since when is bending a few rules cheating?" He laughed.

"Oh you." She pulled open the door and he tumbled inside with his eyes squinched tightly closed. "What is it?"

"I have a present for you." He grinned. "Where are you?"

"I'm right here." She tapped him on the shoulder. "Couldn't this wait?"

"Nope." He extended a long slender jeweler's box in her direction.

"What is it?"

"Open it up and find out."

Maddie unwrapped the box. Nestled in the tissue paper was a gold heart necklace.

"David," she whispered.

"I know it can't replace the one you lost in Spain," he said. "And I couldn't find that half-a-heart design. But this is it, babe, I'm giving you all of my heart."

"And you said you weren't any good at this sentimental romantic stuff."

"Come here, you." With his eyes still tightly closed, he reached for her.

He kissed her long and hard while his hands pushed up underneath her dress. Passion swept over them and the next thing Maddie knew, they were sprawled across the window seat breaking all the rules.

Several minutes later, breathless and sated, they lay against each other, listening to their hearts thump in unison. True to his word, David's eyes were still shut.

"I love you, Maddie Cooper," he whispered.

"Soon to be Maddie Cooper Marshall," she whispered back. "And I love you too."

"Soon to be Maddie Cooper Marshall, Olympic gold medalist," he added. "Now let's go get married."

Ten minutes later, before God and their loved ones, Maddie and David vowed to love and cherish each other and they both knew that this was a vow they would happily keep forever and ever and ever.

Mission: Irresistible

To my cousin Ginna, you're the best!
Love you bunches.

To the people who painstakingly helped me brainstorm this book—Carolyn Greene, Jamie Denton, and Hebby Roman. Thank you for your high tolerance for my whining. Your insight and talent astound me.

And to my research team who came through like gangbusters—Fred and Maxine Blalock. Keep surfing the Net!

Prologue

Egypt, Valley of the Kings
Sixteen years ago

Who is my father?"

It was late. The oil lanterns burned low, casting flickering shadows against the walls of the tomb of Ramses IV. The air smelled of dirt and musty decay. Nothing met sixteen-year-old Harrison Standish's question but the sound of a shovel steadily scooping sand.

Except for the armed security guards posted outside the pyramid, he and his mother, Diana, were the only ones left at the excavation site. The rest of the archaeologists, dig workers, and college students had long ago returned to their quarters at the university compound.

They were searching for the lost grave of Ramses's oldest daughter, Kiya, and her lover, Solen, a Minoan scribe sold into slavery to the Egyptians. According to lore, Solen and Kiya had been separated by Ramses's vizier Nebamun. The Egyptian title of vizier was a very important position, administratively just under the pharaoh himself. In fact, a vizier could even be elevated to pharaoh, often by marrying into the royal family.

For his loyal service, Ramses had promised Nebamun

Kiya's hand in marriage, but when the vizier found her in Solen's arms, he poisoned them in a jealous fit of rage.

Nebamun had buried each lover separately with one-half of a magical brooch amulet in an attempt to avoid the curse Solen cast upon him with his dying breath—even though he'd been too superstitious to destroy the amulet entirely. Mythology held that if the two rings of the brooch were ever brought together again, Solen and Kiya would be reunited in the Underworld, and Nebamun's descendants would be forever damned.

For months Diana had been working from dawn until midnight. She was immersed, focused, fixated on her goal. She glanced over at Harrison. Her eyes shone with a feverish light.

He pushed his glasses up on his nose and held his breath. Would she answer him this time?

She did not. Her jaw tightened and she returned her attention to what she was doing, squatting on the ground, meticulously sifting through sand.

"Was my father Egyptian?" he asked. "Is that where I get my coloring?"

Scrape, scoop. Scrape, scoop.

"Mother?"

"He was an asshole," Diana said. "You're better off not knowing him."

"What about Adam's father?" Harrison asked, referring to his younger half brother.

"What about him?"

"How come he gets to know his dad?"

Diana groaned, rocked back on her heels, and lifted a dirt-stained hand to brush a lock of blonde hair from her forehead. "Because Tom Grayfield insisted on being part of Adam's life."

"And my father didn't insist on being part of mine?"

It was a rhetorical question. The absence of a father was explanation enough.

"No. Your father was already married. Already had a son. Although I didn't know that when I met him." The bitterness in Diana's voice echoed throughout the cloistered chamber.

"Oh."

He swallowed the ugly information. His biological father was married to a woman who wasn't his mother. His father had another son. A son he obviously liked better than he liked Harrison.

Disappointment weighted Harrison's shoulders. Slowly, he rose to his feet.

"Look, son." His mother's tone softened. "You've got to trust me. For your own good, stop asking questions."

"But I need to know the truth."

"Why?"

"Because everyone deserves to know where they come from," he said.

"Does this have something to do with your little friend Jessica? Are her hoity-toity parents refusing to let you date her because they don't know your heritage?"

His face flushed hot. He fisted his hands.

"I must be right," Diana scoffed. "You're blushing."

He did not reply. He was too angry, too frustrated, too confused. He sucked his emotions deep inside his lungs, held them down with the indrawn breath, and stared at his mother. He couldn't believe she had withheld such vital information from him for so long.

"I deserve to know. I'm sixteen now. A man."

"Okay." Diana relented after a long pause. "I'll tell you this much. Your father was born of noble blood, and he holds a very powerful position."

Harrison expelled his breath along with his emotions. He felt as drained as if he'd sprinted fifty miles without stopping.

And as empty.

"Did you ever love my father?" he asked.

Diana snorted. "Love is for suckers. What you're feeling for Jessica is nothing more than raging hormones and teenage angst. Take my advice. Forget about her. Concentrate on your work, your schooling. Science will free your mind. Not love."

It was as if his mother had sliced open his head, peered inside his brain, and voiced his greatest fear out loud. He loved Jessica with an intensity that scared him, but he didn't like out-of-control feelings. They clouded a man's reason, and he thought of himself as a reasonable man.

But his heart refused to stay silent. Something unexpected inside him rebelled against logic. Something wild and scary and exhilarating.

"You're wrong. I love Jessica, and she loves me."

Diana shook her head. "My poor, naive boy."

"If you don't believe in love, then how come you've spent your entire life searching for Kiya and Solen to prove the legend of the star-crossed lovers?"

"Is that what you think we've been doing?" She looked surprised.

He shrugged. "What else?"

"Harrison, all these years I've been trying to *disprove* the legend."

"I don't understand." He frowned. For as long as he could remember, his mother had been consumed by the story. How could he have been so mistaken about her motives?

"Haven't you been listening?" Diana clicked her tongue. "There's no such thing as soul mates and undying love. No such thing as love at first sight, or even second sight, for that matter. It's all romantic bullshit concocted to entertain the masses. When we find Solen and Kiya and join the two pieces of their amulet together again, absolutely nothing is going to happen."

He blinked at her, incredulous. "You dragged Adam and me to Egypt when we could be having a normal life, staying in one place, making friends, all to prove nothing?"

"Exactly! Now you understand."

"Nihilism. How Nietzsche of you, Mother."

"Don't get smart."

"Why not? Apparently intelligence is the only quality you value." Harrison pivoted on his heel and stalked toward the exit.

"Where are you going?"

"Back to the campus. To see Jessica. To tell her how much I love her. Because I'm not bitter like you. I do believe in the legend of the star-crossed lovers. I do believe in love."

"Don't do it, Harrison. It's a mistake," she called after him, but he just kept marching.

Tonight he would take a chance. He would give Jessica the promise ring he'd been carrying in his pocket for three weeks. Waiting for the courage to speak what was in his heart.

In the illumination from the fat yellow full moon high in the velvet-black sky, he rode his bicycle into town. His stomach was in his throat. He wanted this. He did, he did. He was no longer afraid.

I love you, Jessica.

Thirty minutes later, he pedaled through the gates of the university, his pulse pounding in his ears. He parked his bike in front of the girls' dormitory.

He intended to sneak around the side of the building and throw pebbles at her window to wake her up, the way guys did in romantic movies. He stuck his hand in his pocket, fisted his fingers around the delicate promise ring. The smooth feel of it gave him courage.

Jessica, Jessica, Jessica.

He started across the veranda, but then he spied a couple locked in an embrace on the porch swing. He shuffled to the right, giving them a wide berth, but a familiar scent caught his attention and stopped him in midstep.

Cherry blossom cologne. Jessica's signature scent.

He froze, rooted to the spot, to that horrible moment in time. Harrison stared while the young lovers kissed.

They must have sensed his presence, because they raised their heads, and in the bright moonlight he saw clearly the thing he most did not want to see.

Jessica in the arms of another guy.

And not just any guy, but his half brother, Adam.

The emotions were too much to handle. Betrayal, anger, disappointment, bitterness.

He shut down his feelings. Shut down his heart and stalked away.

"Harrison, wait," Adam cried out. "It's not what you think."

But it was. They both knew it.

At that moment Harrison realized his hand was still clenched around the promise ring. With a curse, he pulled it from his pocket and flung it into the darkness.

Mother had been right all along.

Love was for suckers.

Chapter 1

No question about it. The mummy was following her.

Cassie Cooper slipped past King Tut, who was chatting up Nefertiti beside the lavish hors d'oeuvre table, and cast a surreptitious glance over her shoulder.

Yep.

There he was. Peeking from behind the Sphinx's chipped nose, his mysterious dark eyes following her as she meandered around the main exhibit hall of the Kimbell Art Museum.

Stifling a triumphant grin, she readjusted her Cleopatra Queen of the Nile headdress, which kept slipping down on her forehead and mussing up her wig. Just to tease, she moistened her lips with the tip of her tongue.

Who was lurking beneath the swaddling linen?

Her pulse quickened. She had a lot of admirers. No telling who was in the costume.

Maybe it was an old flame. Maybe a new one. Maybe it was even a stranger.

Goose bumps dotted the nape of her neck.

A mystery. How exciting.

Don't let yourself get diverted. Forget the distractions; you've got a job to do.

The voice inside her head sounded exactly like her straight-arrow twin, Maddie.

Cassie sighed in wistful longing. Apparently she missed her sister's lovable nagging so much that her own conscience had taken over the job. She was happy Maddie had married her true love, hunky FBI agent David Marshall. What she wasn't so thrilled about was David's getting promoted and dragging Maddie off to live in the urban wilds of Washington, D.C.

Focus on your goal.

Okay. All right. She was focusing.

Cassie turned her back on the mummy and managed to tamp her libido down a smidgen. If she had any hope of landing her dream job in the public relations department of the Smithsonian, she would have to make sure this charity masquerade to promote the legend of the star-crossed Egyptian lovers exhibit went off without a glitch.

After getting laid off as the PR director for *Art World Today* magazine four months ago, she'd been grateful just to get her old job back at the Kimbell, but now her wanderlust had kicked up again. She was hungering for something new and different. Cassie wanted the change not only because bagging the Smithsonian represented the pinnacle of her career, but also because she would get to live near her twin again.

Unfortunately, achieving her dream job would require a glowing recommendation from her new boss, Phyllis Lambert. And old Prune Face was not her greatest fan. In fact, if Cassie hadn't been instrumental in helping capture the charming art thief who had robbed the Kimbell the previous year, she knew Lambert would have convinced the board of directors to show her the door.

She must perform flawlessly. All she had to do was keep her mind off Mummy Man and firmly fixed where it belonged.

On the party.

With a discerning eye, she assessed the room. Exotic Egyptian music trickled through the state-of-the-art surround sound system. Large navy blue banners with ivory lettering adorned the walls of the exhibit hall. Underneath the lettering on each banner was the amulet's double-ring emblem, encircling an embossed silhouette of two lovers kissing beneath a blanket of golden stars.

"UNDYING LOVE," declared the banner along the north wall. "INTRIGUE" bordered the south. "DANGER" flanked the west. "BETRAYAL" along the east wall, completed the quadrangle.

Tuxedoed waiters moved throughout the assembly carrying trays of champagne. Armed security guards manned the exits. Caterers dished up bacon-wrapped water chestnuts, assorted puff pastries, grilled prawns, Russian caviar, and the finest pâté.

Cassie had spared no expense. A hundred patrons of the arts had shelled out a thousand dollars apiece to witness the reunion of the ill-fated lovers separated in death for the past three thousand years.

Great. Perfect. Everything was running like a precision Swiss timepiece as they anticipated the arrival of the guest of honor, the illustrious Dr. Adam Grayfield from Crete, who was bringing with him Solen's portion of the exhibit.

Until then, Cassie found her concentration drawn irresistibly over her shoulder again. She scanned the guests, searching for the mummy.

Impromptu romance had landed her in trouble more times than she cared to count, but she couldn't seem to help herself when it came to the first rich blush of potential amour.

Putting an extra wiggle into her walk just in case the mummy happened to be watching, Cassie sashayed over to where several high-profile patrons, an eminent Egyptian from the Ministry of Antiquities, and various members of the press were clustered around a red velvet cordon. They were oohing and aahing over the feminine segment of the main attraction.

Princess Kiya's sarcophagus and the section of amulet found among her artifacts.

The amulet, displayed on black velvet draped over a granite pedestal, was nothing spectacular to look at. After all the fanfare, seeing the amulet in person was a bit of a letdown. The talisman was a simple half-dollar-sized copper brooch, and there was a small jagged tear in the pliable metal ring where a second circle had long ago been ripped away.

Kiya was patiently awaiting the return of her Minoan lover, Solen.

Tenderness clutched Cassie's heart. Damn, she was a sucker for romance. But secretly, while at the same time she dreamed of finding her own true love, deep down she was conflicted about the reality of such intimacy. The whole one-man-for-the-rest-of-your-life thing gave her the heebie-jeebies. For crying out loud, how did a girl ever know for sure if the grass wasn't greener in another pasture?

From her peripheral vision she caught furtive movement through the crowd. The mummy was creeping closer. He was most definitely following her. He edged around a collection of canopic jars before ducking behind a guy in a hawk mask dressed as Horus the Sky God.

Aw, he was shy. How sweet.

She was normally attracted to bold, daring types, but there was something about shy guys that made her feel all soft and squooshy and maternal inside.

Face it, Cassie, Maddie's voice teased inside her head. *You have a talent for finding something to like about any member of the opposite sex.*

True enough. She did love men.

Well, except maybe for the annoying Dr. Harrison Standish skulking at the back of the room. He was petulantly tossing from palm to palm that odd miniature replica of an ancient Egyptian battery that he always carried with him. She tilted her head and met his gaze. He glowered at her through the smudged lenses of his round, dark-framed glasses.

Dr. Standoffish. That was what Cassie called him behind his back.

The truth was, the guy intimidated her with his intellect. He was a Rhodes scholar, and he used so many big words, she often felt the need to lug a dictionary around with her just so she could figure out what he was saying.

Harrison had arrived from Egypt the previous Monday with Princess Kiya and her artifacts in tow, giving Cassie dark and brooding looks right from the beginning. Two years ago he had resurrected Ramses IV's oldest daughter in the Valley of the Kings, and ever since then he had been diligently searching for her eternal soul mate, Solen.

But Dr. Adam Grayfield had beaten Standoffish to the punch. Harrison had to be irked over Dr. Grayfield's coup d'état. Perhaps that was why he was so pissy.

Standoffish was younger than she had expected. His youthful face placed him in his early thirties, but still, he seemed much older. Stodgy. Set in his ways.

And Cassie was stuck with him.

He was the sole reason the Egyptian government had allowed the exhibit into the United States. The Kimbell had gotten lucky because Standish was a Fort Worth native, and he'd chosen to host the exhibit in his hometown.

Cassie and the obstinate Egyptologist had had several heated disagreements over the publicity of the star-crossed lovers. She'd had to remind him on more than one occasion of the politics of economics. If he wanted more grant money for his digs, then, like it or not, Harrison would have to play footsie with both the media and the museum's benevolent benefactors. You'd think after so many years in the archaeology game, the guy would have already bought a clue or two.

They'd also argued over his refusal to wear a costume for the masquerade party.

The spoilsport.

Cassie might have won the publicity war, but Standish had triumphed in the costume department. As usual, his dark hair was disheveled, looking as if he'd combed the unruly locks with a tuning fork.

He was attired in his quintessential nerdy professor clothes. Rumpled orange-and-white-striped shirt, hideous purple tweed jacket with worn leather elbow patches, a god-awful chartreuse bow tie, and five-pocket, pleated, baggy khaki Dockers. Hadn't anyone ever told him that pleats were out, out, out?

And omigosh!

She just now noticed he was wearing one brown tasseled loafer and one black one. The clueless guy had to be either color-blind or severely fashion-impaired.

Or both.

What a geek.

Cringing, Cassie rolled her eyes and prayed that no one else had noticed. He was destroying the exotic atmosphere of ancient Egypt she'd worked so hard to re-create.

His gaze held hers, and Cassie forced herself not to glance away. She didn't exactly know why, but something about the man made her jittery. Maybe it was the way he habitually handled that toy of his. Or perhaps it was because he seemed immune to her charms. She was accustomed to batting her eyelashes, crooking her little finger, and having men fall at her feet.

But not this dude. He just kept scowling and tossing that stupid artifact reproduction.

Did he want a staring contest? Was that the deal? Oh, he had sure picked the wrong gal for that. She was the master of the staredown. The only one who could trump her was Maddie.

Let's have a go at it, Poindexter. Cassie narrowed her eyes and sank her hands onto her hips.

He didn't blink.

Neither did Cassie.

She'd heard Standish was known as old Poker Face around the digs, but she wasn't intimidated. The game was on.

He narrowed his eyes.

She responded in kind.

One minute passed.

Two.

Then three.

Okay, now she'd see how he responded under pressure. She stuck out her tongue.

Real mature. He cabled the message with his eyes and didn't crack a smile. Apparently he wasn't going to let the sight of her tongue unnerve him.

She laughed, flipped her straight dark wig over her shoulder, and gave him a quick flash of her natural blonde hair beneath. The peekaboo was no accident. His face flushed as if he was having thoughts he had no business entertaining.

"Ahem." Phyllis Lambert cleared her throat. The middle-aged curator was also dressed as Cleopatra, but Phyllis didn't possess the pizzazz to pull it off.

"Uh-huh," Cassie mumbled without glancing over at her boss. She didn't want to break eye contact with Standoffish and default the game.

"If you're all done exchanging meaningful glances with Dr. Standish, might I have a word with you, Cassandra?"

Meaningful glances? As if!

First off, she wouldn't be caught dead flirting with a pointy-headed intellectual like Einstein Poindexter Standoffish. Second, before Cassie could ever successfully flirt with him, he would have to read the comprehensive volume of *Flirting for Dummies* cover to cover.

Twice.

From what she had seen of Standoffish so far, the dude possessed few social skills and zero talent for coquetry.

"Cassandra," Lambert repeated.

No one except the annoying curator ever called her by her given name. Not even her own mother when she was displeased with her.

Cassie directed her gaze to the potato-chip-thin woman who wore too much makeup and not enough clothing. Powder foundation had settled into the numerous wrinkles lining her disapproving mouth. The air-conditioning was cranked a couple of degrees too low, providing indisputable evidence that the fifty-something Lambert wasn't wearing a bra under her flimsy white gown.

Not that her "girls" needed a harness, but barf, this was

a classy event. At the very least, a couple of strategically placed Band-Aids were in order.

Be nice. Lambert has the power to make all your dreams come true.

Or crush them into dust.

Cassie forced a smile and ignored both the curator's comment about exchanging meaningful glances with Dr. Standish and her unbound ta-tas.

"How may I help you, Phyllis?"

Lambert pursed her lips and tapped the face of her wristwatch. "The presentation starts at eight o'clock. It's now fifteen minutes until the hour, and there's no sign of Dr. Grayfield. Have you heard from him?"

Seven-forty-five. Really? Time flew when you were being shadowed by a mysterious mummy.

Cassie frowned. Where *was* Adam?

He had called her from New York the previous afternoon, promising that he and Solen would arrive at the Kimbell with plenty of time to set up for the reunification ceremony. Even if Dr. Grayfield appeared right now, fifteen minutes wasn't nearly enough time to get things set up and rolling.

She had offered to send a car and an assistant to help him unload the crate at DFW Airport, but Adam had refused. For the sake of secrecy, he'd insisted on handling the details himself. Because she was a big fan of the dramatic, Cassie had acquiesced. In retrospect, it wasn't such a hot idea.

Had something happened to him? Could he have been robbed? Accosted? Worse?

Anxiety clutched her, but then she blew out her breath and brushed her fears aside. Her twin sister, Maddie, was the worrywart, not she.

Everything would be fine.

Adam would show. No doubt he just wanted to make a grand entrance. And who could blame him? He had a big surprise in store. Imagine being the first person ever to decipher the hieroglyphs of the ancient Minoans, on top of discovering the lost tomb of Kiya's beloved Solen.

Cassie felt especially honored because she was the only one Adam had told about the hieroglyphs. He'd said it was on a need-to-know basis, and because she was in charge of the party, she was the only one who needed to know in advance that he had an addition to the program. He'd sworn her to secrecy. Which wasn't a problem. She liked being in on secrets.

From over Phyllis's shoulder, Cassie spied the mummy again. He was waving, trying to get her attention. When his dark, enigmatic eyes met hers, he inclined his head toward the exit door leading to the garden courtyard. Was he telling her to meet him outside?

A sudden thought occurred. Could Adam Grayfield be the mummy? He'd told her he would be wearing a special costume. Was he playing flirtatious games with her? Or did he have an urgent message to relay?

"Well?" Phyllis demanded.

"Hmm?"

"Have you heard from Dr. Grayfield or not?"

No point putting the woman in a snit before there was something to snit about. "I heard from Adam." *Last night*, Cassie mentally added. "Everything is on schedule."

"He better be here by eight." Phyllis tapped her watch again. "Because if anything goes wrong tonight—"

"Nothing," Cassie interrupted the curator, "is going to go wrong."

"Then do me a favor and put my mind at ease. Locate Dr. Grayfield."

"Okay, fine."

Jeez Louise, don't get your panties in a bunch.

"Go. Now." Phyllis made shooing motions.

"I'm going, I'm going."

Cassie started after her purse, where she'd stashed her address book. She had taken only a couple of steps before Lambert dropped the nuclear bomb.

"Oh, and Cassandra," Phyllis called after her.

Cassie forced herself not to sigh. She turned around and plastered a perky smile on her face. "Yes, Phyllis?"

"If you return without Dr. Grayfield and the remainder of the exhibit, you can kiss your coveted recommendation to the Smithsonian good-bye."

Chapter 2

Dr. Harrison Standish hated parties.

No, *hated* was too mild a word. He loathed them, despised them, abhorred them. He would rather have a root canal, a major tax audit, and a prostate exam—all on the same morning—than attend one of these exorbitantly expensive, butt-kissing cultural affairs.

He'd already scoped out every exit so he could make a quick and clean getaway as soon as feasibly possible. He never went anywhere without an escape route mapped out.

Worst of all, it was a masquerade party. How pathetic—a group of grown people dressing up in silly costumes, pretending to be some ridiculous characters from history or literature. And as the icing on the cake, there in the center of the room, glomming on to attention, was the flamboyant Cassie Cooper. Looking as if she owned the world in her regal Cleopatra costume, heavy eyeliner, and thick dark wig. The kohl made her big eyes look even wider than they were, emphasizing that compellingly innocent-yet-naughty quality of hers.

Harrison was irritated with himself because each time she sashayed by, every intelligent thought bounced right out of his head, to be replaced by a drooling, Cro-Magnon, monosyllabic beat.

Me want.

This wasn't like him at all, dammit. But whenever Cassie appeared he could not seem to stop himself from fantasizing about her. And he hated his unexpected weakness almost as much as he hated this party.

He had to stop thinking about her because she was, quite frankly, the most mesmerizing yet infuriating woman he had ever met. He could not afford the luxury of falling under her spell. However, it was far more than her fair complexion, light-colored eyes, and voluptuous figure that drove him around the bend.

Her scattered thought processes made no rational sense. Just when he thought he had her figured out, she would do something totally illogical. Harrison suspected the woman possessed a serious case of adult attention deficit disorder.

She strutted across the room, hips swaying with primal rhythm. In his head he heard the hissing whispery sound of metallic brushes whisking over brass cymbals, reverberating with each roll of her fabulous ass. *Tss-tta-tss-tta-tss.*

A guy could get whiplash from watching her.

The woman was nimble. He would give her that. She was Lepidoptera *Danaus plexippus*, flashy, colorful, flitting from flower to flower. Here, there, everywhere. Never lingering in one place, always on the move.

Working with her over the course of the past nine days had been a royal pain in the butt. Whenever she wanted to get her way on an issue, she would ply her womanly wiles. Flirting, teasing, cajoling.

Harrison had pretended to be underwhelmed by her charms, even though he was as bedazzled as the stammering college students helping them set up the exhibit. But he refused to let her know the extent of her power over him. He'd learned from hard experience you couldn't trust lust.

Face it, Standish, it's just been too long since you've had sex.

The pressure of celibacy, that's all this was. Because he and Cassie were total opposites in every way imaginable. She was a bubbly optimist. He was an eternal pessimist. She was sensual. He was cerebral. She was a romantic. He was a cynic. She was laid-back. He was tense. She sought the silver lining. He was always waiting for the other shoe to fall. And whenever he looked into her eyes, he could tell exactly what she was thinking.

Nerd. Dork. Geek.

Harrison knew, without a word being said, what kind of man she normally went for. Suave, debonair, charming dudes with expensive sports cars, ostentatious wardrobes, and toothpaste-commercial smiles.

Guys like his devilish half brother, Adam. Who upstaged him at every turn. The way she had gone on and on and on all week, chattering about how excited she was that Dr. Grayfield was coming to the Kimbell, really stuck in his craw. What was he? Chop suey? He was so irritated by her obvious adoration of Adam that he hadn't even told her they were brothers.

Harrison ground his teeth. He was trying to suck up his disappointment and be the bigger person. So what if Cassie seemed enamored of his half brother? So what if Adam had found Solen before he did? No big deal. Adam and his gregarious personality had been able to raise the financial backing while introverted Harrison had not.

Story of his life.

But he was suspicious of his brother's financial support. Although Adam's father, Ambassador Tom Grayfield, was rich, Adam, forever the rebel, raised his own money so he wouldn't have to do things his father's way. In the past, Adam hadn't been too choosy about where he got his funding, often running afoul of loan sharks and other unsavory characters.

Harrison would hate to see his younger brother in trouble again. Because as much as they disagreed, they did share an unbreakable bond. They'd both survived a nomadic childhood with Diana Standish.

Besides, he didn't care about the fame that came with finding Solen. The discovery was what mattered. Not their sibling rivalry.

Where was his brother, by the way?

He glanced around the room. Adam should be making his grand entrance anytime now. He was all about grand entrances and grand gestures and grand romances that flared hot but never lasted.

All style and no substance. Come to think of it, Adam was essentially a masculine version of Cassie Cooper.

Harrison snorted. What a spectacular pair those two would make.

The yin and yang of glitz and flash. If Adam and Cassie ever hooked up, it would be like spring break, New Year's Eve, and Mardi Gras all rolled into one. Of course, when reality reared its inevitable head, bye-bye hot tryst. Neither one of them had the staying power for cleanup after the party was over.

"Excuse me, young man," said an elderly woman with an Isis headdress. She was peering at the display of an ancient Egyptian battery found in Kiya's tomb. "Do you know what this is?"

"It's called a *tet* or a *djed*." He pointed to the label mounted on a plaque above the display. "A wireless battery."

"They had batteries in ancient Egypt?"

"Yes, ma'am, they did."

"What did they use them for?"

"We don't know for sure, although there's a lot of speculation. Some believe it was for religious rituals, others think it was used for medicinal purposes."

"Really?"

Harrison's personal theory was that the ancient Egyptians used the djed as a transmitter of electromagnetic waves. He'd been very excited about finding one in Kiya's tomb and had even constructed a miniature replica of his own so he could test his theories. "Would you like to see a reproduction?"

"Why, yes." The aged Isis peered at him curiously as Harrison placed his homemade djed in her hand.

"It has a bit of a phallic appearance, doesn't it?" Isis ran her hand along the tube.

"Uh, yes, ma'am."

The woman gave it back to him and winked. "Very interesting."

He pocketed the djed and decided to move away from the exhibit to forestall future questioning. He strolled over to the central display, eyeing Kiya's sarcophagus and the amulet. Ahmose Akvar, exalted son of a former Egyptian prime minister and himself a high-ranking official with the Ministry of Antiquities, moved to stand beside him.

Ahmose wasn't much older than Harrison, and while they possessed similar olive-toned complexions and were about the same height and build, the resemblance ended there. The Egyptian's features were much more patrician than Harrison's, and he wore tailor-made silk suits and expensive Italian shoes. Ahmose was there to make certain nothing happened to Kiya. Over the years, many precious relics had been stolen from the Valley of the Kings, and the Ministry of Antiquities took their artifacts very seriously.

Ahmose shook his head. "You know, Dr. Standish, I am worried about the lax security."

"Lax security? There are armed security guards posted at every exit."

"Yes, but I did not realize the amulet would be displayed right out in the open. It should be in a locked case."

Harrison had similar reservations concerning the display, but Cassie had insisted that the guests, who had paid an excessive amount of money to attend the event, would demand to see the amulet without the restriction of a locked case. Against his better judgment, he'd allowed her to have her way, simply so he wouldn't have to watch her lips plump up in a pout. Those pouty lips clouded his reason every single time.

God, he was a fool.

"As you know," Ahmose said, "I've never approved of reuniting the star-crossed lovers. What if something unexpected occurs?" The Egyptian's English was flawless. He held a bachelor's degree from Harvard and a master's from Oxford.

"Don't worry. It's just a myth. There's no magic, no charm, no curse. Nothing to be afraid of."

The furrow in Ahmose's otherwise smooth brow deepened the longer he stared at Kiya's sarcophagus. "There are more things in heaven and earth than mortal man understands, my friend."

Terrific, here was another gullible believer in that idiotic star-crossed lovers legend. "I didn't realize you were such a sentimentalist, Ahmose."

"You do not know everything there is to know about me, Dr. Standish."

Apparently not. Harrison had presumed that Ahmose was a man of science. Instead, he had just discovered he was as susceptible to the ludicrous fairy tale as everyone else.

"No need for alarm," he reassured the Egyptian. "Everything is under control."

Well, except for the small detail that his brother had yet to show up with Solen's remains for the reunification ceremony. What was taking Adam so long?

Ahmose glowered. "For your sake I hope you are correct, Dr. Standish."

"That sounds like a threat. Are you threatening me, Ahmose?" Harrison squared his shoulders.

"It is not a threat. It is a guarantee. If anything happens to the amulet, the djed, or any of Kiya's artifacts, your visa will be rescinded and you will never again be allowed inside Egypt."

Alarm shot through him. Surely Ahmose couldn't be serious about this.

"Nothing's going to happen," Harrison reiterated.

Why was Ahmose acting so strangely? He wasn't by nature a dramatic man. Usually the Egyptian was quite reserved. His dark mood seemed infectious. The crowd shifted restlessly. People peered at their watches and mumbled negative comments.

"Dr. Standish?"

Harrison glanced over to see one of the young college students who had spent the past week helping him and Cassie assemble the exhibits. The lanky kid's name was Gabriel Martinez, and he had a rare enthusiasm for archaeology. Harrison had considered inviting the young student to participate in his next dig.

"Yes?"

"A man asked me to hand this to you." Gabriel passed him a white business-sized envelope with Harrison's name printed in block lettering. It looked like Adam's handwriting.

"What man?"

"That dude over there." Gabriel pointed.

"Where?" Harrison squinted at the crowd.

"In the Indiana Jones hat."

The Indy hat stood out among the cluster of Egyptian headdresses. Immediately, Harrison knew whose head was under it, because he'd been there when his brother had bought the hat on a trip to London.

But Adam wasn't hanging around. He was headed for the front entrance at a fast clip.

Where was he going?

Clutching the envelope Gabriel had slipped him, Harrison jostled through the throng. He didn't want to shout and attract undue attention, but he didn't want Adam to get away either.

"Excuse me," he apologized as he careened into Isis, whose oversized headdress bobbled precariously. He'd had his gaze so fixed on keeping the Indiana Jones hat in sight that he hadn't seen her meander into his path. He zigzagged around her, just as the moving Indy hat reached the foyer.

The crowd was even thicker here because this area was much smaller than the main part of the exhibit hall. He had to move quickly, or his brother was going to disappear. To hell with his dislike for drawing attention to himself.

"Adam!" he called.

People turned to stare. Harrison pretended not to

care that he was being watched. He had never been a center-stage sort of guy, and collecting stares made him uncomfortable.

The front door opened.

"Wait!"

The hat disappeared and the door clicked shut.

Harrison was still a good twenty feet and twenty people from the entrance. What parlor game was his brother playing? From the time they were small kids, Adam had had a penchant for pirate treasure maps and secret spy codes and fantasy role-playing.

His fondness for outlandish pranks and schemes lasted into adulthood and frequently plunged him into trouble. One year, when they were collage students on a dig site in Peru, Adam had cooked up a scheme to fake a famous religious artifact. It had started out as a joke. He'd never meant for people to take it seriously.

For several days he was touted in the media. He achieved instant celebrity status and actually started to believe he'd honestly found a real artifact. He had a way of buying into his own bullshit. When the artifact was proved a fraud and Adam found himself threatened with legal action, Tom Grayfield rushed in, threw his money around, and hushed everything up.

Adam had confessed to Harrison that those few days of notoriety had been well worth the ass-chewing he'd received from his old man.

Was his brother up to his old tricks? Could he have faked Solen's discovery? But that was impossible. Solen's tomb had been authenticated by highly trained specialists. Experts Harrison knew and trusted. Still, he wouldn't put it past his brother to pull some crazy publicity stunt.

He reached the door, pushed through it, and ended up

on the sidewalk outside the main entrance of the Kimbell. The streetlamps glinted off the smudged lenses of his glasses and the reflected glare blocked his view.

He whipped off his glasses and wiped them on his shirttail. One of these days he was going to have laser eye surgery and throw the damned spectacles away forever. His brother had been nagging him to do it for years. Adam was fond of saying, "Girls don't make passes at guys who wear glasses."

Still rubbing his lenses, he squinted into the darkness. The grounds were empty. The street was deserted except for a nondescript white delivery van parked at the corner. No one else was around.

Adam had vanished.

Where'd he go?

He heard the roar of a motorcycle engine, and just then a souped-up Harley, customized with lots of chrome and specialty tires, zipped around the corner. The powerful machine buzzed past him on the street, Indiana Jones seated behind the handlebars.

Quickly jamming his glasses back on, Harrison waved his arms. "Adam!"

His brother never glanced back.

The balmy April night air greeted Cassie as the double-glass door snapped closed behind her, muting the laughter and voices from inside the museum. Suddenly, she felt very far away.

Isolated. Alone.

Tingles skated up her spine.

Her breath came in short, raspy gasps. Anticipation escalated her excitement. She looked right, then left. Where had the mummy gone?

Maybe she'd misunderstood his intentions. Maybe he'd been signaling to someone else. Nah. She knew when a guy was sending signals. And the mummy had been telegraphing her big-time. Who was he?

Old boyfriend? New boyfriend? Friend? Lover? Enemy? Adam Grayfield?

The suspense was excruciating. And totally irresistible.

Ambient lighting from quaint low-voltage streetlamps illuminated the courtyard. Well-manicured trees and dense shrubbery cast dark shadows over the walkway.

"Yoo-hoo." Cassie wandered around the maze of chest-high bushes. "Anybody here?"

No sound except for the echo of her high-heeled sandals clicking against the flagstones.

What if Adam *was* the mummy? What if he needed to tell her something important about the exhibit? What if someone had been following him, and he had dressed up like an extra from an old Hammer Films horror movie so he wouldn't be recognized?

"Don't be silly," she growled under her breath and plopped down on a stone bench. More than likely the mummy was just teasing her, heating things up a notch, escalating their flirtation. "Everything is just fine."

To prove it, she would call Adam right now. She took her cell phone from her purse, along with a tin of cinnamon Altoids and her address book. She looked up his number, punched it in, and then popped one of the curiously strong breath mints.

The phone rang. Once, twice, three times.

"Come on, Adam," she muttered. "Pick up the phone. Lambert's looking to serve my behind on a platter over you."

When his voice mail answered after the tenth ring, Cassie sighed and switched off the phone without leaving a message. She stuffed the cell back into her purse and crunched the remainder of the cool cinnamon mint between her teeth.

A rustling noise emanated from the bushes behind her. Her stomach nose-dived. She turned her head and saw the mummy silhouetted in the light.

"Hello?"

He shuffled toward her.

"Adam?" She stood, dropping her purse on the ground beside the stone bench. "Is that you?"

He nodded, or at least she thought he did. His head barely moved, but she could have sworn it was a nod.

"What is it? Is something wrong?"

He made a rough, gurgling sound.

Cassie sank her hands onto her hips. "I have to tell you, this isn't earning brownie points with me. Everyone is waiting for you inside the museum."

He lumbered closer, his hands outstretched, reaching for her. He mumbled something indecipherable in a foreign language. She was fluent in Spanish, but he certainly wasn't speaking that. Neither was he muttering French or Portuguese. Greek? Latin?

"Adam," she repeated. "Is that you?"

Maybe she'd made a boo-boo and this wasn't him after all. She'd never met Adam in person.

"Beware...," he whispered hoarsely, and then he started coughing.

"Are you okay?" She took a step toward him. "Do you need a glass of water?"

"Beware..." He raised a linen-wrapped hand to his throat and coughed again.

"Beware of what? Dry crackers?"

He repeated the foreign phrase.

She strained to listen. If she squinted real hard and turned her head in his direction, it sort of sounded like he was saying, "Wannamakemecomealot."

"Pardon?"

"Wannamakemecomealot."

"Oh, I get it, you're flirting with me." She grinned.

During their numerous transatlantic telephone conversations over the course of the past few weeks, as they made preparations for the exhibition, Cassie had nonchalantly let it slip that she adored surprises and fantasy role-playing games. Perhaps Adam had taken her suggestive comments to heart and decided to use the occasion of their first face-to-face meeting as an opportunity to seduce her.

Too fun.

"Let me guess. You're pretending we're in jeopardy. Bad guys are after us. Danger heightens the sexual attraction," she said. "It's a good game. You really had me going there for a minute."

He drew in another gurgling breath. He was doing a great job of sounding creepy.

"Is it the vizier's men? Are we pretending to be Kiya and Solen? Are they after us?"

"Beware of the . . ." He wavered on his feet, just inches from her.

Was he drunk? She hoped he wasn't drunk. She didn't like drunks.

"Spit it out, man. Stop being so cryptic. I know it's a game, but I can't get into it if you don't move things along. I have a short attention span. Everybody says so. Beware of what?"

But he didn't answer.

Wait a minute. Something wasn't right.

Ever since her near-drowning accident as a kid when

she had spent three months in a coma, she occasionally experienced a weird sort of hotness at the very base of her brain. The sensation almost always preceded an unexpected turn of events. And right now her medulla oblongata was sizzling like skillet bacon.

Her nerve endings scorched a heated path from the nape of her neck to the tips of her ears. Burning, tingling, stinging.

Run, leave, get out of here.

Suddenly, the mummy pitched forward and Cassie thrust out her arms to catch him before he smashed face-first onto the stone walkway.

And that's when she saw the wicked, black-handled paring knife protruding from his back.

Chapter 3

An ominous feeling swept over Harrison. Something wasn't right, but he had no idea what was going on.

Stay calm, stay cool, stay detached from your feelings. He repeated his life mantra and exhaled slowly. Gradually his sense of dread abated.

That's when he realized he was still clutching the envelope Gabriel had given him. He ripped the flap open and dumped the contents into his palm. For some strange reason, he had expected to see Solen's half of the amulet. Instead, he was puzzled to find an airport baggage claim ticket.

Huh?

What was his brother trying to tell him? Why had he given the envelope to Gabriel rather than delivering it himself? What did the ticket mean? Had Adam left Solen and his artifacts in baggage claim at the DFW airport?

But why?

Considering Adam's look-at-me personality, whipping up an elaborate exploitation of the reunification ceremony was not a far-fetched notion. Harrison had a flash of insight. Although Adam claimed to believe wholeheartedly in the legend of the star-crossed lovers, his innate fear of ending up with egg on his face like Geraldo Rivera with Al Capone's empty safe could explain his motives. Adam would have to make sure *something* happened when the pieces of the amulet were joined together.

Harrison pulled out his cell phone. He hadn't talked to his brother in so long he'd forgotten his number, and it took him several seconds to remember it. Adam's voice mail answered, and Harrison left a message for him to call ASAP.

He wondered when Cassie had last heard from his brother and decided to go ask her. On the way to the courtyard, he palmed the ticket into his jacket pocket. He shouldered past King Tut, who was lip-locking Nefertiti behind a replica of a Minoan sailing ship from 1100 BC, and moved toward the side entrance.

He stopped with his hand on the exit door. Did he really want to meander into the courtyard and find Cassie in flagrante with a mummy?

If the door handle had been made of plutonium, he couldn't have jerked his hand away faster. He stepped back.

The room was uncomfortably hot and getting hotter by the minute. The party was too loud. He was breathing too fast. He felt claustrophobic. More than anything, he longed to be alone in a library studying ancient Egyptian lore, or knee-deep in sand at a new excavation site.

Calm down. Don't let the crowd rattle you.

He got his breathing under control just as a woman's screams erupted from the courtyard, and then the lights in the museum went out.

And all hell broke loose.

Panicked, Cassie backpedaled. The injured mummy slumped to the ground. She turned and ran full-out for the museum, her shoulder throbbing from the weight of his body, her nostrils filled with the smell of his blood.

Sprinting wasn't easy, considering the most rigorous exercise she got on a regular basis was blow-drying her hair straight, but she was scared witless and wanted out of there.

Now.

She reached the entrance and the lights winked out at the same time. The entire building was plunged into instant darkness. She couldn't see whose chest it was that she slammed into when she barreled through the door, but she could tell it was a masculine one.

Strong male arms embraced her.

Safe.

She couldn't see anything. The room was totally black. She heard people gasp. Then came the exclamations of fear and concern. Everyone was in a tizzy.

But she was all right. She felt the hardness of the man's honed chest beneath her fingers and she trembled, not with fear, but with something just as elemental.

"I'm here," he said.

It was almost as if he were inside her head and his mind was wrapped around hers. As if their hearts were beating to the same tempo. As if his breath were hers and hers his.

Bizarre.

Something about him arrested her. Something about his calm-in-the-storm aura filled her with a strong sense of déjà vu. She'd never felt such a compelling mental connection to any man in her life. She hadn't even believed such a bond was possible. And yet, here it was. Deep inside her, something monumental stirred. Something long-buried. Something hoped for and dreamed of but never dared spoken aloud.

Soul mate.

All the headlong giddiness and impulsiveness that had defined her life to this point vanished. As if for the first time since birth, she was sobered.

This was no mere flirtation. This was no simple tease. This was no ordinary male-female reaction.

Her skin tingled as the warmth of his breath feathered the minute hairs on her cheek. Her heart lub-dubbed frantically. The rough material of his jacket lightly scratched her bare arm. His masculine scent, an odd but pleasing combination of sand, soap, and old parchment paper, soothed her.

He smelled intriguingly like the Prado museum in Madrid where Cassie had worked as a foreign exchange student when she was in college. Bookish, old-worldy, solid. He was as hard and firm as she was soft and pliable. He tightened his grip on her shoulder, squeezing gently.

Her trembling increased.

"Cassie," he murmured. "Don't worry, I've got you. You're all right."

His voice was rich and earthy. He sounded the way mushrooms tasted, she found herself thinking dizzily— *shiitake, cremini, enoki, portobello, chanterelle.* But unlike mushrooms after a rain, his words did not sprout willy-nilly. He did not speak again, even while others crashed into things around them, cursing and complaining.

He was a rock. Gibraltar. Atlas.

Strong, present, unmoving.

She heard Phyllis Lambert urging everyone to stay still and remain calm, reassuring the panicky crowd that the backup generator would kick on momentarily. But Cassie wasn't listening to the curator. She wanted to hear *him* speak again.

She curled her fingers around his wrist and whispered, "I'm scared."

"Nothing to be afraid of." His tone was low, measured, controlled. "I've got you."

His quiet, deliberate words inspired her. She fought an urge to beg him to fling aside those precise vocal notes and let loose in a careless, heartfelt rush of verbiage. She wanted to hear him breathe a cornucopia of language. Each sound falling upon the next, like kernels of corn slipping through a tin funnel.

Speak to me. Talk. Feed my ears.

Her twin sister, Maddie, teased her because she compared so many things to food, but Cassie embodied sensual experiences. She saw nothing wrong in associating a man's virile baritone with the lush sumptuousness of delicious mushrooms.

She loved to taste and smell everything. To lick and sup and dine. It was probably the main reason why she wore a size 14 instead of a 9. But who cared? She'd take sated over skinny any day. Plus, she'd never had any complaints about her cushy upholstery from her numerous suitors.

Cassie felt the heat of his hand at her waist, the pressure of his hip resting against her pelvis. She was disoriented, lost. All senses distorted. Thrown off balance by the lack of sight.

That had to be what this feeling was all about. It couldn't be anything more.

Could it?

Sounds were either too distant or too close, smells too sharp or too muted. The lingering cinnamon taste on her tongue was too immediate and too raw. The texture of his nubby jacket beneath her fingers too authentic and yet at the same time too surreal.

Her mind spun topsy-turvily.

For the moment, she forgot there was a mummy lying in the courtyard with a knife in his back. She forgot all about the botched party and the missing guest of honor and the nervous horde surrounding them. She forgot about everything except the feel of this stranger's virile arms around her and the echo of his sexy voice fading from her ears.

She was lost in time. Lost in the moment. Lost in the dark. It was the most erotic sensation she'd experienced in recent memory. Her reaction to the stranger was potent.

Whoa. Wait a minute.

Hadn't he called her by name? He couldn't be a stranger. He must know her. Who was he, her mysterious protector?

The pulse in her neck kicked.

At that precise moment the lights flickered on, and she found herself in Harrison Standish's arms.

Holy crap.

She stared at him.

No, it simply could not be. She could not be having such stunning feelings for this geeky intellectual who dressed funny. Somewhere, somebody's wires had gotten seriously crossed.

Harrison peered at her curiously through the lenses of his dark-frame glasses as if she were an interesting fossil he had just excavated.

"You," she whispered.

Immediately they jumped apart as if they had received a simultaneous electrical shock. Cassie couldn't have been more disconcerted if she had discovered she'd been French-kissing a boa constrictor.

Harrison glanced at the ceiling, the floor, out the glass

door leading into the courtyard. Everywhere but into her eyes.

Everyone else seemed startled by the light as well. People stood around blinking and rubbing their eyes and shaking their heads.

And then Cassie remembered why she'd run screaming into the museum in the first place.

The mummy. His cryptic message. The knife.

"Murder," Cassie croaked. "In the courtyard. There's been a murder."

The mummy lay in the courtyard, barely breathing. In his palm he clutched a half-dollar-sized copper circle that exactly matched the ring in the museum display.

He had to hide the amulet. The consequences would be dire indeed if he failed.

Because *they* were coming for him. *They* would stop at nothing. And *they* would assassinate anyone who got in their way.

The pain was so blinding he could barely see, but he could not get caught with the amulet. Desperately, he tried to raise his head, to look around for some kind of hiding place.

His gaze fixed on a bright red shoulder-strap purse resting against the stone bench.

There. Perfect.

Not much time. Hurry, hurry.

But each tiny movement jarred his back, stabbed throughout his entire spine. His body throbbed and ached and burned. He drew a shallow breath and his lungs cried out.

Fight it off. You can't fail.

Gritting his teeth, the mummy pulled himself up on

his elbows and dug them into the cobblestone walkway. Painstakingly, inch by awful inch, he dragged his body forward.

He didn't know if the streetlamps had flashed off in unison or if he had suddenly gone blind, but all at once he could not see.

He bit down on his bottom lip, urging himself onward. Go, go, go.

In the distance he heard noises, loud voices, crashing sounds. But he wasn't concerned with that. One thing dominated his mind.

Get rid of the amulet.

The pain was so agonizing that he didn't know if a minute had gone by or if it was a millennium, but at long last his hand reached out and struck against the supple leather handbag.

He fumbled inside.

His hands, wrapped in white linen like mittens, were clumsy and cold from shock. His search yielded a zippered compartment.

He opened the hiding place and slipped the amulet ring inside the pouch. He zipped it shut again and then shoved the purse as deeply as he could reach into the nearby bushes.

Later he could come back for it.

If there was a later.

He lay there panting, hoping he had outsmarted his attackers. Sweat dripped into his face; salt burned his eyes. He blinked even though he could not see.

And that was when two pairs of rough, careless hands reached down, grabbed him by the upper arms, and hauled him away in the darkness.

All the occupants of the exhibit hall erupted into the courtyard.

Osiris, Horus, two Nefertitis, three King Tuts. Anubis, Seth, Isis, and Ra. Harrison lost count as the courtyard filled up with more than a hundred curious guests. All the gods and goddesses of ancient Egypt converging upon Fort Worth, Texas.

And then he caught sight of Ahmose, the real Egyptian royalty, standing off to one side.

Harrison followed the group, but his brain was back there in the dark, holding a trembling Cassie close to his chest. He would have bet hard cash she was truly frightened and not putting on, but he wasn't about to place his trust in her.

Still, her sweet, delicate perfume enthralled him, clung to his clothes. She smelled like a garden, a bouquet, a spring event. Like some ripe, rich fruit in full bloom.

A scent like, oh, say, cherry blossoms?

The unexpected memory of that long-ago night in the Valley of the Kings when he had caught Jessica smooching Adam washed over him, and Harrison remembered why he'd started out to the courtyard in the first place.

To find out if Cassie knew what was going on with Adam.

But that had been before he'd held her in the dark, before the lights had come on and she'd looked both shocked and disappointed to discover he was the one holding her.

To Harrison's own mind, in the darkness, he had been someone else. Someone more like Adam. An easygoing guy with a fun-loving grin. A swashbuckling hero who knew how to dress, could court the ladies as easily as he could pick out the right wine for a gourmet feast, and wasn't so color-blind he couldn't tell blue from green.

Enough.

He had to stay mentally tough. He couldn't forget the woman was the antithesis of everything he valued.

"Well?" Phyllis Lambert said to Cassie. "Who got murdered? Where's the body?"

The crowd murmured, echoing the curator's questions. The courtyard was empty.

No body. No blood. No sign of a struggle.

Harrison pushed his glasses up on his nose and watched Cassie peer down at the cobblestones where she stood near the hedges. She looked confused.

And heartbreakingly vulnerable.

She nibbled her bottom lip and shifted her weight from foot to foot. She kept bobbing her head as if to convince herself she was right and everyone else's eyes were deceiving them.

"He was here before the lights went out, I swear," she declared. "A guy in a mummy costume, and he had a knife sticking out of his back."

"So who was this mysterious stranger?" Phyllis sank her hands on hips so narrow her palms slid right down her outer thighs.

Harrison had never seen Cassie distressed. He had the strangest urge to shove himself between the two of them and tell the curator to step off.

"I don't know," Cassie admitted.

For a minute the earnestness in her voice almost had Harrison believing that she was telling the truth, that there really was a backstabbed mummy crawling around in the bushes.

"You expect us to believe some guy with a Ginsu in his back just got up and toddled off?" Phyllis tapped her foot.

"I never said it was a Ginsu. It very well could have been a Henckels. I really didn't look that closely."

"That's not what I meant," Phyllis snapped. "Where's the damned mummy?"

Cassie's eyes widened. "Why don't we search the courtyard? He could be lying in the shrubbery, slowly bleeding to death."

Several people made a move to do just that.

Her urging aroused Harrison's suspicions. Why was she so interested in having the guests search the courtyard?

Had Adam planted a surprise? Was Cassie in on his publicity stunt?

"I found a purse," Osiris said, pulling a leather handbag from the bushes. He stood on tiptoe and peered down over the back of the hedge. "But I don't see any dead mummies lying around anywhere."

"That's mine." Cassie snatched the purse from him. "Thank you."

"Where's the blood?" Phyllis demanded, clearly growing tired of the charade. "Do you see any blood?"

"He wasn't bleeding much. The knife blade must have stanched the flow."

"A likely story." Phyllis narrowed her eyes. "What do you take me for? An idiot?"

"It's true. I came out here to meet him and..."

"You came outside to meet a man you didn't even know, when you were the hostess of the party and I explicitly told you to locate Dr. Grayfield?"

"I thought the mummy *was* Dr. Grayfield."

Now that was total bullshit.

Harrison stroked his jaw with a forefinger and thumb. He knew full well Adam couldn't have been in the mummy costume, because he'd been tearing through the exhibit hall in his Indiana Jones hat not fifteen minutes earlier. There hadn't been nearly enough time for him to park his motorcycle, swaddle himself in linen, run to the courtyard, get stabbed in the back, and then disappear again.

"Now why on earth would a man of Dr. Grayfield's distinguished stature slink around the courtyard in a mummy outfit?" Phyllis questioned.

Cassie's face flushed. "We've sort of been flirting with each other over the phone for the past few weeks while we made plans for the exhibit."

It figured. Harrison snorted silently. Adam was probably pulling some kind of stunt to impress Cassie. She was the kind of woman men did foolish things over.

"I've had it with your impetuousness," Phyllis snarled. "You know what I think?"

Cassie shook her head. Gone was her normally ebullient smile, and Harrison couldn't figure out why that would cause his stomach to knot. Impatiently, he shoved aside the unpleasant sensation.

The crowd shifted, glancing from Phyllis to Cassie and back again, waiting to see what was going to happen next.

"I think you made the whole thing up because you're a drama queen who can't stand it when you're not the center of attention."

"No." Cassie's bottom lip quivered.

"And I never believed that line of malarkey you fed the FBI last year when you took off with that art thief. I think you were in on the deal all along, and when it looked like you were about to get caught and hauled off to prison, you pretended you were on the good guys' side."

Harrison couldn't tolerate watching anyone get raked over the coals, but neither did he like confrontation. Normally, he just walked away from a fracas. But with every passing moment, he was becoming more and more certain that Adam was involved in some kind of publicity exploit gone awry.

One question remained. Was Cassie part of Adam's scheme or not?

She looked pretty innocent with her wide, susceptible eyes and her silly Cleopatra wig knocked askew. Had Adam set up this mess and then disappeared on her? Or was Cassie a consummate actress who knew exactly what she was doing to elicit sympathy?

Either way, Adam had flown the coop, leaving only the baggage claim ticket in way of explanation. He'd put Harrison in something of a bind.

If the reunification ceremony didn't come off as scheduled, the Egyptian government would get testy. And if the Egyptian government got testy, the university backing his excavations would end up looking bad. And if the university ended up looking bad, he could kiss his funding good-bye.

Dammit, Adam. Thank you so much for screwing me over yet again.

"I wanted to fire you the minute I took over this job," Phyllis continued to harangue. "But the board of directors wouldn't allow it. Well, this time you've gone too far. You're out on your keister, Cooper."

Cassie gasped. "Ms. Lambert, please, you don't know the whole story. Let me explain."

"I don't want to hear it." Phyllis held up her palm in a talk-to-the-hand gesture.

Harrison couldn't allow Cassie to get fired. He might regret his decision later, but he had to do something to bail her out. He had to make her beholden to him. Then she couldn't refuse to answer when he asked her some very pointed questions concerning her involvement with his brother.

"Excuse me, Ms. Lambert." Harrison cleared his throat and fiddled with his bow tie. He had no idea what he was going to say.

"What is it, Harrison?" Phyllis's tone quickly changed from waspish to syrupy.

The curator had to suck up to him. Without Harrison there would be no Kiya, no star-crossed lovers exhibit. No one hundred well-heeled guests willing to shell out a thousand dollars apiece to see the show.

"Call me Dr. Standish," he said sternly. He didn't like brownnosers.

"Of course," Phyllis replied. "If that's what you'd prefer, Dr. Standish."

"I do prefer."

The guests had gone curiously quiet. One hundred bated breaths.

Waiting.

Quick! Astonish her with your brilliance.

Damn. He was lousy under pressure.

It turned out he didn't have to dazzle her with bullshit. At that moment a security guard came rushing from the building. The man pushed through the crowd, panting and gesticulating wildly. "Ms. Lambert, Ms. Lambert!"

"What is it?" Phyllis snarled

"Come quickly. Kiya's amulet. It's been stolen!"

Chapter 4

The myriad gods and goddesses filed back into the museum with a grim-faced Phyllis Lambert marching at the head of the pack. Cassie brought up the rear, anxiously nibbling her bottom lip.

Which wasn't like her.

She never lagged behind and she rarely fretted, mainly because she didn't like thinking about anything that bummed her out. Plus, she hated chewing off her lipstick because she indulged too lavishly at the Neiman Marcus Lancôme counter. At twenty-eight dollars a tube, she'd learned to make her lipstick last.

But she'd just been fired. She was out of a job. So long, Smithsonian. Good-bye, Maddie.

Cassie swallowed the lump in her throat and told herself she would not tear up. She wasn't about to give Phyllis the satisfaction of making her cry.

Just ahead of her in the multitude, she spied Harrison and her heart thumped illogically. She didn't even like the guy. Why was her pulse speeding up?

As if sensing her gaze on the back of his head, he turned and glowered at her. Apparently he wasn't any fonder of her than she was of him, but he had stepped in and interrupted Phyllis when she'd been reading her the riot act.

The question was, Why?

She searched his face, looking for answers, but found none. The man was a master at hiding his emotions. Which in this instance was probably a good thing.

The entire group skidded to a halt in front of Kiya's now-empty display case. Phyllis took one look, narrowed her eyes, and spun around.

"Cooper!" she bellowed.

Cassie took a deep breath, marshaled her courage, and stepped forward. How much worse could it get? She had already been canned. What else could the irritable curator do to her?

"What is it, Phyllis?" she asked, making sure her tone sounded light, casual, and untroubled as she toed off with the woman.

"Now I realize what you were up to." Lambert shook a finger in her face. "Screaming and claiming there had been a murder in the courtyard. You were creating a distraction, luring us outside, while your accomplice shut off the electricity to deactivate the security alarms and stole the amulet."

The crowd inhaled a collective gasp of surprise. She could feel a hundred pair of staring eyes.

"Oh, no," Cassie denied. "You're wrong. That's not what happened at all."

She had been quite mistaken. Things could get worse. A lot worse.

"Detain her," Phyllis barked to the security guard, "while I alert the police."

The brawny security guard moved to firmly take hold of Cassie's arm.

"What a minute," Harrison blurted, nudging aside the

guests until he was standing beside them. "Phyllis, obviously you didn't get the memo."

The curator looked puzzled. "Er, what memo?"

Cassie gaped at him, totally confused. What was he talking about? What was going on? Why was he trying to help? The guy hated her. She narrowed her eyes suspiciously.

Harrison sent her a look that said, *Just go along with me on this.*

As a rule, she wasn't a liar. She did not prevaricate without a darned fine reason. And she wouldn't allow someone to step in and take the blame for her. Especially not someone like Standoffish, who wasn't even pleasant to her under normal circumstances.

"Phyllis, I don't know what memo he's talking—" she started to say, but then Harrison gently but firmly trod on her toe.

Shut up, his chocolate eyes insisted.

Hey, hey, hey!

Purposefully, she jerked her foot out from under his brown tasseled loafer. She couldn't believe he was behaving so out of character. What was up?

"What Cassie means is that she doesn't understand why you didn't receive your memo," he said, muscling in and interrupting her in midsentence. "She sent it four days ago, after we cemented the plans."

"Clyde, did you get their memo?" The curator glanced over at her executive assistant, a pie-faced balding man in his early fifties.

Clyde Petalonus was dressed as George of the Jungle in a cheetah-spotted loincloth with artificial kudzu vines draped around his neck. Poor Clyde didn't really have the figure for the ensemble. Cassie presumed he'd either gotten his Brendan Fraser movies mixed up, or his sense of geography was so terrible he actually thought there were jungles in Egypt.

"Sure thing. I got the memo," Clyde lied.

His reply took Cassie by surprise.

Why was Clyde lying? She knew he liked her and that he really disliked Phyllis. The curator had the annoying habit of sending him on "essential" errands the minute the man sat down for a meal in the employees' lounge. And the sneaky woman would always wait until Clyde had a cherry Pepsi poured over ice and his sandwich unwrapped or his frozen Hungry Man zapped in the microwave before she sprang the urgent assignment on him. But that wasn't explanation enough for him to risk his job over her.

She looked at him, and he gave her a quick smile that said, *Don't worry, I'll cover for you.* But she was worried. Why would he cover for her?

Maybe he wasn't covering for her. Maybe he was lying to protect himself. He was in charge of overseeing the crew that had set up the lighting for the exhibit. Maybe he was afraid Phyllis would accuse him of some culpability in the crime when she got done chewing out Cassie.

She might get fired, she might even get accused of stealing the amulet, but she knew she was innocent. Whatever Clyde's and Harrison's motives might be, she simply could not allow them to prevaricate on her account. She'd done nothing wrong. Phyllis couldn't pin a thing on her.

Could she?

"What memo?!" Phyllis's voice jumped an octave, and the tip of her nose turned blotchy red. "What are you talking about? What did this memo say?"

"Interactive murder mystery theater," Harrison supplied. The tone of his voice was calm and steady, but Cassie caught the jerk of a subtle tic at his right eyelid. He was nervous.

A general titter of delight undulated throughout the gathered crowd.

"What a marvelous idea," murmured Lashaundra Johnson, a reporter for the Arts and Entertainment section of the *Fort Worth Star-Telegram*. Lashaundra had written a feature on Cassie last year after she'd helped the FBI capture the art thief.

"I adore murder mystery theater," exclaimed a very prominent, very moneyed museum patron dressed as Isis. "Will there be prizes for the winner?"

Murmured speculation rippled throughout the room as the guests eagerly exchanged ideas and discussed suppositions. Harrison's fabrication was a huge hit.

"I don't understand." Phyllis impatiently tapped her foot. "Explain it to me."

"Give us more details," one of the King Tuts said. "Who is the mummy? Why was he in the courtyard? How is he connected to the legend of Kiya and Solen?"

"Wait, wait," Nefertiti said. "I'll need a pen and paper to keep this all straight."

"Me too," piped up Horus the Sky God.

"But what about Dr. Grayfield?" Phyllis asked dubiously. "What about the reunification ceremony?"

"Oh, that's not tonight." Harrison shook his head. Cassie admired his grace under pressure. To the casual observer he seemed totally composed, but she noticed he was squeezing his replica djed so tightly the muscles in his wrist bulged.

"Not tonight?" Phyllis repeated and frowned.

Not tonight? Cassie wondered.

"It's all in the memo." Harrison gave Phyllis a gosh-are-you-out-of-the-loop expression.

On the surface, he did not look like a man whose life's work had just jumped off that display case and

walked out the door. He was pretty darn good at bluffing. But Cassie detected the telltale signs. His lips were
pressed thin, and she saw a single bead of sweat glisten on
his forehead.

"Let me get this straight, Dr. Standish. What you're
telling me is that the amulet is not really missing. No one
stole it?" Phyllis asked.

"That's correct."

Cassie adjusted her cumbersome headdress. What had
happened to the amulet? She shot him a surreptitious
glance, and the look he returned was so desperate that she
knew for certain the amulet *had* been stolen and he was
covering up the theft.

But why?

Because of her?

But that made no sense. Harrison barely knew her, and
until tonight he'd acted as if he didn't care for her methods
or her personality.

Was he simply using this opportunity to steal the amulet for himself? But why would he do that? He'd discovered the amulet. If he'd wanted to steal it, wouldn't he
have done it when he first excavated it?

Should she back him up in the lie or blurt out the truth?
What were Harrison's motives? Who had stabbed the
mummy? Who was the mummy? Who'd turned off the
lights? Who'd stolen the amulet? And most of all, where
was Adam Grayfield? Things were weird and getting
weirder by the minute.

"Where is the amulet?" Phyllis inclined her head
toward the empty case.

"It's secured in a bank vault. The amulet on display
was a copy made for the sake of the murder mystery theater. It was all in the memo."

"I wish I could see this memo. Clyde, do you still have your copy?" Phyllis crossed her arms over her chest.

"I deleted it from my e-mail," Clyde said.

"Since there doesn't seem to be a copy of this elusive memo, then you won't mind taking me to the safety-deposit box at the bank vault tomorrow morning and showing me the real amulet, Dr. Standish."

"I wish I could, Ms. Lambert, but Adam Grayfield has the key. He'll bring both halves with him to the reunification ceremony," he said.

"Dr. Grayfield is in on this too?"

"You could say it's his brainchild."

Was Adam party to this farce? Cassie frowned. Pondering these questions was giving her a headache. She didn't like thinking this hard.

"Oh. Well. Then I'll take you at your word." Apparently Phyllis was willing to give them enough rope to hang themselves. "What happens next?"

"The guests will have a chance to solve the mystery on their own, and then when everyone returns with their guesses, we'll give out the prizes and have the reunification ceremony," Harrison supplied.

Cassie realized he was trying to buy them time to figure out who took the amulet. She only prayed it worked before Phyllis became suspicious and called the police. She didn't know who Harrison was protecting or why, but if she went along with his plan, she would be up to her eyeballs in the conspiracy with him.

And the last thing she wanted was to be eyeball-deep in anything with the contentious, but oddly compelling, Harrison Standish.

She had to speak up.

But how?

"And when is everyone supposed to return for the reunification ceremony?" Phyllis raised an eyebrow.

"Anyone who's interested in returning for the second part of the show will meet back here on Saturday night. Eight o'clock," Harrison said.

"What about the logistics of all these people returning?" Phyllis waved a hand. "Will there be another party?"

"Absolutely." Harrison nodded. "It was in the memo."

Another party on Saturday night! Cassie didn't have the budget for a second party, and it was only three days away. Would they be able to find Adam and the amulet in seventy-two hours?

"But I can't make it on Saturday," one of the King Tuts whined. "Will I get a refund?"

"This event is a charity fund-raiser for the Kimbell," Harrison said. "You're one of the most influential men in Fort Worth. Surely you will still want to make your contribution, even if your schedule doesn't permit you to return for the second party."

That shut King Tut up and put an end to a possible mass rush for refunds.

"Dr. Standish," Cassie said. She took his elbow and squeezed it meaningfully. "May I speak with you in private about our mystery theater?"

"Right now?"

"Yes, right now."

"Phyllis," Harrison said and smiled at the pickle-faced woman, "could you give us a minute?"

"Of course." The curator's return smile was frosty. Clearly, Phyllis didn't want to go along with their story, but the guests were so excited about the murder mystery theater concept that she had little choice.

"Out in the courtyard, Standish," Cassie hissed.

She flounced away through the murmuring crowd. Harrison followed at her heels.

"What gives?" she demanded once they were outside. "What's with this interactive murder mystery theater crap?"

"I'm trying very hard to save your skin, along with my brother's miserable hide."

"Who in the heck is your brother?"

"Adam Grayfield."

"For real?" That was a shocker. Charming, romantic Adam was kin to this pigheaded cynic? The plot thickened. "But you have different last names."

"He didn't tell you?"

"If he'd told me, then I wouldn't be surprised that you two were siblings, now would I?"

"We're half brothers. We have the same mother, different fathers."

"That's all well and good, but please don't do me any more favors. I didn't ask you to do me any favors. Why *are* you doing me favors?"

The man was a certifiable nut job. Why was he under the mistaken impression that she needed saving? And even if she did need saving, she wasn't his to save. If she *was* searching for a Sir Galahad, she certainly wouldn't turn to Sir Gripes-a-Lot as a consolation prize.

Harrison's jaw hardened in that stubborn clinch she'd come to recognize and dread over the course of the past nine days. Whenever he set his mandible at that fight-or-die angle, Cassie had learned she was in for a protracted battle.

"I know what Adam's up to, and the way you've been waxing rhapsodically about him all week makes me wonder if you two might be in on this together. As far as I know, you might even be his lover."

"How can I be Adam's lover? I've never even met your brother in person, you ass," she snapped.

Harrison's cheeks flushed. Was he embarrassed over his false accusations? Or was he mad because she had called him an ass? He was lucky she hadn't called him worse.

"Besides, I have no clue what you're talking about," she finished.

"I'm talking about you two staging a publicity stunt involving Solen and Kiya as a way to milk the museum benefactors out of more money to fund Adam's future excavations."

"You are a petty, suspicious man, you know that?" Even though she felt a little guilty for sounding so harsh, Cassie refused to budge. She crossed her arms over her chest and glowered at him. To think that for one brief millisecond back there in the dark she had actually been sexually attracted to him.

Heaven forbid.

"I'm not petty and suspicious," he denied. "Not at all. But I do know my brother. He's a trickster. He loves games and treasure hunts. When it comes to Adam, I know exactly what to expect. You, Miss Cooper, are the wild card."

"I might be wild," she agreed, "but I don't pull stunts to dupe people out of their money. And I can't believe you think so little of your own brother."

Cassie was breathing hard and she didn't know why. For the longest moment, they glared at each other, gazes locked, temperatures rising.

"Why don't you try to call Adam and see if you can wring a confession from him?" she challenged.

"I will." Harrison took out his cell phone and punched in his brother's number. Voice mail answered. He hung up.

"Is he still incommunicado?"

"Apparently."

"Guess you'll just have to take my word for it that your brother and I are not in cahoots."

She could tell he didn't want to buy it, but at last he relented. "All right, I'll take you at your word, and I apologize if I offended you in any way."

He did have the good grace to look chagrined, and when he humbled himself he was less like a high-minded pompous ass and more like a real human being.

"Your apology is accepted," Cassie relented, uncrossing her arms.

"Thank you for not holding a grudge."

"Don't get too comfortable. You're on probation with me." She shook an index finger at him.

"As are you with me." His eyebrows bunched darkly. "I don't trust you."

"I don't even like you." She hardened her chin.

"Nor I you."

"You're arrogant and judgmental and contentious."

"And you're self-centered and overly opinionated and self-destructive."

"Obviously we don't get along." She wondered why she was so breathless.

"Not so much." He frowned and shook his head. He looked a little winded too.

"Great, as long as we have that established, could you clue me in? Where do you think your brother might be? Seeing as how my livelihood is on the line and all."

"Adam was here just a little while ago."

"You saw him at the museum?"

Harrison nodded.

"Did you talk to him?"

"I tried. He ran outside."

"Why'd he do that?"

Harrison shrugged. "I don't know. I thought you might have the answer."

"Not me. What did you do?"

"I followed him. Just as I hit the street, he took off around the corner on a custom Harley. He had Gabriel Martinez slip this to me."

Harrison pulled an envelope from his pocket, extracted a small rectangle of paper, and waved it under her nose.

"Looks like a baggage claim ticket from American Airlines," she said.

"Exactly," he crowed, like he was Columbo or Hercule Poirot or Perry Mason. Her mother was a huge mystery buff. Cassie had cut her teeth on late-night Charlie Chan reruns and could recite verbatim every title Agatha Christie ever wrote in order of publication date.

"I had to tell the white lie in order to buy us time with Phyllis, so we could figure out what the baggage claim ticket means," Harrison said.

"It means there's baggage at the American Airlines terminal that needs picking up." What was the deal? She thought the guy was supposed to be some kind of Mensa genius.

"But whose baggage? And why hasn't it already been claimed?"

Cassie shrugged. "I dunno."

"If we get the baggage," he continued, "we might find the answer to Adam's whereabouts. Or a clue to who took the amulet, but we don't have time for honesty. Police rigmarole would slow us down for hours."

"There's something more you're not telling me. You're not too upset about the missing amulet. You're thinking that Adam's the one who took it, and you don't want to get him into trouble."

"No, I'm just good at cloaking my panic."

"Had me fooled."

"Actually I'm praying like hell that Adam *did* take it. If the amulet is truly missing and it's not part of my brother's crackpot ploy, then my life's work has vanished in a whiff of smoke." He snapped his fingers. "The Egyptian government is going to be extremely unhappy with me. If the amulet is not recovered, I'll lose not only my funding, but my visa to Egypt. My entire future is on the line."

"So that's your real motive for lying. To save your career. This isn't really about your brother. This is personal."

"Yes, okay," Harrison admitted. "It's personal. What's wrong with that? But I'm not as selfish as you want to believe. Even though the amulet represents everything that I treasure deeply and hold dear, that's not what's important. The real travesty would be the loss of a precious artifact that gives us new insight into the ancient Egyptian culture. There's nothing more important to the future than an understanding of history. I've devoted my life to it, and I'll do anything to preserve it."

"Even lie?"

"Even lie."

Cassie blew out her breath, letting everything he'd told her sink in.

"Meanwhile, your boss is getting edgy." He nodded toward the exhibit hall. "So like it or not, we're in this mess together."

She peeked over his shoulder to see Phyllis standing behind the glass door, hands on hips, lips pursed disapprovingly.

"I'm not in the habit of lying," she whispered. "Not even to keep myself out of trouble."

"I don't lie either, dammit. But this is important. I just blurted it out. Believe me, I'm not an impulsive guy. I hate this as much as you do, probably more so. But this has to be done. For me, for my brother, for Egypt, for Kiya and Solen, but most important, for humankind."

What a moving speech!

She'd had no idea such passion lurked beneath his cool exterior. The moonlight glinted off Harrison's honed cheekbones, giving him a surprisingly knavish appearance in spite of his scholarly spectacles. An unexpected shiver tripped down her spine.

"You're cold," he said and removed his jacket.

Before she knew what he intended, he'd already slipped the hideous purple tweed jacket over her shoulders. She wanted to protest and hand it back to him, but she was cold. The jacket smelled of him, and the pleasantness of his scent caught her off guard.

She stuck her hands in his pocket and felt a cylindrical tube. It was the replica he'd made of the djed found in Kiya's tomb. Harrison had once told her that he was determined to discover the true use of the djed. Considering the size and shape, Cassie often wondered if it hadn't been anything more than an Egyptian sex toy, although Harrison would probably be horrified if she suggested such a thing.

"Please," he said. "I know this is not an optimal situation, but just go along with me."

"I'm sorry." She shook her head. "I can't lie."

"What happens," he asked softly, "if my brother has stolen the amulet and you're left holding the bag? You two planned this event together. You expect Phyllis to believe you weren't part of it? Especially after that stabbed, disappearing mummy escapade you pulled."

"I didn't pull anything. A mummy *was* stabbed in the courtyard."

"Either way, Phyllis is gunning for you."

"You noticed that too? I'm not just paranoid?"

"Who could miss the animosity? She almost hisses whenever you walk by."

Well, thank you very much. At least someone else had confirmed Cassie's suspicion that Phyllis hated her guts.

"Would Adam hang me out to dry?" she asked. "He doesn't seem the sort of guy who would do something like that."

"I would hate to believe it of him, but honestly I don't know. The murder mystery theater is our best temporary solution. If Adam is just pulling a publicity stunt, we successfully nip it in the bud. If not..." He didn't complete the sentence, leaving the rest of his unspoken words up to her vivid imagination.

Cassie's pulse spiked and a surge of excitement shot through her. Her exploits with the art thief last year had given her a taste for crime solving.

"All I'm asking is for three days to locate my brother," Harrison continued, "and straighten this whole thing out. It's probably a simple misunderstanding."

"And what happens if we can't find Adam or the amulet by Saturday?"

"I'll report it to the police and explain what happened. I'll tell them I coerced you into going along with me. In the meantime, you'll still have your job, and the guests will get a big kick out of playing sleuth. And if everything turns out okay, I'll make certain you get that recommendation to the Smithsonian. Adam's father is Tom Grayfield, the U.S. ambassador to Greece, and he has a lot of influence in Washington. He could pull strings."

"I don't know what to do."

"Whichever way you decide to go," Harrison said, "lie or tell the truth, you're already in trouble."

That was true. Even though she wasn't involved with the theft of the amulet, Phyllis was ready to hang her from the highest tree based on circumstances alone.

"So what do you say?" He argued a good case, but she was still afraid to trust him.

"I'm not sure I can."

She saw that he wasn't a man accustomed to asking for favors. But she could also see he was very worried about his brother and his career. She was worried too. Empathy could do terrible things to a woman.

"And if everything doesn't turn out the way you foresee it?" Cassie murmured, bracing herself for the answer she did not want to hear.

Harrison grimaced and shook his head. "Then we're both royally screwed."

Chapter 5

Royally screwed indeed.

How had he gotten entangled in such an abysmal state of affairs?

Impulsive behavior didn't solve problems, it created them. Rational men thought before they spoke. Tonight, he had been anything but rational, and now he was paying the price.

Following the disappearance of Kiya's amulet, Ahmose Akvar had taken him aside and privately reiterated his earlier warning: *If anything happens to the amulet, your visa will be rescinded and you will never again be allowed inside Egypt.*

Exiled.

For Harrison, who had devoted his life to the study of ancient Egypt, banishment from his adopted country was unimaginable. To top things off, Phyllis Lambert had cornered him and issued a similar veiled threat, whispering that if she discovered he was covering for Cassie, she would report him to the head of the archaeology department at the University of Texas at Arlington, where Harrison taught as an adjunct professor. Hinting that she would make certain he lost his job.

Thanks a lot, Adam. I hope you have a damn good reason for absconding with the amulet. Because if you're not in trouble now, you will be when I get my hands on you.

The guests had finally departed the museum after Cassie's briefing. She'd concocted a spur-of-the-moment murder mystery tale so brilliant in detail, she'd mesmerized even Harrison. Her cock-and-bull story was one-third legend of the lost lovers, one-third reality, and one-third creative fabrication. Grudgingly, he had to admit the woman, however irritating, possessed an incredible talent for adapting to shifting circumstances.

A skill he sorely lacked.

He resented his need for her help. If he had his way, he would ditch her posthaste and go in search of Adam on his own.

But other than Gabriel Martinez, who'd merely been given the white envelope from his brother, Cassie was the last known person to have spoken at length with Adam. And even though she professed otherwise, Harrison still wasn't sure he could trust her.

Was she lying to protect his brother? She claimed they weren't lovers, and for some asinine reason he wanted to take her at her word.

It was all too coincidental. The mummy stabbed, his brother missing, the lights going out, the theft of the amulet. Cassie had to have more information than she was letting on, whether she consciously knew it or not.

"Hey, Harry, why so down in the mouth?"

They were the last ones left in the building except for the armed security guards and the janitors. Phyllis Lambert had just walked out the door with one last ominous word of warning that they had better produce the amulet come Saturday night or there would be hell to pay.

"Excuse me?" He scowled.

Cassie slung her purse over her shoulder, and she was still wearing his jacket. "You look like your best buddy just ran off with your wife and squashed your favorite puppy under the tires of his jacked-up monster truck on their way out the gate."

"Colorful analogy," he said. "If somewhat country-and-western-songish in nature. But I don't have a wife. Or a puppy."

Or a best buddy.

His friends were his colleagues. Outside of work he didn't hang around with the guys. He didn't enjoy shooting pool or drinking beer or yelling insults at football players on television. Harrison knew he was an odd duck, but he couldn't help the way he was. He liked being alone with this thoughts and his books. His time was precious. He didn't waste it on trivial pursuits.

Or trivial emotions.

Cassie rolled her eyes. "It was a joke, for heaven's sake. Ha-ha-ha. Lighten up, dude. Do you always have to take everything so literally?"

"I don't know any other way to view the world." Harrison held the exit door open for Cassie to walk through.

"I take that as a yes." She sighed.

"You find my objectivity tiresome?"

"Exasperating," she said. "There's no fun in logic."

"Maybe not, but there's logic in logic."

She gave him a sidelong glance, and he did his best to ignore the suggestive look she angled his way. He wasn't getting involved with her on a personal level. No way, nohow.

"Then again, I'm guessing you've never been accused of having too much fun."

Harrison ignored the comment. Ignored her. Well, as

much as he could. Ignoring Cassie was a bit like ignoring a major force of nature.

The security guard locked the door after them and Harrison realized their cars, his ten-year-old Volvo and Cassie's late-model Mustang convertible, were parked at opposite ends of the lot. He couldn't distinguish shades of colors well, but he would bet the baggage claim ticket in his pocket that her car was a flaming "ogle-me" scarlet.

"So what's the plan, Stan? What's on the agenda, Brenda? Where do we start to sleuth, Ruth?" She was jumping around, swinging her arms, acting like a nervous thoroughbred eager to shoot from the starting gate.

"Are you always so hyper?"

"Always," she promised.

"Remind me never to give you sugar."

"As if I'd remind you of that. Chocolate is my middle name."

"Explains the hyperactivity," he muttered.

"Anyway, what's the scheme, Kareem?"

"I've calculated that the best use of time would be to head for the airport tonight and check out this baggage claim ticket. Put our heads together and see if we can determine what might have happened."

She gave him a thumbs-up. "I'm with you."

"Whose vehicle should we take to the airport?"

"Not mine, unless you don't mind stopping for gas," she said. "The empty light flashed on just as I was pulling into the parking lot this morning."

"You don't fill up when your gas gauge gets to the half-way mark?"

She squinted at him, incredulous. "Good God, no. Do you?"

Yes, he did, but Harrison wasn't about to admit it when

she was staring at him like he had just sprouted a second head. He had a momentary flash of insight into Cassie's driving. He could just see her careening down the highway, talking nonstop on her cell phone, rock music blasting from the stereo speakers, her eyes everywhere but on the road. Anyone that drove around with their empty light flashing had to be an irresponsible driver.

"Never mind," he said, taking her elbow and hustling her toward the Volvo. "I'll drive."

"Oooh, Harry." She batted her eyelashes at him. "I never imagined you were the forceful, take-charge type."

"Knock off the eyelash batting. It won't get you anywhere with me."

"You think I'm flirting with you?"

"Yes."

"Please, don't flatter yourself. I flirt with everyone. You're no more special than the checkout boy at Albertsons."

Harrison's cheeks burned. She did flirt with everyone. "Just don't do it with me."

"Don't worry, chum. The last thing on earth I'd want is to 'do it' with you."

Dammit. She'd twisted his words.

"Listen, since we're forced to spend time together, could you please keep the sexual innuendos to a minimum?" he said.

"Aww, whazza matter, Harry? Get up on the wrong side of the bed this morning?"

When and why had she switched from calling him Standish and started addressing him as Harry?

"Stop calling me Harry," he growled. "I don't care for that particular moniker."

"Harrison's too uptight."

"I like uptight."

"I never would have guessed."

"You're big on sarcasm too."

"When it suits me." She stroked her chin with her thumb and index finger pensively. "Hank, then? You like Hank better?"

"Hank is a nickname for Henry, not Harrison."

"Yeah, but I could call you Hank if I wanted to, right? It's a free country." She blithely waved a hand.

"Don't call me either Harry or Hank." He gritted his teeth. "It's Harrison. Just Harrison."

"Okay, Harry's son." She shrugged and grinned mischievously. "Whatever you say."

With a grunt of displeasure, Harrison thrust a hand in his pocket, plucked out his keys, and opened the passenger door so she could slide in. *I won't throttle her, I won't throttle her, I won't throttle her.*

She wasn't worth a murder charge. That much was certain. Normally he was slow to anger, but there was something about this woman that rubbed him the wrong way.

Unfortunately, his testosterone was shouting, "Wrong way, right way, who cares, just as long as she rubs you."

He slammed the door after she got in. Briefly, he closed his eyes and swallowed hard.

Stay calm, stay cool, stay detached from your feelings.

The chant soothed him the way chocolate chip cookies soothed a carboholic. He felt his anger lift as he mentally disengaged from the moment. With a cool inner eye, he watched himself walk around to the driver's side and then ease behind the wheel.

That was better. No pesky anger to muddle his thinking.

"Hey, Harry," Cassie said huskily, her voice a velvet stroke against his ears as he started the engine.

"It's Harrison." He forced himself not to clench his

teeth over her use of the unsavory nickname. Clenched teeth indicated irritation, and he wasn't irritated. He was aloof, far above his base emotions. This flighty woman couldn't touch him.

"Anyone ever tell you that you're really cute when you're pissed?"

"I'm not pissed," Harrison denied, and told himself the sweat pooling under his collar had absolutely nothing to do with her frank teasing.

"Coulda fooled me," she said lightly. "Oh, by the way, we have to stop off at my apartment."

"Good grief, what for?" Against his better judgment, he glanced over at her.

She had her stiletto sandals peeled off and her feet propped up against the glove compartment. He hated that she had her bare feet on his dash, but at the same time he loved the sight of her delicate toes, painted a light, pearly hue, wriggling in the dome light.

"I can't go to the airport dressed like this." She blithely swept a hand at her skimpy Cleopatra costume. The skirt hem had ridden up when she'd sat down, exposing a long expanse of round feminine thigh.

He swallowed hard. "You know, this is rather urgent. We've got less than seventy-two hours to find my brother and solve this mystery."

"I hafta go home and change. Hang a left at Seventh Street. My apartment is on the next road over." She had a point about traipsing around in public in that diaphanous Cleopatra garb.

"My brother's missing," he said. "Kiya's amulet's been stolen, and my life is unraveling before my very eyes."

And, he mentally added, *I'm stuck with a free-spirited fruitcake of a woman.*

"It won't take ten minutes, I promise."

He wanted to be adamant and say no, but Cassie was so damned irresistible with her perky, expectant smile and her goofy, yet strangely winsome ways, he found himself doing exactly as she asked.

Five minutes later they were at her apartment.

"To speed things up, I'll just wait for you in the car."

"You're gonna sit out here in the dark all by your lonesome?" she picked at him.

He patted his dashboard. "I can listen to NPR."

"What is it, Harry? Are you just antisocial, or are you too scared to be alone with me?"

"I'm in a hurry, that's all."

"Prove you're not scared of me. Come up to my apartment."

He gritted his teeth. Damn, the woman could vex a Zen monk. To prove her wrong, he shut off the engine and followed her up to the second-floor landing.

It had been a long time since he'd been alone with a woman at her place, especially a woman as sexy as this one; maybe he was a little nervous. But he didn't want her to know that. He tried his best to look composed and nonchalant, but ended up tripping over the doorsill because he was too busy watching her derriere sway.

Cassie put out a hand to stop his forward momentum. "Are you okay?"

He nodded, feeling like he was back in high school, standing at his locker next to the gorgeous prom queen who dated the first-string quarterback that used to beat him up on a regular basis.

Would he ever stop feeling like a wimpy nerd when it came to women? Probably not. Especially with a woman like Cassie who could have any guy she wanted.

She wrapped her hand around his bicep and her eyes widened with surprise. "Why Harrison, you dawg, you work out."

He shrugged and pushed up his glasses, unnerved by the teasing awe in her voice. "Now and again."

"Now and again doesn't give a man muscles like these." She squeezed his arm. "You're hitting the weights at least three times a week. I should know. My identical twin sister is an Olympic athlete, and she's a rock."

"I didn't know you had a twin," he said, mostly to change the subject, but also because he was fascinated to learn this tidbit. There were two of her?

"But Maddie and I are nothing alike. She just won a gold medal in track and field, and me, I'd rather get forty licks with a wet noodle than sprint from here to my mailbox. We're as opposite as twins can get."

Well, that was a relief. He couldn't imagine two identical Cassies let loose on an unsuspecting world.

"Have a seat," she said. "I'll go change."

"I don't need to have a seat. It's only going to take you a couple of minutes, remember?"

"Suit yourself." She waggled her fingers and ambled down the hall.

"Hurry. We need to get a move on." Harrison cleared his throat and tried not to fidget. No matter how hard he fought to block the visage, he kept visualizing her slipping out of the silky white goddess toga-thingy she was wearing.

"You can turn on the TV if you want."

"We're not going to be here that long," he called as she disappeared into her bedroom.

He ended up plunking down on the couch because he didn't know what else to do with himself. Cassie's apartment was as harum-scarum as she was. The cluttered decor was in sharp contrast to his own austere living quarters, where everything was monochromatic and totally bric-a-brac free. His house contained no extras except for his home office, which was filled with neatly cataloged artifacts.

No doubt about it. He would go crazy if he had to live in such chaos. He resisted the urge to get up and start cleaning.

Knickknacks lay jumbled across every bit of available cabinet space. Porcelain kittens decorated a wall shelf. An overgrowth of ivy spilled from a plant stand and curled along the window ledge. In the corner stood three umbrellas, one of them open. Books sprawled on the bar between the living area and the kitchen, and a roll of unopened triple-ply toilet paper leaned against a bottle of extra-hold hairspray.

Clearly, she had never heard the phrase "a place for everything and everything in its place."

There was a half-finished jigsaw puzzle on the coffee table and a three-quarters-empty glass of chocolate milk. In a tote bag beside the couch he spied a half-knitted afghan. Twinkle lights were stapled to the mantel, and Harrison didn't know if they were left over from Christmas or simply part of her willy-nilly decorating scheme.

He was beginning to see a theme emerging. Cassie had a difficult time finishing what she started.

He glanced at his wristwatch. Ten-forty. Time was wasting. What in the world was taking so long?

"Hurry," he hollered, and when she didn't respond, he took out his phone and tried to call Adam. Voice mail again. He left another message.

"Harry?" Cassie's voice drifted from the bedroom.

He jumped as if he'd been caught doing something illegal. He closed his cell phone. "Uh-huh?"

"Um…" She paused. "Could you come in here a minute? I could use a hand."

She required his help in the bedroom? What did that mean?

In his head, he heard the sound track from one of those cheesy soft-core porn movies that came on Cinemax late at night. Not that he watched them. Much.

Dow-shicka-dow-now.

"Harry?"

"Ulp…er…" Jeez, he was sweating. He adjusted his glasses and shifted uncomfortably on the couch.

"Please," she coaxed in that breathless way of hers that could turn a man's insides to soup. "I'm in something of a pickle."

Dow-shicka-dow-now.

This was sounding more and more like a bad script for some X-rated flick. Why was his heart knocking like a jalopy engine? He hadn't violated his personal code of ethics.

Well, as long as you didn't count sexual fantasies.

"I need you…," she wheedled.

His instincts urged him to hit the door at a dead run. If Cassie had hanky-panky on her brain and she intended on seducing him, there was no way he could resist. But why would she choose this moment to come on to him? Particularly when she didn't even seem to like him very much.

Hell, who could know why the loopy woman did anything?

"Harry," her voice drew him.

Mesmerized, Harrison left the couch and edged down the hallway.

Her bedroom door stood slightly ajar as he approached with the mind-set of a warrior going into battle. If she was stretched out naked across the bed, giving him a come-hither look, he would retreat.

Um-hmm, yeah, sure. Uh-huh.

He would!

And when was the last time a delicious woman threw herself at you? Yep, never. Dream on, Romeo. If Cassie is buck naked on that bed, with lust for you gleaming in her eyes, you ain't about to turn tail and run.

He reached the door and hesitated.

"Could you possibly hurry it up? I'm in something of a compromising position."

Holy jeez, she *was* trying to seduce him.

The hairs on his arms lifted. He felt simultaneously panicky and thrilled and immediately tried to squelch the feelings. But they were unsquelchable.

Are you a man or a mouse, Harry?

Aw hell, now she had him calling himself by that atrocious nickname. Conflicted, he just stood there.

From inside the bedroom he heard a thumping noise.

"Did you leave?" Her voice sounded faraway and a little tremulous now. Like she was sad or in trouble or both.

And that's what got to him. The lost-little-girl quality in her voice and the notion that she needed him.

Emboldened, he marched into her bedroom.

Only to learn she was nowhere in sight.

He glanced around at the unmade four-poster bed covered by a canopy of some sheer girly-looking material. At least ten different pairs of shoes littered the floor, along with a blouse or two. A plaid miniskirt was thrown over the television set perched on a wicker dresser in the corner.

Talk about your lurid Catholic schoolgirl fantasies.

He jerked his head away, desperate for something less provocative to stare at. Three curio shelves lined the north wall, all three stocked with a variety of scented Yankee candles, and even though they weren't lit, the scents were still potent. The cacophony of aromas assaulted his nose. Peach parfait, freshly laundered linen, hazelnut coffee, pineapple-coconut, summer rose garden.

Hadn't anyone ever told the woman you weren't supposed to hodgepodge scents? The smell was too sweet, too intense, too overwhelming.

Much like Cassie herself.

What he lacked in visual acuity, God had made up for by supplying him with a highly attuned sense of smell. To Harrison's nose, her bedroom smelled the way a thirty-piece orchestra would sound if all the instruments were playing a different tune at once.

Olfactory bedlam.

Squinting, he noticed a collection of mini-collages tacked onto the wall behind each candle. Morbid curiosity, the quality his mother had sworn would be his ultimate downfall, propelled Harrison toward the candle wall for closer examination.

The collages were displayed in three-dimensional, eight-by-ten picture frames. In the center of each assortment was a photograph of Cassie with a different guy. Various memorabilia surrounded the photographs. Movie tickets, sports team pennants, lapel pins, charms, scrapbook lettering, stickers, swatches of fabric, and even a Top Forty playlist for the time period.

He counted the candles and framed memorabilia. Eighteen. Six on each shelf.

What in the heck was this?

Suddenly, Harrison realized what he was looking at. The wall was a shrine. To the men Cassie had known. Startled, he leaped back and ended up stumbling over a silk pillow thrown haphazardly on the floor. He lost his balance and crashed into the dressing table, knocking over a lamp in the process.

"Harry, is that you? I thought you'd run out on me and left me stranded. Are you all right?"

"Fine, I'm fine," Harrison muttered. "But where are you?" He righted the lamp, ran a hand through his hair, and struggled not to think about the significance of her candle wall.

"I'm in the bathroom."

Not good. Not good at all.

"The bathroom?" he repeated, because he did not know what else to say. Goose bumps spread up his arms like a bad case of the measles.

The *dow-shicka-dow-now* music twanged inside his head again.

"Yep."

"Why are you hiding in the bathroom?" he asked, even though he did not want to know.

"Because I'm embarrassed."

"Embarrassed?" he echoed.

"Before you come inside, I gotta know something. Do you shock easily? I get the feeling you shock easily, and this is a job for a man who doesn't shock easily."

"I don't shock *that* easily." Good God, what was happening in there?

"You sure?"

"For heaven's sake, just tell me what's going on. Nothing could be as shocking as my imagination."

Her voice turned teasing again. "Harry, just what *are* you imagining?"

Enough coyness.

Mentally girding his loins, he prepared his eyes for whatever unexpected sight might greet them. He placed a hand on the bathroom doorknob and slowly twisted it open.

Cassie was standing beside the vanity, her back to him, her shoulders slumped. A pair of hip-hugger jeans and a long-sleeved T-shirt had replaced the Cleopatra costume. The tight pants molded snugly against her well-rounded bottom, and the pockets were boldly embroidered with the Cadillac emblems.

Instantly, he understood the message. Here was a plush ride.

As Adam would say, *bootylicious.*

No matter how hard he tried, he could not stop ogling that fabulous fanny. The Flemish artist Rubens would have salivated for the opportunity of capturing such a lovely backside on canvas. Harrison found his own mouth growing moist.

"Cassie?"

She did not move. "Before I turn around, you have to promise me something."

"What's that?"

"You won't laugh."

"I promise I won't laugh. Please, just let me see what's causing you so much distress."

Slowly, she turned toward him.

He was so busy watching her facial expression, which was a touching combination of embarrassment, chagrin, and discomfort, that at first he did not notice that her blue jeans were only halfway zipped up.

First his gaze hung on the tiny heart tattooed at the level of her hip bone. It was no bigger than his thumbnail, discreet, tasteful, and yet it was still a tattoo. Wild women got tattoos. Or at least that's what he supposed.

Sexual awareness so strong it jarred his fillings zapped from his brain straight to his groin. He'd never found tattoos sexy before. Why now?

Was this what she'd called him in here for? To show him her tattoo?

Dow-shicka-dow-now.

It was only when she shrugged helplessly and splayed her hands in front of her fly that he realized the silky material of her skimpy black thong panties was wedged firmly in the teeth of her zipper.

Chapter 6

I was trying to hurry up for you, and look what happened," Cassie said.

Harrison dropped to his knees in front of her, the manicure scissors she'd retrieved from her makeup vanity clutched firmly in his hand.

"I hate that you have to cut them," Cassie muttered. "These panties are from Victoria's Secret, and I'm not about to tell you how much they cost."

"The material is jammed in tight; there's no other way around it unless you can shimmy out of those jeans."

"Don't you think I already tried that? The zipper isn't down low enough for me to edge the pants over my hips."

His breath was warm against her skin as he leaned forward and grasped the zipper. Cassie looked down at the top of his dark head planted startlingly close to her most private area. His hair grazed her bare belly and she just about came undone.

How did she keep getting herself into these sticky predicaments?

She closed her eyes against the hot, moist sensation gathering low inside her. She was forced to brace her palms against the counter at her back to keep from top-pling over on legs suddenly gone to Silly Putty.

What in the hell was the matter with her? Why was Harrison Standish, of all people, making her weak in the knees?

"Hold still," he muttered.

"I wasn't moving," she denied, not wanting him to know how much he affected her.

"You were swaying like a palm tree."

"Was not."

"I'm not going to argue with you. Just hold steady unless you want to get poked with these scissors."

She wanted to get poked, all right, but not with scissors.

Cassie!

She'd shocked even herself. How come she was so turned on? She had never been sexually attracted to a dude that she didn't even like.

It felt weird. It felt kinky.

It felt like sex outside in a lightning storm.

Unbidden, she had a sudden visual of the two of them doing the wild thing in a rowboat on a lake in the summer with a light spring shower pelting their heated skins.

Stop it.

The boat was bobbing. Birds twittered in the trees along the shore. The cotton-candy pink dress she wore was pushed up around her waist, the gauzy material cling-ing to her hard nipples as Professor Standish studiously explored every nook and cranny of her willing body.

In real life, his fingertips skimmed lightly over her skin and Cassie inhaled sharply. Yeah, baby. More of that. Oh, she was an unrepentant slut puppy!

"I'm sorry," Harry said rather gruffly. "I didn't mean to hurt you."

Hurts sooo good, her audacious side wanted to say, but

luckily she was prudent enough to keep her mouth shut. Nevertheless, a shudder ran through her.

"You okay?" he asked, tilting his head to peer up at her.

"Just a little chilled with myself so exposed."

He made a noise that sounded like someone being strangled.

Turnabout was fair play. "You okay?"

"Just clearing my throat."

"You need a glass of water or something?"

"I'm fine," he mumbled. "I just want to hurry and get this over with."

Aw, don't hurry, whined her impish voice. *I like things nice and slow.*

Knock it off, she scolded herself. Think of something besides the fact his touch is so tickle soft it's giving you goose bumps.

Let's see. What could she think about? She wasn't much of a protracted thinker.

Hmm. She'd never noticed before how broad his shoulders were. He'd be a dazzler in a tux if he had a decent haircut and contact lenses.

There you go again, imagining him as a sexy stud. He's not a hidden hunk in geek's clothing. He's a nerd with a capital N.

Okay, okay. How's this? Think about the difference between Harry and Adam. While she had never met Adam in person, she knew ten times more about him than she did about Harry.

Adam was an outrageous flirt who loved to take chances. And just like her, he enjoyed driving flashy cars really fast. His favorite food was lobster. His favorite color was aquamarine. His favorite video game was *Grand Theft Auto*. In high school, he'd won the starring role in *Damn Yankees*. And in college, his GPA had been the exact same as hers, 2.75. Adam read *GQ* religiously, owned the latest and greatest electronic gadgets, and he'd never once told her he had a brother.

What she knew about Dr. Harrison Standish could fit in a tube of lipstick. He was a bad dresser, and he mumbled under his breath a lot when things didn't go his way. He drove a white Volvo, and apparently he filled up whenever the gas gauge reached the halfway mark.

Ack! What a blah, safe car. Come to think of it, the Volvo was much too clean. No fast-food wrappers stuffed in the side door pockets, nothing cute dangling from the rearview mirror, no smushed bug guts on the windshield.

She would go crazy if she had to drive around in his spick-and-span-mobile.

"All done."

"Huh?" Cassie blinked.

Harrison had risen to his feet and was staring at her kind of funny. As if she had spinach in her teeth or something equally gauche.

"You're free. Panties clipped out of the zipper." Awkwardly, he handed her the manicure scissors.

She completely understood his awkwardness. She too was feeling decidedly ill at ease. Her idiotic hormones wanted to tango with Harry something fierce, while mentally she was much more in sync with his brother, Adam.

Her eyes locked onto his butt, which somehow managed to look sensational in spite of the baggy Dockers, as he walked out of the bathroom. She had to stop getting herself into these sticky predicaments.

At least for the next three days.

Across town in an abandoned warehouse, the man in the mummy costume slowly regained consciousness. The throbbing in his back was almost unbearable. Each tiny movement sent jolts of pain shooting down his spine. His lips were cracked, and his mouth was so dry that he could hardly swallow.

He frowned, and even that tiny movement caused intense pain. He realized he was lying facedown in metal shavings on a cement floor that smelled of rat excrement, and his wrists were duct-taped behind his back.

Not a good sign.

Nausea roiled his stomach. God, he couldn't puke. He must not puke. He moved his head to get his nostrils out of the metal shavings, before he accidentally inhaled them, and stared glumly across the floor.

The room was badly lit by a dim fluorescent bulb. He saw large sheets of corrugated tin stacked in piles all around him. Beyond the stacks he could make out heavy, double-rollered doors. The sharp bite of pain that blasted into his head wouldn't allow him to look any higher. He felt shapeless.

Boneless.

As desiccated as a mummy.

Pulp. Living mush. Mashed. Squashed. Pulverized. Hot. Red. Burning.

His back was a furnace. He could not think. Could scarcely breathe.

No.

He could not allow himself to be consumed. There was something he must do. Something vitally important. Except he couldn't remember what it was.

Think.

But his mind was a blank. He closed his eyes. Think, think, think.

Where was he? Why was he here? Why did his back hurt like the belly of Hades?

He lay there for what seemed an eternity, his mind a sticky cobweb of jumbled thoughts. None of it connecting. None of it making sense. In his mind's eye he could see a red purse lying beside a stone bench, but he had no idea of its significance.

Awareness came and went in waves. First he was acutely aware of every physical ache, and then he would nod off, sleeping in brief snatches. Then he'd awaken, confused all over again.

Finally, there came a sharp intrusion to his mental meanderings.

He heard noises.

Footsteps.

Voices.

Low and argumentative. Originating from somewhere beyond his blurry field of vision. Speaking in a language he recognized, but not his native tongue.

Concentrate.

He strained to listen.

Greek. He recognized the language now. The men were speaking Greek. But they were too far away for him to hear what they were arguing about.

It's Greek to me, the mummy thought giddily and almost laughed.

Were they friend or foe? Considering he was tied up in a rat-infested warehouse stocked with sheet metal, it would be a good guess that they weren't his best drinking buddies.

Sweat trickled down his neck as they drew closer. Then the footsteps stopped just outside the door.

"Hold on to your temper this time, Demitri," a man who sounded like a bullfrog with a bad cold said in English. "You almost killed him when you stabbed him."

"I can't believe we are treating him with kid gloves," the man presumably called Demitri retorted. "He's trying to destroy everything."

Their voices sounded vaguely familiar. Especially the Louis Armstrong soundalike. But their identities wavered just out of reach. Maybe he didn't know them. He could be mistaken.

"Patience," said Croupy Bullfrog Man. "If you ever want to advance beyond apprentice then you must develop patience."

Who were these guys? Did he know them? Should he know them?

The mummy strained against the duct tape, but it would not yield. There wouldn't have been time to run even if the tape had given way. Plus, he wasn't in any condition to fight off a Girl Scout, much less two grown men.

He heard the mechanical whirring noise of the door being hoisted on its rollers. Squinting in the dimness, he saw two sets of feet round the corner of the metal stacks. One wore dirty Nike sneakers; the other guy had on patent-leather wing tips.

Wing Tips hung back.

Mr. Nike approached.

He had an awful feeling that the backstabbing, temperamental Demitri was the one in the sneakers. He closed his eyes, slowed his breathing, and pretended to be unconscious.

The tip of an angry Nike caught him hard and low in the rib cage.

The mummy grunted, biting his bottom lip against the pain. It wasn't only his ribs that took the jolt, but his entire spine.

The man squatted, peered at him. It was the face of a

ruthless thug, scarred and hard. He grinned and licked his lips.

Alarm charged through the mummy. Even though he did not recognize the man, he had a sense that he had run afoul of this unsavory character in the past, and their encounter had not been cordial.

"Eh, you're not asleep," Nike said in English, then suddenly grabbed him by the neck and dragged him to his feet.

The mummy screamed in shock and agony. He'd only imagined that he had been in pain before. Nothing matched the fiery train wreck that was now chewing through his body like it was a toothpick.

"Take it easy, Demitri," Froggy croaked. "If he passes out again, it will be that much longer before we can coax his secrets out of him."

The mummy's eyes flew to the man illuminated in the path between the door and the stacks of metal on both sides of them. The man with the deep, hoarse voice of an ailing bullfrog. His coal-black eyes showed not the slightest glimpse of mercy. His face was as emotionless as marble.

He stepped closer.

Bullfrog Man was short and squat, barrel-shaped yet muscular. His dark hair was slicked back with something oily, and his mouth bore a nasty mixture of cruelty and intelligence.

"The sooner you talk, the sooner this will all be over." His English was heavily accented with Greek flavor. A gyro-eating, wing-tip-wearing, bad-cold-having bullfrog. "Where is the amulet?"

The mummy did not answer.

What amulet? He didn't remember anything about an

amulet or who these men were, but something told him this question was vitally important. His head pounded. His gut roiled again.

Nike yanked his hair.

He yelped. Involuntary tears flooded his eyes. He couldn't help it. The pain was that bad.

"Please, don't make me ask you twice," Bullfrog said, pulling a pointy metal nail file from the pocket of his suit jacket and slowly dragging it across his nails.

The thought of what an evil man could do with a sharp metal fingernail file squeezed the mummy's breath right out of his lungs.

"I . . . I don't know," he whispered, his legs swaying as he struggled to remain standing. Demitri's breath burned hot against his neck. He just dangled there, too weak to fight.

Bullfrog nodded. Demitri pressed a thumb into the aching wound at his back.

Blistering tides of agony lapped over him. His knees gave way. His eyes rolled back in his head.

"Where is the amulet?"

"I don't know what you're talking about."

Bullfrog sighed and passed the metal file to Demitri. "You know what to do."

"Please," the mummy babbled. "I swear, I don't remember. My thinking is fuzzy."

"Then Demitri will sharpen your memory for you. One way or the other, we will have both halves of the amulet. Never doubt that."

Demitri stroked the file against the mummy's cheek, stopping when he reached his eyes. "Where's the amulet?" he hissed, his breath thick with garlic.

The mummy whimpered. If he could remember, he

would tell him. But his mind was a blank screen and the harder he tried to conjure something, the more elusive it became.

The file was at the corner of his eye now.

"Where's the amulet?"

Dear God! the mummy thought just before he lost consciousness. He couldn't remember anything. Not even his own name.

Not even to save his life.

Chapter 7

The American Airlines agent at the main ticket counter confirmed Cassie's inquiry. Yes, Dr. Adam Grayfield had arrived at DFW Airport on the eleven-twenty-five flight from JFK twelve hours earlier.

"What about Dr. Grayfield's cargo?" Cassie asked.

Harrison shot her a quelling glance. *Zip it*, his fierce glare warned.

She figured he was mad because she had asked the question before he could. Fine. She shrugged. No skin off her nose if he wanted to play big man in charge.

"What happened to my brother's freight?" Harrison addressed the man behind the ticket counter. "Did it arrive safely? Or did you lose it?"

The ticket agent—who looked like a strange cross between Bill Clinton and Mr. Rogers with his lush gray hair, hound dog nose, long slender neck, and wooly red cardigan—went on the defensive. Cassie recognized from his stiffening body language that his self-protective instincts were kicking in. Squarer shoulders, narrowing eyes, clenched jaw, petulant expression. She understood that a good part of the ticket agent's day must be taken up by people bitching about their lost or damaged luggage.

"As far as I know," the man said to Harrison in a tone as warm as an Alaskan glacier, "we've received no complaints from Dr. Grayfield."

"Did he pick up his luggage?" Harrison fished the baggage ticket out of his jacket pocket. "I have the claim stub."

"Then I'm assuming he did not pick it up. Check with baggage claim."

"Where's that located?"

"Near the baggage carousels, but they closed at ten and it's now eleven-thirty. Guess you'll just have to come back tomorrow morning." The ticket agent looked anything but disappointed.

"This is an urgent matter that can't wait until morning. Dr. Grayfield never showed up for an important engagement this evening," Harrison said.

"Not my problem," the ticket agent replied. "Now if you'll excuse me, it's time for my lunch break."

Cassie couldn't keep quiet. Not when the ticket agent was about to walk away. Not when they had less than seventy-two hours to find Adam and the amulet.

"Excuse me." She bellied up to the counter, not caring if Harrison got mad because she was taking over. She glanced at the ticket agent's name tag and gave him the friendliest smile she could muster. "Jerry."

Jerry stopped and turned toward her. "Yes?"

"Please excuse my friend. He's very irritable because his only brother is missing." She told him who Harrison was and explained about the star-crossed lovers exhibit, and she elaborated on how Adam hadn't shown up for the event.

"He has no right to take it out on me," the man grumbled and shot Harrison a dirty look.

Cassie nodded in agreement. "You're absolutely right about that, Jerry."

"I'm just doing my job."

"Of course you are." She lowered both her voice and her eyelashes seductively. "Could you please find it in your heart to check your computer and see if Dr. Grayfield's freight was picked up? It could be a clue to his whereabouts."

For the coup de grâce, she reached out and lightly touched Jerry's forearm.

The ticket agent stood up a little straighter. "I could do it for *you*."

"Thank you ever so much. I really appreciate your effort."

Jerry returned to his computer monitor and typed something in on the keyboard. "Dr. Grayfield's freight is still in the airport. It was never picked up."

"Is there any way that someone, a supervisor maybe, could open baggage claim for us?"

"I could ask, but don't get your hopes up." Jerry sounded doubtful.

She pursed her lips in the sexiest pucker she could muster. Pamela Anderson had nothing on her. "Please."

"All right," he agreed. "I'll call a supervisor and see if we can't get those bags for you."

She rewarded Jerry with a stupefying smile and a gentle squeeze of his forearm. She could practically see the man's knees weaken. "Thank you so much."

"No problem, Miss..."

"Call me Cassie."

Damn if Jerry's face didn't flush red and perspiration

break out on his forehead. Quickly, he grabbed for the house phone.

And that, Harrison Standish, is the way you handle people.

"You don't have to act like a centerfold queen to get people to do your bidding," Harrison growled softly in her ear while the ticket agent was on the phone to baggage claim. "I was handling things my way."

"And getting nowhere."

"I was about to demand to see his superior when you decided to butt in."

"Maybe you were, sugar," she whispered, keeping her smile pasted firmly in place even when she wanted to tell him to kiss her fleshy fanny. "But my way turned out to be faster and a whole lot nicer."

"And a whole lot more manipulative."

"A girl's gotta do what a girl's gotta do."

"You're justifying your means."

"What is your problem, Standish? Why do you care if I'm flirting with the guy to get my way? You reap the benefits."

"It makes me feel like a pimp."

"Well now, that sounds like a personal problem to me." She tossed her head. Give the man a palace, and he would no doubt bitch because it was too big and drafty.

Jerry hung up the phone. "The supervisor will be with you in a minute, Cassie. Why don't you have a seat? Can I get you anything? Cup of coffee? A soda?"

"I'm fine, Jerry, but thanks a million. You've been such a big help."

Cassie and Harrison seated themselves on the black vinyl chairs. She practiced smiling coyly, preparing to cajole the supervisor into opening the baggage claim office for them.

Five minutes later a tall, muscular brunette woman with plenty of sass stalked from behind a door marked "Employees" on the opposite side of the concourse. Her navy blue uniform fit her like a second skin, and her three-inch pumps made her long, lean legs look even longer and leaner.

Cassie disliked her on principle. So much for her plans to flirt her way into baggage claim.

The woman sauntered over to Harrison and extended a hand. "How do you do," she murmured in a silken voice. "I'm Spanky Frebrizo."

"Dr. Harrison Standish. And this is Cassie Cooper."

Spanky pumped his hand, but she never even glanced at Cassie. "I'm well aware of who you are, Dr. Standish. I'm a huge ancient Egypt buff, and I'm a big fan of the star-crossed lovers. I even attended one of your lectures at UTA through community education. When Jerry told me there was a famous archaeologist waiting to see me, I just about fainted."

Imagine that, Cassie mused. Harry had a groupie. She half expected Spanky to grab a Sharpie and write "I LOVE YOU" on her eyelids.

Harrison beamed. "It's always nice to meet someone with an interest in ancient Egypt, Spanky."

Spanky?

What in the hell kind of name was that anyway? It had to be a nickname. Cassie didn't even want to speculate on how the woman had earned it.

While Spanky totally ignored Cassie, Harrison explained the situation and their dilemma.

"I'll take you over to baggage claim," Spanky said. "Anything I can do to help you, Dr. Standish." She turned and led the way.

Cassie mocked her behind her back, silently mouthing, *Anything to help you, Dr. Standish.*

She and Harrison were walking shoulder to shoulder a few feet behind Spanky. Harrison leaned over to whisper, "What's the matter?"

Cassie shot him an evil look.

"Jealous?"

Ha! Over Harrison Standish?

Why would she be jealous over a color-blind, pompous, nerdy professor who worked out regularly and was damned handy with a pair of manicure scissors? Okay, so maybe she was a teeny bit jealous. Big hairy deal.

Then suddenly she had an inkling into what he might have been feeling when she was flirting with Jerry. Ouch. The shoe didn't fit so well on the other foot.

"Here we are." Spanky unlocked the door to the lost baggage area, flicked on the light, and ushered them inside. "You can wait right here while I go see if I can locate the baggage."

"It's probably a heavy crate. You might need some help lifting it."

"I'm sorry, it's against our company policy to allow customers beyond the front desk." Spanky ran her gaze over Harrison again, and Cassie could have sworn the woman licked her lips. "But I suppose it would be okay to let you in this one time."

"Thank you, Spanky," Harrison said.

"But she has to stay here." Spanky indicated Cassie with a wave of her hand.

Bitch.

Cassie ground her teeth and glared while Harrison trailed off after Spanky. He cast a parting glance over his shoulder, giving her a what-can-I-do shrug. He might act innocent, but clearly he was enjoying turning the tables on her.

She plopped down on a bench. A few minutes later she heard whispering and giggling from beyond the shelves stacked tall with MIA luggage. She rolled her eyes and tried to ignore the churning in the pit of her stomach.

The giggling stopped.

A few seconds later Harrison reappeared. "By any chance do you have a Swiss Army knife?"

"Do I look like the kind of woman who carries a Swiss Army knife? If I needed to, say, oh, slice some Camembert, I'd just call in the Swiss Army."

"There is no Swiss Army," he said.

"Then what do they need knives for?"

"You're incorrigible."

"I know." She grinned. "What did you want the knife for anyway? You and Spanky aren't slicing Camembert back there, are you?"

Harrison looked at her like she was the weirdest person he had ever met. He just didn't get her sense of humor.

"The crate is locked," he said, "and I don't have a key, but I think if I had a Swiss Army knife or something like that I could pick the lock. It looks pretty flimsy."

"I have a fingernail file."

"May I borrow it, please?"

"It's gonna cost you."

"Don't be petty."

"Take it or leave it." She fished the file from her purse but held it out of his reach.

He sighed. "What's it going to cost me?"

"I want to be there when you open the crate."

He looked at her a long moment. "There's nothing going on between me and Spanky."

"Pfft." She waved a hand. "As if I care. I just want to know what happened to Adam."

"Me too," he said soberly. "Come on. If Spanky gets mad, then she just gets mad."

"Really?" Cassie's heart warmed.

He motioned for her to follow. Happily, she sprang to her feet.

"Cassie has a metal fingernail file," Harrison said when they reached Spanky and the coffin-shaped crate that was pulled out into the aisle.

Spanky frowned at Cassie. "I changed my mind. I don't think we should be breaking into it. If you don't have a key, you should come back when you get one."

"We have the baggage claim ticket. It's my brother's freight. I have a right to open it."

"Maybe so, but I don't have to let you open it on airport property."

"Spanky," Harrison said in a wheedling voice.

Cassie suppressed a smile. It was fun watching him try to flirt his way out of a problem.

"Solen's half of the star-crossed lovers exhibit is quite possibly in that crate," Harrison cajoled. "You would be the very first person to see it outside of archaeologists, scientists, and academicians. Patrons of the arts were paying a thousand dollars a head for a private viewing at the Kimbell."

"Really?"

"Really."

"Okay," she relented. "Go ahead and open it."

Harrison knelt on the floor beside the crate and worked at the lock with the fingernail file. After several minutes, the cheesy lock finally clicked open.

He raised his head and met Cassie's gaze. They exchanged a look. What would they find?

Slowly Harrison raised the lid and sucked in his breath. Cassie peered over his shoulder to see what was inside.

Except for some sawdust, the packing crate was empty.

"Well, that was a big buncha hoopla over nothing." Spanky snorted.

Harrison was past the point of trying to get his needs met by charming the supervisor. He had to think. Kneading his brow with two fingers, he stared at the empty crate.

What was this all about? Had Adam screwed up with shipping? Had he somehow dropped the ball and lost Solen in transit? Was that why he hadn't shown up at the museum? Was it because he was too embarrassed to admit his mistake? It wasn't as if Adam was the most reliable person in the world.

And yet, in spite of his doubts, something told Harrison there was more going on here than met the eye.

"This sucks," Spanky complained. "You promised me something cool, and it's nothing but an empty box."

"Hush," he growled.

"Excuse me?" Spanky's eyes flamed.

"He told you to hush," Cassie said.

"Shut up." Spanky made a face at her. "You're not even supposed to be back here."

"What are you gonna do about it?" Cassie challenged, thrusting out her chest.

"Call security."

If their quarreling wasn't getting on his nerves, Harrison would have found Cassie's jealousy endearing. No matter how much she might deny it, she liked him. But as it was, he couldn't hear himself postulate.

"Stop bickering, both of you," he growled and glared up at them. "I'm trying to think."

Women. Throw in a little envy, and poof, you had a

catfight on your hands. Amusing thing was, he'd never been the object of a chick brawl before, and it was something of an ego stroke. Too bad he didn't have time to enjoy being cock of the walk.

"But ...," Spanky started to protest.

"This is serious," Harrison said and pointed an index finger. "Not another word from either of you. Got it?"

Cassie and Spanky exchanged spiteful glances, but thankfully they fell silent.

Harrison ran his fingers along the crate. The outside of it was stickered with labels that proclaimed, *Fragile! Delicate! Don't mutilate!* But the shipping box was cheap, and the lock on it was even cheaper.

The Egyptian government had shipped Kiya's remains in an elaborate crate, escorted by Ahmose and an armed security guard.

Why hadn't Adam or the Greek government taken the same precautions with Solen? It made no sense.

Unless Adam had shipped the wrong crate. Unless Solen had never been in there in the first place.

If that was the case, where *was* Solen and his half of the amulet? And if Adam had screwed up, why had he given Gabriel the envelope with the baggage claim ticket to give to Harrison?

There had to be something he was overlooking.

"Harry," Cassie whispered. "Don't get mad at me, but the clock is ticking and we're running out of time. Maybe we should be on our way."

"No, not yet."

His gut told him there was a message in this box, and Harrison Jerome Standish was nothing if not methodical. He would not leave until he found the clue, and Adam knew that about him.

Damn you, Adam, and your silly games. If you've sent me on a wild-goose chase, I'll wring your neck when I find you.

He plowed through the fine wood shavings. Maybe there was a small artifact, something, anything, buried inside. Sawdust sifted through his fingers. He tossed it from the box, littering the floor, but he didn't care. He was frantic for evidence.

"Hey! Hey!" Spanky griped.

"It sweeps up," he said.

"I'm seriously starting to regret letting you in here," she muttered.

"See what happens when you let hormones do the thinking?" Cassie sassed.

"Oh, like you're one to talk, skank."

"Takes one to know one."

"Ladies!" Harrison shouted. "Shut up."

Minutes later, when he had most of the sawdust in a pile beside the crate, he was almost ready to admit defeat. The box was empty. There were no hidden secrets.

He sighed and rocked back on his heels, perplexed.

And then he remembered one of Adam's favorite possessions when he was a kid.

A box with a false bottom for hiding secrets.

Chapter 8

Without warning, the base of Cassie's skull started its precognitive burn. The freaky sensation always preceded some bizarre occurrence—say, for instance, a mummy stabbing. But she had never experienced it twice in one day. That fact by itself was disconcerting. And when the heat did not abate after a few seconds as it usually did, but actually blazed hotter, she got nervous.

She slapped a palm to the back of her neck and rose unsteadily to her feet. She'd been crouching beside Harrison, watching him dismantle the packing crate in the airport parking lot after Spanky had thrown them out of baggage claim for making too big of a mess.

"Harry," she said.

"It's Harrison," he corrected without looking up. He was intently trying to pry nails out of the board with his car keys.

"We have to get out of here," she said. "Something bad is about to happen."

"Uh-huh."

"Harrison." She raised her voice. "We gotta go."

"Look, look, Cassie!" He was so excited.

"Huh?" She wished she felt better so she could get into his enthusiasm. She'd never seen him looking so passionate about anything. But her head was so miserably hot that she longed to dunk it in a bucket of ice water.

"I was right." He beamed. "There is a false bottom."

"I've got a really bad feeling about this."

But he wasn't listening. He flung the strip of board across the parking lot and lifted something from the false bottom. It was bundled in sheepskin and tied with a cord bearing a wax seal. The seal depicted a Minotaur transposed over a double ring emblem.

"This is important." Her head was burning so hot she could hardly see, much less think.

"So is this." He carefully peeled away the sheepskin to reveal a papyrus scroll. The awe in his voice was perilously close to religious ecstasy. She had an artifact zealot on her hands.

"Dammit, man, listen to me!"

"What?" Finally Harrison raised his gaze and met her eyes.

"I know this is gonna sound crazy, but ever since I almost drowned when I was nine, I occasionally get these twinges."

"Twinges?" He pushed his glasses up on his nose with the index finger of one hand, while the other hand cradled his discovery.

"Premonitions. My brain gets really hot."

"You're joking." He was staring at her as if her mother had dropped her on her head one time too many when she was a baby.

"Nope, not kidding, and I've learned that if I ignore these twinges, it's at my own peril. We gotta get out of here."

"You're talking about premonitions when I have the find of the century in my hands?"

"Your brother found it first," she snapped, getting irritated with his one-track mind. "And if I don't sit down in a cool place soon, I'm going to pass out and crack my head open on the pavement."

"Okay, okay." He finally seemed to snap out of his artifact-induced euphoria. "I'll unlock the car door for you."

"Thanks ever so much." Feeling like a boiled jalapeño, Cassie sank into the passenger seat.

This will pass. Think of something pleasant. Think of your favorite things.

Like Kiss Me Scarlet lipstick and fusilli pasta and reruns of *Sex and the City.* Coffee ice cream and strolling the streets of Madrid and long soaks in the hot tub.

Oooh-no, not hot tubs. Don't think hot.

Cassie took a deep breath and waved a hand in front of her face in a vain attempt to cool herself. This was getting scary. She'd never had one of these ESP-induced brain hot flashes last so long. What she wouldn't give for a tall glass of sweet tea over crushed ice and an oscillating fan set to supersonic speed.

But the sense of urgency pushed at her, as overwhelming as the heat. "Get in the car, Harry," she barked.

He looked at the crate.

"Leave the crate. It won't fit in the car. You've got what you came for. Let's go."

"Okay."

Her face was sweating and she was panting hard. If the guy ever thought about getting married and having kids, he was going to have to learn that when a woman got that particular tone in her voice she meant business.

"Now!"

He wrapped the papyrus scroll in the sheepskin and got in the car. He glanced over at her as he laid his newfound treasure on the backseat.

"You're serious about this. You really are overheated."

"Damn skippy. I'm melting like a box of chocolates, Forrest Gump. Get the air-conditioning cranked."

They drove away from the terminal with the AC blasting as high as it would go. The nightmarish heat inside her head began to recede. By the time they were off airport property, Cassie was feeling almost human again.

"Take the next exit," she said. "There's a bunch of drive-through fast-food joints. I need a large Coke with extra extra ice."

"So these premonitions of yours, what happens when you get them?" he asked as he pulled up to the speaker at a Jack in the Box.

"The back of my head burns, and then something weird always happens. Get me a couple of monster tacos along with the Coke. No, wait, monster tacos have hot sauce on them, and the last thing I want is something hot. Just get me a grilled chicken sandwich and an order of curly fries."

He placed her order, plus he got a salad for himself and a glass of water.

"Sheesh, Harry, what's with the salad? Live a little, willya?"

"It's Harrison, and I prefer to watch my intake of fats and carbohydrates."

"Hey, with the kind of precognitive heat I've been feeling, today could very well be your final day on the face of this earth. Don't go out on lettuce and water."

"I'm happy with my choice of last meals," he said.

Cassie shrugged. "Suit yourself."

While they waited in the drive-through line, Cassie

called home to check her messages to see if Adam had called, but her machine never picked up. She must have forgotten to turn the thing on. Terrific.

They got their food and Cassie tore into the sack. She peeled the paper from her sandwich and took a big bite.

"Hey, you can't eat in my car."

"Watch me. I'm starving."

"No one's ever eaten in my car."

"The old gal is like, what? Ten? I'd say it's way past time to pop her cherry. Wanna french fry?" She dangled a fry in front of his face.

"No, I do not want a fry."

"You might as well pull over and eat your salad. I've already contaminated your car by pigging out in it."

He considered her a moment, then to Cassie's surprise he pulled into the parking lot. With a resigned sigh he said, "Hand me the salad."

She passed it over to him and watched him carefully open the container and cautiously squeeze the packet of Italian dressing over his veggies. They munched in silence for a few minutes.

"How's your brain now?" Harrison asked in between bites. "Still fried?"

"Are you being a smartass?" She sized him up with a sidelong glance. "You don't believe me about the premonitions, do you?"

"Sorry. I'm a seeing-is-believing kind of guy."

"So tell me, Harry, what exactly *do* you believe in?"

"Harrison," he said. "I believe in the power of the intellect. In scientific method. In reason and logic and common sense."

"I take it you don't buy into the legend of the starcrossed lovers."

"I do believe that Kiya and Solen were lovers in real life. Hieroglyphic writing found in Ramses IV's tomb supports the story. But I don't believe that when the amulet pieces are brought back together Solen and Kiya will be reunited in some mythological afterworld."

"That's a shame," she said wistfully.

"What?"

"That you don't believe in magic."

"And you do?"

"Oh, sure. I believe in romance and magic and love at first sight and..."

"Happily ever after," he supplied.

"Oh, no, I don't believe in *that*."

"You believe in magic and in the legend of the starcrossed lovers, but you don't believe that people can find permanent happiness together?"

"For some people, maybe," she said. "But it's not my thing."

"Why not?"

"Because after a while things invariably get dull. The fire goes out. The passion dies down, and you're stuck with someone who leaves their socks on the bathroom floor and expects you to pick them up."

"Ah," he said. "I understand."

His smug expression irritated her. "What is it that you understand?"

"You're a commitment-phobe."

"I am not. I just don't want to be locked down."

He laughed. Really loud and long. "That's the definition of a commitment-phobe. Be honest with yourself. You like the thrill of romance but a real, honest-to-God, mature relationship based on mutual respect scares the pants off you."

Cassie felt as if he'd just driven a push pin through the

center of her forehead. Ouch. He's got you bagged, tagged, and labeled, babe.

"Oh, like you're one to talk. When was the last time you even had a date, Harry? Much less a serious relationship?"

"I've been too busy for a relationship."

"You've been too busy? Doing what? It's been two years since you dug up Kiya." Cassie polished off her last french fry and took a long sip of her Coke. "What's been shaking since?"

"I've been looking for Solen."

"Unsuccessfully."

"Yeah," he said, sounding just a tad bitter. "Unsuccessfully. Thanks for reminding me. But I have also been working on the djed. I'm trying to figure out how it works and what the Egyptians used it for."

"You mean the dildo?"

"It's not a dildo!"

"It looks like it could be one."

"Well, it isn't," he snapped. "It's some kind of electromagnetic transformer."

"Hey, a dildo could transform me."

"You're impossible," he said.

"That's what they tell me."

He gathered up their empty food containers and stepped out of the car to deposit them in a nearby trash can. He got back inside, started the engine, and then motored toward the freeway entrance ramp without speaking.

Okeydokey. Apparently she'd made him mad by belittling his djed thingy.

"I apologize for the dildo comment," she said. "I was just teasing."

"Unlike some people, I'm serious about my work," Harrison grumbled.

"So what's this papyrus thing all about?" Cassie jerked a thumb at the backseat.

"I don't know. I recognized that seal, but is it a real artifact or something Adam's concocted? I didn't get to examine the writing on the scroll closely, but it looked like Minoan hieroglyphics, and no one has ever been able to translate them."

"Adam did."

He jerked his head around to stare at her. "What?"

"Yep. It was supposed to be a surprise. Adam was going to reveal his achievement at the reunification ceremony."

"But that's impossible. The Minoan hieroglyphics are untranslatable."

"Not according to your brother. He was very excited. Your name came up several times in our conversation, but he never let on that you were his brother."

"You're certain that he said he'd translated the Minoan hieroglyphics?"

"Positive."

"This changes everything. What else did he tell you?"

"All Adam would say is that the translation could alter the face of history. But you know your brother better than I do. I gather he leans toward the dramatic."

"That he does, but this time he might be right. It all depends on that scroll."

A car was following close on their bumper. The headlights reflected off the rearview mirror. The base of her skull warmed again, and she reached up a hand to massage away the tingling. Maybe it was just stress. Being around Harry was certainly stressful. Hopefully there was nothing ominous in the offing.

"I'm beginning to think this isn't a publicity stunt," Harrison said quietly. "I'm afraid Adam's gotten himself in serious trouble."

"What kind of trouble?"

Curiosity prompted her question, but it was more than casual interest that had her waiting for Harry's answer with indrawn breath. Maybe the smoldering premonition at the top of her spine wasn't for herself or Harry but for Adam.

"You saw the seal on the cord binding the sheepskin?"

Cassie nodded. "It was two circles with some Greek letters and a Minotaur on top."

"Not Greek letters. Minoan hieroglyphics."

"And?"

"The Minotaur over the double circles is the sacred crest of a three-thousand-year-old secret brotherhood sect that supposedly had perfected both the art of alchemy and the ability to control the weather. Adam's dad, Tom Grayfield, is something of an academic expert on the ancient order. I believe he even did his doctoral thesis on them."

"What were they called?"

"The closest we've come to correctly pronouncing their Minoan name is by using a Cretan intonation." Then he said something that sounded an awful lot like, "Wannamakemecomealot."

"Excuse me?" It wasn't that she hadn't heard him the first time. Cassie just couldn't imagine that she was hearing the same phrase twice in one night.

Harrison repeated himself.

"Omigosh, Harry." She splayed a hand over her mouth, then whispered, "That's exactly what the mummy said to me before he collapsed."

"You're certain?"

Cassie inhaled sharply. "Do you think he was telling me that members of this cult were the ones who stabbed him? He said, 'Beware Wannamakemecomealot.' That was before I knew he'd been stabbed, and I just thought he was trying to be flirtatious."

"It seems a huge stretch, Cassie."

"Harry, the mummy was really weak. Barely breathing. I was so scared he was dying."

In the light from the headlamps of the car following close behind them, Cassie could see Harrison's jaw tighten. "Let's just hope you're wrong."

"Tell me more about this Wannamakemecomealot bunch," she said, quickly changing the subject. She didn't want Harrison dwelling on the fact that his brother might be dead. Best not freak out until there was something to freak out about. That was her motto. If you put off worrying long enough, maybe it would never happen.

"Many people in the archaeological community believe Solen was a member of this cult. Most scholars now refer to it as the Minoan Order. Causes fewer giggles in the classroom than 'Wannamakemecomealot.'"

"I can imagine." She snickered.

She wished that stupid car would pass or drop back. Wasn't the headlight glare bothering Harry? But he seemed totally wrapped up in his story, oblivious to what was going on around him. He had the most intense powers of concentration she had ever seen. It made her want to squirm.

Settle down. This is important.

Fighting her natural ADD tendencies, Cassie rested her elbow against her knee, propped her chin in her palm, and forced herself to really hear what he was saying.

"Go on, sorry for laughing."

"When the Minoan Order was initially formed, they only used their metaphysical powers for good. 'Do no harm' was the foundation of their creed. Anyone discovered using their arcane knowledge for evil purposes was immediately stripped of their magic and exiled from Crete."

"Was that what happened to Solen? Is that how he ended up in Egypt? He did something bad and got banished?"

"No. At least not according to the hieroglyphics we found in Ramses's tomb, although we do know Solen was one of Ramses's scribes. He could have written his own version of history."

"So fill me in. What's the entire scoop?"

"Supposedly, here's what happened," Harrison said. "The village where Solen lived was threatened by a rampaging Minotaur, and even the strongest, most talented warriors could not defeat the beast. Solen was young. He was only fourteen, but he'd been studying metaphysics under a grand master. With the power he derived from his magic amulet and the purity of his soul, Solen was able to slay the Minotaur."

"What happened then?"

"The grateful villagers lauded him with praise and riches. But several young warriors in the Minoan Order were jealous of his triumph. They ambushed him one night, beating him until he was almost dead, but he refused to use his powers against them in anger. He would not violate the code, even to avenge himself. The men put him on a sailing ship to Egypt, where he was sold into slavery."

"Sort of like Joseph and his coat of many colors."

"Similar story, yes."

"From there Solen ended up in Ramses's household, where he fell in love with Kiya."

"And that was his downfall," Harrison said. "There was only one thing that would cause Solen to break the Minoan Order's code and commit an evil act."

"His love for Kiya," Cassie whispered and got goose bumps on top of her hot spot.

"Solen attacked Nebamun when he discovered the vizier had poisoned Kiya. They battled and Nebamun stabbed him with a dagger dipped in asp venom. With his dying breath, Solen cursed the vizier's descendants into eternity, just as Nebamun tore the magic amulet from his hands."

"Thereby preventing the curse from taking place." She sighed deeply and rubbed her palms together. "I love this star-crossed lovers stuff. It's so tragically romantic."

"You only like the legend because their romance ended passionately and luridly and before Kiya ever started to resent Solen for leaving his socks on the floor," Harrison teased.

"Oh, you." Cassie reached across the car to playfully swat him, but the minute her hand made contact with his solid shoulder she realized that touching him had been a major mistake.

He'd stopped at a traffic signal and as her fingers grazed his shirt, he turned to look at her. The reflection of the red traffic light illuminated him in a vermilion hue. He looked alien and unlikely and incredibly potent.

They stared at each other. All levity vanished in the heat of tension stretching between them.

His dark eyes glistened enigmatically behind his scholarly spectacles. For the first time, she noticed a small scar just below and to the left of his right cheekbone. The unexpected defect was intriguing and mysterious and darkly masculine.

Who was he?

She didn't know him. Not really. She was vulnerable. At his mercy.

She suppressed a shiver.

The nerd image was all a ruse, Cassie realized. A defense mechanism he hid behind. He cloaked his real self with thick glasses and bad clothing and disheveled hair. The real Harrison disappeared inside scientific method and mental analysis and complicated ideas. But there was so much more to him than his intellect.

Here, in the close confines of the car, she could feel the emotional surging of this heavier, earthier, more complex personality. She wondered if he even understood the dynamics of his secretive behavior.

She felt herself sucked in by the enticing vortex of unknown territory. They stared into each other, and her world spun.

The car behind them honked and they both jumped, brought back to their physical surroundings. The light had changed. Harrison put his foot on the accelerator, and the Volvo chugged through the intersection.

That furtive moment, the deeper connection, vanished like a whiff of smoke and everything was back like it had been. Neither one of them spoke of what passed between them, but Cassie could not tolerate the awkward silence.

"So this Minoan Order." She nervously licked her lips and then swallowed hard. "Whatever happened to them?"

"Not to get all *Star Wars* on you or anything, but the dark side won. When the elder members of the Minoan Order found out what the young warriors had done to Solen, they stripped them of their powers and banished them from their homeland. But in exile, the warriors banded together. They sought revenge against the original sect for kicking them out. They murdered every member of the old order in their beds to steal their magic. But the new Minoan Order was now tainted with evil. They still had the ability to transmute base metal into gold and to control the weather, but every time they used these skills they grew weaker and weaker."

"Chilling story."

"Many scholars of ancient history feel that Solen held the key to the group's alchemical talents. Some think the power was in his amulet."

"Do any practitioners of the Minoan Order exist today?" Cassie asked.

"The general consensus is they were wiped out by the Greeks," Harrison said.

"But were they?"

"Rumors of their existence persist. One theory postulates that Hitler was a member of the New Minoan Order. But no one has ever proved that. If they are still around, they've kept their presence very clandestine." He shook his head. "But if Adam has translated their hieroglyphics, the papyrus scroll in the backseat could hold the answer to all the speculation."

"It's a seductive thought."

"Very seductive for an archaeologist." Harrison exited the freeway. The high-glare-headlight car that had been on their bumper since they'd left Jack in the Box took the same exit.

"So do you personally believe there could still be a Minoan Order?"

"Anything's possible."

"You don't believe in true love, but you believe there could be mumbo-jumbo weirdos running around trying to turn base metal into gold and brew up tornadoes?"

"I'm a cynic." He grinned and shrugged. "But I'm not totally closed-minded."

"Good to know you believe in something."

The light changed and he turned the corner. Maybe

now they could escape the obnoxious driver who seemed determined to give her a migraine with those unforgiving headlights.

No such luck. The car also turned right at the light.

They were back in Fort Worth and drawing nearer to the Kimbell.

"Just drop me off at my car," she said.

"No way. I'm not about to let you go driving around on empty at one o'clock in the morning. I'll take you to your apartment and come back to pick you up tomorrow."

She started to argue with him but stopped herself. What the hell? If he wanted to cart her around Fort Worth, no skin off her nose. He made a left turn and darn if that blinded-by-the-light car didn't stay right on their tail.

"Harry." Squinting, Cassie glanced in the side-view mirror.

"Yes?"

"I hate to alarm you, but I think we're being followed."

Chapter 9

Harrison had come to the same conclusion about the Ford Focus in his rearview mirror long before Cassie expressed her suspicions. But before he made a move, he had to be certain.

"My head is burning again," Cassie said. "Hate to sound all woo-woo, but this isn't a good sign."

On that point they agreed. Harrison circled the block.

The Focus followed.

This was unbelievable. The driver couldn't be more obvious if he had a neon flasher light proclaiming, "I'm following you," perched atop his hood.

He slowed the Volvo.

The Focus decelerated.

Harrison navigated down a narrow side street.

Here came the compact Ford, practically kissing his bumper.

No doubt about it. Not only were they being followed, but the driver didn't care if they knew it.

Harrison crept along, analyzing the situation. Obviously, the person behind the wheel of the Focus wanted him to pull over.

Why?

He edged over to the curb. The Focus followed suit.

"What's happening? Why are you stopping?"

"I'm finding out who's following us and why."

His pulse kaboomed in his ears. After their conversation about the Minoan Order, he was feeling a little jumpy. *Get over it, Standish.*

They weren't being followed by members of some ancient cult desperate to get their hands on the ancient scroll. No way. It was too incredible. No matter how hot Cassie's brain got.

So who was following them?

His mind jumped to the thought of carjackers and highway robbers. Or maybe it had something to do with Adam's disappearance. Maybe he had taken money from mobster loan sharks to finance his dig and he hadn't paid them back and they'd been watching the crate, waiting for someone to pick it up.

Outlandish, yes. Impossible? Considering his brother, no. But far more believable than a killer secret brotherhood sect.

Stop with the speculation. Make a move, doober. You're not going to discover anything while cowering in the car.

Right.

"Here." He twisted a key off his key ring and handed it to her. "Get the papyrus scroll from the backseat and lock it in the glove compartment."

Cassie did as he asked, retrieving the sheepskin-wrapped bundle, stowing and locking it in the glove compartment. She gave the key back to him.

He reached down at the side of the driver's seat and thumbed open the trunk release latch.

"Are you nuts?" Her eyes widened and her voice shot up an octave. "What if they have a gun?"

"I imagine that is a possibility."

He looked in the rearview mirror. The Ford Focus had not switched off its headlamps. The beams bounced off the mirror, momentarily blinding him.

Harrison could not tell how many people were in the car. It could be one person. It could be four or even more. He had no idea what they were up against.

"This isn't good." Cassie ferociously rubbed the back of her head. "My head is blazing. There's going to be serious trouble. Just drive away, Harry."

"And let them follow us home?" he said. "No thank you."

"I don't scare easily, Harry." She grasped his arm. "But I'm scared now. This doesn't feel right. Don't do it."

"Cassie." He met her gaze.

"Uh-huh." Her voice was barely above a whisper.

He was startled to see exactly how scared she was. Her hands were trembling and her mouth was pressed into a thin, anxious line. His gut twisted. He would protect her, no matter what.

"When I get out of the car, I want you to slide behind the wheel, hit the automatic door locks, and drive immediately to the nearest police station. Do you understand?"

"I don't like this. Don't go."

"I refuse to be intimidated by common thugs."

"What if it's not common thugs? What if they're uncommon thugs? Like members of the Wannamakemecomealots."

He almost laughed at the way she mispronounced the name, but he didn't want to bruise her feelings. "There's no such thing. That cult no longer exists."

"Are you sure?"

"Right now, I'm not sure of anything."

"Whoever it is could hurt you," she said breathlessly.

"My head's never burned this bad. Not even when I was in the rehab hospital."

"Yeah, well." He was trying hard to ignore the twinge of sympathy that sparked whenever he imagined sweet little nine-year-old Cassie in a rehab hospital. "That's why I popped the trunk. I'll use the tire iron as a weapon."

"What if they overpower you?" She laid a hand on his shoulder.

Was that concern in her eyes? Was she worried about his safety? Her touch struck a chord inside him, and then he felt stupid letting himself get so embroiled.

Stay calm, stay cool, stay detached from your feelings.

"That's why you're going to drive to the nearest police station as soon as I get the tire iron out of the trunk."

"I won't go off and leave you to fight them alone."

"You can and you will."

She lifted her hand from his shoulder to caress his cheekbone. Her fingers found the small scar he'd acquired playing Zorro with Adam when they were kids. Harrison's heart knotted. If she only knew how hard his knees were quaking, that venerating expression in her eyes would quickly disappear. He found it so much easier facing the unknown physical menace outside the car than the intimate tenderness inside the Volvo.

Unable to deal with her admiration for his imaginary courage, he ducked his head and fumbled for the door handle. *Round the back of the Volvo, shove up the trunk lid, grab the tire iron, and start swinging.*

"Harry?"

"Uh-huh?" He hesitated.

"Take this with you."

"Wha—"

But that was as far as he got because Cassie unsnapped

her seat belt, leaned across the console, and planted a kiss on his scarred cheek.

He was so startled that he jerked his head toward her, and her mouth slipped from his cheek to his lips.

The next thing he knew he was kissing her.

Full on.

It was hot and wet and moving.

For one endless second Harrison forgot about the Ford Focus parked behind him. He forgot about the Minoan hieroglyphics. He forgot about Solen and Kiya. He forgot about the amulet. He even forgot about Adam.

Whereas before there was danger, now there was nothing but pleasure. His full attention was focused on one thing and one thing alone.

Cassie Cooper's mouth.

Lush and full and ripe and sweet. She tasted of summer. Throbbing and heated and humid. Filled with life and intensity and drama.

He remembered swimming pools and lounging on the beach, smelled chlorine and suntan lotion. He thought of the Fourth of July, heard bottle rockets scream and Black Cats explode. He saw fireflies flickering through pecan trees, and he spied charcoal embers glowing white-hot in the bottom of a barbecue grill.

It all added up to a glorious *wow*.

His mouth sizzled as Cassie's tongue glided over his lips. Wow, wow, wow, wow.

Harrison floated. Caught, trapped, besieged. He was suspended in another time zone, another dimension, an alternate reality. Everything ceased to exist except the taste and shape of Cassie's mouth.

An eternity drifted past his consciousness, but rationally he knew it had been no more than a couple of seconds. He coped with the emotional impact the only way he knew how—by narrowing his focus and attempting to retreat into the sanctuary of his mind.

But it didn't work. He could not isolate his mind from his body. His penis hardened and his mouth moistened and his toes curled.

Pull away, pull away.

But he could not.

He reacted violently against his natural instincts. Something about her tugged at a long-denied, subterranean part of his psyche. Harrison flung himself into the kiss, restless, agitated, forgetful, crazed.

More, more, more.

His mind sped up. His anxieties flamed. Her lips were the single distraction from his escalating uneasiness. Where had his mind gone? Where was the essence of him? Where was Harrison Jerome Standish in all this?

Resist her! Resist her! Remember your mission.

Ah, but she was irresistible.

Her lips were wicked, her tongue even more so. Nibbling, licking, tasting, teasing.

Panic seized him, but Harrison was unable to fight off the very cause of his alarm.

His unquenchable desire for Cassie.

And then a fist knocking hard against his window slammed him straight back down to reality.

A rush of protectiveness, so strong he could taste the briny poignancy, suffused him. He had to shield Cassie. He'd gotten her into this mess; it was his responsibility to extract her.

It was so deeply ingrained in him to mentally disconnect from his body's physical response that he couldn't help himself. He was barely aware that his limbs had gone rigid and his hands were curled into fists.

He jerked his head toward the driver's-side window, fully expecting to see either a knife-wielding carjacker or a brass-knuckle-wearing loan shark, or, bizarrely enough, members of the Minoan Order, their faces hidden behind Minotaur masks.

When instead he saw the smiling caramel-colored face of the *Star-Telegram* reporter who'd attended the Kimbell party, Harrison exhaled in surprise and rolled down the window.

"Hiya," the reporter said, waggling her fingers at him in a friendly wave.

"Hi." He smiled weakly.

"Remember me? I'm Lashaundra Johnson."

"Yes?"

"I know who stole the amulet."

"Pardon?" Harrison had detached his mind so completely from his body that he was having trouble processing what the woman was saying. She repeated herself.

"You know who stole the amulet?"

"Uh-huh." She bobbed her head. "I already figured it out."

"Who?"

"Cleopatra. The thin one. Not her." Lashaundra nodded at Cassie."

"What?" He had no idea why this woman was hanging on to the side of his car and babbling nonsense.

Cassie leaned over to whisper in his ear. "She's talking about the murder mystery theater."

Oh. He'd forgotten all about that.

"Yep," Lashaundra went on. "She doesn't want Solen and Kiya reunited 'cause she wants Solen's handsome bod for herself. I'm thinking old Cleo might even have stabbed the mummy as well, but I haven't quite figured out why or how. I don't trust her. She's too damned skinny. My mama always told me never trust a bony woman. They're just too hungry."

"Amen, sister," Cassie mumbled.

Harrison's pulse, which had jackhammered into the red zone when Lashaundra rapped on the window, dipped back to normal.

"So am I right?" Lashaundra asked. "It's the skinny bitch, isn't it? She's the thief."

"Sorry," Harrison said. "You'll have to wait until Saturday to find out."

"You won't even give me a hint?" Lashaundra gazed beseechingly at Cassie. "I've been following you guys around all night looking for a clue."

Cassie shook her head. "It wouldn't be fair to the others."

"Dammit," Lashaundra said. "Well, I figured it was worth a shot."

"I'll walk you back to your car, Ms. Johnson," Harrison offered, plus he had to shut the trunk. "You shouldn't be out alone at this time of the night."

"Okay," Lashaundra agreed. "I'll let you."

Harrison opened the door to get out and the dome light came on. That's when he got a glimpse of himself in the rearview mirror. His right cheek was branded with the imprint of Cassie's lipstick.

Perfect lips, sealed with a kiss. A stark reminder of how he had lost control.

He reached up to guiltily swipe the imprint away with a hand. The lipstick came off, but he could not so casually erase the taste of Cassie from his tongue or rid the smell of her from his nose or eliminate the primal stirrings in his body.

As he walked Lashaundra to her car, he mentally

berated himself. *Kissing Cassie was a huge mistake. You will not let it happen again.*

What a mess!

He was stuck with Cassie until Saturday night, and yet it was almost impossible to resist her. He had to find a way. There could not be a repeat performance of what had happened in the car. He'd been so swept up by their passion for one another that if it had been a loan shark or a carjacker or even, as laughable as it seemed, a member of the Minoan Order at his window instead of the *Star-Telegram* reporter, both he and Cassie could be dead at this very moment.

From now on, for the duration of their time together, it was totally hands off. No matter what the sacrifice might cost.

Chapter 10

Keep your lips to yourself. Absolutely, positively no more kissing Harrison Standish.

Because when his mouth had landed on hers and his tongue had skimmed along her lips and her pulse had knocked with anticipation, Cassie realized she was traversing a paper-thin ledge in six-inch stilettos.

Tightrope act deluxe.

Her stomach quivered and her hands shook. Her brain scorched hot and her lungs squeezed breathlessly out of control. All the wonderful sensations she loved rained over her. It felt like romance, and nothing got Cassie into trouble quicker than the thrill of the chase.

She couldn't risk pursuing this feeling. There was too much at stake. Her job. Harrison's future. Maybe even Adam's life. They had to stay focused on the mystery. They couldn't afford the distraction of attraction.

They drove in silence. He kept both hands on the steering wheel, his eyes fixed on the road, unaware of what she was thinking, oblivious to the excitement throbbing inside her.

Maybe, she thought, her precognitive brain burn had nothing to do with outside danger and everything to do with Harrison. Perhaps he was the threat.

They were inhaling the same air, sharing the same closed, dark space. He had never looked as sexy to her as he did right now. He'd been prepared to risk life and limb to protect her. Underneath the glasses and the mismatched clothes beat the heart of a hero.

Don't go there. Don't romanticize the dude. Remember how much he gets on your nerves? Just think about his dirty socks on your kitchen table.

Socks, smocks. Who cared about socks when a bona fide hero was driving her home?

And the very fact that he was so smart and private and respectful and he'd kissed her like he really meant it was a total turn-on. She'd never been with a brainy guy before, and she wriggled joyously at the thought of bedding him.

"You okay?"

"Uh-huh." She forced herself not to squirm. She could not let him know how much he affected her. She might have the hots for him, but she wasn't about to hand him that much power.

Harrison parked the Volvo outside her apartment. "I'll see you to the door."

"You don't have to do that," she said quickly, even though she was accustomed to men waiting on her, treating her like a princess.

Cassie had to get out of the car before she did something totally stupid.

Like lick him.

She jumped from the Volvo, red leather handbag slung across her shoulder, and was halfway up the sidewalk before he caught her.

"Whoa, slow down." He took her elbow.

She jerked away. "It's okay. I'm all right. No need for

an escort. Ta-ta, bye-bye, thanks for everything. See ya tomorrow."

Babbling. She was babbling and she knew it. Babble, babble, babble. But the last thing she wanted was to let this man into her house. Because if she let him in, she absolutely knew she could not be trusted to keep her lips to herself.

"I'm not going to let you walk into an empty house at one-thirty in the morning."

"No big deal. I do it all the time."

"Not when you're out with me."

"Excuse me, but I did not hire you as my protector. Buzz off." She waved a hand.

"Give me your keys." He put out his palm.

"No." Damn, why wouldn't that sensitive spot at the base of her skull stop the infernal burning?

"Cassie," he said, "I'm going to unlock your door for you, wait until you get across the threshold, and then I'll take off. I'm not going to shoulder my way inside and rob you of your virtue."

No? Rats. She was big into having her virtue robbed by guys who flipped her switch.

"Listen, Harry...," she started to argue, desperate to get him to step away before she kissed him again. But she stopped midsentence when she realized her front door was ajar.

He saw it at the same time she did.

Without another word, he grabbed her by the shoulders and moved her away from the door.

"Stay behind me."

She wrapped her arms around his slim, muscular waist and held on tight. Nice.

He moved forward and she went with him in a bizarre, backward waltz. He toed the door open wider and reached an arm around to search for the light plate.

A second later the kitchen lit up.

"My God." Harrison audibly sucked in his breath.

His muscles bunched and Cassie felt his tension slip right up her arms, to her shoulders, and then lodge hard against the fiery section of her brain.

What had he seen?

She stood on tiptoes and peeked over his shoulder with one eye shut to lessen the blow of what she might witness.

Aha.

This was the reason her quirky ESP had been sizzling off and on all night. The danger hadn't been at the airport. Nor was it in the car that'd been following them. Nor was it even Harry's sexy proximity that had lit up her brain like a Christmas tree. The menace had been right here in her home.

Her kitchen had been trashed.

Not that it was really all that easy to tell. Cassie wasn't much of a neatnik. The dirty dishes piled in the sink were hers, as well as the stacks of books, Blockbuster movies, and CDs crowding the kitchen table. The clutter of cooking hardware—blender, food processor, bread maker, etcetera—was strewn across the counter because she'd been too lazy to bother stuffing it into the cabinets after her last cookfest.

But what wasn't her own doing were the drawers hanging open and the dish towels tossed around the room and the bottle of Dawn tipped over and dribbling soap down the front of the microwave. Nor was she responsible for the box of smashed sugar-frosted cornflakes littered across the tile floor or the upended garbage can or the broken jar of Russian caviar pooling next to the open pantry door.

Dammit! An admirer had given her that caviar, and she'd been saving it for a special occasion.

And then all at once the reality of the situation smacked

her hard. Her place had been ransacked. Her valuables either stolen or destroyed or both.

"My collage wall," she cried, shoving Harrison aside as she zigzagged around the land mines of spilled delicacies and sprinted for the bedroom.

Wishing she had a shot of tequila to brace her for what lay inside, Cassie flicked on the light.

Not even a quart of Cabo Wabo Milenio could have prepared her for this. The shelving had been ripped off the wall. Her collection of candles lay shattered, the collages yanked from their picture frames and scattered across the room.

Someone had been viciously searching for something. But she had no idea who or for what.

Helplessly, she stared at the destruction. She felt as if she'd stepped into a morgue, surrounded by the corpses of her previous relationships. She stumbled across the room, fell to her knees in the middle of the devastation, and bit down hard on her bottom lip to keep from crying.

The wall was silly nostalgia. She knew it. Maddie had lectured her for years about clinging to the past. But her twin sister had never really understood what the collage wall stood for.

It wasn't that Cassie lived in the past. On the contrary, she was definitely a live-for-the-moment kind of gal. But her memories of the men she had once loved echoed throughout the collages.

It was difficult to explain, but when she had been in those relationships, the anticipation and the passion and the intensity had prevented her from savoring the actual experience. It was only upon reflection when she looked at the collage wall that she realized what an incredible, fun, adventuresome life she'd led.

With time and distance, she could linger in the variety of her experiences. Relish what had been without the pressure of what could be. In a glance, the wall gave her a clear visual of who she was, where she'd come from, the things she valued, and what she believed in.

She'd dated tall men and short ones. Brunets and blonds and even a redhead. Slim men and chubby men. Atheists and Christians. Men from other countries. Men of other races. Scoundrels and saints. Rebels and reactionaries. Crusaders and crackpots.

Some of the relationships had been strictly intellectual. Others only emotional. A few had been purely sexual. But no one guy had ever been able to meet all her needs.

She was driven to seek fulfillment for all the different sides of herself. She could not resist. Her energy was cycled and replenished by the diversity of her men. She was always looking for something better. Scoping out her options.

Cassie knew she could never commit to just one guy. Marriage wasn't in the cards for her. That's why she bailed out of relationships before they got serious. She'd always been the dumper, never the dumpee.

And that's the way she liked it.

No one had to tell her that almost drowning when she was a kid, spending three months in a coma and then nine months in a rehab hospital, had contributed to her need for variety.

She reached for a picture. Peyton Shriver. The charming art thief she'd spent several intense days with in Europe the previous year. She had known he was a very bad boy, and because of that, she'd never slept with him. But she couldn't say she'd regretted their time together. She'd learned a lot about herself from Peyton.

"This wasn't an isolated incident," Harrison said from the doorway. "This break-in is connected to what's been going on. Someone must think you've got something or know something that you're not even aware of, Cassie."

But she wasn't paying him much attention.

The invitation to her junior prom was ripped in two, as was the playbill to her first Broadway play, *Phantom of the Opera*. There was a partial sneaker print stamped across an old love letter, from the guy who'd taken her virginity. Cassie could even make out the brand name of the sorry scumbag's right shoe.

Nike.

Cruel bastard.

Who could have done this, and why? A tear slipped down her cheek. Then another and another.

Oh, crap. She wasn't supposed to do this. She swiped at her eyes and swallowed back a sob.

Distantly, she heard Harrison walk closer, but his presence really didn't register until he crouched down in front of her, his eyes level with hers. "It's okay. I'll help you piece everything back together."

But she couldn't look at him. She didn't want him to see her crying.

Carefully, he reached out and touched her forearm, as if initiating such contact wasn't something he usually did and he wasn't quite sure if he was making a mistake or not. His fingers were hesitant yet firm, his palm warm. He stroked his thumb along the underside of her arm.

"Are you all right, sweetheart?"

Sweetheart.

Her chest squeezed. What a lovely, kind word and so unexpected coming from Standoffish.

Cassie raised her head, met his steadfast gaze. Here he was, offering to help her recreate her past with other men. His smile was faint, but considerate. He looked at her with such empathy that she knew, without another word passing between them, somehow, he understood.

"Thank you," she said.

"You're welcome." The look in his eyes, the touch of his fingers against her skin, the tenderness in his voice made her feel a lot better. For the first time since Maddie had moved to D.C., Cassie felt as if she wasn't alone.

And when Harrison knelt to pick up broken glass, mindful of the photos and memorabilia, Cassie just knew she had to kiss this man again.

He had to escape.

If he didn't, the mummy knew they would kill him. He realized this as surely as he could not remember his own name.

Faint fingers of daylight were pushing through the high, dirt-smudged windows of the warehouse. He had no idea when the men would return, but the consequences would not be good.

The throbbing in his back had dulled slightly, but the fresh wounds Demitri had inflicted upon him with the metal file stung with a fierce and fiery ache. He felt hot and sweaty and dizzy, and whenever he gazed into the distance his vision blurred.

He wondered if he had a fever. Was he delirious? Was this just some bizarre dream?

But no, the sharp teeth of pain tearing through him whenever he tried to drag himself to his feet assured the mummy that this was no dream.

It was a nightmare.

He gritted his teeth and rolled over onto his back. He ended up lying on his bound hands. His wrists were chafed raw from the too-tight duct tape, and his fingers were scarily cold.

Grunting against the pain, he made several attempts and finally managed to get into a sitting position with his shoulders propped against the wall. He sat panting from the effort that tiny accomplishment extracted.

The coppery scent of blood filled the air, and a warm wetness spread over the crusty dryness at the back of his shirt. Bile rose in his throat, and he gagged but did not throw up. He'd aggravated the stab wound, and it was bleeding again.

Once he'd rested enough that the dizziness and nausea abated, he glanced around for an escape route. After the men had tortured him and left the warehouse, he'd heard the heavy snap of a padlock latching the double-rollered doors.

He was locked in. The window was his only way out.

Up, up, up he stared. At the window looming far above his head.

It was only ten feet, but it might as well have been a million miles. He was that weak and debilitated. It was all he could do to keep breathing. How was he supposed to scale a wall with his hands duct-taped behind his back?

He was almost ready to say "Fuck it" and opt for death. At least if they came back and killed him, he would be out of his misery.

But something much stronger than the fear of those thugs and the pain in his body would not allow him to wallow in self-pity. A determination he didn't fully understand spurred him onward.

There was something very important he must do. He felt it straight to his bones. Unfortunately, no matter how hard he tried, he could not remember what it was.

Think, think. Who are you? What is it that you must do?

He closed his eyes. He needed a name. He needed a motivation to keep from giving up and surrendering to the relentless pain.

Froggy Voice had kept asking him about an amulet. Demanding to know where the thing was. He had no idea what the man had been talking about, but each time Froggy asked a question and he did not know the answer, Demitri would twist the metal file deeper into his skin.

A dark voice in the back of his brain murmured, *Find her.*

Find who?

Think, dammit. Think.

The harder he pushed, the more it felt as if his brain had broken into a thousand fragmented pieces, each walled off from the rest. He got snippets but could make no connections. He could not understand how it all fit into a whole.

The sound of a garbage truck rumbled in the alley outside the warehouse. The mummy tried to yell, but his voice stuck in his throat. When he finally forced out a sound, he was alarmed to discover he could not speak above a whisper.

On your feet.

He braced his shoes against the cement floor strewn with metal shavings and pushed himself up the wall.

Intense pain grabbed him in a vise. He stopped halfway to a standing position, hands bound behind his back, panting and sweating and sick to his stomach.

His knees wobbled. His stomach lurched. An icy-cold chill belied the sweat drenching his brow. His eyelids fluttered closed. He tasted the bile in his mouth again and almost lost consciousness.

And then a name popped into his head.

Kiya.

His beloved.

Heart strumming, he suddenly knew who he was and what he had to do.

His name was Solen.

And he had to get to Kiya.

He had to find his secret bride before she drank the poisoned wine.

Chapter 11

This time, he saw it coming.

The look in Cassie's eyes, the way she leaned close and puckered up those lush, glossy lips, left no doubt as to her intention. Panic-stricken, he sprang to his feet, leaving her blinking at the spot where he had just been kneeling beside her. She fingered her bottom lip, hurt and confusion on her face.

Had he been unconsciously leading her on? He shouldn't have touched her. He shouldn't express such sympathy for her plight. Intimate emotions just got you into trouble. Hadn't that message been hammered home enough times?

He cleared his throat. He wanted to tell her they needed to leave. That it was important they get a few hours' sleep so they could start looking for Adam again as soon as possible. But instead he said, "I'll help reconstruct your collage. But you have to promise you won't keep trying to kiss me."

"Why not?"

"Be... because," he sputtered.

"Because why?"

"Because I don't want you to."

"Oh." She considered that for a moment. "Do I have bad breath? I could go brush my teeth."

He raised both palms. Would he ever understand the way her mind worked? "It's not your breath. Your breath is minty fresh."

"So it's me? If I were someone else, then would you want to kiss me?"

"No. I don't want to kiss anybody."

"So it's you?"

"Yes." He would say anything to get the exasperating woman to stop talking about kisses. "It's me."

"You don't like kissing? Is that the deal?"

"I like kissing."

"Then what's the problem?"

"Kissing leads to other things."

"I know. That's the general idea."

This circular conversation was getting them nowhere. Not knowing what else to do to escape her chaotic reasoning, Harrison picked up a photograph of Cassie when she was about sixteen, draped all over some surfer-type dude on the hood of a station wagon. He was certain she must have made out in the backseat of that car. You couldn't miss the lustful gleam in the guy's eyes as he stared at her chest.

The jerkwad.

"Who's this?" He hadn't meant to ask that.

Cassie perked up and took the photograph from him. "Oh, that's Johnny D. He wanted in my panties so bad I thought he was going to explode."

"You didn't sleep with him?" Why Harrison should feel so relieved over something Cassie hadn't done a dozen years ago was beyond him.

"Are you nuts? The guy lived down by the river in his

car. He had crabs like you wouldn't believe. Or that's what I heard from my pal Julie Ann."

"Why'd you keep his picture?"

"He was sweet, and I liked the idea of hanging with a musician. He wrote a love song about me and everything. But then again, the song sort of sucked. It didn't rhyme. He took me to a U2 concert when they came to Dallas back in the early nineties. If you see a U2 ticket stub, it goes in the frame with Johnny D."

"Cassie, we gotta hurry this up. I hate to rush you; I know this is important, but finding Adam and the amulet is even more important. We both have a vested interest in the outcome," he said, realizing the last thing he ever wanted to be was a memory on her collage wall. That's why he'd circumvented her kiss with some fancy footwork.

She nodded. "You're right. I got caught up in my emotions. I can finish assembling the collages later. It was considerate of you to even offer to help, Harry."

He started to correct her, tell her to call him Harrison, but it hardly seemed worth the effort. If she liked calling him Harry, he could live with it for a few days.

"Good night," she said and extended a hand. "What time are you picking me up in the morning? Although technically it already is morning."

"Oh," he said, "I'm not leaving you alone in this apartment. Whoever trashed it might come back. Especially if they didn't find what they were looking for. We gotta get you out of here quickly, so pack a bag."

"What do you suppose they were looking for?" She took a backpack from the closet and tossed it on the bed.

"Adam? The amulet? The papyrus? Who knows?"

"But why come after me? I don't know anything." She headed to the bathroom. Harrison moved to stand in the doorway. He leaned against the jamb, watching while she hurriedly scooped up her cosmetics and toiletry items.

"Maybe you do and you just don't know it. One thing is for sure, it's not safe for you to stay, and as far as I can see there's only one solution."

"What's that?" She maneuvered past him to dump her makeup bag and toothbrush onto the bed beside her backpack.

He resisted making the suggestion. If he was smart he would just foot the bill and put her up in a hotel, but he needed to keep her close. Especially if someone was after her. Harrison took a deep breath.

"You're staying with me."

Harry's place turned out to be much like Harry. Bland, boring, and colorless.

Or rather that was the general impression everyone had about Harry. She'd once thought that about him too.

But the more time she spent with him, the more Cassie realized he was much more interesting than he appeared on the surface. He might be color-blind, but Harry was far from bland and boring.

He was deeply private and intense. The curious adventurer in her wanted to dig past the surface, find out what he was truly like. The adage "can't judge a book by its cover" certainly applied to Harry Standish.

His sterile, monochromatic white kitchen begged for a shot of color. Not to mention food. His pantry had a glass door, and all she could see were tins of tuna, boxes of whole grain cereal, and cans of tomato soup, all neatly stacked. The man was seriously in need of culinary intervention.

"I'm sorry," he said, "that my apartment is so small. I'm rarely here, and I've converted my bedroom into an office."

Cassie looked around and sucked in her breath. A bed-room converted into an office meant the narrow daybed in the living room was where he slept.

Whoo boy.

Why was she suddenly feeling out of her element? She rarely felt uneasy around men. What was it about Harry that rattled her cage? She wished she had something to calm the nervous flutters in her stomach.

"Let me just check my answering machine to see if Adam called," he said and went to the telephone in the corner of the room. He shook his head. "No messages."

"It's looking darker by the minute, isn't it?"

"Yeah."

His expression was grim, and Cassie had an almost irresistible urge to wrap her arms around him and tell him everything was going to be okay, but something held her back.

"Got anything to drink?" she asked.

It was either very late or very early, depending on your definition, but a glass of wine or a bottle of beer was exactly what she needed to help her fall asleep. And to quell her inexplicable attraction to Harrison Standish.

"Sure. I have bottled water and milk and orange juice in the fridge."

"No, that's not what I meant," she said. "Do you have something serious?"

"You mean alcohol?"

"Ding-ding-ding." She nodded. "Beer, wine. I'd even take a shot of tequila if you have it."

Harry frowned. "I know you're reeling from what happened at your apartment, but do you really think alcohol is the answer?"

"Yep, I sure do." She sauntered over to the refrigerator

and popped it open. She sank one hand on her hip and studied the contents.

Well, here was a dearth of choices.

A carton of skim milk that had expired two days ago. A quart of orange juice with pulp—*yuck*—and a six-pack of mineral water. There was also a package of deli-sliced turkey breast in the meat drawer, a jar of maraschino cherries and a bottle of ketchup in the shelf on the door, and in the crisper a chunk of brown iceberg lettuce.

Eew.

She slammed the fridge door closed.

"I have a bottle of peppermint schnapps that Adam gave me for Christmas a couple of years ago," Harry said. "It's never been opened. Would that do?"

"Now we're talking. The schnapps sounds promising. Lead on, Poindexter."

"Poindexter?" He swiveled his head to stare at her.

His expression was deadpan. He might have been insulted or he could have been amused. There was no reading this guy when he didn't want to be read.

"Oops, sorry." She cringed apologetically.

"Sorry for what?"

"Calling you Poindexter."

"You do it behind my back all the time, why not go ahead and say it to my face?"

She opened her mouth to dispute his claim, but it was true. She had called him Poindexter behind his back. And Standoffish. And Egghead.

"May I ask why you call me that?"

Apparently it was time for truth or consequences. "No real reason. Don't take it personally."

"It's because I'm a nerd."

"Yeah, well, kinda."

"Kinda?"

Way to go, Cassie. Pry that shoe out of your mouth. She had just insulted the guy who'd taken her in. She crinkled her nose. "It's not you, really. It's the clothes."

"Oh? What's wrong with my clothes?"

Nothing like brutal honesty to quash any budding romantic attraction into pulp. "You don't match, and everything you wear is out of style."

"I'm color-blind," he said.

"I figured."

"And I don't care about fashion."

"I figured that too, but that's what makes you a Poindexter," she explained.

"Don't forget the glasses." He grasped the nosepiece and lifted his spectacles up and down on the bridge of his nose.

"Here. Let me see what you'd look like without those." She stepped the few feet across the kitchen floor, reached up, and removed his glasses. That's when she realized just how close they were standing.

He held his breath and so did she.

Cassie was acutely aware of his masculine scent, the warmness of his temples where her fingers grazed, the serious set to his intense mouth. She stepped back, tilted her head, and studied his face in the overhead lighting.

"You've got amazing brown eyes. You shouldn't hide them behind glasses."

"I have to see where I'm going." He shrugged, acting like he was unaffected by her touch.

He was a self-disciplined guy, but Cassie was an expert at reading men. She recognized the subtle changes. His shoulders tensed up. His jaw muscles tightened. His fingers curled into his palms.

"You could get LASIK surgery." She set his glasses down on the counter.

"Maybe," he said. "But what's the point? You can't change who you are at heart. Guess I'll always be a Poindexter."

Cassie felt bad for having called him nerdy names. He really was a nice guy once you got to know him. And he was kinda sexy in a disheveled, absentminded-professor sort of way.

"I'm sorry," she said. "For calling you that."

"Don't be. I appreciate your honesty."

Why did his compliment warm her from the inside out? He was giving her that serious, bookish look of his, which she'd thought was due to the spectacles. But his eyeglasses were resting on the counter beside a peppermill. His chocolate eyes glistened with expression, and she could almost read his thoughts.

You interest me.

And that was the true compliment. A smart guy like Harry interested in a ditzy chick like her.

Cassie shook her head. *Don't get any funny ideas about this one, Cooper. With his brains, he's way out of your league.*

Yeah, but maybe he just needed someone to show him how to let loose and have fun. She was good at having fun, and Harry's curiosity seemed to suggest he might be game for whatever intriguing things she cooked up, either out of bed or in it.

Stop it! He already told you, no more kissing.

Aw, but he hadn't meant that. He just hadn't known how to handle his sexual feelings for her. So he'd put a moratorium on kisses. As far as she was concerned, moratoriums were made to be broken.

"The schnapps?" she said, eager to drown the runaway

voice in her head that usually led her into one mess or another.

He dragged a step stool from the pantry and positioned it beside the refrigerator. Climbing up on the bottom step, he opened the small cupboard over the fridge and took out the bottle of peppermint schnapps still wrapped with a festive red ribbon.

"Got any shot glasses?" she asked.

He just looked at her. Dang if he wasn't downright cute without those pesky spectacles.

"Right. You're not the shot-glass type."

"I have coffee mugs."

"That'll do."

He retrieved a mug from the cabinet.

She looked at the lone mug and pursed out her lips in a sexy pout that came as easily to her as eating. "You're going to make me drink alone?"

"Cassie, it's three-fifteen in the morning, and we've got to get up early. We need sleep for our brains to function properly. Can't puzzle out a puzzle if your brain's not game."

"Cute."

"It's something my mother used to say."

"So why do you think they call it a nightcap? To help you sleep. And you've got to admit we've had a rough evening. If the events of the day don't call for a strong bedtime belt, then I don't know what does."

He hesitated and then said, "Aw, what the hell."

"Attaboy." She grinned.

Harry poured a finger of schnapps into each mug.

"Stingy," she accused.

He added another finger's worth.

"That's better." Cassie raised her mug. "Here's to finding Adam safe and the amulet in mint condition."

"To finding Adam and the amulet," he echoed, and they clinked their mugs.

She swallowed the peppermint liqueur with a toss of her head. It burned nice and friendly all the way down. "Whew."

Glancing over, Cassie saw that Harry had taken only a tiny sip of his schnapps and was making a face like he was downing castor oil.

"No, no." She shook her head. "You gotta shoot it down in one big gulp."

"It's going to burn."

"But then you'll feel warm and toasty inside. Trust me on this. Down the hatch," she wheedled.

He made a face.

She could tell he didn't want to shoot it, but the man needed to learn to relax. She gave him the college chant that had usually persuaded her to overindulge: "Chug, chug, chug."

More to shut her up than anything else, Harry slung back the schnapps.

"Way to go." She slapped him on the back.

She was leaning against the counter, her head buzzing sweet and easy, her breast just slightly grazing his arm. She hadn't brushed up against him deliberately, but the results were the same as if she had. One quick glance down and she was honored to discover the bulge in his Dockers.

"You shouldn't have any trouble falling asleep now," she whispered.

"It's not the falling asleep that worries me," he muttered. "It's the getting up."

Cassie grinned at his unintended pun. She tilted her head and lowered her eyelashes for another peek at his fly.

"Oh, I don't think you're gonna have any problem with that either."

Harrison flushed the color of ketchup. "I...er...um... sorry. I don't drink much, and it goes straight to my... er..."

He caught himself this time before he made another accidental pun. Poor guy knew next to nothing about sexual innuendo. She gave him a break and went to retrieve her knapsack from the foyer where she had dropped it when they'd come in. She slung it over her shoulder and padded into the living room.

"Okay," she called to him. "What are the sleeping arrangements?"

"I have a sleeping bag." He came into the living room to stand behind her. "I'll stretch out on the floor in my office. You take the bed."

"Thank you." She beamed at his chivalry. Her twin sister, Maddie, would probably have argued with him, insisting on taking the sleeping bag, but Cassie wasn't the type to bed down on the floor. She appreciated Harry's courtliness. A girl should accept considerate gestures graciously.

She went to kick off her heels, but misstepped and lost her balance. Harry reached out to keep her from tipping over and she fell hard against him.

He wasn't built like an Adonis, but he wasn't half bad. His chest muscles were firm, and the arm he wrapped around her waist was strong and comforting. Her knees weakened and she just melted into him.

"Are you all right?" His breath was warm against her ear.

"The schnapps made me a little woozy, I guess," Cassie admitted.

"Here. Sit down."

Holding her securely, he guided her to the daybed. She sank onto the mattress, and Harry perched anxiously beside her. He kept glancing around as if searching for an escape hatch.

What? Did he think she was going to rape him?

Yeah, well, he was the one with a boner. Can't rape the willing, buddy.

She sneaked another quick peek at his crotch. He was even larger than before. That was why he was so nervous. It wasn't because he didn't trust her, but rather because he couldn't trust himself with her.

Cassie hiccuped and slapped a hand over her mouth. "Oops, sorry," she apologized. "Sweet liqueurs sometimes give me the hiccups."

And then she promptly hiccuped again.

"I know how to stop them."

"How?"

"Rub your diaphragm."

"I use those birth control patches, not a diaphragm." She giggled. "And I carry condoms. Never leave home without 'em. That's my motto."

"Ha-ha. Funny. Does pretending to be an airhead really work on guys?"

She grinned. "You have no idea how well. The condom line is one of the most popular, usually countered by an American Express joke. I learned a long time ago that a woman gets a lot more mileage out of being sexy than she does out of being smart."

"That's a sad commentary."

"Hey, I don't make the rules." She shrugged and spread her hands. "I just play by them. Intelligent women scare most men."

"Not me."

"You say that now." She wagged a finger. "But I bet if a woman you were dating challenged you on something about ancient Egypt and she turned out to be right, you'd dump her in a heartbeat. It's just the way most men are."

"I'm not most men." He glowered.

"I'd puzzled that out already."

"You don't have to pull that dumb-blonde act with me, Cassie."

"At this point, it's something of a habit."

"Habits were made to be broken."

She hiccuped again. "Oops."

"Rub right here." He placed three fingers in the center of his abdomen just below the level of his rib cage and stroked in a circular motion. "Like this."

Cassie leaned over and placed three fingers on his belly and stroked him in rhythmic circles.

Blame it on the schnapps, but oh, she was acting wicked bad!

"What are you doing?" He sounded scandalized, but she noticed he did not move away.

"You said to rub right here." In all honesty, where she ached to rub him was a bit lower.

"Now you're just causing trouble," he said.

"That's my middle name." Her eyes met his gaze and held it, but she did not stop massaging him.

"Cassie...you've been drinking." He forcefully took her wrist and removed her hand from his body.

"So? You've been drinking too, and we've only had one shot of schnapps, so it's not like we're snockered."

"I won't take advantage of you."

"Not even if I wanted you to?" She fluttered her eyelashes seductively.

"No!" he exclaimed, but she heard amusement in his

voice. "Besides, I think you're just bluffing. You don't really want me to make love to you. You just like to tease."

Oh, really? Is that what he thought of her? That she was all come-on and no substance?

They stared at each other, eyes locked.

Her need for him was building faster than she could have imagined. Who'd have thought she'd be all hot and horny for ol' mismatched Harry?

But dammit, she was.

The glimmer in his eyes sent goose bumps marching up and down her arms, and she was wetter than a Slip'N Slide. Need for him, for his kiss, his touch, was a wild thing inside her, sending her heart thrashing wildly against her rib cage, throwing out all common sense.

"You think you have me figured out?"

"I do, or at least as much as anyone will ever have you figured out, Cassie Cooper."

"Go ahead. Get it off your chest. Let's hear it." She jutted out her chin, daring him.

"You sure you're ready for this? You might not like what I have to say."

"Go ahead." She raised a hand. "I'm all ears."

"Remember, you asked for it."

"Just shut up and analyze me."

"Here goes. You act like you're not afraid of anything. You hide behind your charm and your sex appeal and your gregarious talk. You have a hopscotch mind that often gets your body in trouble."

"Oh yeah?" she said, because she did not know what else to say. It was true.

"Yeah. But in spite of your plucky personality, you really have a fear of exploring anything too deeply. You keep everything on the surface, which you mask by a fascination with many subjects. Your flirtation with pleasure is actually a flight away from pain. Ergo, your attempts to get me into bed are in reality nothing but a bluff."

" 'Ergo'? Who in the hell says 'ergo'? It's little wonder you get called Poindexter."

Cassie knew she was being defensive, but she was unnerved that he had figured her out so easily. Not even her own twin sister, Maddie, understood her motivations the way Harry did. It was amazing and a little disturbing.

She didn't appreciate being dissected so accurately, and she wasn't going to let him get away with it.

Cassie knew it was impulsive. She recognized that she was tipsy and that she was still vulnerable over her apartment break-in. And yes, maybe she was using pleasure to cloak her fears. She was on the verge of not only losing her job but potentially going to jail for the theft of a priceless artifact she didn't even steal.

But something deep inside her whispered that this time was different. Harry was an impulse worth acting on.

"Go ahead," she teased, reaching for the hem of her long-sleeved T-shirt. In one swooping motion she pulled it over her head. "Call my bluff."

Chapter 12

Put your shirt back on." It took every morsel of self-discipline Harrison possessed to say the words, but he had to stop Cassie's insane seduction.

He tried not to look at her breasts, but damn him, they were so *there*. The thin material of her skimpy black-lace bra barely supported them, and from where he was sitting they looked solely God-given, not bestowed by a plastic surgeon.

"What's the matter, Harry?" Cassie gave him a deadly wink. "Scared?"

Oh, hell yeah. His knees were knocking and his heart was rocking, but he wasn't about to let her know.

She reached out and walked two fingers over his arm. "See anything you like?"

What didn't he like!

Cassie had been blessed with full, round curves, a thick head of blonde hair, and luscious lips just made for kissing. She was the richest truffle at the confectionery, the fastest car on the showroom floor, the poshest vacation resort in the Caribbean.

Whereas Harrison ate low-carb, drove a ten-year-old

Volvo, and when he'd visited St. Lucia, he had camped out in a pup tent on the beach.

She was uninhibited about her body and quite obviously sexually experienced. He was outclassed and out of his league, and he knew it. His last few relationships had been with colleagues. Calm, studious women who could either take sex or leave it, with no particular feelings about it one way or the other.

The gleam in Cassie's eyes told him she cared about sex and cared deeply. How could he ever hope to measure up to her expectations? Or to satisfy her? She flourished on thrills and excitement.

Face the facts, you're not an exciting guy.

Besides, he had been studying her over the course of the past ten days, and he was slowly starting to figure her out. If he made love to her after her apartment was ransacked, he would just be feeding into her habit of using pleasure in order to avoid dealing with a painful experience.

Ha!

Look who's talking, accused a voice in the back of his head that sounded a whole lot like Adam. *You hide your fears behind the acquisition of knowledge. How come it's okay for you to cloak your fears, but it's not okay for her? That sounds like a double standard to me.*

He had to stop thinking about this. They had no future together whatsoever, and he wasn't a one-night-stand kind of guy. And there was the time crunch. Even if he could bring himself to let go of all his doubts, he simply couldn't afford the distraction.

"Put your shirt back on," Harrison croaked.

He picked up the long-sleeved T-shirt she'd dropped on the floor and handed it to her. He was careful to keep his eyes averted from those mesmerizing breasts.

"Are you that prudish? Or are you just not attracted to me?" Cassie asked.

"How on earth could you possibly believe that I'm not attracted to you?"

"You're not taking advantage of a primo opportunity. There's gotta be a reason why. Is it me?"

"Are you that insecure?"

"Well, if it's not me, I don't get what it is with you."

"Woman, I have a Godzilla-sized boner and sweat is dripping off my forehead."

"So, what are you waiting for?"

"I just can't handle this right now, okay? I'm worried about my brother. Imagine if it was your twin sister who was missing."

"Oh. I see your point."

That was good, because if she didn't cover up soon he didn't know what he was going to do. The pressure was building inside him, low and scorching hot. His penis ached and throbbed. If he wasn't so adept at detaching from his emotions, he would already be pumping into her.

And getting yourself tangled in an intimacy that you can't handle.

Cassie, with her verve and her zest for living, would quickly drain him of his resources. If he couldn't even master his own libido, how could he hope to master anything else? If he lost control with her, he risked losing control in other areas of his life.

And if he lost control in other parts of his life, he would end up looking incompetent, useless, and incapable.

He couldn't take that gamble. He had to stay emotionally distant and mentally on top of things. His ability to disconnect from his feelings had served him well for thirty-two years. No point mucking around with success at this stage of the game.

Cassie, however, was not cooperating with his plan for self-domination. Not only was her chest still bare, but she was audaciously undoing the snap on her pants.

Whoa!

"What are you doing?" he exclaimed. If she took off those Cadillac pants right here in his living room in front of him, he was done for.

"Oh, settle down, Harry. I'm merely headed for the bathroom. I'm just going to take a shower and then pop into bed."

"Really?" He opened one eye, feeling both relieved and disappointed.

"I'm not going to jump your bones. I just unsnapped my jeans to scare you. You can stop sweating. I get the message loud and clear. Your body might want mine"—she flicked a sly smile at his crotch—"but your brain won't let you do the wrong thing, no matter how much fun we might have in the process."

"I...I..."

"No need to explain." She shrugged, hopped off the daybed and reclaimed her backpack from the floor. "Long as you know, it's your loss."

"Button-pusher," Cassie mumbled into the darkness as she lay on Harrison's sofa. "Instigator, rabble-rouser, agitator."

But she wasn't talking about herself and the way she had tried to provoke Harrison into making love to her; rather, she was thinking about the way *he* had inflamed her without even being aware of what he was doing. The man was chock-full of untapped potential. If he ever decided to intentionally use his masculinity to his advantage, heaven help her.

He'd gotten to her so thoroughly, she'd wanted him so

darned badly, she'd brazenly ripped off her shirt in front of him. She'd never done anything that inflammatory—and she'd done a lot of inflammatory things.

But she hadn't lit his fire. At least not all the way.

Just thinking about her behavior made her cringe.

She'd stared him right in the eye and practically begged him for sex, and he'd turned her down cold. What was the matter with her?

Or rather, what was the matter with him? Most guys would have been octopuses. But not Harry.

He'd been a complete gentleman. Drat him.

In her mind's eye she saw him as he'd looked, perched stiffly beside her on the couch. The man was graced with a razor-sharp mind, dark intelligent eyes, and an enigmatic way about him that commanded her attention. He was the trustiest horse at the stable, the wisest insurance policy at the agency, the calmest lullaby in the songbook.

Whereas she rode motorcycles, carried only liability insurance, and when she sang, she belted out rock and roll.

He was smart and quite obviously grasped concepts she would never understand. Half the things he said whizzed right over her head. She'd never been with a man more in touch with his mind than his body. He was brilliant. She could never keep up with him. He thrived on intellectual challenges.

And she was not a scholar.

She should forget all about what had *not* happened here tonight. She should ignore her body, still flushed from the excitement of kissing him. She should deny the ache low in her belly.

Frustrated, Cassie dug her fingernails into her palms. *Just go to sleep.*

But she couldn't.

She flipped. She flopped. She couldn't stand the torture.

If she was going to get any sleep at all, she needed something to take the edge off.

Heave-ho went the covers. Her feet hit the floor. She retrieved her backpack and dug around inside until she found what she was looking for.

Ah, yes. Sweet relief.

Harrison couldn't sleep.

Instead of mellowing him out, the peppermint schnapps had revved him up. Although he was probably giving too much credit to the peppermint liqueur and not nearly enough to Cassie's inherent sexiness.

It was easier to blame the schnapps.

After twenty minutes of fighting the sleeping bag, he decided to get up and take a crack at trying to decipher the scroll. Just one problem. The scroll was still locked in the glove compartment of the Volvo. He would have to creep through the living room, tiptoeing past Cassie snoozing on his couch.

Knowing her, she probably slept in the buff. Without the benefit of covers.

He lay in the darkness a little while longer, but then curiosity got the better of him. He had to take another look at those hieroglyphics. If his brother—who was not the sharpest trowel at the dig site—had been able to decipher the Minoan hieroglyphics, there was no reason he shouldn't be able to figure them out too.

Except that ancient Egypt had been Harrison's only field of focus, whereas fickle Adam went on jags. He pursued whatever subject interested him at the moment. He had dabbled in everything from Egyptian to Greek to Mayan cultures. Grudgingly, Harrison had to admit his brother's versatility might have given him an advantage.

Or maybe Adam's modern sensibility, his very edginess, had lent him the edge.

And, speaking of edgy.

Harrison felt as if he was hiking way too close to a steep canyon drop-off whenever he thought about Cassie. There was something compelling about her. Maybe it was her indomitable optimism that countered his natural pessimism. Even in the face of her ransacked apartment she had quickly rebounded. He wished he possessed such an elastic temperament.

I thought her exuberance got on your nerves.

Well, maybe he'd judged her a little harshly. Harrison had discovered his opinions often mellowed when he was in private. Maybe it was from growing up with a strong, domineering mother; maybe it was his instinctive loner tendencies; maybe it was just that when he got off by himself he really had time to contemplate. But it seemed his real enjoyment of being with other people came when he was alone. When he had adequate time to sit back and reflect on the interactions.

Alone, he could match up his memory with the feelings and try them on without the confusion and clutter of being expected to react in a certain way.

He thought of Cassie's winning smile, her saucy wink, the sexy sway of her hips, and he got a soft, warm feeling in the dead center of his chest.

Okay, stop thinking about her. Focus on what's important.

Resolutely, he turned his mind to the enigmatic hieroglyphics and his missing brother in order to keep it off his lovely houseguest.

But his resolution didn't last long. Cassie was the most—and he was being crude here, but no other word truly fit—*doable* woman he'd ever had the pleasure to kiss.

Which was exactly the quandary.

He wanted her. He couldn't have her. She was all wrong for him, and he was all wrong for her. He didn't do runaway lust, and she didn't do commitment.

He was just experiencing a physical reaction. Chemistry. It meant nothing.

You have a brain, Standish. Use it, for godsake, and keep your dick in your pants.

His dick, however, had a whole other agenda.

He tried to tell himself it was purely an intellectual pursuit that drove him from the sleeping bag, and not the insistent throbbing in his penis. He bought into his own line of bull. He would simply sneak into the kitchen without turning on a light, slip out the door, retrieve the scroll from the glove compartment of his car, and hightail it back to his office. He would not, under any circumstances, even glance over to see if Cassie did indeed sleep au naturel.

Two steps down the hallway and then he heard a soft, feminine moan.

Was Cassie dreaming? Or having a nightmare?

What if she was awake?

He almost pivoted on his heel and fled back to his office, but then she moaned again. It was a low, helpless sound.

Was she in pain? What if she needed his help?

He took a step forward but stopped, not sure what to do next. If she was asleep, he didn't want to wake her; but then again, if she was having a nightmare, she might appreciate being awakened

The moaning deepened, grew more frantic.

She had to be in distress.

Then he heard another sound. It was odd, out of place. A strange buzzing rattle. A shiver played down his spine like fingers on a keyboard. He'd heard that sound before.

On a dig. In the desert.

Rattlesnake.

But how could a rattlesnake have found its way into his apartment?

Harrison froze. His mind spun. He thought of Cleopatra and Cassie. Of asps and rattlesnakes. Of regal women and poisonous vipers.

The rattling buzz grabbed him by the ears and shook violently. Trouble. Danger. Someone had stabbed a guy in a mummy suit. His brother was missing, an ancient amulet stolen, an enigmatic papyrus found. Someone had ransacked Cassie's place. That same someone could have dumped a deadly serpent in his apartment.

"Harry." Cassie called his name in a rough, achy whisper. "Harry, Harry, Harry."

Had she already been bitten?

She must have heard him in the hallway. She was snakebit and calling out to him for help.

Galvanized, he rushed into the living room and flicked on the light.

And that's when he learned that Cassie was neither sleeping nor bitten by a snake.

She was in the middle of his bed, murmuring his name as she pleasured herself with the most sophisticated rattling, buzzing sex toy he'd ever seen.

"Cassie!" Harrison's scandalized voice broke through the sweet fog of her solo sexual adventure.

What? He had never seen a woman masturbating before? From the shocked expression hanging on his face, she deduced probably not.

"Good God, woman!" he exploded. "Have you no sense of personal decorum?"

Truthfully, Cassie was mortified to have been caught

playing with the Rattler, but she wasn't about to let Harrison know that she was anything but honest, open, and straightforward about her sexuality. She tugged the covers over her waist and blinked at him in the bright light.

Oh God, this was the most humiliating thing that had ever happened to her.

"Well," she said matter-of-factly, totally ignoring that her body was burning up with embarrassment. "What did you expect? You turned me down."

The Rattler buzzed and vibrated beneath the sheets, and Harrison's gaze was fixed on the spot where it danced. "I...I...," he stammered.

Cassie blew out her breath. It wasn't the first time she'd left a guy speechless, but it was the first time she'd ever had so much trouble collecting her thoughts. There was only one way to deal with this obloquy—turn it back on him.

"Come on, Harry. We're both adults here. It's okay to tell the truth—didn't seeing me like that turn you on?"

"No!" he denied, but when his gaze, quick and furtive, fell below her waist, she knew he was lying.

Buzz, buzz, buzz, went the Rattler.

"Could you...er...um..." He waved a hand at her sex toy slowly vibrating its way across the mattress. "Could you turn that thing off?"

She shrugged nonchalantly, trying her best to look casual and totally in control of the entire situation when she was anything but. Swallowing hard, she slipped a hand beneath the covers and pulled the vibrator out into the open.

Embarrass him. Make him feel uncomfortable. Can't let him know you're not as sexually liberated as you let on.

"See." Cassie winked, hoping against hope that he didn't notice how her hand was shaking and call her on it. "It's called the Rattler. It's got these little button heads that shimmy and shake and…"

His face was beet red. No fear that he was going to notice her own telltale flush. He cupped his hands over his ears and averted his eyes.

"That's way more information than I need. Thanks."

"Who knows? You never can tell," Cassie teased, while at the same time she imagined the earth cracking open and sucking her down inside and then slamming shut on her, forever keeping her safe and sound from the undignified backfire of her own audacity. "Someday you may end up with a woman who's just dying for a good rattle."

"I seriously doubt that."

She waved the vibrator. "Aw, come on, you're a man of science. You keep toying with that djed thing. This should interest you. Look: here's where you turn it on. And here's where you adjust the speed. The faster it goes, the louder it rattles."

She was pushing him too far but couldn't seem to stop herself. If Harry had any clue exactly how unnerved she really was, he would quickly figure out she was not as candid about sex as she professed.

"Okay, okay."

She jacked up the dial. Now it sounded as if there were three dozen rattlesnakes in the room. "You ought to feel this sucker."

"No, that's all right. It's mechanics. I'm an archaeologist. Totally different sciences. Now put that thing away."

"Prude," she muttered under her breath, but it was only for effect. In reality she was extremely glad to stuff the thing into her backpack and out of sight.

They both simultaneously exhaled their relief.

"I've never met anyone like you," Harrison exclaimed, shaking his head.

She forced herself to grin impishly, when what she wanted to do was flee into the dark of night, never to face him again. "Is that a good thing?"

"Hell if I know."

He ran a hand through his hair and finally met her gaze. She did spy lust shining in those dark pools. She could also see that he was scared of his earthier impulses.

Right this moment, what she wanted more than anything was to pull him in bed on top of her. But the look on his face told Cassie that if she dared to do anything so bold, he would likely have a coronary on the spot. Never mind that he was young and in good shape. He obviously had no experience with daring women who knew their way around their own bodies.

"You flummox me, Cassie. I can't understand how you can be so...so..."

She tilted her head and studied him. He didn't seem judgmental. Not in the least. In fact, below his obvious embarrassment, he'd seemed quite curious about what she'd been doing.

"How can I be so what?"

"Uninhibited about your body," he finished.

"Hey, babe, I'm a *Cosmo* girl," she said saucily, finally regaining her natural sass. "Never miss an issue."

"I've gotta start reading that magazine." He grinned.

"You know," she said. "The two of us would make a spectacular hookup."

"What do you mean?"

"Look at it this way. I'm into romance, but I don't do commitment. You're into commitment, but without the romance-colored glasses. We've got sizzling sexual chemistry, although mentally we're polar opposites. Yet it's the perfect recipe for a lusty fling. Sorta like cinnamon ice cream—sounds like a bad idea, but it tastes really great. Say yes, and I'll give up the Rattler so fast it'll make your sperm swim."

He looked at her speculatively. "I'd have to be out of my mind to agree."

"That's the point, Harry. To get you out of your mind and into your body," she whispered.

He leaned down. Was he going to kiss her? Cassie's heart thumped. Please, oh, please, yes. She raised her chin, pursed her lips, and waited.

His lips hovered just out of reach; he wanted to. She could see it in his face.

"That's it," she egged him on. "For once in your life, let go. Do something wild and reckless and irresponsible. Ask yourself, What would Adam do?"

It was the wrong thing to say.

He pulled back so quickly that he stumbled over the coffee table and fell squarely on his butt. "My brother would cause chaos. Just as he's already done."

"Okay, scratch the Adam thing," she said. "Forget all about Adam."

But it was too late. Harrison picked himself up off the floor and gave her a wry smile.

"While your offer of a wild sexual fling is tempting, here's the reality. We're running out of time. Adam is MIA, whether by choice or not we don't know for sure. Someone trashed your apartment. My livelihood is hanging in the balance and you're this close"—he measured off an inch with his forefinger and thumb—"to ending up in jail. This might not be the most prudent time to start an affair."

Chapter 13

Not long after dawn, the perky sound of Cassie's cell phone playing the digitalized notes of "Girls Just Want to Have Fun" dragged her from a very frisky dream about Dr. Harrison Standish.

In her dream, she'd been systematically dismantling his every sexual inhibition and enjoying herself immensely in the process. In reality, she cracked open one eye to discover she had a pounding headache. She fumbled for the phone and ended up rolling off Harry's couch, sheets tangled around her legs as she clobbered the floor with her hip.

And the cell kept ringing, taunting her.

Give it a rest, Cyndi Lauper.

She finally got the phone freed from her purse and flipped it open. When she saw whose number was on the caller ID, Cassie groaned. She depressed the talk button and, in the same tone Jerry Seinfeld used whenever he greeted his nemesis Newman, said, "Hello, Phyllis."

"Where are you, Cooper? I tried your home phone and got nothing." Don't you have your answering machine on?"

Should she admit she was at Harrison's apartment?

Cassie decided to evade the question. "It's only"—she paused to peer bleary-eyed at her wristwatch—"six-thirty. I don't have to be at work for three more hours."

"Be here in twenty minutes," Phyllis said. "Alone. Or it's your ass."

The dial tone hummed in her ear.

Witch.

She glanced up to see Harrison standing in the doorway. He was sans glasses, his hair sexily mussed, and he had the sweetest sheet crease ironed into his cheek. He wore boxer shorts and a T-shirt, and he was sleepily rubbing his eyes. Dang, the man was downright adorable in the morning.

He stared. "You're not...um...I didn't...er...interrupt anything like last night?"

She realized that she was still lying on the floor with the sheet wrapped around her ankles. Memories of last night flooded her brain, and she got embarrassed all over again. Chagrined, she scrambled to her feet.

"Nope, nothing like that. I just forgot I wasn't at home, and I fell off your couch looking for my cell phone." She waved the phone to prove she hadn't been doing that other thing.

"Oh." He looked as if he didn't believe her.

"It was Phyllis," she said, desperate to get his mind off what he'd caught her doing last night. "She wants me at the Kimbell, ASAP."

"Uh-oh."

"Uh-oh is right. She sounded pissed off. I think we might be busted."

"I'll come with you," he said.

"No, that's okay, it's my problem. I'll deal with her."

"It's not okay. I got you into this mess. I'll get you out."

"I don't need you to save me. Phyllis was gunning for me long before this."

"Don't be stubborn," he said. "I'll go change."

Phyllis had told her to come alone. Although Cassie really wouldn't mind having Harry along for moral support, she didn't want to rile the curator any more than she already was.

"Harry," she said, stopping him halfway down the hall. He turned and looked back at her. "I think our search for Adam would be more efficient if we split up. We've already wasted a lot of time."

He paused, considering what she'd said.

"So you can just drop me off at the museum. I'll call you later and let you know what's going on."

"Or we can meet back here." He went to a drawer in the kitchen cabinet and pulled out a key. "In case you need to get in."

"You're giving me a key to your place. Harry, that's a pretty big step."

"Stop joking for once. Are you sure you don't need me to help out with Phyllis?"

"Positive."

"All right," he conceded. "I've been working on a search strategy. Adam occasionally stays at his father's house in Westover Hills whenever he's in town. I'll head over there while you go to the museum. I can interview the staff. See if anyone's heard from my brother."

"Okay."

Just two minutes shy of Phyllis's twenty-minute ultimatum, Cassie bounded out of the Volvo and hurried up the steps of the Kimbell. She skidded into the curator's office with thirty seconds to spare. She expected to see Phyllis looking like a thundercloud, which she was, but what she hadn't expected was to find Ahmose Akvar sitting behind Phyllis's desk.

When he spotted her, the Egyptian got to his feet and gave a courtly nod. "Miss Cooper."

"Mr. Akvar." Cassie extended her hand. He took it, raised it to his lips, and kissed her knuckles.

"Sit down, Cooper," Phyllis barked.

From the look on her boss's face, she was in much deeper trouble than she'd imagined. Help! She was seriously starting to regret not bringing Harry along with her.

Heart pounding, she sat, as did Ahmose. Phyllis remained standing, arms crossed over her chest as she leaned against the front of her desk, inches from Cassie.

"I'm confused," Cassie said. "Why is Mr. Akvar here?"

"May I address Miss Cooper?" Ahmose asked Phyllis. The guy certainly knew how to get on the curator's good side, asking her permission to proceed.

"But of course, Mr. Akvar." Phyllis flashed him a smile. "Please, go ahead."

Ahmose cleared his throat. "Miss Cooper, I understand that you and Dr. Standish have become quite close over the past few days."

Cassie shifted in her seat. What was he getting at? "I wouldn't say close. We barely know each other."

"But you have been working side by side on the star-crossed lovers exhibit, and you orchestrated this"—he paused—"murder mystery theater together."

"Um," Cassie hedged, not certain how to respond. She cast a sidelong glance at the curator. She didn't want to lie to the Egyptian official, but she didn't want to get herself in an even deeper crack with Phyllis. "I'm not sure what you're asking."

"Knock off the crap," Phyllis exploded. She leaned in close, glowered darkly, and shook an index finger. Cassie half expected her to grab the desk lamp off the table, shine it in her eyes, and mutter in a Gestapo accent, "Ve haff vays of making you talk."

"What?" Her voice came out in a whispered squeak. *Way to stay cool.* Oh man, this was much worse than she'd anticipated, plus she was such a lousy liar.

"Tell the truth. There is no murder mystery theater."

Cassie crumbled like a stale snickerdoodle. "Okay, all right, we made it up."

"Aha!" Phyllis crowed. "I knew there was no memo. I'm calling the police."

She reached for the phone, and Cassie was frantically trying to think of something to say that would make her put the receiver down when Ahmose Akvar reached over and pulled the phone from her hand.

"No," he said. "No police. Not yet."

"What do you mean, no police?" Phyllis glared at him. "We had the display case dusted for prints, and only two sets appeared. Cooper's and Clyde's."

"It is natural for her prints to be on the case. Personally, I believe neither Mr. Petalonus nor Miss Cooper are involved in the theft. The real thief would obviously wear gloves. I do believe, however, that Miss Cooper has unwittingly been manipulated by Dr. Standish and his brother, Adam Grayfield."

You could tell from Phyllis's expression that she was disappointed she wasn't about to see Cassie handcuffed and carted off to the slammer.

"Did you steal the amulet, Miss Cooper?" Ahmose asked.

This she could answer honestly. "No, I did not."

Phyllis snorted and started to say something, but Ahmose silenced her with a scathing glance. "I believe Miss Cooper could be a valuable asset to us."

"Excuse me?" She rounded her eyes and rolled out her best dumb-blonde routine. "I don't understand."

"Was the murder mystery theater Dr. Standish's idea?" Ahmose asked. "Did he ask you to go along with it only after the amulet disappeared?"

"Yes," Cassie admitted. "But I still don't see what you're getting at."

"Think about it, Cassandra," Phyllis said. "I fired you, and then Standish came to your rescue with this murder mystery theater idea. Now, why would he do that?"

"I don't know." Cassie shrugged, but a voice in the back of her mind whispered, *Why indeed?*

"Think, for once in your life," Phyllis retorted.

Ahmose frowned at the curator, and then he spoke to Cassie in a gentle tone. "Here's what I suspect happened. Dr. Standish was quite aware Ms. Lambert was looking for an opportunity to dismiss you. He and his brother, dressed as a mummy, staged a little drama for your benefit. Then Dr. Standish leaped to your assistance with an offer you couldn't refuse."

Cassie gulped. "I don't get it. Why would Harrison do something like this?"

"You are being set up to take the fall for the theft. You'll be the one going to prison, and they'll get off scot-free with the amulet." Phyllis snapped her fingers. "Put two and two together."

"But why would Harrison even offer to rescue me? Phyllis had already accused me of taking the amulet. Why not just let me be arrested?"

"Timing," Ahmose said. "And Dr. Standish needed to plant evidence so the case against you would be airtight."

"Evidence? Like what? If they're keeping the amulet, what could they plant on me?"

"Another artifact from the exhibit."

The papyrus scroll? Cassie wondered. Was that what the baggage claim ticket and the crate had all been about? Was even Spanky Frebrizo in on it? She got a sick feeling in the pit of her stomach.

"I'm clean. Search me." She plucked up her handbag and shoved it at him. "Go ahead. Search me. Search my purse. Search my house. I've got nothing to hide." Then a sudden thought occurred to her, and she jerked the purse back into her lap.

"Hey." She pointed a finger at Ahmose. "Were you the one who ransacked my apartment last night?"

If he *was* responsible, the guy was cagey. His expression never changed. "Your apartment was ransacked?"

"Yeah? Know anything about it?"

"I do not. But perhaps your friend Dr. Standish faked a break-in for the opportunity to plant evidence."

"He couldn't have," Cassie said. "He was with me all evening."

"No, but his brother could have."

There was that.

Ahmose leaned back in his chair and steepled his fingers. "Miss Cooper, have you ever heard of the Minoan Order?"

Uh, not until last night, and Harrison had been the one to tell her about it. "Isn't it an extinct secret brotherhood cult?"

Ahmose shook his head. "Not extinct. The Minoan Order is alive and thriving in modern society."

"Hmm. Imagine that." She tried her best to look completely bored in spite of her racing pulse and mouth gone scarily dry.

"Members of this order believe that once the pieces of the amulet are reunited, a long-dead secret will be revealed. In fact, the Minoan Order has been caught several times trying to sell stolen artifacts. We've known for a long time they've been stealing them, we just haven't known how. Your friend Dr. Standish holds the key."

"What kind of secrets are you talking about?"

"I'm not at liberty to say."

"Alchemy? The ability to control the weather?" *Ka-thump, ka-thump, ka-thump* went her heart.

"Something much more provocative than that, Miss Cooper," he hinted.

"And you believe that?"

"I don't believe it, but that's not the point. The members of this order believe it, and they'll stop at nothing to get what they want. My countrymen and I suspect that Dr. Standish and his half brother, Dr. Grayfield, are both members of the Minoan Order."

"Really?"

"I can see you're having trouble processing this information. Do you know what the symbol for the Minoan Order is?"

"Yes. A double ring with the Minotaur."

"That is correct."

She and Ahmose locked gazes. "And?"

He reached down for the briefcase at his side, opened it, and passed her a college term paper with Harrison's name on it. She briefly skimmed the text. Her hand trembled, but she did her best to control it.

"So he wrote a paper about the Minoan Order. Big hairy deal. Who cares?"

"The Minoan Order cares. And Adam Grayfield has a tattoo of the Minotaur on his left shoulder blade."

"A lot of people have tattoos."

"The brothers own property together in Greece. A tavern. Want to know what it's called?"

"The Minotaur?"

Ahmose gave her a humorless smile. "I know this is not solid proof of their involvement in the Minoan Order, but collectively, these things make one wonder. That and the fact their mother was kicked out of Egypt fifteen years ago for performing a Minoan Order ritual at an excavation site."

No. Cassie couldn't buy into what Ahmose was telling her.

Could she say she trusted Harrison enough to side with him over a high-ranking member of the Egyptian Ministry of Antiquities? Could she so easily dismiss the possibility that Harry was not everything he seemed to be?

"For the sake of argument, say your suspicions are correct. None of that explains why Harrison and Adam would steal the amulet halves from the Kimbell instead of just taking them from the dig sites when they discovered them," she argued.

"You obviously don't understand how excavations work in countries like Egypt and Greece who've had antiquities pillaged for centuries. They're very sensitive about it."

"Please," she said. "Explain it to me."

Ahmose seemed endlessly patient, unlike Phyllis, who kept scowling deeply at her and pacing the carpet.

"There are armed guards at the sites. There's a great deal of paperwork, and everything must be approved and supervised by many people and recorded in many places. The Ministry of Antiquities takes immediate possession. It is very difficult to steal something, either at an excavation site or in the country of origin. The best opportunities for thieves occur when the artifacts are loaned to museums outside their homeland."

"Oh," she said.

"Then there is the political element," Ahmose continued. "One-half of the amulet was found in Egypt, the other in Greece. Neither country was willing to allow the other country access to their half of the amulet. In pieces, the amulet is useless to the Minoan Order. It is only through reunification that they can regain their long-lost secrets."

"Why didn't you come forward last night when the amulet first disappeared? Why didn't you call the police then?"

"For one thing, I do not trust the authorities in your country, and alas, I had no hard evidence against Dr. Standish. But that's where you come in."

"So what's the bottom line?" Cassie nervously drummed her fingernails on Phyllis's desk until the curator shot her a quelling glance.

"We need more evidence before we connect Dr. Standish to either the thefts or the Minoan Order. We want you to get very close to him. Gain his trust. If he thinks you are a fool, his guard will be down," Ahmose said. "It should not be so difficult for a beautiful woman like you."

"I don't know. It's underhanded. Sneaky."

"Your hesitation is understandable."

"I just need a little more time to think this through."

"Bullshit." Phyllis splayed both palms against her desk. "You want me to lay it on the line for you, Cooper? Here are your choices. Cooperate with us, and you'll get your dream job at the Smithsonian. Or side with Standish, and end up imprisoned for stealing priceless relics."

Chapter 14

Harrison couldn't help fretting as he drove to Ambassador Grayfield's mansion in Westover Hills. Why had Phyllis called Cassie at six-thirty in the morning? Had he made a serious error in judgment by letting her go see the curator alone?

It had seemed to make sense to split up. They were running short on time and needed to cover as many bases as possible, but in retrospect it might not have been such a hot idea.

One persistent question circled his brain. What if Cassie cracked and ratted him out? How much did he really trust her? After all, trust wasn't his greatest virtue.

He arrived at Tom Grayfield's front gate, entered the security code at the call box, and the gate swung open. He had expected to speak with the housekeeping staff, to see if anyone had seen or heard from Adam, but he was surprised to find Tom's personal chauffeur, Anthony Korba, puffing a cigarette on the back porch.

The minute Anthony spotted him coming up the driveway, he crushed the cigarette out beneath his heel. "Harrison," he greeted and smiled broadly. "It's good to see you again. It's been a long time. No?"

"A long time, yes," Harrison said and embraced the man who used to drive him and Adam to and from the Athens airport whenever they visited Tom on holiday.

"You look good." Anthony sized him up.

"So do you. Is Tom here?"

Anthony nodded. "He came into town for the museum exhibit, and he's been invited to an event in Austin at the governor's mansion later today."

"Tom was at the museum for the exhibit? I didn't see him there."

"No, no." Anthony shook his head. "Plane delay."

"Harrison, how are you?" Tom's rich voice greeted him like a warm hug as he stepped out onto the back porch. "Don't stand on the stoop gossiping with the help, come in, come in."

"Hello, Tom." Harrison followed him into the house. Tom clapped him enthusiastically on the back. Over the years, the ambassador had been very generous to him, at times even assuming a surrogate father role.

"Let's go to my study." Tom led the way through the foyer, to the great hall, and on into his study. The lavish room was filled with expensive leather furniture, lots of animal trophies, and the finest aged scotch and Cuban cigars.

It had been several years since Harrison had visited the mansion, but not much had changed. He'd always felt uncomfortable in this house. It was too big, too ornate, too filled with dead things.

"Have a seat." Tom nodded at a chair and seated himself on the corner of his desk, fishing a Cuban from the humidor. "How've you been?"

"I'm doing great. How about you? How's the ambassador business?"

Tom laughed and waved a hand at his surroundings. His gold signet ring flashed in the light. "Obviously, I can't complain."

Harrison plunked himself down. A bull moose stared accusingly at him from the opposite wall.

"I did hear through the grapevine that you and Adam had decided to drag out the reunification ceremony with a little murder mystery theater concept. Good advertising ploy." Grayfield nodded and clipped the end off his cigar with special gold-handled scissors. "I'm guessing it was Adam's idea. He is gifted when it comes to bullshit. Takes after his old man."

"There's no murder mystery theater. It was a desperate stall tactic on my part." Harrison wondered exactly how much to reveal about Adam's disappearance. He didn't want to upset Tom unduly, but then again, if his son was in trouble, the man had every right to know what was going on.

"Oh?" Tom flicked his Zippo, lit the cigar, took a long puff, and then blew a smoke ring. "Why's that?"

He decided to tell him. Maybe Tom could help. "Adam never showed up at the Kimbell with Solen."

"What?" Tom groaned. "Don't tell me that kid is up to his old tricks."

"You haven't heard from him either?"

"No."

This had gone beyond pranks and publicity stuff. How could his brother just vanish into thin air? This was serious. "Adam didn't know you were coming into town for the exhibit?"

"It was last-minute. Wasn't sure I could make it in time, and as it turns out, I didn't. My plane was delayed. There were storms over the Atlantic."

Harrison shifted in his seat and clutched the leather armrests with both hands. He thought of his brother. Of the underlying tension that had always existed between them. He had a sudden urge to start over, to absolve Adam. For having a father, for stealing Jessica, for being the fun, charismatic one.

Desperately, he wished his brother was in the room so he could apologize for having been so judgmental and withdrawn over the years. For not being the kind of big brother he should have been. He wanted to ask for a second chance. He didn't know if forgiveness was even possible now.

He felt despondent and somehow responsible.

If anything had happened to Adam, he didn't know how he was going to live with himself.

Tom studied Harrison's face. "Adam left you high and dry again."

"I really think this time is different. I have a gut feeling that he's in real trouble."

"I respect your concern, but let's not beat around the bush, Harrison. You're not a guy who's real in touch with his gut feelings. No offense."

"None taken."

Tom was right. What could he say? He'd been trained to shun his feelings in favor of logic. Anyone who knew Diana knew that. Except the training hadn't taken with Adam.

"Have you told your mother?"

Harrison shook his head.

Tom smiled. He loved being one up on Diana. "So you came to me first."

"Adam wouldn't want me to involve Mom unless I had no other choice."

"Wise move. No one wants an ass-chewing from Diana." Grayfield uncocked his leg and walked to the wet bar in the corner. "What makes you think Adam is in trouble?"

He poured himself a scotch. Drinking at seven-thirty in the morning? Tom must have noticed the look because he said defensively, "It's late afternoon in Greece."

Harrison ignored that comment and instead answered the question. "I can't reach him on his cell phone. I've left a dozen messages, and he's not calling me back. I'm really starting to get worried."

"Sounds like same old same old with Adam to me."

Harrison drew in a deep breath. "Okay. I didn't want to alarm you, but here's the whole story." Then, blow by blow, he told Tom everything that had transpired the previous evening.

Tom took a long pull of his drink. "Let's give Adam the benefit of the doubt, not that he deserves it, and we'll say that there is someone after him. What's your theory?"

"I was thinking he got in deep to loan sharks again. Maybe he gambled the money he borrowed to finance the Solen dig."

Tom shook his head. "Nope."

"Why not? It's happened before."

"Because I gave him the money this time."

Harrison was surprised. Adam had never taken Tom's money for a dig. He didn't like having to do things Tom's way. "Mind my asking why?"

The ambassador grinned. "Because of you."

"Me?"

"Couldn't let you take all the glory. Particularly after you found Kiya; that really fanned Adam's competitive streak. Why do you think I was trying to make it to this exhibit?"

"To see Adam show me up?"

Tom looked like a proud father for all of two seconds. "But once again, the kid let me down."

Conflicting emotions surged in Harrison. Feelings he used to be able to beat back, ignore. But ever since he had started hanging out with Cassie, he was having a harder and harder time suppressing his feelings.

"You're overanalyzing things again." Tom polished off his drink and got up. He came over to clamp a hand on Harrison's shoulder, his signet ring digging uncomfortably into his skin. "Don't worry. Adam will turn up. Always does. And usually with a very tall tale to tell."

Harrison started to ask if Tom knew that Adam had decoded the Minoan hieroglyphics, but he held his tongue. It was Adam's news to break to his father. Especially since Tom was such a Minoan Order buff. It was as big a deal as finding Solen. And for some strange reason, talking about it felt like admitting he might never see his brother again.

"I'm sure you're probably right," Harrison said, wanting to believe Tom's reassurances but deeply concerned that they weren't true. He got up to leave.

"If you hear from Adam, please tell him to call me. As much as he antagonizes me, I do love my son."

The minute Cassie left Phyllis's office, she phoned David, her brother-in-law with the FBI.

"Hey, Cass, how's my favorite sister-in-law?"

"I'm your only sister-in-law, David."

He laughed. "You're still my favorite."

"Flatterer."

"What's up?"

"I need a favor."

"For you? Anything."

"Run a background check on someone."

"Cassie, you aren't in any trouble, are you?" She could hear David rapping a pencil against something.

"Keyed up, Dave?"

"I'm always keyed up. It's dead around here. But stop avoiding the question. Are you in trouble?"

"No. Not really."

"Not really? I don't like the sound of that."

"Will you just do this for me and not ask a lot of questions, please?"

"Come on, don't make me promise that. I ask questions. It's my job."

"I thought you said you would do anything for me."

He sighed. "All right. Give me the details."

"He's an archaeologist named Harrison Standish. Someone in the Egyptian government just gave me bad news about him, and I want to know if it's true."

"What's the deal?"

"This Egyptian official suspects Harrison of being a member of the Minoan Order. You ever heard of them?"

"Yeah, and they're bad news."

"So the Minoan Order really exists?"

"Unfortunately, yes. Honey, I've got just one piece of advice. Run, don't walk, away from this guy. Why take the chance?"

"I can't walk away."

"Somehow I knew you were going to say that. You want to tell me why you need to know this?"

"I can't talk about it. Not now."

"All right," he said. "I'll look into it. In the meantime, if you get into any trouble, you call me. I'm a three-and-a-half-hour plane ride away."

"Thanks, David. I really appreciate it."

"No problem, kiddo."

"Um, there's just one other thing."

"What's that?"

"Please don't tell Maddie. She'll just think this is Duane Armstrong all over again."

Over at the warehouse, the mummy finally found his sarcophagus.

He'd spent the night gathering his strength, trying fruitlessly to recover his memory, and sawing the duct tape off his wrists with the sheet metal. He'd sliced his wrists to ribbons, but he didn't care. He had to get out of here before his captors returned to torment him anew.

And he had to find Kiya.

The men had hidden his sarcophagus behind a tall stack of corrugated tin sheet metal. Because he had been forced to make concessions for the piercing pain between his shoulder blades, it had taken him more than three hours to crawl his way around the warehouse looking for an escape route. His initial intent had been to grapple enough sheet metal over to the window and stack it high enough to reach the ledge.

Rationally, he had known that wouldn't work, that the sheets of metal were too large and unwieldy for him to handle. But he had no other plan, so he'd clung desperately to his illusion.

And then, when he was wrangling the metal, he'd discovered the sarcophagus.

A pleasant surprise.

If he could drag his ornate coffin to the window, it would make a much more effective ladder than sharp-edged, slippery, flat pieces of tin.

The unpleasant surprise came when he tried to move the damned thing. With his diminished strength, it wouldn't budge more than a few inches at a time. He sat panting on the floor and staring at the sarcophagus, his lungs almost bursting from the strain.

Kiya. He had to rescue Kiya. Had to get to her before Nebamun discovered his secret scroll.

He did not know where the thought about the scroll sprang from or what it meant. He closed his eyes and tried to concentrate.

Think.

A fleeting wisp of memory floated. Just out of reach.

Come on, come on.

In an instant the ephemeral remembrance was gone. And yet he could not shake the feeling of impending doom winding its way around his heart.

Why couldn't he remember?

Just get out of here. You can worry about your recall later. Out. Out. Out.

Get to Kiya.

He braced himself against the floor with his hands, bent his knees, and used his feet to push the sarcophagus forward through the narrow lane between the tall stacks of sheet metal. This time he moved it three inches instead of one.

Never mind the ripping sensation in his shoulder blades. He had to get out of here. The mummy wriggled forward on his butt, cocked his legs against the coffin, and shoved again.

And again.

And again.

And again.

An hour later, the sarcophagus was positioned beneath the window, a springboard to the world outside his warehouse prison.

He almost giggled. He felt that giddy. Grasping the

gilded faceplate with both hands, he hauled his trembling body up onto the coffin. Once he reached that small four-foot summit, he lay resting, head tilted upward as he studied the window.

Sweet freedom.

He could almost taste it.

Except the window was still several more feet above the top of the sarcophagus. He stood on tiptoe, rested his chest against the cool wall, and stretched for the window ledge.

His fingers were just millimeters short of it. He was going to have to use the sheet metal after all. That meant climbing down, hoisting those hunks of sharp unfinished metal onto his raw, aching back, and dragging them across the warehouse space many, many times.

The wound in his back was already a boiling cauldron of pain.

He felt like crying. He clenched his teeth to stay the tears stinging the back of his eyelids. He'd never felt so alone, so empty, so hopeless.

At least not that he could recall. He had a hard time remembering.

To hell with self-pity. Get off your ass and get moving.

He didn't know where the tough inner voice came from, but it galvanized him. He slid off the sarcophagus, steeled his mind, and set off again.

Hours later, he was back atop the sarcophagus with a stack of sheet metal draped over the top and dipping over onto the floor. It was enough to boost him an extra foot if he didn't slip off his precarious perch.

This time when he reached for it, his fingers found the ledge. Now all he had to do was drag his body weight up to the window.

Fourteen attempts later, he lay on the floor, bloody, sweating, nauseated, and ready to die.

Just let 'em kill you. Death couldn't be any worse than this.

But Kiya needed him. She was waiting. She'd always been waiting.

The thought bolstered his flagging spirits and he tried once more, crawling up on the metal-draped sarcophagus. He took a deep breath, gathered the very last ounce of his physical reserves, and lunged for the ledge with every bit of love for Kiya he possessed inside him.

He made it.

His chest hit the window ledge and his fingers found a secure hold on the window frame. He curled his feet against the wall, using them to propel him higher.

The metal sheets slithered off the sarcophagus and fell to the floor, but that was okay. He didn't need them anymore.

He was almost there.

And then he heard the ominous clicking and whirring rasp as the metal warehouse doors began to roll upward.

Cassie stood outside Harrison's apartment, staring at the key in her hand.

This was a defining moment.

Did she really trust him? Could she take him at face value? Should she just walk away, pick up her cell phone, call him, and tell him what had happened?

Or should she believe Ahmose Akvar?

At this point it wasn't a matter of faith. If she did not do this thing that Ahmose and Phyllis were asking her to do, if she did not spy on the man who had trusted her enough to give her a key to his apartment, then she was going to end up taking the fall for the stolen amulet.

Besides, whispered that part of her that distrusted all men, *what if Ahmose is right? What if Harrison is playing you for a fool?*

There was only one way to resolve the issue. Go look for proof. If she found nothing incriminating, she could report back to Ahmose with a clear conscience.

But if you snoop, aren't you betraying Harry?

And yet, she had to know.

She pushed the key into the lock but didn't twist it, still hung on the twin horns of her dilemma. She thought of all the men in her life—her father, Duane, every guy on her collage wall. They'd all let her down in one way or another. How could Harrison be any different? She didn't owe him anything.

Resolutely, she unlocked the door and stepped inside.

"Harry?"

The silence in the apartment was as deep as a moat.

"Yoo-hoo, Harry, you home?"

No answer.

Cassie's heart chugged and her throat went so dry she could hardly swallow. Like a sneak thief, she furtively edged down the carpet, headed for Harrison's office.

A floorboard creaked and she jumped half a foot.

Stop freaking out. He's not here.

His door was shut tight.

Another barrier to cross. Another wrangle with her scruples, but she'd come this far, she might as well see what was on the other side of that door.

The room, although crowded with books and papers and Egyptian artifacts, was tidy. Bookcases lined three walls. The fourth was taken up by a desk and computer equipment. A digital camera was perched on a shelf above his monitor, and stacked on the closest bookshelf were several photo albums. There was a mini-fridge positioned next to the computer desk. Cassie cracked it open to find nibbles and bottled water and soft drinks.

His space was his haven. He hid out here.

She studied the collection of artifacts but quickly understood she could be looking at evidence and not even recognize what she was seeing. She leafed through a few scholarly journals and her eyes glazed over. The material was way over her head. The room smelled of him, studious and worldly. It smacked her then, the extent of his intelligence, how much smarter he was than she.

Sitting here looking at his things, she felt so inadequate. A guy like Harry could never be interested in her for long. Once the sexual chemistry abated, there would be no common interest to hold them together. No glue to make them stick.

Who cares? It's not like you're into commitment.

Where the hell were these thoughts coming from anyway? It was probably nothing more than a case of wanting what she couldn't have.

Cassie thought about flicking on his computer and searching his files for evidence that he and Adam had orchestrated the theft of the amulet to set her up, but she wasn't quite ready for that.

Instead, she turned to the photo albums. She liked pictures. Photographs generally captured the good times in people's lives. She wanted to see Harry when he'd been happy.

The first photo album contained nothing but pictures of dig sites and artifacts. Here or there you'd see someone's shoe or an elbow, but this collection wasn't about Christmases or birthdays or summer vacations.

It wasn't even about people.

Disappointed, she stuffed it back on the shelf and opened the next album. Now this one was more interesting. These were pictures of Cairo. The shots were packed with people, but it was all crowds, no individuals, as if he'd been walking the streets of the ancient city snapping photos of buildings and vehicles and bustling streets. The pictures were artistic, displaying above-average skill with lighting and form and framing.

As she flipped through the books, it became clear that Harrison had a proclivity for observing life through a filter. Whether it was from behind a camera lens or through abstract theory or via ancient history, Cassie instinctively understood that he used these things to distance himself. His need for privacy isolated him. She felt at once sorry for him and ashamed of herself for intruding upon his sanctuary.

She almost did not pick up the third album, but in the end she was eager to find at least one picture of Harry with someone he loved. This album was older than the other two.

Inside, she found what she was looking for—baby pictures of Harry.

Her heart melted. He was such an adorable toddler in his diaper and a cowboy hat. Then a few pages later as a first grader with a missing front tooth. The glasses appeared on his face in the next year's school picture and her heart ached. It must have been tough having to wear glasses so young. He'd probably gotten called "Four-Eyes" more times than he could count.

There were a few pictures of him with a younger boy she assumed was Adam. Frequently they were glaring at each other. The pictures tapered off around his teenage years. There was one shot of a sixteenish Harry beside a battered Mustang, smiling his head off. Ah, so he hadn't always been a Volvo aficionado. She noticed a clear absence of girlfriends. He'd probably been a late bloomer when it came to dating.

Toward the back of the album she came across a photo of what appeared to be Adam's graduation from college. In the foreground stood Adam, wearing a cap and gown, and Harry on the rolling green lawn of the University of Athens in Greece. There was an older, burly man positioned between them. She wondered if this was Adam's father, Ambassador Grayfield. She'd seen him in a few of the other photos too.

Adam, with his arm slung over the older man's shoulder, was grinning and making the V-for-victory sign. Harry, as usual, looked rather taciturn. Cassie had an illogical urge to crack a joke and make him smile.

If she hadn't reached out a finger to trace the outline of Harry's face, she wouldn't have seen the man lurking there in the background. In fact, she almost didn't recognize him with a full head of hair.

She brought the album closer to her face and squinted. He wasn't looking at the camera, but instead was studying Adam intently.

Alarm shot through her.

He was ten years younger and thirty pounds lighter, but she recognized him.

There, at Adam's college graduation, was none other than Phyllis's executive assistant, Clyde Petalonus.

Chapter 15

Right smack-dab in Harrison's parking lot, Cassie ran out of gas just as she was preparing to zoom over to Clyde's for a showdown. She sat in her Mustang, staring woefully at the gauge. She'd driven around with the empty light on plenty of times, and this had never happened.

Fine. Great. She could handle it. She would just call the auto club. She reached for her cell phone.

A car pulled to a stop beside her. She glanced casually over her shoulder and then did a double take when she spotted the white Volvo.

Uh-oh, busted.

Her pulse jumped. She had to stay calm and act as if she was completely innocent. As if she'd never been upstairs rummaging through his office. As if there wasn't an incriminating photograph in her pocket of him with Clyde Petalonus.

Harry sauntered over. Cassie rolled down the window.

"Hi," she said, trying her best not to look like a spy for the Egyptian government.

"Hey, you just drive up?"

"Uh-huh," she squeaked, hating that she had to lie, but

taking the easy way out. She wasn't prepared to confront him head-on with the damning evidence.

"How come you didn't call and let me know you were leaving the museum?" Harry leaned against the door-frame and smiled down at her.

Her heart hammered. "I thought you were supposed to call me."

She hated this whole subterfuge. Especially since Harry was being so sweet. Damn, why was he being so sweet? He could not be a Wannamakemecomealot guy. He turned her on too much. She wouldn't get turned on by a bad guy.

Ahem? What about Peyton Shriver? And Duane? Let's not forget Duane.

"Guess we got our wires crossed," he said mildly.

"Did you find out anything about Adam?" She rushed to change the subject.

Harrison shook his head. "Tom Grayfield's in town, but he hasn't heard from Adam either. What about you? How'd it go with Phyllis?"

"Um, okay."

"Okay?"

Did he sound suspicious or was it just her guilt-ridden imagination?

She shrugged. "To be a pain in my butt. You know Phyllis."

"What'd she want?"

"What is this?" she wanted to snap, but instead she said, "She wanted to know more particulars about the plans for the second party on Saturday night. She told me to spend the day ironing out the details."

"So you're free to come with me to see Clyde Petalonus?"

"Clyde?"

"Yeah, in the nuttiness of last night I forgot that he lied for us about the memo. As I was driving back over here, I kept asking myself why," Harry said.

"I wondered the same thing."

The midmorning sun was beating down through Cassie's window, but that wasn't why she was starting to perspire. Rather, it was Harry's proximity and the topic of conversation that had moisture beading her neck.

"And he disappeared really quickly last night. I never saw him leave."

"You...um...didn't know Clyde before meeting him at the Kimbell, did you?"

Come clean. Tell me that, sure, you've been acquainted with Clyde for years and years, and then I'll know the photograph doesn't mean a thing.

He looked at her strangely. "No. What? Were you thinking he lied to protect me?"

"It crossed my mind."

"I was thinking he lied for you."

"Nope," Cassie said. "He wasn't lying for me." She met his gaze and telegraphed him a message with her eyes. *Please tell me the truth.*

Harry said nothing.

Apparently he wasn't going to confess. How could he stand there and fib to her? Crushed, Cassie fisted her hands. She felt as if she'd just learned her favorite chocolates contained strychnine.

What if he's not lying, her hope whispered. Maybe Adam was the one who stole the amulet. Maybe Clyde was protecting him, not Harry.

But Adam wasn't the only one in that graduation picture. Harry had been there too, and he had just denied knowing Clyde back then. The question was, Why would

Harry want to confront Clyde about the fabricated memo if they were conspirators?

None of it made sense.

"Should we take my car or yours?" he asked.

Cassie swallowed. How was she going to play this?

He looked so endearing in his mismatched clothes and unruly hair that she just had to trust him. She would operate on the motto that had served her well throughout her life—when in doubt, smile and deny reality.

"Okay, Clyde, let us in."

Ten minutes later, Cassie was pounding on the door of Clyde's cracker-box palace in Arlington Heights, two doors down from a Taco Bell. The smell of breakfast burritos and lard wafted on the morning breeze. She knew where Clyde lived because she occasionally gave him a lift to work when his aged Buick Regal acted surly.

"We know you filched Kiya's half of the amulet," she said. "So cough it up."

Clyde did not respond.

She slid a sideways glance over at Harrison to see how he was reacting to the accusations she was hollering at the door, but as was often the case with Harry, she couldn't read his expression.

Holding the screen door open with one hand, she stood on tiptoe and tried to peer through the small diamond-shaped window at the top of the wooden outer door.

"You can run, but you can't hide, Clyde. Don't make us go to the police. Or worse yet, we'll sic Phyllis on you." Cassie figured, if nothing else, *that* threat ought to have the curator's assistant swinging the door open pronto.

But no dice.

She couldn't see much through the window in the door.

For one thing, even at five foot eight she was too short to get an unobstructed view. Obviously the cutout was for lighting, not for spying. Plus, the window was dusty and coated with grime. Clyde wasn't married, and apparently he kept house with a typical "Windex? I don't need no stinking Windex" bachelor mind-set.

"Spptt, Harry."

"What is it?"

"You're a good four inches taller than I am. Take a gander through the window and tell me what you see inside."

"To what end?"

"To the end of finding out what in the hell is going on around here."

He sighed, shouldered past her, and peered through the window. Cassie tried not to notice how he smelled like soap and toothpaste, or how cute and intellectual he looked in his round, dark-framed glasses. Sort of like a grown-up Harry Potter.

Stop ogling him. The guy could be a high priest in the Minoan Order. But even as she thought it, she still couldn't reconcile the Harry she knew with the cunning mastermind Ahmose Akvar had made him out to be.

"Well?" she asked.

"I don't see anything."

Cassie rolled her eyes. "What do you mean, you don't see anything? You have to see something."

"No," he corrected her. "There's nothing to see."

"You're kidding."

She muscled him aside, stretched as tall as her toes would allow, but she still couldn't see anything except the foyer wall. And it was a truly icky shade of latte. "We've got to get in."

"What?"

"How else are we going to learn anything?"

"We could be mistaken," Harry said. "Just because Clyde lied to Phyllis for us doesn't mean he stole the amulet."

Oh yeah? What does it mean when he's in an old photograph with you and Adam?

She waved a hand. "Look around and see if Clyde's the kind of guy who stashes a hide-a-key. Try under the welcome mat. We need to get inside and see if he left any clues."

Harrison grimaced. "This idea doesn't appeal to me."

"How come?" Was it because he might have left clues implicating him?

"I'm a private guy, and as such, I respect other people's right to privacy."

"Luckily, I don't have such misgivings. I'll do whatever I have to do to stay out of jail. I'm not taking the fall for Clyde's sticky fingers," she said.

"You've got to stop jumping to conclusions."

"Well, at least I jump. You spend so much time hugging the shore, too cautious to stick a toe in the water, that you never make a move."

"Yeah, well, what if there was a drop-off in the water? Or a deadly undertow? Who would be dead and who would be alive?"

"And who would have had fun while they were alive and who wouldn't?" she challenged.

"Why are we arguing about this?"

"You got me. Just check the welcome mat for a key."

"Fine."

"Fine." Hardheaded man.

Harrison lifted up the corner of the dusty welcome mat with two fingers. "Nothing here."

He let the mat flop back down, sending dirt scattering

across the porch. Cassie peeked behind the mailbox and underneath an empty flowerpot but came up empty-handed.

"Looks like Clyde's not a key stasher," he said.

"Let's check around back. Maybe you can pry off a window screen so I can wriggle inside—and don't give me that long-suffering look."

"I don't see the point in breaking into the man's house."

"Hello? The guy stole Kiya's amulet and left me to take the blame."

"We don't know that."

She met Harry's gaze and he didn't flinch. What was going on behind those dark, enigmatic eyes? She didn't know what to think or whom to believe. "Clyde lied."

"People lie for all kinds of reasons." His eyes were locked on hers.

Was he lying to her? She was certainly keeping secrets from him. A tremor afflicted her, a slight thing, nothing terribly noticeable. At least she hoped he didn't notice. But it was in her legs and then her arms. She steadied the quivers by locking her knees, dropping her gaze, and nervously tucking a strand of hair behind one ear.

"You're acting differently," he said. "What's changed between us?"

Cassie hung a nonchalant expression on her face. "Changed? Nothing's changed."

"What happened with Phyllis?" He reached out a hand to touch her shoulder and she drew back. "See? That's changed. Yesterday you wouldn't have pulled away from me."

Dammit, why did she have to be such a lousy liar? She had to sidetrack him from talking about Phyllis. She couldn't keep fibbing, or she'd soon give herself away. She had to tell him something that was true to throw him off the scent.

"Maybe I'm still embarrassed about last night."

"Aw, Cassie, you don't have to be embarrassed about that. You were just being yourself. I like how open and honest you are."

If he only knew. Right now she felt about as open and honest as an alcoholic Enron executive. And as guilty.

"I'm going in," she said and nodded at the house, desperate to get out of this conversation.

"And what if some nosy neighbor decides to notify the police?" he asked.

"We'll just say we dropped by to see an old friend. He didn't come to the door. He's plump; he's middle-aged. He doesn't eat right. He's a heart attack waiting to happen. We were worried."

Cassie didn't wait for Harry to follow. She took off around the side of the house. The grass whimpered for a good mowing, and her sandals sank deep into the dewy foliage. The itchy Bermuda seeds tickled her ankles, and several narrow blades lodged between her toes.

Ugh. The sacrifices she made for her job.

She cornered the house and was pleasantly surprised to find the back door standing open. No breaking-and-entering charges needed. Well, no breaking anyway. Technically, she supposed she would still be entering. She started up the back stoop, but a hand reached out and snagged her elbow.

"Are you crazy? Buy a déjà-freakin'-clue. Didn't we just go through this last night?"

She turned to look at Harry. "Hey, I like the déjà-clue thing. Way to reference pop culture. Didn't know you had it in you. Now let go of my arm."

"Woman, don't you have even a whisper of common sense? An unknown man in a mummy costume has been stabbed, an ancient amulet has been stolen, and your apartment was plundered. Figure out the appropriate response. Danger. Proceed with caution."

"Fiddle." She blew a raspberry. "If his place is empty, Clyde is long gone."

"There could be someone else inside instead of Clyde."

"Oh." He was right. She hadn't considered that.

"I'll go first. You stay right behind me."

"Can I wrap my arms around your manly waist?" she teased, to lessen the tension and to keep him from noticing any more changes in her behavior.

"Are you physically incapable of going five minutes without flirting?"

"Pretty much."

A grin tugged at the corner of his mouth, but he managed to fight it off. "Just follow me."

Harry ascended the stoop, Cassie at his heels. He pushed the door open. The hinges creaked ominously.

She made spooky horror movie noises.

"Shh." He frowned and whispered fiercely, "What if someone is in here?"

"The cow already got out of the barn on that one. I don't think our presence is going to come as a news bulletin."

"Good point," Harry admitted and stepped over the threshold.

The kitchen was lit only by the morning sun dappling through the bare window. Except for the refrigerator and stove, the room was vacant. No dining table, no toaster on the counter, no dirty dishes in the sink. But there was dust on everything. It looked as if Clyde didn't live here anymore.

Very strange.

They moved into the tiny living room. Harry led the way, and it was all Cassie could do to keep from resting her hands on his shoulders. But she was still anxious about trusting him. She wanted to believe in him, but Ahmose had raised enough doubts in her mind.

They skulked down the narrow hallway and into the first bedroom. It was as dusty and empty as the rest of the house. They took a quick peek into the adjoining bathroom.

Nada.

One room to go.

The room at the end of the hall.

"If this was a horror movie, this is where the audience would be screaming at us not to go into the room. You realize we're the too-stupid-to-live people."

"I promise you that Freddy Krueger isn't in there."

"What about Jason?"

"Him either."

"Michael Myers?"

"Nope."

"Leatherface?" Cassie asked. "He's the scariest of all with that chain saw. Rrrrrrrrr." She pretended to slice him up with a chain saw.

"Knock it off." Harrison squared his shoulders and moved toward the door. Cassie crept after him.

He turned the knob.

Blood swooshed through her ears.

Harry edged the door open.

Something darted out.

Something small and gray and fast.

A mouse!

Cassie shrieked, wrapped her arms around Harrison's neck, and jumped into his arms. "Omigod, omigod, omigod. I would have preferred Leatherface."

"You're afraid of mice?"

"Petrified."

"He's more afraid of you than you are of him," Harrison said.

"I seriously doubt that. You're incredibly lucky I didn't pee my pants."

He was holding her and chuckling. Cassie could hear his laughter deep inside his chest.

She didn't want to get down. It felt kinda nice in Harry's arms, and there was a mouse lurking in the house. But she wasn't a lightweight and she didn't want to break his back, so she let go of his neck and set her feet on the floor, all the while casting a suspicious gaze in the direction of the mouse.

"Let's wrap this up." He stepped into the room the mouse had come out of. Tentatively, Cassie crept in behind him.

It had a short stairway leading down into a cellar.

Oh no. She wasn't about to go down there. She quickly backpedaled.

"Where you going?" Harry started down the steps.

"That's okay, you go on, report back to me."

"What? You chicken to go down to the cellar?"

"No." Terri-fickin'-fied.

"Brock-brock." He made chicken noises and flapped his arms like wings.

"Don't make fun of me. I'm claustrophobic."

"And after that big speech about jumping headlong into the water."

Why did he have to call her on this? She hadn't been in a cellar in eleven years. She never wanted to be in one again.

"You know the only way to get over a fear is to face it," he said.

"I know."

Crap. He was going to goad her until she went into the cellar. With no windows and only one door to escape through.

"We'll leave the door open. I'll be right with you." Yeah, famous last words. Probably what Ted Bundy said to his victims.

Don't exaggerate. Harry's not a serial killer.

Maybe not, but he could very well be a thief who was trying to frame her for his crime. If that was the case, why had he brought her to his conspirator's house?

Maybe he had wanted to lure her here so he could lock her in the cellar. That thought froze her.

He extended his hand. "Come on."

Don't go!

"You can do it." His smile could have melted the polar ice caps. She was such a sucker for a great smile. How pathetic was that?

"Can't I just wait here?"

"That doesn't sound like the Cassie I know."

"All right," she said. "But if I do this, the next time I want you to do something adventurous, you can't hold back."

"Deal."

She could do this. No problem. Just a simple cellar. She gulped and eased down the stairs.

"Now that wasn't so hard, was it?" He reached up and pulled the dangling cord on the bare lightbulb. It took every ounce of courage she possessed not to fling herself back up those steps.

"Hey, look here." He squatted on the dirt floor. Cassie could clearly see the imprint of what looked like a coffin delineated in the dirt.

Their eyes met. "Solen's sarcophagus."

Harry trod across the floor, headed for a cabinet positioned in the corner beside a cedar hope chest.

"Where you going?" she asked, quickly covering the gap between them.

"We're here. We've come this far. Might as well check out every nook and cranny."

"Such a thorough little scientist."

The expression on his face was somber. "I've got to be honest with you, Cassie. I'm really getting worried about Adam. What if he's"—she could tell he was having trouble even saying the word—"dead?"

His voice cracked, and the sound of it squeezed her heart. There was no doubt in her mind that he cared about his brother. He wasn't lying. This wasn't an act. Ahmose had to be wrong. Harry would never put either his job or his brother in jeopardy by stealing an ancient artifact.

Unless he's just a damned good actor. It's not like you're the best judge of a man's character.

But she could not deny the look of concern in his eyes. He was extremely worried about his brother.

Harry reached for the handle on the cabinet door.

"Ooh, wait, wait." She shook her hands like she was drying her fingernails after a manicure. "Let me brace myself in case there's another mouse in there."

"Tell me when."

She gritted her teeth and tensed her shoulders. "Go."

Harry wrenched the cabinet open, and they found themselves staring down at a bolt of white linen.

The mummy hit the ground rolling.

Ooph.

Stunned, he lay there gasping like a guppy. It was a long drop for a three-thousand-year-old guy with a leaky stab wound in his back.

Get up. You ain't got time to laze around.

He heard shouts from inside the warehouse. Knew his absence had been discovered by Nike and Froggy Voice. Frantically, he rolled over on his side, tried to force his legs to obey.

After a couple of wobbly attempts, he managed to drag himself to a standing position.

Get the hell out of here.

Right. Which way?

If he took off in the wrong direction, he could easily run into Nike and Froggy, and if he did, he knew there would be no getting away. In his present condition, he couldn't outrun an infant.

He swung his head around, spied a delivery van parked on the street at the end of the alley. Maybe he could hide behind it until the coast was clear.

Hurry, hurry.

Something brushed against his leg. He looked down and saw he was starting to unravel. A long strip of linen was dangling from his elbow. If he wasn't careful, he'd trip himself. Tucking the material into his fist, he took off at a lope, headed in the direction of the van, but just as he reached it he tripped in a pothole and went tumbling head-long under the vehicle.

He bit down hard on his bottom lip to keep from crying out. He was underneath the van's back tire, and when he rose up he bonked his head on the axle.

Son of a wh—

Something fell off the undercarriage.

He peered at it, blinking. It was a small oblong black box with a magnet on one side.

A hide-a-key. He smiled. He was saved.

Hope spurring his recovery, he scooted from underneath the van, slid open the box, and retrieved the key.

He was just about to hop behind the wheel and take off when he heard a pounding noise coming from the back of the van.

Was someone in there?

You don't have time to mess around. Get moving. Get out of here.

Bam, bam, bam.

Get in the van. You can look in the back later.

He hopped inside, started the engine, and drove away just as Froggy Voice and Nike came bursting from the warehouse. Cutting the corner so short that the van bounced up onto the curb, he stomped the accelerator and careened three blocks through heavy traffic. All the while the knocking in the trunk was growing louder and louder.

Damn, shut up.

What if it was Kiya? The thought suddenly occurred to him.

Okay, that did it.

He pulled over to the shoulder, left the engine idling, and got out.

Vehicles blew past him. Someone honked.

Cautiously, he inched his way to the rear of the van. He grabbed hold of the door handle. Preparing to run at the first hint of trouble, he gingerly pulled the door open and peered inside.

The person bound and gagged on the floor looked familiar, but he couldn't place the name. Slowly, the mummy approached. A pair of gray eyes beseeched him.

"Hey," said the mummy. "Am I supposed to know you?"

Chapter 16

Clyde's the mummy?" Harrison fingered the bolt of linen.

"No." Cassie shook her head. It reassured her that he looked genuinely confused, and reinforced her trust in him. "There's no way. The mummy was stabbed in the back."

"Unless the stabbing was faked."

"No. It was real blood, and Clyde was in the museum looking fine just minutes after I found the mummy in the courtyard."

"Could he have stabbed the mummy?"

"Maybe."

"Or," Harrison said.

Their eyes met.

"Clyde and the mummy were working together," they said in unison.

Cassie was certain that Harry was as surprised by this insight as she was. Ahmose had to be wrong about him, that's all there was to it.

"I'm guessing the mummy created the distraction while Clyde doused the lights and snatched the amulet," Harrison said.

"But if Clyde and the mummy were in cahoots, then who stabbed the mummy?"

"Could it have been a third party?"

"Somebody horning in on Clyde and the mummy's caper?"

"But who?"

"Maybe it's the same person who ransacked my apartment."

"Or maybe Clyde ransacked your apartment. Maybe the mummy double-crossed him. Or perhaps Mummy Man was the one who trashed your place." Harrison set the bolt of linen back in the cabinet.

"I'm telling you that mummy was in no shape to do anything more than breathe—and he was doing very little of that—much less ransack and double-cross."

"And then there's the central question." Harrison brushed his fingertips against his pant legs.

"Yeah," Cassie said. "Who's the mummy?"

"Adam?"

"What now?"

Harry took the djed from his pocket and fingered it, a faraway look in his eyes. He seemed to use the thing to help him think. "My brother's in trouble," he murmured.

"Call him again." Cassie handed Harry her cell phone. "I'll check out the cedar chest."

Palming the djed, Harry accepted her phone and pulled out the antenna. Cassie sank to her knees beside the cedar chest, praying there were no mice inside there either.

She undid the clasp and cautiously eased open the lid, not sure what to expect. She was slightly disappointed to find sweaters. She lifted them out one by one.

"I can't get any reception down here," Harry muttered.

About halfway to the bottom of the chest, underneath

all the sweaters, Cassie found something disturbing. It was a Minotaur mask and a wax seal with the sign of the Minoan Order engraved into it. She caught her breath. The implication was clear. Clyde was a member of the Minoan Order.

She started to call out to Harry to tell him what she found, but then she hesitated. As much as she did not want to believe Ahmose, the part of her that had trouble trusting any man whispered in her head. What if Harry and Clyde were in this together?

But then why had Harrison brought her here?

She pivoted in her squatting position to see where Harry was and if he was watching her, and that's when she realized she was alone in the cellar.

And the door at the top of the stairs was swinging closed.

It clicked shut with an ominous sound.

Cassie freaked. She totally lost it. Terrified, she flew up the steps and charged the door. No, no, she could not be locked in a cellar. She would die. No place to go to the bathroom. No food to eat. Not enough air.

Help!

Her knees were rubber, her body instantly drenched in sweat. She slammed both palms hard against the door. "Let me out! Let me out! You can't lock me in here!"

Two seconds later, Harry wrenched the door open and she tumbled out onto the floor, gasping frantically. He stared down at her. "It wasn't locked."

She swatted his leg. "I told you I didn't like cellars, and you left me down there alone."

"I thought you were following me. I had my mind on Adam and I—"

"You forgot me," she accused. She was *not* going to cry. She would not.

"Not on purpose. Why are you clenching your fist? You gonna hit me?"

"Maybe." No crying. Stop sniffling.

"Jeez, Cassie, I had no idea you were so claustrophobic." He bent down to help her up, but she squirmed away from him.

"You forgot me." Her bottom lip trembled.

"Okay. I forgot you. I'm sorry. I was focused on calling my brother, and when I focus on something I get absent-minded about everything else."

He looked remorseful, but she wasn't letting him off the hook. Five minutes ago she'd been sure Ahmose was completely wrong about Harrison; now she wasn't so sure.

"Just calm down," he soothed. "Take a deep breath."

"Don't tell me what to do." She pushed past him, headed for the back door. For fresh air and freedom.

He followed her. "I didn't mean to make you cry."

"I'm not crying," she said, drawing in great gasps of air, the morning sun warming her face as she walked out into Clyde's backyard.

"What's this then?" He caught up with her and reached out to stroke her cheek damp with tears.

She jerked her head away and glared. "I'm not crying."

"Oookay, if you say so."

"You can be a big ol' jerk, you know that?"

"Do you want to tell me why you're overreacting?" he said calmly.

His calmness made her want to punch something. "None of your damned business."

He raised his palms. "All right, obviously you have a thing about getting locked in a cellar, and you don't want to talk about it."

"Damn skippy." She rubbed a tear from the end of her nose with the back of a hand.

"Please forgive me for leaving you down there. Sometimes I get so caught up in my mind, I forget what my body is doing."

"Gee, way to make a girl feel special, Einstein. Explains why you're not married."

"I suppose I deserved that."

She felt safer now, less haunted, more like her cocky self. The farther she got away from the cellar, the faster the past receded. She shouldn't have freaked out on him. It wasn't Harry's fault. He didn't know about Duane and the cellar.

Taking a deep breath, she opened her mouth to tell him about Duane, but got no further because a man darted out of Clyde's back door.

"Harry!" she cried as the man in Nike sneakers slammed into her and knocked her to the ground.

Immediately, Harry took after the guy. Cassie struggled to her knees. The guy was holding something in his hand that looked sort of like the keyless entry remote from a set of car keys. The man had a small head start, but Harry was closing the gap.

"Stop!" Harry hollered.

And to Cassie's amazement, the guy did.

But no one could have predicted what he would do next. The man pressed the button on the remote in his hand, and Clyde's house exploded.

The force of the blast blew out the windows and knocked Harrison sprawling to the ground.

"Cassie!" He crawled back across the lawn.

"I'm here; I'm okay."

He reached for her and tucked her body under his,

protecting her from the debris raining down around them. His heart was thumping madly and his mouth was bone dry.

Harrison had trained his mind not to react to his body's emotions so well that he was able to feel the spurt of adrenaline rushing through his system but still process his thoughts rationally. They'd checked every inch of the house, and it had been empty. The man had clearly slipped in the back door while they'd been in the cellar and set the bomb.

But who was he, and why had he blown up Clyde's house? What did all of this have to do with Adam and the missing amulet?

He didn't know, but he was determined to find out.

First, they had to get out of here. The police would be arriving soon, and they'd be hard-pressed to explain their presence here. They had no time for police questioning.

"Sweetheart," he said, the strength and clarity of his voice surprising even him. His chest was pressed into her back. "Are you all right?"

She nodded. He clambered to his feet. She rolled over and looked up at him, her eyes dazed. He held out a hand to help her up, but she scooted away from him on her butt.

"Stay away from me."

What was the matter? Was she shell-shocked? Had something hit her on the head? She appeared to be okay. He took a step toward her.

"Don't come any closer."

"Cassie, I'm not the enemy."

"Aren't you?"

The look in her eyes rattled him to the bone. She was scared of him.

"You were going to lock me in the cellar so your accomplice could blow me up in the house."

"No!" He said it more vehemently than he intended

because her fear of him tore a hole in his heart. When she cringed, he dropped his voice. "How can you even think that about me?"

"There was a Minotaur mask in Clyde's cedar chest and other things that looked like they could belong to the Minoan Order."

"There is no Minoan Order." Had she hit her head? Did she have a concussion? Was that why she was accusing him of such crazy things?

"Oh yeah? Then who detonated the house?" She stared at him as if he'd sprouted a pitchfork and devil horns.

"That guy in the Nikes—you just saw him."

"How do I know it wasn't staged for my benefit?"

"Look around. I think the bomb was real."

She blinked. "I'm so confused."

"Please believe me. I didn't try to hurt you. I'm on your side."

Siren screams. The emergency vehicles would be here soon.

"Let's get out of here. I'll take you somewhere quiet and safe. We don't need to get tangled up with the police."

"I don't know what to believe." She drew her knees to her chest. She looked so lost sitting on Clyde's debris-strewn lawn with bits of grass in her hair.

He kept his hand extended. "You're just going to have to trust me."

"I'm not good at that." She shivered and rubbed her hands over her upper arms.

He squatted in front of her, took her chin in his palm, and forced her to look him in the eyes. "Cassie, I swear, I would never, ever hurt you."

Poor kid. She was shell-shocked. He couldn't blame her for jumping to ridiculous conclusions. He had left her alone in the cellar after she'd told him she was claustrophobic. He had been caught up in his own agenda, and he hadn't paid attention when the cellar door swung shut behind him.

He'd treated her like an afterthought.

When he thought about it from her point of view, he could understand why she'd come uncorked. A woman never wanted to feel trapped by a man. Had he learned nothing from having a mother like Diana? If she knew what he'd done, she would give him hell.

And then it hit him like a kick to the gut. Cassie had almost died in that house.

So how are you going to make it up to her? He had to do something to gain back her trust. He had to apologize. Big-time.

"I'm an ass," he said. "An A-number-one dillhole for being so insensitive, but we've got to get out of here before the police show up. Are you coming with me?"

He held his breath, waiting. The sirens screamed nearer.

Cassie reached out and took his hand.

A crowd had gathered on the lawn, but everyone was so intent on staring at the devastation that no one really took note of them as Harry gently escorted her toward the Volvo parked on the street by the Taco Bell. The first fire truck arrived just as Harry started the engine. By the time the second truck pulled to a stop, they were turning the corner onto a main thoroughfare.

"I feel like we've done something wrong, sneaking off like this," she fretted

"We don't have a choice. The police would question us for hours, and we simply don't have the time. We have to find Adam. Besides, how would we explain being in Clyde's house?"

He was right and she knew it. She did her best to throw off her anxiety. She'd never been much of a worrier. That was Maddie's job. Everything would turn out all right. She had to believe that, and since she'd chosen to go with him, she had to trust her instincts and believe in Harrison, no matter what Ahmose suspected him of.

"Where are we going?" she asked.

"It's a surprise."

"I'm not really in the mood for any more surprises," she said. She'd had enough of the unexpected for one day, thank you very much.

"It's nearby. Just a short detour. I want to go somewhere we can relax and catch our breath for a minute." He took University Drive to the Fort Worth Zoo.

"We're going to the zoo?"

"Uh-huh."

He parked the car, paid the entry fee, and they went inside. Cassie kept glancing at him, torn in two conflicting directions. Part of her wanted to break down and tell him everything Phyllis and Ahmose had sprung on her, but her ears still rang from the echo of the explosion, and she didn't know what to believe.

It was just before noon on Thursday. The crowd was light and consisted mainly of mothers with strollers, waving juice boxes and Lunchables.

"It's this way." Harrison took her elbow, guided her down the narrow asphalt path toward the rear of the grounds.

"There's nothing out here." She hadn't been to the zoo in a long time, but she was pretty sure they were walking away from the animal attractions.

"Special exhibit," he said.

A howler monkey screamed, and an eerie coldness blasted down Cassie's spine. She was still high-strung from what had just happened at Clyde's and still feeling mistrustful.

She glanced over at Harrison.

He was sprouting a five o'clock shadow and his hair was scruffy, but he looked kinda good. And he smelled even better. Like soap and sunshine. She caught the aroma of cigar smoke on him. She liked cigar smoke. Her daddy smoked cigars when she was little.

Duane had smoked cigars too.

Well, hell, Duane had smoked a lot of things.

They had to circle around the construction zone, and just when Cassie was certain they'd reached the end of zoo property, she saw a temporary building constructed out of a tentlike material and mesh wire.

"What's this?" she asked.

He pointed at the sign that she'd failed to notice in her paranoia, and then she remembered reading about the two-week exhibit. In fact, there were banners up all over town advertising it. She'd just forgotten.

The building was a butterfly hatchery.

Harrison opened the screen door and they scooted into a small area, where they paid a small extra fee for the attraction and were greeted by a butterfly expert who gave them a short lecture.

"Go right on through." The perky lady guide handed them a color brochure. "Pick out a butterfly emerging from its cocoon, watch it hatch, and you get to name it. After that, walk on through to the butterfly garden. Please make sure the doors close securely behind you."

They walked into the hatchery area where another tour guide, this one a lanky male, greeted them. The humidity was high in this area. Cassie could just feel her hair frizzing, but she soon forgot about her hair as they watched the butterflies hatch.

"Which one do you want to claim?" Harrison asked.

Cassie heard the excitement in his voice and she was surprised to discover she was excited too, watching new life uncurl into the world.

"That one." She pointed.

"You've chosen Lepidoptera *Danaus plexippus*. The monarch." The guide grinned. "You've made an excellent choice."

A few minutes later, their butterfly was born.

"She's beautiful," Cassie breathed.

"She'll sit on that twig for a while to pump up her wings. What would you like to name her?" the guide asked.

Cassie looked at Harrison. "What do you think?"

"There's only one name for her." Harrison's eyes met and held hers. "She's a vibrant beauty who's only in your life for a short while. We'll have to call her Cassie."

"Cassie it is," the tour guide said and entered the name in his log.

Cassie's throat felt full and scratchy. She blinked and had to drop Harrison's gaze.

"Step on through into the butterfly garden," the guide said. "We'll bring Cassie in as soon as her wings have fully opened."

They moved into the garden ripe with lush fruit and vegetation. The climate was tropical, warm and damp, and the air was filled with all manner of butterflies.

Cassie had never seen so many of the lovely creatures. They were every color under the rainbow. Small, medium, large. Everywhere she looked she saw butterflies.

She glanced over at Harrison. Butterflies fluttered

above his shoulders, landed on his head. One was even walking along the top of his ear.

"Look at you." His eyes crinkled.

Butterflies were all over her as well. Lightly kissing her skin with their spindly legs. She giggled and then pressed a hand to her heart. "It's so breathtaking. Thank you for bringing me here."

"My gift to you," he said. "To apologize for being such an inconsiderate ass."

"You weren't an ass. I went schizo."

"No. You had every right to be upset with me. In my single-mindedness I did let the cellar door close on you, and I'm sorry."

"Oh, Harry."

"Please, forgive me. I hate to think you're mad at me."

"There's nothing to forgive."

"You folks want a picture with Cassie?" The tour guide came in from the other room with Cassie the monarch perched on his finger.

"Yes." Harrison nodded. "We do."

"Give me your hand," the butterfly wrangler tour guide instructed.

Cassie held out her hand, and he transferred the monarch onto her finger. Cassie the butterfly flexed her wings.

"Hurry," Harry said. "She's about to fly."

The tour guide snapped the Polaroid picture just as Cassie the monarch took flight. Harry was smiling and the tour guide was smiling and, aw hell, Cassie the woman was gonna cry.

Chapter 17

Harrison had wanted to do something nice for her, to apologize for being such a lunkhead and scaring her. But he hadn't expected this simple trip to the butterfly hatchery to affect her, or himself, so profoundly.

"That's the sweetest, most romantic thing anyone's ever done for me," Cassie said for the fifth time and stared down at the Polaroid in her hand. She'd kicked off her sandals and propped her feet on his dashboard. She had such adorable feet.

They had left the zoo and were headed down University toward I-30 in search of lunch. He wanted to find a quiet place where they could talk. They needed to hash out the significance of what had happened at Clyde's, but Cassie still had that goofy, sentimental expression on her face, and it was starting to unnerve him. He'd wanted to make her happy. He just wasn't sure he'd wanted to make her *that* happy.

"Obviously that creep who blew up Clyde's house was the same one who ransacked yours. Surely there aren't two Nike-wearing criminals causing us problems," he said. "What I can't figure out is why he blew up Clyde's place."

Cassie said nothing.

"Unless he was trying to kill us. What do you think?"

"Harry, I can't hide my secret anymore," Cassie said. "There's something important I have to tell you."

"What?" He jerked his head around to stare at her. "What secret?"

"I can't keep this up. Suspecting you is killing me, so I'm putting my cards on the table."

"Suspecting me? Of what? What are you talking about?"

She took a photograph from her pocket and laid it on the console between them. "I know about you and Clyde, so you can stop lying to me."

"What?" he said for the third time, and momentarily took his eyes off the road to glance down at the picture.

It was the snapshot of him and his brother and Tom at Adam's college graduation in Crete.

"Where did you get this?" he demanded.

"Don't make this about me. That's Clyde Petalonus in the background, and you denied ever knowing him before you came to the Kimbell."

Harrison picked up the photograph and squinted at it. By gosh, she was right. It was Clyde. "I swear to you, I had no idea Clyde was in the picture."

"And you expect me to believe that?"

"You were snooping through my apartment," he accused. "You got this photo out of my office."

"Yes," she admitted.

He stared at her, stunned. He couldn't fathom that she would violate his privacy. He clenched his jaw. "Why?"

"I'm going out on a limb by telling you this," she said. "You don't know how much it's costing me to trust you."

"No more than what it cost me to trust you." He waved the photograph at her. "And you betrayed me."

"Harry, I'm sorry."

"My name is Harrison."

She flinched. "I can understand your anger, but I had no choice. Ahmose Akvar and Phyllis told me I'd go to prison for stealing the amulet if I didn't spy on you. There were only two sets of fingerprints on Kiya's display case. Mine and Clyde's. So I spied and I found the photograph."

"And you impulsively jumped to conclusions about me."

"It wasn't a big leap."

"Why did Ahmose recruit you to spy on me? What does he suspect me of?"

Cassie's gulp was audible. "He speculates that you're a member of the Minoan Order."

"And you believed him?"

"No. Yes. I don't know," she said miserably.

"We're going to get this straightened out," he said. "We're going to confront Ahmose."

At just that moment, a customized chrome Harley zipped around them.

Harrison did a double take, unable to believe what he was seeing. "There he is! There's Adam!"

"Where? Where?"

"On that Harley."

"How can you tell? It zoomed by so fast, and the guy is wearing a helmet."

"It's the same motorcycle I saw outside the museum last night. I would bet my doctorate on it." Harrison made an erratic U-turn. Car horns blared. He tromped the gas pedal and followed the Harley out onto the freeway.

"Hey, slow down. I like adventure, but there's adventure and then there's foolhardiness."

"I'm not letting him get out of my sight." He gritted his teeth determinedly.

They were too far away for him to get a good glimpse

of the rider to see if it was indeed his brother, but Harrison knew that was the motorcycle. He changed lanes, edging out a U-Haul with New Jersey plates.

"Get back over," Cassie shouted. "The Harley's taking the Rosedale exit."

Harrison obeyed, turning on his blinker and cutting sharply in front of the U-Haul, earning himself a double-whammy middle-finger flip from the driver and his passenger. Cassie blithely waved at them, smiled broadly, and called out, "Thanks for letting us in."

"When in doubt," she told Harrison, "assume that getting flipped the bird is just the way people say howdy wherever they're from."

Ah, the sunny, illogical philosophy of Cassie Cooper.

The street they drove down was littered with potholes. Vagrants squatted outside liquor stores. Many buildings were boarded up, vacant. Women in very skimpy outfits sauntered up and down the sidewalk, waving at passing vehicles.

"Don't worry," Cassie said, apparently not even noticing they'd entered an unsavory neighborhood. "We'll catch up to Adam. I can still see the Harley. Wait, wait, he's pulling into the parking lot of that bar. Lemme see." She rolled down the window and craned her neck out of the Volvo. "The place is called 'Bodacious Booties.' Hmm, is your brother into seedy strip clubs?"

"Not that I'm aware of," he said grimly, but then again, who knew?

Nothing made sense anymore. Harrison was the quintessential reluctant hero journeying through the mythological woods with his very own, very sexy Trickster sidekick. When or how his life had started diverging wildly out of control, he could not exactly pinpoint, but all roads led right back to Cassie.

And the scary thing about it: he was enjoying the ride. Until a man in a filthy overcoat threw a brown paper bag wrapped around an empty wine bottle at his hood when he stopped for a red light.

"Asshole," the guy swore at him.

Harrison honked his horn.

"Hey, Harry, don't get so upset. It wasn't anything personal. The guy was aiming for that trash can next to the streetlight. See, there." Cassie waved at a graffitied trash barrel positioned at the curb. "He can't help it if he's a bad shot."

Harrison glanced over at the bum. The guy bared his teeth and shook a fist. Yeah, right, he was just aiming for the trash can.

Not for the first or even the tenth time, he wondered how Cassie had survived well into her twenties with those rose-colored glasses glued so firmly to her face.

He didn't even wait for the light to change. Once he was sure no traffic was coming, he floored it through the intersection.

"Whoo-hoo!" Cassie sat up straight and grasped the armrests with both hands. *"Breakin' the law. Bad boys, bad boys,"* she sang, the theme song from *Cops*.

He wished she'd stop making him grin at the most inopportune times. He bumped into the parking lot of Bodacious Booties and cut the engine, glancing over his shoulder to make sure the bum hadn't trailed them from the intersection.

The chrome-customized Harley sat out front along with numerous other motorcycles. In peeling paint, the silhouette of a naked woman adorned the side of the building. The provocative beat of pole-dancer music throbbed from inside the club.

"Are you certain that's the bike you saw Adam drive

away on?" Cassie asked in a squeaky voice. She sounded as nervous as Harrison felt.

"Positive."

He had no idea why Adam was inside this den of iniquity, but he was determined to find out. No matter how scared he might be to walk through that door.

But what to do with Cassie?

He couldn't very well leave her alone in the car in this neighborhood. Yet the thought of taking a woman like her into a place like that shoved icicles through his veins. The men in there would be on her like wolves on a newborn lamb.

It's up to you to protect her.

Okay. He could do this. He would do this. Adam was inside. His brother could help if things got dicey. But he had to think this through, get it right in his head so he wouldn't make the wrong move.

Cassie, however, had different plans. Before Harrison even realized what she intended, the crazy woman was out of the car and heading for Bodacious Booties, her own bodacious booty bopping up the steps.

He leaped from the car and charged after her. Lord, she'd be the death of him. He caught her elbow just as she stepped over the threshold into the smoky, dimly lighted strip bar.

A lanky, bored woman with breasts she had definitely not been born with spun listlessly on a small stage. To one side sat three pool tables. A gaggle of guys in leather and chains stood around drinking beer, chalking their cues, and occasionally casting glances at the dancer.

Harrison spotted the Indy hat immediately. Adam was sitting at the bar with his back to the door. A burly dude with a bandanna on his head was seated on the stool to his right. The barstool to Adam's left was empty. Harrison decided to approach from that side.

"There's your brother." Cassie nudged him in the ribs. "Go get 'im."

He hated to be rushed, but he'd seen the way the men were eyeing Cassie. Best to claim his brother and get out of here as quickly as possible. But then he thought of all that had happened, how Adam had been leading them on a wild-goose chase, and anger took over.

Stay calm, stay cool, stay detached from your feelings.

To Harrison's confusion, his never-fail mantra failed. No matter how strongly he told himself not to do it, he could not seem to stop himself from stalking over and slapping a hand on his brother's shoulder.

"Just what in the hell kind of game do you think you're playing?" he demanded.

Adam turned his head.

Only it wasn't Adam.

The guy had a face like a car accident. His cheeks were crisscrossed with pockmarks and scars. His nose had been broken at least twice, and his eyes were so small and close-set that he looked cross-eyed. Life had not been kind.

Without a word, the man pushed off the barstool and rose to his full height. Harrison was forced to look up and up and up. At six feet, Harrison was by no means short. But this dude was a sequoia.

"You startin' somethin' with me?" The cross-eyed guy leaned down and blew his hot, beer-and-pork-rind-smelling breath in Harrison's face.

"No, no," Cassie rushed to say. "He's not starting any-thing. Case of mistaken identity."

Why couldn't she have let him handle this? He might be terrified, but he didn't need her to rescue him.

"You let your woman do your talkin'?" Pork-Rind Beer Breath asked.

"Hey baby," said the bandanna-headed guy on the barstool to the right. He made smooching noises at Cassie. "I wanna start a little sumpin' with you."

"Let's discuss this like rational men," Harrison said. "I thought you were someone else. Please excuse my blunder. I'm sorry if I caused you any inconvenience."

"Rational?" Bandanna Head hooted. "You think Big Ray is rational?" Then he winked at Cassie. "After Big Ray kills your boyfriend, wanna go out back and get it on with me, baby?"

"Before you pound me senseless, could you answer one question?" Harrison said to Big Ray, who was clenching his fists and grinding his small, crooked teeth. Harrison's mind raced, searching for a way out of this mess.

"Yeah?" Big Ray grunted, slamming his right fist rhythmically into his left palm.

"Is that your customized Harley out front?"

"No," Big Ray said, jerking his thumb at Bandanna Head. "It's Freemont's. But I borrow it sometimes."

"Did you borrow the Harley last night? Were you near the Kimbell Art Museum?" Harrison asked.

"Nah," Freemont supplied. "That wasn't Big Ray. That was me at the Kimbell last night."

"Were you wearing Big Ray's Indy hat?" Cassie asked.

"It's not Big Ray's hat. He likes to borrow stuff," Freemont volunteered. "Like other men's women."

"Whose hat is it?" Harrison asked, doing his best to ignore that last comment.

Freemont shrugged. "I met a guy in the airport who gave me that hat, a hundred bucks, and a white envelope with the name 'Harrison' printed on it. He said I should show up at the Kimbell wearing this hat and give the envelope to someone who worked there. What's it to you?"

"You said just one question," Big Ray said. "That's a bunch of questions, and they're starting to sound pretty damned nosy."

Harrison pulled five twenties from his wallet and slapped them on the bar. "How many questions will this buy me?"

Big Ray's eyes lit up and he reached for the cash. Just when Harrison thought that maybe they had a chance of waltzing out of there without Big Ray pounding him into talcum powder, Freemont picked that moment to grab Cassie's butt.

"Honey," Cassie said glibly and wriggled away from him. "I'm not up for grabs."

"Then you shouldn't have been wagging that gorgeous ass in front of me," Freemont said and then smacked her fanny so hard the sound of it echoed above the stripper music.

Harrison saw red.

And for a color-blind guy, that was quite a feat.

All logic flew out of his head. He was an animal gone wild. He ignored Big Ray and turned on Freemont. Curling his lip, he snarled, "Get your hands off my woman."

"Make me, Four-Eyes."

At that moment, Freemont was every bully who'd ever called Harrison a wimp. He was every jock who'd gotten the girl by pushing around a weaker guy. He was every petty tyrant who'd ever sexually harassed a woman.

Harrison smacked his hand around Freemont's wrist and yanked the man off Cassie. Then, before he even knew what he intended on doing, he punched Freemont square in the jaw.

Old Bandanna Head went down like a sack of cement.

Harrison blinked, amazed at what he'd done. Freemont sprawled on the floor at his feet, the bandanna half off his chrome dome. Harrison's fist throbbed, but Cassie was gazing at him like he was her own personal superhero. Archaeology Man to the rescue.

Unfortunately, everyone else in the place was looking at him too.

"Get him!" Big Ray hollered, and then it was a free-for-all.

They were beating the living crap out of Harry. Not only that, they were beating the living crap out of one another. Guys fighting for the sake of fighting.

The stripper and the bartender had taken cover, but everyone else was slinging punches and throwing beer bottles and bouncing pool balls off each other's heads.

Men.

Cassie stood in the midst of it, hands on her hips. She had to do something to save Harry, or they were going to kill him. She could call the cops, but that would take too long. She needed a plan and she needed it now.

Okay, think logically. What would Harry do?

Her mind tumbled with possibilities, but she quickly rejected them. She needed something that would make everyone stop fighting so she could grab Harry and make a clean getaway.

Think, think, think.

Big Ray grabbed Harry by the collar and threw him against the bar.

"Ooph," Harry grunted, and the pain in his voice tore a hole right through her heart.

Impulse urged her to jump on Big Ray's back and start slapping him about the head, but for once something held her back. Harry was depending on her to remain composed. She couldn't go off half-cocked and possibly land them in even more dire circumstances. Was this what it felt like to be prudent?

But she wasn't accustomed to thinking things through. Acting out was her basic defense mechanism. How did she make the shift from spontaneous to structured thought?

A beer bottle whizzed over her head.

Hurry, think quick!

Play to your strength, use your talents.

What the hell were her talents beyond flirting? Things had gotten a little too out of hand for that tactic to work at this late date.

Cassie groaned. What was she good at?

Everyone said she excelled at thinking out of the box. Terrific, what out-of-the-box solution could stop three dozen pissed-off, half-drunk, badass bikers in their tracks?

Harrison was on his feet, swinging wildly, desperately at Big Ray and missing his target completely. Big Ray laughed and punched him in the gullet.

A pool ball rolled under her foot. She could pick it up and bean Big Ray, or she could do something really spectacular and arrest the attention of the entire bar.

Whatever it is, do something, anything, before Harry gets clobbered to a pulp.

And then the answer came to her.

Cassie had left him.

When things had gotten too tough for her to handle, she had turned and run out the door. A small part of him was disappointed, but most of him was happy she was out of harm's way.

He told himself that her adiosing from the bar was a good thing. He wanted her clear of the fray. She'd done the only thing she knew to do, and he couldn't blame her for that. With any luck, she was out in the Volvo on her cell phone calling 911.

If only he could hold on until the cops got there.

His right eye throbbed where Big Ray had just planted his fist. His glasses were broken, dangling from one ear. Freemont had roused, and Big Ray was holding Harrison's arms behind his back.

Freemont was still a little wobbly but determined to get even. He drew back a fist, took a deep breath, and aimed for Harrison's sternum.

Oh, shit, this is going to hurt.

Harrison gritted his teeth, clenched his jaw, and braced for the fresh assault.

But the punch never came.

Instead, the front door slammed open and Cassie strode into the room, carrying her backpack in front of her. The loud buzzing sound of diamondback rattlesnakes filled the room.

"Okay, boys," she yelled and held the bag aloft. "Y'all hear that?"

Everyone froze.

When Harrison realized what she intended, he almost started grinning at her craftiness.

Helluva creative woman. Using her vibrator to save his bacon.

"That's right," she said. "I have ten diamondback rattlesnakes in this knapsack. Everyone raise your hands and step back against the wall, or I'll let 'em loose."

Bzzz, bzzz, bzzz, went the bag.

No one made a move.

"Do it!" She unzipped the bag.

The rattling sound was much louder now. Dozens of hands shot into the air.

"Now step against the wall."

Like the usual suspects in a police lineup, the men all backed up.

"Come on, Harry," Cassie said. "Let's get out of this joint."

In spite of his jelly legs, Harrison sprinted happily toward her.

"Now, nobody do anything stupid, and we'll all get out of this without getting snakebit."

Slowly, buzzing bag still held aloft, Cassie and Harrison edged backward out the door.

Chapter 18

Your poor eye." Cassie made a soft hissing noise of sympathy and tenderly applied a chunk of cold beefsteak to Harrison's battered face.

His right eye was swollen shut and his head throbbed. Even his teeth hurt. But they were alive and in one piece, which after the bar brawl was saying something.

He was on Cassie's couch, and she was seated next to him with her soft, round breast pressed into his side. She'd taken a shower and changed into silky black lounging pajamas, and she looked good enough to eat. If he were to keel over dead at that moment, his life would be complete. Which was a totally stupid thought, but he couldn't help the way he felt.

Since when? You've always been able to distance yourself from your emotions.

What in the hell had the woman done to him?

"How did you think of using the Rattler as a decoy?" he asked.

She grinned and tilted her head at him in the cutest way. "I just asked myself, 'What would Harry do?'"

"And *that's* what you came up with?"

"Uh-huh."

"Wow, were you off base. I would never have thought of using a dildo as a weapon."

"Maybe not, but you would have thought first, reacted second. So that's what I did. Me, normally I'm the other way around."

"I think we made a good team."

"Me too." She beamed. "You hungry? I can fix us something to eat. I'm starving."

He wanted to say no because he didn't want her to get up. He wanted her to keep sitting right next to him. He wanted to feel her breast rise and fall against his arm as she breathed. But the mention of food made his stomach rumble and she heard it.

"Got the message." She grinned. "Food it is. Here, hold this." She took his hand and used it to anchor the raw steak in place against his eye. "Come into the kitchen and talk to me while I cook. I like company."

And he liked being her company.

Obediently, he followed her into the kitchen, trying not to wince against the jarring body aches, but he must have given himself away, because after he had plunked down at her dining room table, she brought him a glass of water and a couple of ibuprofen.

"Here, swallow these."

He didn't argue.

"Luckily for you and me," she said, digging around in the freezer, "I cook in huge batches once a month and then freeze the extras with one of those vacuum-sealer thing-amajiggies. All I hafta do is drop the bag in boiling water and toss a salad, and voilà, instant home-cooked meal."

"I feel like we should be out there looking for Adam," he muttered. "Not eating dinner."

"We have to eat, and you have to recuperate, and we have to plan our next move."

"That's the problem. I have no next move. I'm all tapped out of ideas."

"Not for long. You're great at coming up with ideas."

"Not with this headache."

"We could try calling his cell phone again." She fished her own phone from her purse and handed it to him.

He didn't hold out much hope on that score, but while Cassie set a pan of water on to boil, Harrison called Adam's number.

No answer. He left another voice mail message and hung up. He sighed, pressed the steak against his eye with the heel of his hand, and looked up just in time to see Cassie bent over the vegetable crisper.

Nice. Very nice.

Even with a bum eye and blurry vision, there was no ignoring Cassie's fanny.

Great, now he was acting like that jerk-off Freemont. Just the thought of the way that guy had touched Cassie made him mad all over again.

She took the butter lettuce to the sink and rinsed it under running water. Harrison's good eye was glued to her fingers, watching her stroke the soft fresh leaves.

"You're not still thinking I'm a member of the Minoan Order, are you?" he asked.

"No. You've convinced me."

"Now I just have to figure out why Ahmose suspects me. I've known the guy for years."

"You're probably just the most likely suspect. Finding Kiya was your life's work. You have a lot invested."

"All the more reason not to steal her amulet."

"More and more, I believe Clyde is the one who's really in the Minoan Order."

"You're probably right," Harrison conceded.

"So let's go over this again, try to jog the brain cells and piece this jigsaw together. What did we learn tonight?"

"Stay out of biker-bar strip clubs and away from guys named Big Ray."

She giggled and sent the lettuce for a ride in the salad spinner. "No, I mean about your brother."

"He wasn't the one in the Indy hat who passed Gabriel the envelope."

"The next logical conclusion is that Adam is the mummy."

"Which means he got stabbed."

"He could be dead," Cassie whispered. She looked over her shoulder at him with such sadness that Harrison had to glance away. "I'm so sorry."

"I don't think he's dead." Harrison refused to consider the idea. "He's not dead."

"But then where did he go? What happened to him? He could barely walk. How did he get out of the courtyard?"

"Better yet, who stabbed him, and why?"

"And if he isn't dead, then why hasn't he tried to contact us?"

They looked at each other. They were no closer to the answers than they'd been last night at the masquerade party.

Had it only been twenty-four hours ago? That meant they had forty-eight hours left.

"Let's walk through it one step at a time," Harrison said.

The steak was getting warm, so he took it off his eye and went to wash up at the sink. As he leaned over for the hand soap, his hip casually grazed against Cassie's. He glanced down to where their bodies made contact.

"You're not fooling me." She chuckled. "I've been to Europe. I know when I'm being groped."

"I'm not groping you." He moved his hip away.

"Your eyes are."

"Correction, my eye is groping you. One eye is swollen shut. Besides, eye groping doesn't count. If eye groping counted, you'd have to slap nine out of ten men you came into contact with."

"Good point."

"I couldn't be married to you," he said. "I'd be blind from the black eyes and the busted glasses over defending your virtue."

"Nobody asked you to marry me."

"That's good." He snorted.

"You're mad. Why are you mad?"

"I'm not mad."

"Then why are you snorting?"

"I don't like the idea of all that eye groping going on."

"It's not your problem," she said. "Go sit back down."

He did. Not because she'd told him to. He just didn't have anywhere else to go, and he was starting to feel a little woozy. He managed to make it back to the table without breaking into a sweat.

Cassie placed a steaming bowl of ziti with meat sauce and grated Parmesan cheese in front of Harrison, along with a garden salad and a glass of red wine. He had no idea he was so hungry until he got a whiff of the food.

"That was fabulous." He pointed at his bowl with the back of his fork after he'd polished off the food. The wine was good too. He took another long swig. "You're a helluva cook."

"You want dessert?" she asked. "I'm up for dessert."

"Whatcha got?" He let the change of subject go.

"Strawberry shortcake."

"My favorite."

"No way." She beamed at him. "It's my favorite too."

Cassie couldn't say for sure how it happened, but one minute they were eating strawberry shortcake, and the next minute Harry was staring at her as if she were the dessert.

"Hmm," she said, knowing it sounded forced, but she felt compelled to cushion the sexual tension with a barrier of words. "Strawberries are really plump and juicy this time of year."

Great, that came out all wrong.

"Yes, they are."

She slipped him a surreptitious glance and her heart committed hara-kiri, slamming suicidally against the wall of her chest.

Every time she looked at Harry, he got cuter and cuter. She hardly noticed his mismatched outfits anymore. Clothes were just clothes, right? And she no longer thought of his unruly hair as unkempt, but instead found it just-rolled-out-of-bed sexy.

This was an alien experience, and she wasn't sure how to respond. In the past, she was either attracted to someone or she wasn't. If she wasn't instantly attracted, then things went no further. But if she was attracted, she would immediately romanticize the guy. In the beginning, the men she loved were always taller, smarter, better-looking than in reality, but as the relationship progressed, she bumped up against that reality and quickly lost interest.

But it was different with Harry. From the moment she'd met him, she'd found him irritating and elusive. And while his serene, self-contained isolation had initially intrigued her, she hadn't been bowled over by the sexual chemistry. He was the reverse of every man she'd ever been with. The more she got to know him, the more attractive he became.

Until, *pow!* All she had to do was look at him, and her libido rocketed through the ceiling.

Whoa. Slow down. What if Phyllis and Ahmose were right, and Harry was in this weird Minoan Order cult thing? She didn't want to get involved with a guy like that.

Except she couldn't imagine introverted Harry joining any kind of group organization, much less a secret society that probably dressed up in silly costumes with robes and hoods and such. No matter what proof Ahmose claimed to have.

Nope, Harry was not a costume-wearer. When she'd tried to get him to dress up as Mark Antony for the masquerade party, you'd have thought she had asked him to wear a purple tutu and march in a gay pride parade.

"Why are you looking at me like that?" she asked.

"Like what?"

"Like you want to eat me up."

"Maybe I do."

"Last night I would have been all over that offer," she said. "But tonight you're bunged up. You should be resting. You need to heal."

"I need TLC." He lowered his voice, lowered his eyelids, and gave her a sultry masculine stare.

"You've had too much wine." She took his glass away and deposited it in the sink with the rest of the dishes. "I can't take advantage of you when you're in a compromised position. Wasn't that what you told me last night?"

"I'm not drunk." He got up and walked toward her, palms held wide. "See, no stagger."

No stagger but lots of swagger. He looked so rough and rugged with that black eye. Like a proud tomcat. His battered face shouldn't have been a turn-on, but it was. Did that make her seriously twisted?

Probably.

He had gotten into a fight protecting her honor, and that's what was turning her on. Not his poor wounds.

All righty then.

She had to keep him out of her bed. As much as she wanted him, it wasn't the right time. He was beat up, and she was feeling too susceptible. It would have been okay if all she felt was lust for him, but things with Harry were too complicated to muck up with sex.

"You're much too inhibited for me, Harry. I need a spontaneous guy."

"I can be spontaneous."

His Godiva brown eyes glistened with a very masculine agenda. He had had too much wine. His mind was on serious mattress moves. She had created a monster. Where were those damned silver bullets and wooden stakes when you needed them?

"No, you can't."

"Yes, I can. See?"

He stripped his shirt over his head and threw it on the floor. Immediately, her eyes were drawn to his chest. Not movie-star ripped, but not bad by any means.

"What are you doing?" she asked.

"I'm calling your bluff."

"You're going to regret this in the morning."

"Who cares about the morning? We've got tonight." He hummed a tune with similar lyrics.

"Oh, please, don't start singing."

"*We've got tonight,*" he warbled and came toward her.

Cassie grabbed for the can of Reddi-Wip on the table. "Stay back, or I'll shoot."

He stepped menacingly around the table.

Cassie's heart galloped, and damn her, but she kept staring at his naked chest. "I'm warning you . . ."

"Warn all you like. You're the one who plied me with ibuprofen and merlot. And now, sweetheart, I'm taking you up on your offer."

"That was last night. The offer has been rescinded. The coupon expired."

Harrison unbuckled his belt and walked toward her. He pulled the belt off and it slithered through the loops with an erotic, whisking sound. "Oh, I get it. You want to be the one to call the shots."

"Stay back," she teased, when what she really wanted was for him to advance. But what had happened to change him? Why had he been so reticent last night, but now he was so frisky? Was it merely the wine? Or was it something else. Something more?

He grinned seductively, not looking the least bit nerdy, and unzipped his pants.

"Don't you dare take off your pants."

"Don't play coy. You want me."

"I don't." She giggled, completely blowing her denial.

He lunged for her. She jumped back. "Don't make me use this."

"Bring it on." He kicked off his pants.

Holy smokes!

"You're naked," she gasped.

"Don't ever let anyone tell you that you're not observant." The expression on his face was purely wicked.

She extended her arm, depressed the nozzle on the Reddi-Wip. A long white stream shot across the room, slapping his brow.

But getting a face full of sugary whipped cream did not

stop his forward motion. He swiped the Reddi-Wip out of his eyes and flung a foamy wad at her. She ducked just in the nick of time. The goop hit the wall behind her.

She squirted him again.

It grazed the top of his head.

A third squirt and she was backpedaling for the door, but no dice. Strawberry shortcake topping was not strong enough to hold him at bay. She attempted another futile spurt in self-defense, but the aerosol can was out of oomph.

Harry strode across the room, his hair spiked up and sticky with whipped cream. "Come here."

She shook her head, exhilarated.

"Don't run from me."

But she was already running, skipping through the living room, body on fire with excitement and lust. What a game. What fun!

She wondered if Solen and Kiya had ever played "your pyramid or mine?"

"Your punishment will just be that much more severe the longer you postpone it," he threatened.

"How much worse?" she squeaked.

"I'm going to give you the most thorough tongue-licking you've ever received."

Omigod. She almost fainted on the spot.

Who'd have thought boring old Harry would be the most fun she'd ever had?

She bolted for the bedroom, but he was far quicker than she ever imagined. He scaled the back of the couch, climbing over and dropping to the other side, almost cutting off her wily escape.

But somehow she managed to wriggle past him. Her pulse was pumping with enough endorphins to kick-start

Freemont's customized Harley. She was high on adventure and ready for action.

Without really meaning to, she had thrown down the gauntlet and invited him to engage in a sport guaranteed to supercharge any heterosexual man's libido—the pursuit of a woman.

He caught her arm just as she reached the bedroom door. Her excitement was like a bird bashing frantically against her rib cage, desperate to get out. To burst free.

A giggle exploded from her, high and nervous. Their eyes met and Cassie stopped breathing.

What was he going to do? Wicked intent was in his eyes. A jolt of pure, raw sexual energy rushed through her, and her world narrowed into agonizing slow motion.

They were ensnared in the web of each other's gazes, transported to an endless time and space. They had reached the point of no return. They were about to become lovers.

And she feared the intimacy almost as much as she craved it.

In the muted hallway lighting, his complexion glowed golden and exotic. With his shock of black hair (never mind the whipped cream, of course), his proud patrician nose, and his sinewy build, he could have been Solen.

But she was no Kiya.

Cassie was too blonde and too soft and too flighty. Harrison needed someone more like himself. Someone dark and exotic and cerebral.

Disturbed by her thoughts, she pulled away.

But he would not let her go. It was as if he'd read the trepidation in her eyes and understood it.

"Tonight," he said, "you're mine."

And that was exactly what she wanted to hear. The whipped cream glistened like new-fallen snow against his ebony hair. Cassie's gaze tracked down his face to his chest to his flat abdomen and beyond.

She inhaled sharply.

His penis and testicles, heavy with desire, dangled between his thighs. He was wholly, unreservedly male. The sight of him tightened her lungs until she could barely force the air out.

She inspected him from head to toe, but he stared only at her face. Finally, when she felt brave enough, she lifted her chin and met his gaze full-on.

He peered straight into her, his brown eyes shining so intensely they were almost black.

She realized he was trembling. It was subtle. Barely noticeable. But his little finger quivered oh-so-faintly against her skin.

How sweet.

She was blind for believing Ahmose Akvar even for a second. There wasn't a larcenous bone in this man's body.

His vulnerability yanked her up short. He might have initiated this game, but he was as scared about the follow-through as she was. He was totally exposed, standing naked before her while she was fully clothed. He was open to her. Hiding nothing.

Cassie realized at once what a precious gift he was offering, even though he did not speak of it. Harrison Standish wasn't a guy who easily dropped his guard. He spent a lot of time by himself for a reason.

And yet Harry had chosen to trust her.

She felt more privileged than words could express. Her body grew warmer, moister.

His shaft stirred thicker, harder, jutting up ferociously, arcing toward his belly.

Irresistibly, Cassie's eyes were drawn downward. Her

knees melted and her mouth watered. She gulped but found she could not swallow. She hadn't expected him to be so impressive. She'd had her share of men in her life, but none of them had ever captured her imagination the way Harrison did.

His erection crooked slightly to the right. The shaft of him was fuller than the spherical throbbing head. His tip was already moist, ready for her. She heard a rough groan of desire and was startled to realize the sound had slipped from her own throat.

Her pulse throbbed in the hollow of her neck. Tentatively, she reached out and touched him there for the very first time. She was shocked at how big he felt in her hand. Her breasts swelled, grew warm.

He unbuttoned her blouse, undressed her with care. By the time he was finished and Cassie was standing naked before him, they were both trembling.

"You have the most gorgeous figure," he breathed, running a hand from the curve of her breast down the cinch of her waist to the flare of her hip. "Hourglass, curvy, a real woman's body."

"Thank you," she said.

"I love the way you love your own body. Most women don't, you know."

Her cheeks heated, and she suddenly felt shy. Impossible, improbable, illogical. Cassie didn't do shy. She ducked her head, confused by her feelings.

Why did she suddenly feel so incredibly weak-kneed and defenseless? What was this strange hesitancy, this unexpected quietness?

Harry caught her chin, lifted her face up, and forced her to look at him. "I want you," he said, and with those three words her shyness disappeared.

There was nothing slow or lingering about his kisses. They started out hot and hard and quickly jumped to a frenzied pace. Passion poured out of him, poured out of her; it mingled, flowed, and became one blinding, driving force.

He tenderly caressed her breasts, and the space between her legs went hot and wet. His kisses slowed, then turned languid. He was changing things on her. His tongue licking hers was like fire dancing in the darkness.

He walked her backward until her butt bumped the edge of the bed.

"Lie back," he commanded. "And wrap your legs around my waist."

She did as he asked, curling her spine into the mattress. Her pulse thundered in her ears. What was he going to do next?

His cock bounced playfully against her belly. He was standing on the floor, looming over her.

She was on the bed, her butt almost hanging over the edge, her legs wrapped tight around his waist. She grinned. Once he was inside her, she would have control over his thrusting. What a great arrangement.

But then he surprised her completely.

He slipped his hand down and gently massaged between her thighs. She flinched. The sensation was so invariably sweet. He leaned down and his mouth fastened onto hers, kissing her as he tickled her slick feminine folds.

And then he inched his finger inside her, easing in and out until she thought she might scream from the superbness of it all.

Harrison slipped a second finger inside her while his pinky stayed on the outside, doing some very interesting tricks. His wrist swayed back and forth to a smooth, balanced rhythm. All the while, his ambitious pinkie was circling lower, around and around and around, increasing the tempo and thoroughly glazing her with her own wet, honeyed essence.

"Oooh," Cassie said and shifted her hips upward, definitely wanting more of that technique.

And then he took it one step further and rimmed her tight, puckered rosebud. Caressing it carefully, pressing in with a light, steady pressure.

She groaned and grabbed the bedcovers with both fists. He did not stop. He kept up the warm, provocative finger glide. In and out and over and around. On and on and on he went, until she was dazed with need and desperate to sate her hunger.

"Where," she gasped, and then had to stop to catch her breath before she could continue with her question—"did you learn how to do that?"

Never in a million years would she have guessed that a guy who spent so much time with ancient artifacts would be so knowledgeable about a woman's body. She hadn't given Harry nearly enough credit for versatility.

"Poindexter reads a lot." He grinned.

Mental note to self. Date more intellectuals.

"But you ain't seen nothin' yet, sweetheart." Harrison eased his hand from her and then dropped to his knees so that her legs were wrapped around his neck and his mouth was level with her most tender assets.

She hissed in her breath through clenched teeth, and her entire body tensed with exquisite pleasure.

His hair tickled her inner thighs. He plied his mouth delicately over her tiny straining ridge. He sank his hot tongue inside her, licking insatiably.

Wickedly his tongue controlled her. She was his puppet. He could do with her whatever he wished.

The slippery sensation was beyond anything she'd ever

experienced. His tongue glided into her molten center and he worked his diabolical magic.

She moaned and arched toward him, providing him with easier access. The quivering sensation was indescribably, scrumptiously private.

How had their relationship progressed to such intimacy so quickly?

The affair that burns the hottest, fades the quickest.

It was something her mother used to say when Cassie had asked why she'd dropped yet another boyfriend.

But Harrison's devilish tongue soon shook such thoughts from her head. He grasped her hips with both hands, holding her pinned to the mattress as she thrashed and writhed. Her body absorbed his heated breath.

Oh, she was done for.

She rode his tongue, pushing and pulling, rocking and bucking. She was searching, grasping, desperate to make it happen.

Her orgasm erupted from the very core of her soul. Exploding outward through her center, flinging into her limbs. Her muscles tightened, then went instantly slack. Her pulse pounded, and she saw a rhapsody of red-white starbursts.

Wet heat spilled out of her, flowed over him as the sound of his proud laughter filled the room.

Well, she thought, dreamily. She'd done it. She'd kept him out of her bed.

He had been standing on the floor the entire time.

Chapter 19

Thanks. I needed that." Cassie sighed contentedly.

"You're welcome."

They were piled up in the middle of her bed. Her head resting against his shoulder, her body curled into his side. A smug smile played across his lips.

She traced the smile with her fingertips. "You're pretty proud of yourself, aren't you?"

"Aren't you proud of me?"

"What do you think?"

His grin widened and her heart just sort of splintered into two pieces, and in that moment she knew she had to tell him about Duane, even though she didn't understand why.

"Harry?"

"Uh-huh?" He sounded drowsy, self-satisfied. She noticed he'd stopped telling her to call him Harrison. Slowly but surely she was wearing him down.

"Can I tell you something?"

He turned his head and peered at her with his good eye. "Absolutely."

"Would you really want to know why I freaked out on you today?"

"You don't owe me any explanations."

"Yeah, I do. You gave me that beautiful butterfly apology, and it wasn't even your fault."

"Shh," he murmured. "It's okay. Honest. Forget about it. I don't care."

"I do. I acted like a crazy woman, and I want you to understand why. It's important to me."

"Okay."

"I was married once."

Harrison didn't say anything. Cassie gulped back her fear and plunged ahead. It was still difficult to talk about, even after eleven years.

"His name was Duane Armstrong. And I was madly in love with him." She had been apeshit crazy for Duane in that sick-in-the-head-obsessive-teenage way. It was humbling to admit it now. That she'd been so wrong about what love was.

"Uh-huh." Harry didn't sound any too enthused to hear about this.

"I wanted to marry him more than anything else on earth. He was handsome and fun and daring. He was twenty-one and I was seventeen. Everyone in my family was against it. Even my dad, which surprised me, because he and Duane were two of a kind. But I was young and headstrong and wildly in love, so I married him anyway. For the first couple of months it was great. One good time after another."

"Then what happened?" On the surface his voice was teasing, but underneath she heard the tension. He was jealous. "After a while did you discover you didn't like picking up his socks off the bathroom floor?"

"It's not so much his socks I minded picking up," she confessed. "It was his crack pipe."

"Dammit, Cassie, are you serious?"

She felt his muscles tense beneath her. "I was an utter fool."

"No, you weren't a fool. You might have made foolish choices, but you were never a fool." He sounded so vehement. Like he really believed what he was saying.

"I was so ashamed. I didn't tell anyone what I was going through. Not even Maddie."

"It must have been really hard for you, handling that all alone, hiding such a secret from your family."

She nodded. "The drugs really took their toll, and quick. Duane got crazy jealous. Possessive. The straw that broke the camel's back was when he locked me in the cellar while he went off on a two-day drug binge." She shuddered, remembering.

"Damn my hide." Harrison hissed in his breath. "And I had my head so far up my ass I let the cellar door slam shut on you. And that guy could have blown you up inside there." His voice hung on a clot of emotion.

"It wasn't your fault, Harry. I was having a post-traumatic stress flashback. There's no way you could have known. I just wanted to explain so you could understand me better."

"How'd you get the courage to leave?" He softly stroked her hair, and his touch was so incredible her heart just ached from the sweetness of it.

"I tried to help Duane. I really did. Tried to get him to join Narcotics Anonymous, but he denied he had a problem. I couldn't stick it out. I flaked. I didn't have the stamina for the long haul."

"Is that why you don't want to ever get married again? Because you think you did something wrong?"

Cassie nodded and clenched her jaw to keep from crying. Revealing her most shameful secret to him was much tougher than she'd thought it would be.

He gently slipped her head off his shoulder, threw back the covers, and got out of bed. He marched over to the remnants of her collage wall, his bare buns flexing in the light from the bathroom. Her heart fluttered. He was so magnificent.

He fisted his hands. "Which one is he?"

"Oh, Duane's not on my collage wall. I only put happy memories up there." Cassie sat up in the bed, curled her knees to her chest.

He looked over at her. The expression on his face plucked at her heartstrings. "It tears me up inside to think that someone hurt you. I'd like to kill the bastard."

"You don't have to," she said. "He died in a car wreck the day after I left him."

"God, Cassie, sweetheart, I'm so sorry you had to live through that." Harrison stalked across the room, sat on the edge of the bed, and drew her into his arms.

She was trembling.

"It's okay," he murmured and pressed his lips to her forehead. His soul caved in for all she had suffered. He tried to mentally cut off his rational mind from his emotions, but he couldn't stop sympathizing with her pain. "You're all right."

She clung to him and buried her face against his chest. Harrison had never felt so needed, so manly.

"I felt so responsible," she said. "I kept thinking that if I'd never married Duane, never *committed* to a relationship, he might not have gotten drunk and driven into that bridge abutment. He might still be alive today."

"Duane was a troubled man. Surely you've figured that out by now. His death had nothing to do with you and whether or not you stood by your wedding vows. You were only seventeen, Cassie. A kid."

Harrison rubbed circles on her back, wishing he could

make her see the problem had been with her ex-husband, not with her, not with marriage or commitment. He felt her tears on his skin. He took her chin in his hand and tilted her face up until she met his gaze. Then he kissed her.

Slowly, sweetly, gently.

But it didn't stay slow, sweet, and gentle.

Things changed quickly, as they usually did with his quixotic, quicksilver Cassie.

Her body loosened, but her grip on him tightened. She increased the tempo of their kiss, stepping it up several degrees when she slipped her tongue past his teeth.

Their body heat mixed, mingled. Sharp need for her burrowed under his skin, fiery and fierce, spreading through his veins, taking him over.

What had started out as a comfort kiss ripened into a frantic, insatiable coupling of their mouths.

His hand went to the soft curve of her waist and his fingers sank deliciously into her flesh. He liked her meaty ripeness, loved caressing her full, rich curves.

She threaded her fingers through his hair, murmured low in her throat. He paid attention to her sounds and moved his fingers accordingly, sliding up from her waist to lightly stroke her lovely breasts.

She was so gorgeous. He was fully aware of how lucky he was to be here. He wanted her so badly. Wanted to bury himself deeply inside her and never emerge.

He dragged his kiss from her mouth, down over her chin, to the underside of her supple throat. He knew he'd discovered an erogenous zone when her body tensed and a small helpless moan escaped her parted lips. She arched against him, her body pleading for more.

Supercharged, Harrison dipped his head lower, his tongue seeking those sweet, rock-hard nipples she thrust at him. He wet them both with his mouth and then rubbed the pad of his thumb over one nipple, while gently suckling the other.

She gasped and writhed.

He was on fire for her. His body was an inferno; he was so hard he didn't think he could go one more minute without sheathing himself inside her.

And when she reached down and slipped her hand along his inner thigh, he had to close his eyes and fight hard to keep from losing control completely. He was so scared he was going to screw this up.

"You relax and enjoy this," she said. "Stop playing with my nipples, roll over on your back, and just relax."

Music to every man's ears. He groaned and rolled over.

"Do you like for me to touch you like that?" she whispered, kneading his leg, moving closer, ever closer to his hard, flushed penis.

"Oh, babe, yeah."

It was so extraordinarily erotic, her hand on him. He lifted his head and looked at her, watching the lusty emotions play across her face.

Inch by agonizing inch, she worked her way to his primal spot. When she finally arrived, she took firm hold, wrapping a hand around his throbbing shaft, while at the same time gently scratching his scrotum with her little finger.

He couldn't stand it. Wouldn't let things finish this way. He had to be inside her. Didn't want to come without her.

"Come here," he groaned and pulled her up to straddle his waist, his penis pulsating against her behind.

He kissed her again, building her up, raising the tension until they were both crazy for it. They thrashed against each other, breathing hard, trembling and tingling, their bodies filled with lust and passion and desire.

"Ride me," he begged.

Cassie pulled her mouth from his, her long blonde hair trailing over his chest.

"Condom," she gasped and splayed a palm against his chest. "We gotta have a condom. Hang on. I'll be right back."

He groaned and grasped his hair with both hands as she slid off him and padded away in the dark. Seconds later she came running back into the bedroom, fumbling with her purse, fingers grasping at the clasp.

"Ooh," she wailed. "You've got me so charged up I can't get it open."

He propped himself up on an elbow. "Here, let me help."

"I've got it, I've got it."

The clasp popped open and she dug around inside, pulling out lipstick and cash register receipts and ink pens. She excavated loose change and a set of car keys and a tin of cinnamon Altoids.

"I know I have a condom in here."

"Try the zippered pocket," Harrison said, amazed he could stay so calm.

"I never put anything in there." She frowned, but slid the zipper open anyway. "Ooh, ooh." She pursed her lips and her face lit up. "You were right. I feel something."

Me too, babe; me too.

And for once, Harrison did not want to deny what he was feeling.

Then Cassie pulled a round, flat object from her purse.

"Hey!" Her nose crinkled. "This isn't a condom."

She held the ring up to get a better look at it in the light seeping from the bathroom, and Harrison recognized it instantly.

It was one-half of the magical brooch amulet.

*   *   *

"But I don't understand." Cassie ran a hand through her hair. "How did it get into my purse?"

Had she stolen it? Harrison immediately felt disloyal for the thought. How could he believe that about her after everything they'd just shared? There had to be another explanation. He knew in his heart of hearts that she was not a thief. Come what may, he was on Cassie's side.

They turned on the overhead light and sat in the middle of the bed. Cassie put on her bathrobe, and Harrison tugged the sheet over his waist. With their ardor cooling, he felt suddenly vulnerable being so naked in front of her.

"I'm guessing Adam must have put it in your purse. You took it with you into the courtyard when you went to meet him, remember? Osiris found it in the bushes after the lights came back on at the museum."

"That's right," she said.

"This is absolute proof that Adam is the mummy. That's not Kiya's half of the amulet. The markings on the rings are different."

"So this is Solen's half." She turned it in her hand. "Adam must have had to put it in my purse before Kiya's half was stolen."

"I'm certain of it."

"And I've been running around with it in my handbag all this time?"

"I'm willing to bet that's why your place was ransacked and why we were followed to Clyde's place."

"I don't understand how anyone knew I had it."

"Maybe they didn't. Maybe it was just a stab in the dark because you'd been helping Adam make arrangements for the exhibit."

She met Harrison's eyes. "But then where's the other half?"

"That's the million-dollar question."

"We have to put Solen's amulet in a safe place," she said. "Right now."

"Yes."

"But where can we put it until morning? It's eight o'clock at night, the banks are closed, and so is the museum. I'm not about to get Phyllis or Ahmose involved. I want this thing as far away from me as I can get it. It's caused nothing but trouble."

"Tom Grayfield has a safe. We can ask him to keep it for us until we can get it back to the museum in the morning. Where's your phone? I'll give him a call."

"The battery on my cell needs charging. I'll go get the cordless from the living room."

"Never mind. I'll come with you." He threw back the covers and tried to act nonchalant as he slipped from her bed to search for his pants. He wasn't accustomed to strutting around a lady's apartment buck naked and having her appraising eye on him.

When they reached the living room, she picked her cordless phone from its docking station on the end table and passed it to Harrison.

"Hey," she said. "My answering machine's unplugged."

"It must have happened when your place got ransacked."

"No wonder I haven't been able to check my messages. I thought I'd forgotten to turn it on." Cassie plugged the machine in. The red message light winked.

"Look. I've got a message." She checked the caller ID. "Blocked call. It came through at four-fifteen yesterday afternoon, when we were preparing for the party. Hold on. Let me check the message before you get on the phone."

She hit the play button.

"Cassie." The voice was low and urgent, but Harrison

recognized it right away. "It's Adam. Lost your cell number but luckily had your home number programmed in my speed dial."

On the tape, Adam hesitated. In the background they could hear the roaring sound of an airplane taking off.

"Adam must have been at the airport when he called," Cassie said.

"I've discovered something very disturbing," Adam continued after the plane had passed over. "This is vitally important, so listen carefully. I'm being followed, and my life is in grave danger. I'll be at the party wearing a mummy costume to give you the details. If something happens and I don't get to see you, then you've got to get a message to my brother, Dr. Harrison Standish."

Why had Adam called Cassie instead of him? Harrison wondered.

"Tell my brother the secret to the Minoan scroll is in the math. He'll know what I'm talking about. Don't say a word about this to anyone else. Harrison is the only one you can trust. Did you—"

The answering machine beeped and then fell silent. It had cut him off.

"Did he call back?" Harrison asked. "Was there another message?"

Cassie checked the machine and shook her head. "What was he talking about? What math?"

"I have no idea, but I'm going to find out."

He went out to the Volvo, got the scroll from the glove compartment, and brought it back up to Cassie's apartment. He spread it out on her coffee table atop the half-finished jigsaw puzzle of New York City.

The secret is in the math. The secret is in the math.

Harrison stared at the scroll, his fingers tracing the

impenetrable hieroglyphics. Did his brother honestly expect him to decipher something no one else in history had ever been able to decode?

Adam had done it.

The secret is in the math?

What in the hell was he talking about? Harrison took the djed from his pocket and passed it from palm to palm. The electromagnetic properties helped him think.

Math had been the one subject Adam had excelled in over Harrison.

Okay. So? How did math help translate the scrolls?

He paced Cassie's living room, hands clasped behind his back rubbing the djed, his thoughts totally absorbed by the task. Cassie sat curled up on the couch, her legs tucked underneath her. She looked so gorgeous he had to remind himself to keep his attention on the job at hand.

The secret is in the math.

What math? Solen's birthday? Kiya's birthday? The day of their deaths?

Dammit. He didn't have time for parlor games.

Except it wasn't a parlor game. Adam was in serious trouble over whatever he'd learned from deciphering the scroll.

Think.

The secret is in the math.

The Minoans were seafaring people and merchants. Most scholars believed their hieroglyphics were nothing more than ledgers and accounts.

Math.

Harrison clutched a handful of hair in desperation and started to push his glasses up on his nose before he remembered that Big Ray had busted them in the fight and his extra pair was in his locker at the museum.

Solen had been a Minoan scribe. Until he'd been sold into slavery and ended up in Egypt. Until Ramses IV had recognized his talents and sent him to learn Egyptian hieroglyphics. Solen would have acquired much new knowledge in the pharaoh's house. He would have honed his skills, obtained new ways of communicating.

What if Solen had combined the old skills with the new? What if the scroll Adam found in Solen's tomb was a hybrid of Minoan and Egyptian hieroglyphics? What if the scroll had been written by Solen himself?

The secret is in the math.

Numbers. Numerology. The stars and moons and planets. Astrology.

The sun.

In the time of Ramses IV, the Egyptians had worshiped the sun.

Yes, so what, big deal.

Math of the Sun: The Immortal Egypt.

The title popped into Harrison's head. It was the name of a book Diana had given both him and Adam when they had graduated from high school.

"It's the seminal work on how math affected religion in ancient Egypt," his mother had said. "Read it."

He'd found the work deadly boring and never looked at it after the initial attempt. But he still owned it. It was on the top shelf of the bookcase in his apartment.

The secret is in the math.

Could the answer be in that book?

But the book Diana had given them was about Egypt. This was a Minoan scroll in Minoan hieroglyphics.

And Solen had been a displaced Minoan in Egypt, learning the culture, absorbing the religious beliefs. It was worth a shot. He didn't have anything else to go on.

"I think I might have a chance at translating this thing," he told Cassie.

"Okay," she said.

"The problem is that it could take me a long time, and even then I might not be able to translate it. Should I waste time even trying, or should we just be out there looking for Adam?"

"We don't know where to look, and at least you do have a clue on how to translate the hieroglyphics. I think you should do it."

"We also need to get the amulet locked up someplace safe before the people who were after Adam figure out we've got it and come after us. We already know they're ruthless."

"I could take the amulet to Tom Grayfield while you translate the scroll," Cassie offered.

He liked the idea. She would be out of her apartment. Both she and the amulet would be safe with Tom. Then he could totally concentrate on unlocking the secret of Solen's scroll, knowing Cassie was in good hands.

"I'll call Tom," he said, "and let him know what's going on."

While Cassie got dressed, Harrison called Tom's cell phone number.

"Ambassador Grayfield's phone," Anthony Korba answered in his distinctive gravelly voice.

"Anthony. It's Harrison. Am I disturbing you?"

"No, we're on our way back from a meeting with the governor in Austin."

"May I speak to Tom? It's urgent."

"But of course."

Thirty seconds later Tom came on the line. "Harrison, what's up?"

Quickly Harrison told him what had transpired, except he did not tell him about the scroll. It was pride that held him back. He would hate to admit defeat where Adam had succeeded if he failed to translate the hieroglyphics. "I need someone to look after Cassie while I take care of a few things. Can you keep her and Solen's amulet safe for me?"

"You don't even have to ask. I'm there," Tom said. "We're still an hour out of Fort Worth, but give me her address. We'll drop by and pick her up on the way."

"Thanks, Tom, I owe you big-time."

Tom laughed. "We'll work it out. See you later."

Harrison cradled the receiver and looked up to see Cassie in the doorway, dressed in her Cadillac jeans and a sexy turquoise tank top. Her hair shone in the light. Even without his glasses he could see she was a knockout.

She crossed the room toward him and his heart careened in his chest. He took her hand and pressed the amulet into her palm. "Tom's sending a car for you."

"Thank you for looking out for me." She curled her fingers around the amulet. "I promise to guard it with my life."

Chapter 20

Harrison's heart was pumping hard and fast when he let himself into his apartment with the scroll tucked under his arm. Part of his erratic pulse was due to the excitement of trying to translate the scroll, but most of it was attributable to his changing relationship with Cassie.

He was having feelings he shouldn't be having, and he didn't know what to do about them. He had always protected his heart by disengaging from tender feelings. He analyzed his emotions. He did not wallow in them.

Except he was wallowing now, and he'd never felt anything this intense.

It's just the thrill of the danger. Don't worry about it now. Find that book. Translate the scroll. Figure out what had Adam running scared. Later. You can think about Cassie later.

He hurried into his office, spied the book he needed on the top shelf. He stood on his toes, stretching to reach it. It hit the floor with a solid *thunk*. He picked it up and opened it on his desk. Then carefully, reverently, he unrolled the scroll. Somewhere, among the old books and the arcane knowledge, he was determined to find the answers.

He was determined to find his brother.

And he was determined to shut down these inappropriate feelings for Cassie before they got completely out of hand.

Cassie was in the backseat of Tom Grayfield's black stretch limo making small talk with the ambassador when her cell phone rang. Thinking it might be Harry, she smiled at Tom. "Do you mind if I take this call? I know it's rude to talk on the cell phone when you're having a conversation in person, but this might be important."

"Not at all." Tom smiled. "Go ahead."

What a nice man, she thought. Considerate and generous. Imagine, someone as important as the ambassador to Greece going out of his way to pick her up so she wouldn't have to drive around by herself late at night.

She pulled out the antenna and flipped her phone open. "Hello?"

"Cassie, it's David." Her brother-in-law's voice was low and rushed.

"Hi, David. Now's not really a good time for me to talk."

"You're with someone."

"Yes."

"Is it your friend Dr. Standish?"

"No." Cassie smiled at Tom and mouthed, *I'll just be a minute.*

"Listen to me, Cassie; this is very important. I know you have a habit of not fully listening, but please make an exception this time. Do it for me."

Had he found out something negative about Harrison? Could Ahmose be right after all? But no, she could never believe that about Harry. Not after everything they'd shared.

"Is it related to what we discussed yesterday?" she asked.

"It is. I checked out your friend, and he's as clean as they come. The guy could have been an Eagle Scout."

What a relief. Cassie blew out her breath. "Whew, you really scared me there for a minute. So everything checks out?"

"Not exactly."

"What not exactly?"

"Did you know Standish has a half brother named Adam Grayfield?"

"Uh-huh."

"His father, Tom Grayfield, is the ambassador to Greece. Not a nice guy. He has a tavern in Adam's and Harrison's names. It's called the Minotaur. The Minoan Order holds meetings there. He's under investigation by the Greek government. He moves a lot of gold bullion out of the country and they can't figure out where he's getting it, but they suspect he's laundering it through the Minotaur Tavern and Grayfield's scrap metal companies in the U.S."

Cassie gulped. Alchemy. The ability to turn base metal into gold. Members of the Minoan Order were supposed to know the secret of alchemy.

"Um . . . ," she began, trying not to get nervous, "as a matter of fact, I'm in Tom Grayfield's limo right now as we speak."

"Aw, shit, Cassie, no." The timbre of David's voice changed so quickly, she felt her fingers grow icy cold.

"What is it?" she whispered. "What's wrong?"

"I don't want to panic you, but whatever you do, you must get out of that man's car!"

But it was too late. The back of her head burned fiery hot. Cassie turned to look at the ambassador.

Tom Grayfield was still smiling, but now he had a

derringer clutched discreetly in his hand. "It's time you hung up the phone, Cassie."

Harrison worked feverishly, playing with myriad combinations of the number sequences that he found in the math book and drawing on his knowledge of Egyptian hieroglyphics.

Three hours into the ordeal, he finally broke the code.

The ancient Minoan Order had used numbers to represent the characters from the Egyptian hieroglyphics. Their system was obviously influenced by Solen's association with Egypt. Once Harrison understood which number related to which character, he was able to start translating the scroll.

It was a slow, painstaking process. He had to go from Egyptian hieroglyphics to Minoan number symbols to English. It was after midnight by the time he completed the conversion. He read what he'd written. Blinked. Rubbed his eyes and read it again.

No. He shook his head. *It could not be.*

There, in black and white, was the reason why the amulet was so important to the Minoan Order. It meant far more than reuniting star-crossed lovers, and it possessed much greater power than merely cursing a vizier's descendants. The secret was even more stunning than the ability to turn base metal into gold or to create thunderstorms.

And it explained everything.

With dawning horror, Harrison realized what his brother must have understood the minute he translated the scroll.

Tom Grayfield would kill for the amulet. Even if it meant murdering his own son.

The truth was a sledgehammer.

Harrison had not only delivered Solen's half of the

amulet into Tom Grayfield's deadly hands, he'd also placed Cassie in imminent danger.

There had to be a way to put a positive spin on this.

No point feeling terrorized or distressed just because she was staring down the barrel of a gun. What good did it do to panic or freak out? Life with Duane had taught Cassie that the more you focused on negative things, the more they grew. No negative thoughts allowed. She wasn't going to end up in a ditch with a slug through the center of her head. No sirree. So she was just going to stop picturing that.

Being taken hostage by the U.S. ambassador to Greece was just a minor inconvenience. A little misunderstanding. A tiny blip in the huge scheme of things. It would all work out in the end.

Except no one else knew that Tom Grayfield was a homicidal maniac.

Stop it.

He wasn't a homicidal maniac. He was just misguided, misdirected, or misinformed. It was up to her to set him on the right path.

"Tom," she said, purposefully using his first name in hopes of putting him at ease. "You look really tense. Maybe you should have a tipple of something from that minibar." She nodded at the small fridge tucked in the back of the limo.

"I don't want anything to drink," he snapped. "Just sit back and shut up."

"A little vodka and tonic? A slug of gin and ginger ale? A snort of bourbon and branch?"

"Nothing!"

"Jeez, okay." She raised her palms. "I was just trying to be helpful."

"Well, don't. Now, hand over the amulet." He waved the gun at her.

"Is that what this is all about? Well, why didn't you just say so? I would have given it to you without all the gun-brandishing. Sheesh."

Cassie reached into her purse, pulled out Solen's ring, and handed it over to him, because she didn't know what else to do and she didn't want to get shot. Not when she and Harry were just now getting to the good part of their relationship. The wild, hot sex.

"Seriously, Tom, you don't want to kill me. Think of your reputation. Think of everything you'll lose."

Tom Grayfield flicked the dome light on, and he was staring at the ring with such rapture that Cassie almost asked if he needed a private moment alone with the amulet, but decided against being flippant.

He actually licked his lips. "No, I'm thinking of everything I'll gain."

"So you're an optimist. Me too."

"Stop being friendly," he said and slipped the amulet into his pocket while still keeping the derringer aimed at her heart. "I don't want to like you."

"It's okay to like me. Everyone likes me."

Well, except for Phyllis Lambert, but she was in the minority.

And Harrison. He didn't like you either.

Maybe not at first, but he liked her now. In fact, he liked her a lot. She could just tell. Cassie grinned, remembering.

"Why are you smiling? You're in deep trouble, young lady. Stop smiling."

"I can't talk, I can't be nice, I can't smile. What can I do?"

"Face reality, woman."

"I've never been very good at that."

"How about this: if you don't shut up," he threatened, "I'm going to shoot you on general principle."

"If you're gonna get testy about it, all right, all right. I'll shut up."

"Thank you." Grayfield blew out his breath in exasperation and turned off the dome light.

"You're welcome."

"I thought you were going to shut up."

Cassie made a motion of zipping her lip.

"I'll believe it when I hear it." Grayfield sighed.

They traveled in silence. Cassie peered through the tinted windows and tried to see where they were going. She didn't recognize this part of Fort Worth. There were lots of warehouses and scrap metal places. It was a dimly lighted, secluded area.

For the first time, it hit her how truly isolated she was and that she might not make it out of this alive.

The driver turned down a narrow road filled with potholes. There were no streetlights. The darkness around the limo loomed thick, lumpy, and profound. Anything or anyone could be lurking around the next corner.

Harry, if you can read minds, I'm in deep trouble. I need ya, babe.

She sent the mental vibration into the ether, crossed her fingers, and prayed. She was tapped out of positive thoughts.

The limo stopped at the end of the road, next to a large warehouse with an empty parking lot. The headlights played across a man lounging against the dock. He was smoking a cigarette. When the lights hit him, he dropped the cigarette on the cement steps, crushed it out beneath his sneaker, and leered at the car with a sinister smile.

A chill shot straight to the heated core in Cassie's head. Here was a dangerous man.

The limo stopped and the man sauntered over. She recognized him at once. He was the man who'd come running out of Clyde's house and knocked her down. The one who'd detonated the bomb.

Tom Grayfield rolled down the window. "Do you have what we need?"

"Uh-huh," the man grunted.

For one surreal moment, it felt just like when Duane used to swing by his dealer's location to pick up drugs.

The limo driver cut the engine. Apparently they were getting out.

The ransacking bomber opened the back door.

"Demitri," Tom Grayfield said, "this is Cassie. I want you to take good care of her."

The way he said "good care" made it sound like anything but.

Demitri held out a hand to help her from the car. She shied. His fingernails were dirty, and the look on his face was even dirtier.

"You were the one who ransacked my apartment," she accused, staring down at his scuffed Nikes. "And you set off a bomb in Clyde's house."

"At your service." He was still extending his hand, and she still wasn't taking it.

"That was a really crappy thing you did, wrecking my collage wall, blowing up Clyde's place. He doesn't make a big salary, you know."

He shrugged. "Had to make sure you hadn't hidden the amulet inside your pictures. What's that wall all about, anyway? Those all the guys you laid?"

"Demitri, there's no need for vulgarities," Tom Grayfield prodded. "Ms. Cooper, do as I say. Take Demitri's hand and get out of the car."

She didn't want to but she didn't have much choice, seeing as how Grayfield had just positioned the nose of the derringer right under her rib cage.

"I'm going, I'm going; don't get so pushy with the gun." Reluctantly, she took Demitri's grimy hand and he hauled her from the car. The limo driver was standing outside the car with a flashlight and what looked to be a garage door opener in his hand.

"What are we gonna do with her?" the driver asked. His voice was deep and croaky. He sounded like a frog with throat cancer. She knew the thought was uncharitable, but at this point Cassie was over being kind.

Tom Grayfield smiled. "She's going to be Kiya's stand-in."

"Good idea, Boss." Demitri snickered.

Cassie didn't even want to imagine what that meant.

The driver pressed the button on the garage door opener and the thick double-rollered doors on the warehouse rumbled open. The man moved into the warehouse and flicked on the overhead lights. Demitri strong-armed Cassie, shoving her inside. Tom Grayfield followed and closed the door behind him.

Locked in.

Trapped.

No way out.

Shades of living with Duane Armstrong.

Cassie was trying hard not to flip out when she spied what was sitting in the middle of the vacant, foul-smelling warehouse.

At first she thought it was just an ordinary coffin.

Her coffin.

But when Demitri pushed her deeper into the room, she realized it was Solen's sarcophagus.

*   *   *

Harrison didn't even think to call the police. That's how insane with fear he was. He was a man without a plan, acting from gut instinct. Feeling and reacting instead of analyzing and evaluating. There wasn't time to think. If there was ever a time for action, it was now.

He goosed the Volvo, exceeding the speed limit. He looked down at the instrument panel. The gas gauge needle had dropped past half-empty. But in spite of his deeply ingrained habit of filling up at the halfway mark, the idea never even entered his mind.

Only one thought existed.

Cassie.

He didn't know if he was headed to the right place or what he would do when he got there. All he knew was that he was going to rescue his woman.

He had to find her.

Because if anything happened to her, he would die. He would cease breathing, his heart would literally stop beating, and he would leave this world a much better man for having known her.

Cassie sat on a stack of cold sheet metal, her hands and feet bound with duct tape. There was sheet metal to the left of her. Sheet metal to the right of her. And sheet metal behind her.

What was with all the sheet metal? Then she finally got it. Alchemy. That's how Tom Grayfield had gotten rich. So if he already had the formula for turning base metal into gold, why was he after Kiya and Solen's amulet?

Ahead of her, Demitri, the froggy-voiced limo driver, and Tom Grayfield donned Minotaur masks, black-hooded robes, and started performing some kind of bizarre ritual dance around Solen's sarcophagus.

What a lot of bull-loney.

After several minutes, Grayfield positioned himself at the head of the coffin, pulled a piece of paper from the pocket of his robe, and began to chant something in a very strange language.

Outside, the wind kicked up. It howled through a hole in the broken glass of the window above her.

So this was the Texas contingent of the Minoan Order? Frankly, she wasn't impressed. She had expected more. More people. More action. Something more *Eyes Wide Shut*.

Grayfield went on and on and on.

Lightning momentarily illuminated the warehouse in a hot blue flash. Thunder grumbled. Rain spattered the tin ceiling. Funny, the storm had gusted in awfully fast. The midnight sky had been cloudless when they'd hauled her into the warehouse. Must be an unexpected norther.

The chanting continued.

"Good grief," Cassie called out. "How long is this gonna take? I hafta pee."

"Silence!" Tom Grayfield yelled, and pointed a finger at her like the grim reaper on a really bad PMS day with no Midol in the house.

"Excuse me for living." She wondered if Adam knew his dad was such a huge jackass.

"Gag her," Grayfield said to Demitri. "We will have no more interruptions."

There was a brief time-out while Demitri came over, peeled a strip of duct tape from the same roll he'd used to tie her up, and slapped it over her mouth.

That was gonna hurt coming off.

"Anthony," Grayfield barked to the limo driver. "Help Demitri drag her over here."

Good grief, what now? Wasn't it bad enough she was

trussed up like a Christmas goose, forced to watch a really bad floor show with the piquant taste of duct tape on her tongue?

Anthony trotted over and eyed her speculatively from beneath his mask. He tried to slip his hands underneath her armpits, but because she was bound he kept having trouble. He squatted, his chest pressing against the back of her head, his fingers brushing along her rib cage.

Dude, stop tickling me or I'll pee on you.

Finally he got his arms underneath hers. "You grab her legs," he said to Demitri in his froggy voice.

"No fair; her bottom half is a lot heavier than her top half," Demitri complained.

"Obviously," Anthony croaked, "you have not noticed the size of her bazoombas."

Okay, you bozos, nix the sexual comments. She glared at them, hoping to get her point across.

Grumbling under his breath, Demitri grasped her feet and they hoisted her off the floor.

Cassie considered wriggling around and making them work for it, but they would probably just drop her, and it wasn't like she had much chance of getting away with her ankles hobbled.

"She's heavy," Anthony grunted.

Ha! I'll have you know I have big bones. One sixty is not considered overweight for a woman who's five foot eight.

"You could drop a few pounds, sister," Demitri concurred.

What? She should be stick-thin and make it easier for these nimrods to lug her around? They were damned lucky she was gagged, or she'd have given them a protracted lecture about the unrealistic body images modern society projected onto women.

But she soon got over her pique when she realized Grayfield was standing directly over her, his eyes glowing darkly from behind the bull head mask. He raised the sarcophagus lid.

"Put her inside."

The Volvo screamed like a constipated banshee for a good three minutes before Harrison figured out that somehow he'd managed to bump the shifter into second gear while driving seventy-five miles an hour through pouring rain in Fort Worth's warehouse district, running one stoplight after another.

What if Cassie was already dead?

No. He couldn't afford to think like that. He wouldn't. He would make it in time to stop Grayfield from carrying out his ritualistic human sacrifice.

On Cassie.

Harrison cringed, imagining the man he'd once considered a surrogate father doing something so unthinkably heinous. But the Minoan hieroglyphics told the truth. He'd found the answer lurking in the occult scroll.

Ambassador Tom Grayfield had named both his sheet metal business and the tavern in Greece after the Minotaur, the symbol of the Minoan Order. His interest in the order had not been strictly academic. Tom had financed Adam's excavation for the first time. Not because he wanted to see Adam best Harrison in competition, as he claimed, but because he wanted Solen found after Harrison had excavated Kiya. He wanted his hands on both pieces of the amulet. The rings themselves were the last step in an earth-shattering prescription.

Because the papyrus Adam had found in Solen's tomb had been the formula for immortality.

The last few cryptic lines of the translation were burned indelibly into Harrison's brain:

Whosoever commands the double circle holds the key. Believe it is true and it is. The one element that transmutes all others? Blood.

He rounded the corner. Drawing closer. Almost there.

Please, God, let me be there in time to save Cassie.

He squinted as the road narrowed. In the mistiness of a damp dawn, without his glasses, with one eye swollen shut, he could barely see where he was going.

From out of the fog a sudden shadow loomed.

The mummy!

Stepping right into his path.

He twisted the steering wheel hard. The Volvo swerved, tires screeching. He slammed headlong into a deep pothole.

His front tires blew. The noise exploded in his ears. He felt the jolt to his teeth. He went for the brakes, but his foot slipped and he hit the accelerator.

On busted tires the Volvo shot forward and plowed into a stop sign.

Chapter 21

No, no, don't put me in a dark, cramped, airless space with a three-thousand-year-old dead guy! Shoot me, stab me, run me over with a car. Anything but this!

Cassie fought against them, arching her body, bucking hard, trying to crack Anthony, the froggy-voiced limo driver, in the face with the back of her head. She cocked her knees and aimed to kick Demitri in the gut but only ended up squirming like a helpless worm unearthed by torrential rains.

They swung her up and over the side of the coffin.

And she came down hard on top of poor old Solen. He crunched louder than a sack of Cheetos. He had an old, dusty, dirty-feet smell to him.

Eew, grotty.

But she really didn't have time to get grossed out,

because Tom Grayfield slammed the lid and she was trapped.

Shut in.

Closed off.

Sealed.

Her wrists were bound in front of her, her ankles taped.

She was powerless, at the mercy of her captors. She was, as Harry would say, royally screwed.

She rapidly sucked in the fetid air through her nose, unable to expel it in her panic. A scream gurgled up to her lips, but the duct tape held it back. Terror lodged inside her mouth, knotted down her throat to her sore, aching lungs.

Ice sheathed her body.

No, no. What were they going to do? They couldn't bury her alive. She couldn't tolerate that. Never, ever.

She flashed back. To being restricted, restrained, controlled. To the time Duane locked her inside the storm cellar and left her for two days. She did not want to go back to that awful place. She'd come too far. She would not go back into the darkness.

But she was already there, and the coffin was even smaller and tighter than the cellar had been.

Cassie gagged on her hysteria and it was rough and chalky and sour.

No, no.

You have to calm down. You have to stop freaking out.

Tom Grayfield was talking to his henchmen, but the sarcophagus was thickly constructed. His voice was muffled. She could not make out his instructions.

What were they going to do to her?

Oh, Harry, where are you?

In her heart, she knew she couldn't count on him for rescue. He had no way of knowing his half brother's father was an evil, twisted monster. He thought she was safe. He thought he'd done well by turning her over to Grayfield.

Believe in yourself, Cassie. Maddie and David can't help you. Harry can't help you. It's up to you.

But how was she going to get out of this? She was

bathed in darkness, unable to move, unable to shout. And some part of Solen's ancient anatomy was poking hard into her upper back.

Were they just going to leave her here, slowly suffocating to death on the bitter flavor of her own fear?

Frantically, she shifted from side to side.

Let me out of here. Desperately she heaved in more air. In her panic, she hyperventilated. Her heart thumped heavily. Her head ached. Her lungs felt twisted, drained of breath.

The sarcophagus moved.

Cassie realized she was being hoisted and carried. Breathe, breathe; she could not breathe.

You're hyperventilating. You're not running out of oxygen this soon. Get hold of yourself.

But she could not. She was too excitable, too manic, too hyperactive for her own good. If only Harry were here. He was good for her. He kept her grounded. Calmed her down.

Harry, I'm sorry I failed you. I was supposed to keep the amulet safe.

Hot tears wet her cheeks. She would never see her dear, steadfast Harry. She wouldn't kiss his tender, inquisitive lips again. Nor would she ever make love to him fully, completely, the way she longed to make love with him.

Oh, Harry. It could have been so good.

And that was the last thought that slipped through her mind just before Cassie blacked out and embraced sweet oblivion.

"Adam?" Dazed, Harrison staggered out of the crumpled Volvo. The mummy was up ahead of him in the fog. Harrison could barely see where he was going. "Adam, come back."

But Adam did not heed his call. Was the mummy not Adam after all?

The mummy stopped at the corner. Harrison squinted, desperate to see where he was going. He motioned for Harrison to follow.

He wanted to shout, "I don't have time for delays. Cassie could already be dead." But he didn't want to think about that, even though he knew it deep in his bones. Cassie was in trouble. The worst kind of trouble, and he was to blame.

"Where are you going? What is it?" he called as he trailed after the mummy.

He rounded the corner, in the darkness, in the fog, felt an arm slip around him and draw him flat against the cold brick of the warehouse.

"Shh," said the mummy, pressing a finger to his lips. "They've got Kiya, but if they don't know we're out here, we can take them by surprise."

"Kiya?" Harrison stared deeply into the mummy's eyes. It was Adam all right, but he seemed different, sort of dazed and out of it. His mummy linen looked like hell, grimy with dirt and blood. Plus he smelled a bit gamey. "Don't you mean Cassie?"

"Kiya," he said quarrelsomely. "Are you going to help me save her or not?"

Kiya it is then. Harrison nodded.

"Come on."

They crept toward the double-rollered doors of the warehouse. They whirred open.

"Don't let them see you," Adam murmured and pressed himself against the building, hiding in the swirling fog. Lightning flickered and thunder growled. Harrison imitated his brother, pressing his body against the wall and narrowing his eyes as two men in black hooded robes and bull masks exited the warehouse carrying a sarcophagus.

"It's Wing Tips and Nike with my sarcophagus," Adam whispered. "Where are they going with it?"

Wing Tips and Nike? Had his brother gone completely mental?

The men hauled the ancient Egyptian coffin to the car parked at the curb. That's when Harrison realized it was Tom Grayfield's limo.

His pulse leaped. What to do? He had no weapon. If the men had guns, they would just pull them out and shoot him if he tried anything heroic at this juncture.

More important, where was Cassie? Was she inside the warehouse? Inside the limo? Or—and the fear that blasted through his veins was blistering and thick—was she in the sarcophagus?

From out of the warehouse stalked Tom Grayfield, also wearing a black robe. He carried in one hand a bull's head like the one a college football team mascot might wear, a derringer in the other.

"Nebamun." Adam spit out the word.

Huh?

"I will kill him," Adam said.

Harrison had to grab his brother by the scruff of his swaddling linen and hold him back. "He's got a weapon; you don't. He'll kill you, and then where will Kiya be?"

He understood Adam's anger. His vehemence. It took everything he had inside him not to succumb to his rage and charge Grayfield. But he could not afford to act on impulse. Cassie's life was at stake.

What was his weakness was also his strength. While his ability to detach from his emotions might cause him problems in intimate relationships, in instances like this it was a valuable talent. He needed a plan and he needed it fast. Wing Tips, who was really Grayfield's driver, Anthony Korba, unlocked the trunk.

"My sarcophagus," Adam whimpered as the men loaded it into the trunk.

Don't just stand there, do something. Harrison froze. His brain froze. He couldn't react. *Do something, do something.*

Korba got behind the wheel. The other guy held the back door open for Grayfield to slide in, and then he hopped into the passenger seat.

They were going to get away. And his Volvo was smashed into a stop sign half a block over with two flat tires.

Adam took off running in the opposite direction just as the limo started.

"Where are you going?" Harrison called out.

"To the chariot. We must catch them."

The chariot? Something very weird was going on with his brother.

Adam disappeared into the fog, and Harrison had to sprint to keep up with him. He heard a car engine roar to life. From out of the mist drove a delivery van, the mummy at the wheel. He screeched to a halt beside Harrison.

Harrison jumped in, and Adam floored it before he even had the door closed. The delivery van leaped forward, in hot pursuit of the limousine.

It was only after they spied the limo's taillights glinting through the drizzling fog that it occurred to Harrison that Cassie might still be in the warehouse. No time for second-guessing, although it was his instinct to question, question, question. He was committed to this course of action. Cassie had to be in the sarcophagus.

A loud thumping noise came from the back of the van. Startled, he looked over at Adam. "What's that?"

Adam shrugged. "Boreas. Ignore him. He's been doing that all day."

"Boreas? The leader of the group of warriors who sold Solen into slavery?"

"Yes," Adam hissed. "That traitor Boreas."

Thump, thump, thump. Who was really in the back?

"Adam, you have to stop the car. You have to let Boreas out."

"Can't," Adam said grimly, bandaged hands clamped on the steering wheel, eyes fixed on the car ahead of them. "Nebamun's got Kiya."

He had a good argument.

Thump, thump, thump. What in the hell was going on back there?

They were approaching a railroad crossing. Harrison could hear the warning bells of an oncoming train. He saw the flashing lights glaring against the fog. In the distance, the train blew a long, mournful whistle.

The limo scooted across the tracks just as the signal arm started to descend.

Thump, thump, thump.

The train whistle blew again, louder, closer. The headlights cut through the rain and fog.

Adam never slowed. He stayed right on the limousine's taillights.

"Adam, no!"

"He has Kiya." Adam's jaw was a rock of determination.

The signal arm was level with the top of the car. The warning whistle was earsplitting, the headlights blinding.

Harrison stopped breathing as the train hit the intersection.

Cassie touched that dark, empty place inside her. An ugly place she hadn't been to in years and had hoped never to go to again. She was submerged by the fear. It consumed her and she was lost.

But then a funny thing happened.

She made friends with the darkness and the closed, cramped space. Came to grips with the fact that she was probably going to die without ever seeing her twin sister or her mother or Harry ever again.

But once she let go and accepted her fate, the fear vanished. She felt no attachment, only peace.

And forgiveness.

Pure, unconditional forgiveness for both herself and her mistakes and for the whole of humankind. She was filled to the core of her being with the wonder of it.

She forgave her father for running out on the family after her childhood accident.

She forgave poor old Duane, that lost soul, for locking her in the cellar.

She forgave everyone she'd ever known. Friends, lovers, enemies, and all those in between.

She forgave Demitri and Anthony and Tom Grayfield, who were so blinded by greed and lust for power that they did not understand what really mattered. She felt pity and she forgave them.

But most of all, she forgave herself. For the wrong roads taken, the foolish mistakes made, the people she'd unwittingly hurt.

Her heart swelled with forgiveness.

Forgive me, Harry, for not keeping the amulet safe. For not trusting you completely. For not fully appreciating you for who you are.

She lay in the constrained darkness of the sarcophagus and she was filled with a bright, expansive lightness.

Harry, she thought. *Harry, Harry, Harry.*

How she wanted to see him again. To touch him, kiss him, taste him.

Would she ever?

The limo stopped. She heard the men get out. Felt them lift the sarcophagus. Saw the gray swirling mist, the leering bull masks and black hoods as they opened the coffin lid and dragged her out in the rain.

Adam braked to a stop just in the nick of time. A second later, and they would have been delivery van roadkill.

But the limo had gotten away.

Cassie was lost to him. Harrison's heart wrenched.

The train sped by, *clickity-clickity-clack*. He watched the cars slide past, dread mounting as the train continued on and on and on and the clock on the dashboard went *tick, tick, tick*.

Would they be able to find the limo? Was Cassie lost to him forever?

Thump, thump, thump sounded from the back.

"While we're stuck here, we might as well let Boreas out." Harrison sighed.

Adam shook his head.

Harrison reached over and pulled the keys out of the ignition. "Yes."

"Hey." Adam glowered.

Harrison got out and unlocked the back door to find Clyde Petalonus tied up inside.

Anthony and Demitri had carried the sarcophagus to the middle of the spillway of the Trinity River. A metal mesh fence had been erected across the cement barrier to prevent misdirected boaters from falling over.

The water was shallow at the top of the spillway, but

swift. It rushed under the coffin, which was wedged tight against the fence, tumbling over the embankment into a mist of steamy fog below. The sound was a dull roar in Cassie's ears.

They had taken her out of the sarcophagus and laid her on top of it, still bound and gagged. They dropped her in the water a couple of times in the process, and now she was shivering wet.

Tom Grayfield was positioned behind the sarcophagus, bracing himself against it to keep from losing his balance on the slick cement. Anthony stood to her left, Demitri on her right. The fence at her feet. Both Anthony and Demitri were clinging to the metal posts in order to stay upright. In their hoods and masks, they looked like dark creatures from a *Star Wars* movie.

Rain pelted them all. Lightning streaked across the bitter black sky.

"Do you have the rings?" Grayfield shouted over the noise of the river and the rumbling thunder.

Both Demitri and Anthony held up one-half of the amulet.

Grayfield spouted some more chants in a bizarre foreign language. Cassie inhaled sharply. He was performing his own perverse version of the legend of the star-crossed lovers' reunification ceremony.

Solen was here, but there was no Kiya. That's what Grayfield had meant when he'd said she would be Kiya's stand-in. She wasn't certain exactly what all that entailed. If the rings were rejoined now, would her soul forever be melded with Solen's?

But how could that happen when Solen was long dead and crunched up like a smashed potato chip bag and she was very much alive?

"Get ready to meld the rings," Grayfield cried and raised his right hand high over his head.

Lightning lit up the sky.

Cassie stared helplessly. A flare of lightning lit the knife blade clutched in Tom Grayfield's upraised hand.

"Your brother believes he's Solen," Clyde said.

"What happened to him?" Harrison had commandeered the driver's seat, even though he couldn't see worth a flip without his glasses. He preferred his own driving to Adam's kamikaze charioting.

"Adam's got amnesia or something. He doesn't recognize me a bit."

"Yes, I do." Adam scowled at Clyde. "You're Boreas. You sold me into slavery and stole my birthright."

"Boreas was a young and strapping warrior. Do I look like a strapping young warrior to you?" Clyde patted his paunch and ran a hand through his thinning hair. "I mean, honestly."

Adam narrowed his eyes at Clyde and then glanced over at Harrison. "He's Boreas. Right?"

"No, Adam, he's Clyde. Clyde Petalonus."

Adam pondered this, but said nothing.

"I don't know what happened to your brother," Clyde said. "But I can tell you what happened to me."

The train finally came to an end, and the signal crossing arms rose. Harry bumped the delivery van over the tracks. They were near Forest Park on the Trinity River. There was a break in the overcast sky, the full moon playing a quick game of tag with the churning clouds. One minute the park was illuminated in a glow of light, the next minute cloaked in a bath of shadows.

Cassie, where are you?

Harrison fought off the black depression weighing

down his lungs. He thought of her and remembered what they'd been doing when Cassie had found Solen's half of the amulet.

They'd been so close to making love. Joining their bodies completely. Fused.

Now he might never get to be with her.

The sadness was too much to handle. He shut down his emotions, closed off his feelings, hid from himself. This was why he had stayed detached for so many years. It hurt too damned much to get close to someone.

"What did happen to you, Clyde?" he asked.

Anything to keep his mind occupied and off the stark reality that time was running out. Harrison guided the van through the park, straining his eyes to search for the limo. He wished for his glasses. He wished for a gun. He had neither. "How'd you end up in the back of this van?"

"Demitri," Clyde grunted. "He roughed me up and stuck me in the back. If Adam hadn't stolen the van out from under him and Korba, I don't know what would have happened to me."

"You know Demitri and Anthony Korba?" Harrison's hands were clenched tight on the steering wheel. They'd lost a good five minutes waiting for the train. Anything could happen in five minutes. Cassie could die.

"And I know Tom Grayfield. We roomed together in college when he was dating your mother."

"You knew my mother?"

"I knew you too," Clyde said. "Most serious toddler I ever met in my life. You never played with toys, but you were always taking things apart and putting them back together again."

"Did you know my father?" Harrison held his breath.

"No. I just knew he broke your mother's heart.

Grayfield was a rebound fling for her. And Grayfield was just using your mother's passion for the star-crossed lovers to help him get his hands on the amulet."

"You were at Adam's graduation from the University of Athens," Harrison said. "You were in the photograph, in the background."

Clyde nodded. "I couldn't miss his graduation, even if he didn't know I was there. I was as proud of him as if he were my own son."

"Did you know about the Minoan Order?"

Adam perked up. "Minoan Order? I know the Minoan Order."

"I heard rumors about Grayfield. I tried to warn your mother, but he was financing her dig and she didn't want to believe the rumors. Later she did, and that's why she asked me to look after Adam whenever he was in Greece with Tom. Mostly I had to do it from afar."

"I didn't know my mother was in Greece looking for Solen when I was a baby," Harrison said.

"I'm Solen." Adam raised a hand. "I'm right here."

"You're not Solen. You're Adam Grayfield."

His brother just stared at him.

Hoo-boy.

"How come I never met you before?" Harrison asked Clyde, trying hard to ignore his sagging spirits. They'd come to the end of Forest Park, and there was no sign of the limo.

"Tom and I had a huge falling-out over your mother. I was in love with her, you see," Clyde said. "But Tom was the one with the money, and nothing meant more to your mother than her work." He sounded sad, regretful.

Harrison left the park and turned onto University Drive. He had no idea where to look for the limo. The streets were empty. Lightning streaked across the sky.

Raindrops spit upon the windshield. He turned on the wipers. They squeaked against the glass—*Cassie, Cassie, Cassie.*

The streets were empty. No traffic anywhere. He took University Drive to the freeway. If he circled around the overpass and headed east, he would have a bird's-eye view of the park.

Cassie, where are you?

His heart wrenched. He could no longer deny his pain. He was going to lose her before he'd ever really had the chance to know her.

Adam tugged on his shirtsleeve and pointed out the window. "Look, look."

A thick, hot blast of lightning electrified the sky.

Harrison glanced south toward the spillway of the Trinity River and his heart lurched.

There, in the middle of the river, were three men and a coffin.

Chapter 22

Whipping the van around in a dangerous and highly illegal freeway U-turn, Harrison prayed as he'd never prayed before. He lumbered over the median, crashed down into the westbound lane, and took the University Drive exit at twenty miles over the speed limit, tires squealing in protest.

"What is it? What's going on?" Clyde exclaimed.

"Kiya," Adam said at the same time Harrison said, "Cassie."

What were Tom and his henchmen doing with the sarcophagus on the spillway?

A fragment from the scroll translation lodged in his brain:

In the elements lies the progression to immortality. Earth, air, fire, water. Two rings, two hearts, lovers reunited always. Life becomes death, death becomes life. Full circle.

He didn't fully understand what it meant, but water had to be part of the ritual. He wheeled toward the spillway, heart in his throat, pulse pounding.

"There's Grayfield's limo," Clyde yelled.

It was parked near the river's edge. Harrison pulled the

van up beside it. Lightning speared through the air, thick with ions, and smacked with a horrific jolt into a nearby tree.

They jumped and ducked their heads.

The tree burst into flames.

"This way, this way," Adam said, running along the bank toward the spillway ahead of Harrison and Clyde.

Harrison knew what was happening. He felt the dread, the chill, the horror of it shoot straight to his bones.

They reached the spillway. The awful scene was back-lit by the flaming tree.

Cassie lay bound and gagged on top of the sarcophagus. Anthony and Demitri were positioned at her sides, each holding a copper ring, extending them forward. Tom Grayfield stood over her, wearing the bull's head. He had a large gold ankh on a chain around his neck. He was the Minotaur, and there was a vicious knife clutched in his upraised fist.

The wind whirled. The water swirled. The air was rich with the smell of damp, fertile earth; the lightning hot and brilliant.

If Harrison made one move toward Cassie, Grayfield could stab her through the heart before he was halfway across the water.

I can't save her, he thought, and the despair was too much to bear. But he couldn't let her go without a fight. Couldn't lose her forever. Couldn't let Grayfield win.

Think, think.

He had no gun. No weapon. No clue what to do.

The djed. Use the djed.

The thought rose in his mind, clear and strong. *Use the djed.* He pulled the djed from his pocket and raised it over his head, aiming at Grayfield's ankh.

Harrison held his breath.

Grayfield finished his chant.

Anthony Korba and Demitri leaned forward over Cassie's body to connect the rings.

Grayfield brought the knife down.

"Kiya!" Adam screamed and dashed into the water.

"Adam, come back," Clyde called.

A bolt of white-blue lightning descended from the murky black clouds.

It hit the djed with a force so strong that it dropped Harrison to his knees, but he did not let go. Would not let go. Nothing could make him let go.

The lightning sparked, jumping the gap from Harrison's homemade djed to the ankh around Grayfield's neck. It shot veiny branches of voltage straight into his chest.

Grayfield's body quivered as the electricity passed through him, welding him to the water.

But the lightning did not stop there. The energy frequency snapped and crackled as it leaped both right and left. It struck the two copper rings that Anthony and Demitri held in their hands.

It also fingered down from Grayfield's legs, illuminating him in a ghostly blue glow that shimmered and danced over the water.

The water that Adam was trudging through trying to get to Cassie.

Horrified, Harrison watched as the electricity jolted up through his brother's body.

The heat around her was intense, as was the eerie blue-white light. Cassie blinked, not understanding what was happening. Tom Grayfield stood above her, his body shaking, his eyes rolled back inside his bull's head, the knife fused to his palm.

And then the blue electrical light was gone and Grayfield's heavy frame slowly toppled forward.

Cassie raised her bound hands in a defensive reflex to block the blade that descended as Grayfield fell. She rolled her head to one side to keep from getting smacked · by his bullish brow.

The duct tape stopped the knife. Grayfield's head thumped against the sarcophagus and his body slowly slid into the water.

Lightning lit the sky again. Thunder cracked.

Frantically, Cassie began sawing her wrists back and forth against the knife blade, desperate to get free before Grayfield's hand slipped down into the water with him.

To the left of her came another thump as Anthony Korba collapsed onto the sarcophagus as well, his cheek coming to rest against her knee. She almost kicked him off her, but then she saw that Solen's half of the amulet was still clutched in his outstretched fingers.

The duct tape broke free, and she shook it off. She pried the knife from Grayfield's hand and then ripped the gag off her mouth. Plucking the amulet from Anthony's fingers, she tucked the ring into the pocket of her blouse. She was leaning down to cut the duct tape from her ankles when she felt an iron grip clamp around her wrist.

"Not so fast, sister."

It was Demitri, Mr. Nike himself. He looked a little dazed, but his eyes were deadly. In his other hand he held Kiya's half of the amulet.

"Cassie!"

She turned her head to the right, saw Harrison and Clyde splashing toward her in the swift running water, and spied the mummy floating facedown in the water several feet from the sarcophagus.

"Harry!"

She tried to twist away from Demitri, tried with everything inside her to get to Harry, but Demitri applied so much pressure to her wrist, she feared the bone would snap. Helpless, she dropped the knife. It splashed into the river.

Demitri yanked her from the sarcophagus and through the water. He dragged her toward the opposite bank, scraping her knees against the cement spillway in the process.

She gasped against the coldness, against the pain, confused and frightened.

"Cassie, hang on. I'm coming!"

"Harry!" she called over her shoulder.

Demitri jerked her hard. "Shut up. Keep quiet."

They'd made it across the spillway. She tried to look back, to see how far away Harry was, but Demitri kept tugging at her so hard, pulling her so fast, she could not see what was happening behind her.

Demitri's got Kiya's half of the amulet. I have to get it from him.

He was hauling her up an embankment, through a cluster of trees. Somewhere in all the madness she had lost her sandals. Thorns and twigs pierced her bare feet. Her knees stung from the cement burns. She kept stumbling and falling down. Demitri was relentless, never stopping, never even slowing.

What she needed was a plan. Unfortunately, she had nothing. If she could just slow him down long enough for Harry to catch up.

"Hey, Demitri, wanna blow job?"

"Huh?" Demitri paused.

Just as she'd hoped, natural male instinct momentarily outweighed the urgent need to escape his pursuers. But a moment was all Cassie needed. As soon as Demitri turned to see if he'd heard correctly, Cassie plowed her knee into his crotch with as much force as she could muster.

Demitri screamed and clutched himself with both hands, letting go of her and dropping Kiya's half of the amulet as he sank to the ground, writhing in pain. The amulet made a faint clinking sound as it bounced off a rock.

"A blow to your man parts. Blow job, get it?" Cassie stepped over him and pulled back her hair with one hand so it wouldn't fall on her face as she searched in the pre-dawn haze for the amulet.

She spotted the ring and leaned down to pick it up. Just as she reached for it, a man's hand appeared from the shadows.

Breathing hard, clothes soaking wet, Harrison scaled the embankment.

Cassie. I have to save Cassie.

The ground felt like wet cement, dragging him down, slowing him. He pumped his arms and pushed himself harder. The river was directly below him. If he slipped and fell, he would plunge into the deep pool of turbulent water tumbling off the spillway.

Got to get to Cassie.

He crested the hill, heard someone moan ahead of him in the copse of trees. Spurred on, he zigzagged around stumps and boulders, broke through into a small clearing. He found Demitri on the ground, holding himself and rolling from side to side. Cassie was kneeling a few feet away, clutching something tightly to her chest in her knotted hand.

Her face was lifted upward, and she was gazing into the barrel of a gun.

Harrison blinked, unable to believe his eyes, but he understood at once what had happened. She'd racked

Demitri, he'd dropped the amulet, and when she'd gone to retrieve it, Ahmose Akvar had pulled the gun on her.

The question was, Where had Ahmose come from, and what did he have to do with Tom Grayfield and the Minoan Order?

"Give me the amulet," the Egyptian demanded, extending his palm.

"Cassie, sweetheart," Harrison called out. "Are you all right?"

"Could be better," she said ruefully. "I'm not a huge fan of having firearms pointed in my face."

"What are you doing, Ahmose?" Harrison stepped around Demitri, who whistled in a low, keening wail. Cassie must have gotten him good. He moved purposely toward Ahmose, acting as if he was unarmed, acting as if this were all perfectly normal. He didn't want to escalate the situation by injecting unnecessary emotion into it. But he wanted to rush Ahmose and pound the shit out of him for scaring Cassie.

"Stay back, Harrison." Ahmose waved the gun at him.

"What's going on? Let's talk about this."

"Nothing to talk about," Ahmose said. "Give me the amulet."

"No." Cassie shook her head. "I won't."

Ahmose cocked the gun. "Please, do not make me shoot you."

Harrison could tell from the determined set to his jaw that Ahmose would pull the trigger if forced. Harrison had no idea why, but he was certain Ahmose was deadly serious. Sweat popped out on his forehead despite the fact he was drenched and shivering cold down to his very marrow.

"Give him the amulet, Cassie."

In the distance, sirens wailed.

"Give me the amulet."

The sirens goaded the urgency in Ahmose's voice. The Egyptian stepped forward and pressed the nose of the gun flush against Cassie's temple.

Her eyes widened and she looked over at Harrison, the fear on her face ripping a hole through him more vicious than any bullet.

"Give it to him," Harrison whispered. "It isn't worth your life."

"But Kiya and Solen," she whimpered.

"To hell with Kiya and Solen. You're the one I care about."

"Do as Dr. Standish says."

Reluctantly, Cassie unknotted her fist and allowed Ahmose to pluck the ring from her hand.

Without another word, the Egyptian stalked to the top of the embankment and stared down at the churning river below. He cocked back his arm and flung the amulet into the Trinity.

They all watched it hit the water and quickly disappear into the thrashing foam. Ahmose stuck the gun in his waistband and turned to go.

Harrison stared in disbelief. His entire life's work had just been thrown away. Impossible, unbelievable. He couldn't let it go. He had to know. He moved in front of the Egyptian, blocking his way.

Their eyes met.

"Why, Ahmose? Why?"

"Ask your mother," Ahmose said and then shouldered past him and disappeared into the wet, stormy night.

The sirens screamed nearer.

Stunned over what had just happened, Cassie stared at Harrison.

"Ahmose threw the amulet away. Why would he throw it in the river? And what did he mean when he said to ask your mother?"

"It doesn't matter," Harrison said, moving to close the gap between them.

Her bottom lip trembled as emotion swept through her. "Kiya and Solen." She choked back the tears. "They'll never be reunited now."

"Shh, sweetheart, it's okay." Harry reached out to cup the back of her head in his palm, threading his fingers through her hair. "Are you all right?"

"Fine." She forced a shaky smile. "I'm fine."

He lowered his head and tenderly kissed her lips. She'd never tasted anything sweeter than the flavor of his mouth. Fifteen minutes earlier she'd thought her life was over, that she would never see him again. She wrapped her arms around his neck, and he scooped her up against him. She never wanted to let him go.

"We better break this up," he murmured softly against her lips. "Demitri's getting away."

She sighed and stepped back. Harrison went after Demitri, who was trying to crawl off through the trees.

"Not so fast, dirtbag." Harrison grabbed Demitri by the collar and started dragging him, kicking and clawing, back into the clearing. Then Demitri tripped Harrison, knocking him to the ground. They rolled around, punching each other.

"Stop it! Stop it!" Cassie cried.

"Don't anybody move," came a voice from the mist. "FBI."

"How did you find us?" Cassie asked her brother-in-law, David Marshall, several minutes later.

She, David, Harrison, and Clyde were standing on the banks of the Trinity. They'd quickly filled David in on what had happened, each telling their part of the story.

Paramedics loaded Tom Grayfield, Anthony Korba, and Adam into ambulances. All three were unconscious from the refracted electrical discharge of Harrison's djed transformer. Demitri, who hadn't been as severely affected by the voltage because he'd been wearing sneakers, was shackled and had been led off to a waiting police cruiser. None of the uniformed officers with David had been able to find Ahmose Akvar, although they were still scouring the nearby woods and the perimeter of Forest Park.

"The burning bush." David indicated the tree still smoldering from the lightning strike. "Someone saw it flaming and called the fire department. When they got here, firemen spied Tom Grayfield's limo and radioed the police. I had them put an APB out on you the minute you told me you were with Tom Grayfield. Do you have any idea how frantic I've been, Cassie?"

Cassie crinkled her nose. "I'm so sorry, David. I didn't mean to involve you in all this."

"Hey." David smiled and shrugged. "What are brothers-in-law for?"

"You didn't tell Maddie, did you?"

"I had to. Maddie's my wife. We don't keep secrets from each other. She's catching the next flight out from D.C."

"Maddie worries too much." Cassie sighed. Although she might complain about her sister's fierce protectiveness, she would secretly be overjoyed to hug her twin close after tonight's ordeal.

"Your sister just cares about you," David said.

"I know." Cassie nodded and turned to Harrison. Their

eyes met and her stomach clutched. Here was someone else who cared about her too. And she cared about him in return. Cared more than she ever thought possible. "I owe you an apology, Harrison."

"What for?"

"For believing Ahmose's lie. For doubting you even for a moment."

"Why did you doubt me?" he asked.

"Because of the photograph with Clyde in the background. Why did you lie about knowing him?"

"Harrison didn't know that I knew him," Clyde interjected. "He never realized it was me in the picture."

Cassie's eyes never left Harrison's face, and he was studying her just as intently. She couldn't wait to get him alone so she could show him exactly how sorry she was for misjudging him.

"What's going to happen to Tom Grayfield?" Clyde asked. "And his henchmen?"

"Both the CIA and the Greek government are waiting to talk with him about myriad offenses and violations. He'll be going to prison for a very long time," David said. "Anthony Korba and Demitri Lorenzo will face kidnapping and attempted murder charges along with Grayfield."

Harrison gazed after the ambulance that whisked Adam away. "Do you think my brother will be all right?"

"Come on." David clapped a sympathetic hand on Harrison's shoulder. "I'll drive you to the hospital."

Chapter 23

It was eight o'clock on Friday morning when they got back to Harrison's apartment. David had raised an eyebrow when Cassie told him there wasn't any need for him to take her over to her place, because she was staying with Harry.

Adam still hadn't regained consciousness. The doctor had advised them to go home and get some rest. He said Adam's prognosis was good, and he expected him to make a full recovery.

But once the front door had closed and she was totally alone with Harrison, Cassie was surprised to discover she felt shy and a little awkward.

He smiled at her, stretched out a hand, and her uncertainty vanished. In spite of his black eye and bruises, or maybe even because of them. No one had ever taken her breath the way that he did. How was it she'd never really realized exactly how handsome he was?

"Let's get you tended to."

"Huh?" She felt dazed from staring into those rich brown eyes.

"Your legs." He nodded.

Cassie peered down at her feet. They'd given her a pair

of paper booties to wear at the hospital, but there was dried blood on her skin from her knees on down.

Harrison filled the tub with water and quietly undressed her. She appreciated the care he took, tenderly helping her off with her blouse. When he dropped it to the floor, Solen's ring rolled out.

"You have the other half of the amulet," he said.

"Little good it does now." She felt incredibly close to tears again. "Solen and Kiya will never be together."

"It's just a silly legend."

"Still, you never know."

"I understand," he said. "I feel the loss too. I never believed in the legend, and until now I never realized how important reuniting those rings was to me."

"It's sad."

"Shh, let's not talk about it." He finished undressing her about the same time the tub had filled. He turned off the water and helped her into the bath.

Sinking gratefully into the warm water, she told him everything that had happened to her in the warehouse. He told her what he'd discovered in the scrolls. How the cryptic message had led him directly to Tom Grayfield.

She spoke of her fear of never seeing him again, her terror at being locked in the sarcophagus, and then she told him about the strange and wonderful peace that had come over her. The forgiveness she'd felt for everyone.

He whispered of his dismay at learning he'd delivered her into Grayfield's hands. Emotion caught in his throat when he spoke of the horror he'd felt when he realized Grayfield intended to use her as a human sacrifice in his quest for immortality.

Harrison undressed and climbed into the tub with her. They said nothing more, just gazed into each other's eyes, fully experiencing the moment. Both happy that they were together and alive.

She stroked his cheek with a washcloth.

He soaped her breasts.

She massaged his tense shoulders.

He brushed his fingers through the strands of her hair.

When the water grew cold, they dried each other off. He had Cassie sit on the counter and he knelt on the floor, tenderly cleansing her wounds. After first applying antiseptic ointment, he then put Band-Aids on the cuts and scrapes on her feet and knees.

They were completely naked in front of each other in the stark bathroom light, and neither was embarrassed.

It felt too right.

He kissed her and she kissed him back. He took her hand and guided her into his bedroom, dropping kisses on her face along the way. His dear face was battered and bruised, but Cassie had never seen anything as touching as the expression in his eyes when he gazed at her.

They sat together on the edge of the bed, kissing, stroking, licking, tasting. The tempo increased as their passion escalated. They lay back on the mattress. Cassie broke his kiss and nibbled a trail down his chin to his throat to his chest and beyond.

When her mouth touched his jutting penis, he sucked in his breath. She raised her head and met his gaze. His eyes filled with wonder and fascination and desire as he watched her stroke him. He looked so vibrant, so alive, so unlike the standoffish professor she had first met. She'd misjudged him and his ability to experience passion.

The heat of desire in his eyes was so stark, so hungry, it took her breath away. He wanted her.

She could see it written across his face. She tasted it in

his kisses. Smelled it on his skin. He wanted her in a way no other man had ever wanted her.

While she was stroking him with her mouth, he gently reached for her, his fingers skating over her hip bone. She closed her eyes as she felt energy melt up from her feminine core into her breasts and into her throat. She tasted her own desire, hot and rich, mingling with the earthy flavor of him.

A silky moan escaped his lips. He carefully twisted away from her, breaking her gentle suction on his erection.

Her eyes popped open and she saw he had shifted onto his side, propping himself on his elbow. He was peering at her, and she saw the raw, animal intensity of need in eyes the color of Guinness.

He kissed her, his mouth urgent. His energy filled her, shocked her. He was more powerful than a charge of white-hot lightning.

When he lightly grazed her most tender spot, a desperate sweetness suffused her body, full of sumptuous delight. And all the capacity of her desire sprang alive. She reached for him, clutching, devouring.

She had no more restraint. Abandon claimed her, and she thrust herself against his hard body.

But he was tender. So very tender. He acted as if she were going to break into pieces if he so much as breathed on her hard.

"I want to get lost in your eyes as I make love to you, Cassie," he whispered, and it was exactly what she wanted to hear.

"Condom?"

"Right here." He dealt with the details, then poised himself over her. Harry looked down into her face. "You're so incredibly beautiful. So brave."

"Not too shabby yourself, Professor."

She wrapped her legs around his waist, and with a reverential groan he sank into her. She felt so incredibly safe with him. She was able to let go of control and allow him to sweep her along with his masculine rhythm. She gave herself away, fully, completely, without hesitation. Unleashed her heart and surrendered. Forfeited everything to him.

"Harder," she cried and bucked her hips upward.

He rode her hard just as she wanted. Pushing into her, giving her glorious, inescapable pleasure.

Give it to me, give it to me. I want to feel you come.

Then it broke. Her thunderstorm. Her lightning. Her hurricane.

It was large inside her. So large. Spreading and growing. The air was a choir. Singing, vibrating his praises. *"Harrison, Harrison, Harrison."*

The sensation rushed through her, sweet, deep, hot, intense, flaming, burning like a slant of brilliant light far up inside her, diffusing through her and fanning the telltale rash of passion spreading up and over her breasts.

She shuddered against him as he shuddered into her.

"Oh, Harrison," she breathed.

"It's Harry," he whispered into the curve of her throat. "Call me Harry."

Cassie woke before Harry. She rolled over onto her side, stacked her hands under her cheek, and watched him sleeping.

She studied the way the sunlight fell across his bruised face. She held her hand poised above his hip, feeling the power of his body heat radiating up through her palm. She paid attention to the texture of his skin, so smooth and thick and tanned. She noticed how the very quality of the air in the room seemed different because they were breathing in tandem.

Tears filled her eyes and a strange tightness swelled her chest. She was overcome with a melancholy so intense she feared she might die from it.

Her natural instinct was to laugh, to move, to sing. Anything to buoy her mood and block out the sadness. But she did not do that. Instead, she lay beside Harrison, letting the melancholy fill her up.

Their time together was at an end. It was over.

As she fully experienced the sorrow of loss, a very strange thing happened.

All these years what she thought passed for happiness, activity, fun, parties, dates was so different from this unflappable sense of certainty. Her understanding of real and lasting happiness had changed. She had changed.

Something clicked deep inside her as she reconnected with the self she'd misplaced so long ago. Her habitual goals, scripts, and agendas dropped away in the realization of this better self, and suddenly she could see and hear and feel, both internally and externally, with greater clarity.

In that shimmering moment, she knew what she had to do. She had to stop hiding her pain. Had to fully live it, experience it, and then let it go. What she had been running from had already happened, and she'd survived. She was still here, still living her life.

She had so much to be grateful for. She didn't need that job at the Smithsonian to be happy. Didn't need parties or fast cars or constant stimulation. Everything she'd ever truly wanted or needed was within her reach. It was all right here.

All she had to do was make room.

He woke at 2 P.M. to find his bed empty. Cassie was gone. She'd crept away while he slept.

His sheets still smelled of her, vibrant as a summer

garden. He squeezed her pillow to his chest and inhaled the scent of her.

Where had she gone? Why had she left?

The bedside phone rang. He snatched it up, his pulse bumping. Was it her?

"Hello?"

"It's Clyde. I'm at the hospital."

Simultaneously, Harrison sat up and dropped the pillow. "Adam—is he . . ."

"Awake, and he's regained his memory."

"Thank God."

"He wants to see you. He won't tell us what happened to him. Not until you get here."

"Us?" Was Cassie at the hospital already? Was that where she'd gone? But why would she go without him?

"I called your mother," Clyde said. "She's here."

Ten minutes later, Harrison walked into Adam's hospital room. On the drive over, one specific memory from the night before had stuck in his brain.

Ahmose, flinging Kiya's amulet into the Trinity, and saying, "Ask your mother." He hadn't known what Ahmose meant, but he did know his mother had been keeping too many secrets for too many years. It was long past time for a showdown.

But first things first. He had to speak to his brother.

Adam was sitting up in bed. Dark circles ringed his eyes, and his cheeks were sunken. He had an IV in his arm and he wore a hospital gown.

"You look as bad as I feel," Adam said.

"Dude." Harrison grinned and touched his blackened eye. "If you feel as bad as I look, you are so screwed."

Adam blinked. "That doesn't sound like you. You never say 'dude.' Or tease me."

Harrison shrugged and felt his cheeks heat. "Guess I've been hanging out with Cassie Cooper too long, searching for your sorry butt."

"I like the changes. She's good for you."

"Where's Mom?" He plunked down in one of the chairs for visitors at the side of Adam's bed.

"Right here."

Harrison looked up to see Diana and Clyde walking through the door carrying a Burger King bag. Adam held out his hand. "Thanks, Mom, you saved my life. The hospital food is bad enough to kill a guy."

Diana handed Adam the sack, then turned to Harrison. "Hello, son."

"Hello, Mother."

This is how it had always been between them. Distant, tentative, wary. He wished it did not have to be this way. He used to long for the sort of mother you could throw your arms around and wrap in a bear hug. But Diana was who she was.

Diana took the chair next to Harrison. Clyde went to stand at the back of the room, his arms folded on his chest, his eyes on Diana. Adam focused on wolfing down his food.

"So tell us everything that happened," Diana said. "Start from the beginning."

"Well," Adam said, "I was born in a—"

"Don't be a smartass," Diana interrupted. "You'd think after everything you've been through, it would have taken some of the starch out of your sails."

"Or some of the spunk out of the punk," Harrison muttered.

His mother grinned at him. Hey, for once they were on the same wavelength. Adam didn't seem to mind that they were ganging up on him. He waved a hand. "You guys are just jealous because I have an amazing ability to bounce back."

"So talk."

"All right." Adam wiped a smear of mustard off his cheek. "Here's where it started. Dad put me up to searching for Solen. I wasn't really interested. Had a hot girl I was dating and she was trying to get me to move to France with her, but Dad kept telling me how I had to beat Harrison. He said he would finance the dig, no strings attached. He'd never done that before. I thought it might be a chance to mend fences between us." He polished off the last of his hamburger, and with a free-throw toss landed it in the trash can. "He shoots; he scores!"

"Don't get distracted," Diana said.

Adam sighed. Harrison could tell this was painful for him, vocalizing the truth about his father.

"Dad had a lot of detailed information about Solen's tomb and where it was located. He refused to tell me where he got the info, and for the longest time I thought the data must be totally bogus and I wouldn't use it. I kept reminding him that he'd told me no strings were attached to the money."

"Harrison," Diana interrupted, giving him the once-over. "You're not wearing your glasses."

"Broke them in a bar fight. Long story."

Diana looked taken aback. "A bar brawl? You?"

"Dude." Adam gave him a thumbs-up. "Way to go, bro."

"Sorry, go on. I didn't mean to interrupt." Diana shook her head but looked at Harrison differently, as if she suddenly respected him more.

"Anyway, I finally followed Dad's instructions because I didn't know where else to look, and hey, I found Solen right where he said I would."

"And among Solen's artifacts, you found the scroll," Harrison supplied.

"Yeah, written in Minoan hieroglyphics. And I translated it," Adam boasted. "Took me several weeks of trying, but I did it. Dad pressured me." His face sobered. "Once I knew what it said, I wished I hadn't."

Diana fisted Adam's covers in her hands. "And what did you learn?"

Harrison caught the recriminating look his brother sent his mother. "You've known all along about Dad," Adam accused.

"Not known. Suspected. But I never knew for sure."

Harrison was startled to see tears misting his mother's eyes. He could never remember seeing her cry.

A nurse came in to take Adam's vital signs, and they had to wait until she was finished before he could continue his story. The tension in the room was palpable.

"Everything was in Solen's scroll," Adam said. "The legend of the star-crossed lovers. The curse he'd placed on Vizier Nebamun's family. And the reason my father wanted Solen resurrected. The formula for immortality."

The room fell silent for a long moment as Adam's words echoed off the walls.

"There were sayings in that text." Adam took a swallow of water. "Things my father often said. And the symbols that match the signet ring he wears. Since the hieroglyphics had never been translated, only someone versed in the oral tradition of the Minoan Order could have possessed such knowledge. That's why he had funded my dig. That's where he'd gotten his information. I had no idea what he was going to do with the formula, but I knew I couldn't turn it over to him. Not if he was in the Minoan Order."

"Adam called me when he got in trouble. He remembered

me from his childhood and thought I could help since I worked for the Kimbell," Clyde interjected. "His plan was to split up the artifacts. Ship me Solen in his sarcophagus. Hide the scroll in a crate with a false bottom and leave it for Harrison to find, and keep the amulet on his person."

"When I got to Fort Worth," Adam picked up the story again, "Clyde wrapped me in the mummy linen. I had to be unrecognizable. I went to the museum masquerade party to tell Harrison what was happening, but I was afraid to approach him directly because Ahmose Akvar kept hanging around. I had no idea whom I could trust, who might be watching, and the last thing I wanted was to put them on his tail too. In the meantime, Dad sent Anthony Korba and Demitri Lorenzo to bring me back to Greece. Demitri cornered me in the courtyard at the Kimbell and tried to get me to tell him where Solen's half of the amulet was. When I resisted, he stabbed me in the back with a knife he'd filched from the caterers. Only Cassie's arrival in the courtyard saved my life."

"I've got to meet this Cassie," Diana said. "She sounds special."

Special wasn't the half of it. "You'll like her," Harrison said.

Adam kept talking. "I was in the courtyard bleeding, slowly losing consciousness, and I saw this red leather handbag. I dragged myself over to it and hid the amulet inside."

"It was Cassie's handbag," Harrison said.

Adam brightened. "So she has the amulet? Everything is okay? We can still reunite the rings?"

Harrison glanced over at Clyde. "You didn't tell him?"

Clyde shook his head.

"What?" Adam looked from one to the other. "What is it?"

Harrison blew out his breath. "We have Solen's half of the amulet, but Ahmose Akvar destroyed Kiya's half." He looked over at his mother. "Ahmose said to ask you why."

"What?" Diana looked startled.

Then, because he was beginning to suspect the answer, Harrison asked her the question he hadn't asked her in sixteen years.

"Who's my father?"

Chapter 24

You've already started to figure it out, son. Why else would Ahmose Akvar destroy one-half of the amulet?"

Harrison's gaze locked with Diana's. "Because he's descended from Vizier Nebamun. Ahmose destroyed Kiya's ring in order to prevent the reunification. He was desperate to prevent the curse."

"Exactly."

"What does that have to do with me?" he asked.

Clyde came over and placed both hands on Diana's shoulders. She leaned against Clyde and squarely met Harrison's glare. "You're upset about losing the amulet."

"How could I not be? It was my life's work. Your life's work too. Aren't you upset? Your opportunity to disprove the legend is gone forever."

"What does it matter if Solen and Kiya are reunited? If you don't believe."

"What if I do?"

Diana smiled faintly. "Which is it, son? Do you believe in the legend or don't you?"

Odd, but when he tried to think of Kiya, it was laughing, outrageous, fun-loving Cassie who popped into his head. And when he tried to imagine Solen, he saw only his own face. He shook his head, feeling disoriented. What was wrong with him? He turned the tables, answering his mother's question with the eternal question that so badly needed answering.

"Who is my father?"

"Are you certain you want to know?"

"I wouldn't be asking if I didn't." Harrison curled his fingers into his palms, bracing for the news he'd waited thirty-two years to hear. His heart curiously slowed. "I've always wanted to know."

"He was Egyptian. As you've always suspected. That's where you get your olive complexion."

Reaching up, Harrison touched his cheek. Half Egyptian. Somehow he'd always known this. Egypt was in his blood. It was as much a part of him as his color-blindness.

"Your biological father is dead. He passed away four or five years ago. I think it was a heart attack." She said it so emotionlessly, as if she had never made love to the man, had never given birth to his child out of wedlock.

And Harrison realized he'd been like his mother for far too long. Holding back, denying his feelings, living too much in his head and not enough in his heart.

He had not expected the news of his biological father's death to hit him so viscerally. He hadn't known the man, but he couldn't shake the feeling of having been cheated out of something vital.

"What was his name?"

"Mohammad Akvar."

He sucked in his breath as the impact hit him. "The former Egyptian prime minister?"

"Yes."

"Ahmose is my brother?"

"Your half brother, yes."

The full implication finally sank in. "That means I'm also descended from Vizier Nebamun. The man who poisoned Kiya and Solen."

"You are. So I ask you again, son. Do you believe in the star-crossed lovers or not?"

He recognized what she was getting at. If he believed in the star-crossed lovers, then he must believe in the curse. You couldn't have one without the other. But he did not believe in the legend. There was nothing to fear from the curse. As his mother had once said, there was no such thing as soul mates and undying love. No such thing as love at first sight.

What about Cassie? whispered a voice in the back of his head.

"It's a moot point. Kiya's half of the amulet is no more. Ahmose threw it into the river. We'll never be able to prove the legend of the star-crossed lovers one way or the other."

"Don't be so sure about that."

"Enough secrets." Harrison jumped up from his chair, no longer able to tolerate his mother's games. "Just tell me. Tell me everything."

Diana hesitated.

"You've got to let me have control over my own life. Stop withholding information."

"Are you certain?"

"Positive."

"As you wish." Diana nodded. "After you discovered Kiya's remains, I couldn't help worrying. What if I'd been wrong about the legend? What if it really was true? And what if either you or your brother one day found Solen and the other half of the amulet? You were extremely determined, and Adam is very competitive. Throw Tom Grayfield into the mix, and I knew it was inevitable that one of you would find Solen."

"What did you do?"

"I had a replica of Kiya's amulet made."

"You're telling me that you switched the amulet?"

"Yes."

"But when and how?"

"Ten days ago. When you first arrived. Clyde made the switch at the Kimbell while you were setting up the exhibit."

Excitement took hold of him. All was not lost. The pieces could still be brought together, the amulet made whole. Solen and Kiya reunited.

"Ahmose did not destroy the real half?"

His mother reached into the pocket of her sweater, pulled out a small white jeweler's box, and pressed it into his hand. "I can't protect you anymore. It's your decision to make. If you're willing to take the gamble, then reunite the lovers."

Cassie had just finished burning the last memento from her collage wall when the doorbell rang. She rocked back on her heels and watched the picture of Peyton Shriver go up in smoke. She had thought that burning the photographs and memorabilia would be bittersweet.

But it was not. She felt empowered. She felt excited. She felt free.

The bell chimed a second time.

She closed the fireplace screen, dusted off her palms, and rose to her feet. She figured it must be Maddie and David. She was expecting them any minute.

She was surprised but very pleased to find Harrison standing on the landing.

"Harry!" She flung her arms around his neck and hugged him tight. She was so happy to see him, she barely noticed he did not hug her back. "What are you doing here?"

He held out a white jeweler's box.

For one heart-stopping moment she wondered if it was an engagement ring and her hopes leaped with joy. But the box was wider and flatter than a ring box, something more like what a bracelet or a brooch would be in.

"You brought me a present? Aw, Harry, you didn't have to do that."

"It's not a present."

"What is it?"

"Open it up."

She lifted the lid and stared down at an ancient copper ring. Confused, she glanced at Harry. "What?"

"It's Kiya's half."

"The half Ahmose threw into the river?"

"No. The real half."

"Excuse me?"

"Can we sit down? This conversation is going to take me a while."

"Sure, sure." She ushered him into the living room.

He sniffed the air. "You had a fire."

"Yes." She wanted so badly to tell him she'd destroyed her collage wall for him, but the timing had to be right and she wasn't sure this was it. "I was burning a few things."

He sat down on the couch and Cassie curled up beside him, kicking off her flip-flops and tucking her legs underneath her.

"Have you talked to Phyllis yet?"

"No." Cassie shook her head.

She'd procrastinated, not wanting to face the curator

and tell her that not only was the reunification ceremony not going to take place, but the amulet stolen from the display was gone forever. Her dreams for the Smithsonian were officially over. But she realized she didn't feel so bad about that. She studied Harry's face and her pulse leaped. She had other dreams now.

"Good," he said.

Then he told Cassie everything he had learned from his mother. How she'd been madly in love with his father and been heartbroken when she'd discovered he was married and she was pregnant. He told her how Diana had left Egypt and gone to Greece to search for Solen and had met Tom Grayfield. He had been the rebound guy for her, and she had been a means to an end for him.

Harrison told her that he'd learned he and Ahmose were half brothers and that they were descendants of Vizier Nebamun. He even told her about Jessica and his teenage feelings for her and how he'd caught her in Adam's arms.

"So if we reunite the pieces of the amulet at the reunification ceremony, then you will be forever cursed."

"I don't believe in the legend, remember? I don't believe in curses."

"You want to do this?"

"I want you to have everything you've ever wanted, Cassie. If we make this right with Phyllis, you'll get your recommendation to the Smithsonian. Kiya and Solen are reunited. Everyone is happy."

"Well, except for Vizier Nebamun's descendants. Even if you don't believe in it, clearly they do. Belief can do strange things to people."

"Like the belief in immortality? Tom Grayfield was ready to kill his own son over it. Call Phyllis, tell her that everything is a go for the reunification ceremony. Your brother-in-law even got the police to release Solen and his sarcophagus. Clyde's gone over to pick up the mummy."

Cassie glanced at her watch. "It's five-thirty."

"We have plenty of time."

"No. I can't let you do this."

"I want to do it. I've spent my life chasing this legend. The rings belong together."

"But you could be cursed. Are you willing to take that risk?"

"Yes," he said. "I am."

He got to his feet and so did Cassie. "I'm going to miss you when you're off to Washington."

She looked at him, not certain what to say. She wanted to tell him that she wanted *him*, not the Smithsonian, but he was holding himself stiffly, hiding his feelings.

"I brought you something to remember me by," he said.

"Oh?" She didn't want to be a memory. She wanted to be part of his life. *But what if he doesn't want you?*

He took something from inside his jacket pocket. It was a photograph the nature guide had taken of them with Cassie the monarch at the butterfly hatchery and a copy of the brochure.

"For your collage wall," he said.

Cassie bit back her tears. This was good-bye. He was giving her the big kiss-off. She'd never been dumped, but she'd done enough dumping to recognize the signs.

"No." She shoved the picture back at him. "I can't accept this. I won't put you on my wall."

He looked as if she'd smacked him hard across the face. Well, she wasn't going to make this any easier for him. She wasn't going to let him salve his ego with a paltry picture and a butterfly brochure.

"Cassie, I—"

"No," she said again as the doorbell rang. Relieved to have a good excuse to end the conversation, she rushed to answer it.

Maddie and David tumbled through the front door. "Cassie!" Maddie squealed.

"Maddie!"

They threw themselves into each other's arms and hugged as if they hadn't seen each other in four hundred years.

"Guess what?" Maddie's eyes danced. "I'm pregnant!"

"With twins," David added.

Maddie and Cassie squealed and hugged all over again, dancing around the kitchen. Then they hugged David.

It was only after the excitement died down that Cassie realized Harry had slipped out the door without even saying good-bye.

Chapter 25

She had turned down his gift. Apparently he wasn't good enough for her collage wall. And the only other face that Cassie had not put up on her wall was the face of her abusive ex-husband. In Cassie's mind, he and Duane were in the same category. They were the ones who had caused her the most pain.

He squeezed his eyes shut as despair washed over him. He sat parked in Diana's car outside Cassie's apartment. He'd borrowed it from her at the hospital. He was weak-kneed and aching, suffering much more than when Big Ray had beaten him up at Bodacious Booties.

Why should her rejection hurt so much? So she didn't want him on the wall. What was the big deal?

The big deal was he felt as if his insides had been ripped out. The big deal was he couldn't conceive of the idea of not having her in his life.

The reality of his feelings hit him harder than the lightning bolt he'd channeled with his djed. That's when Harrison knew that in spite of all the jockeying he'd done to hide his emotions and keep his heart safe, he'd fallen hopelessly in love with Cassie Cooper.

*   *   *

Everyone had returned for the reunification ceremony. The guests were there. Phyllis was there, as were Clyde and Diana and Adam, sans the mummy costume. The only one missing from the original group was Ahmose, who was cooling his heels in jail for attempting to destroy a priceless Egyptian artifact and Harry.

She feared Harry wasn't coming.

To stall, Cassie had given away the prizes for the faked murder mystery. She'd planned to award first prize to the most authentic solution, but since none of the guesses could touch reality, she'd picked Lashaundra Johnson as the winner for her sheer tenacity.

It was eight-thirty-five and still no Harry.

Everyone was gathered around the two sarcophagi positioned in the middle of the exhibit hall. The twin sections of the amulet were in separate display cases at the head of the sarcophagi, and between the cases sat the original djed unearthed from Kiya's tomb.

Cassie glanced at her watch again.

Eight-thirty-seven.

Adam leaned in close to her. "I can stand in for Harrison."

"That won't be necessary," Harry said. "I'm here."

Cassie looked at him and her heart leaped. He'd found his extra pair of glasses and he was wearing mismatched shoes again, but she'd never seen a more handsome sight in her life.

His eyes met hers. "I need to speak with you in private."

"Now?" She glanced at the crowd, which was staring at them expectantly.

"Now."

"Can't it wait?"

"No, it can't." Manfully, he took her elbow and hustled her into the hallway.

"What is it? What's wrong?"

"This," he said and then kissed her with more passion and need than he'd ever kissed her. "I love you, Cassie Cooper."

Her heart flipped. "Then why did you try to give me that picture for my collage wall? If you loved me, why were you walking out of my life?"

"Because you don't do commitment, remember? And besides, you turned down my picture. The only other man in your life who wasn't on that wall was Duane. Explain that one, Cassie. Do I cause you that much pain?"

"You silly man. I turned down the picture because I want so much more from you than a stupid photograph. I tore down my collage wall. For you. I burned everything. That's what I was trying to tell you when Maddie and David showed up. What I would have explained to you if you hadn't gotten afraid of your feelings and taken off."

"I'm not afraid of my feelings anymore."

"How can I believe that, Harry?"

"You'll just have to trust me on this."

"I'm not sure I can," she said.

"Cooper." Phyllis poked her head into the hallway. "The natives are getting restless. Let's get this sideshow on the road. Chop-chop."

"We better go," Cassie said.

"This isn't over." Harry held on to her arm until she looked him in the eyes. "Mark my word."

"Move it," Phyllis bellowed.

They went back into the exhibit hall.

Adam was retelling the legend of the star-crossed lovers. "And now," he said, "for the reunification of the rings of the amulet."

As they'd rehearsed the way it was supposed to happen the first night, Cassie picked up Kiya's half of the amulet. But instead of Adam taking Solen's ring, Harry picked up his section.

They came together between the two sarcophagi.

"Are you sure you want to do this?" Cassie whispered. "You're Vizier Nebamun's descendant. Are you sure you're willing to risk the curse?"

"Are you?" His eyes met hers.

She shook her head.

Adam began to read from the scroll. When he came to the line about blood transmuting all, Diana stopped him. "Whoa, wait a minute," she said.

"What?" Adam looked at his mother.

"You must have translated that wrong. Let me see it." Diana took the scroll from him. The crowd murmured with speculation.

"The translation is fine, Mother," Harrison said. "I got the same thing."

"And you used the *Math of the Sun: The Immortal Egypt* to translate it?"

"Yes, we both did," Adam said.

"Here's your problem. Your sun calculations are off. The word isn't 'blood,' but 'love.'"

"What does that mean?"

"The one element that transmutes all others," Diana read, "isn't blood, but love. It's not a human sacrifice that's needed in the formula for immortality. But love. And the way it is used at the end of this passage means that love transmutes everything else. In other words, the way to lift the curse is through love."

Cassie's eyes met Harry's. "We can transmute the curse through love."

"I love you," he said fiercely, and she could see the truth of it in his dark brown eyes. "Do you love me?"

"Just join the amulet," she said, "and find out. If you're willing to take the chance."

Harry stepped forward, slipping Solen's section of the amulet into Kiya's. The minute the amulet halves touched, a bolt of blue-white lightning shot from the djed and into the copper amulet.

The crowd gasped.

The rings melded.

Electricity shot through Cassie and Harry. Their gazes fused as surely as the amulet.

Cassie tumbled down, down, down into the glorious abyss of Harrison's dark eyes, and she was awakened. She had known him always. In a bridge across time they were joined.

Cassie was his Kiya, and he was her Solen.

She grounded him. With her sensuality, her earthiness, her authenticity. He'd always been like a kite, mentally flying high above his body, soaring over his feelings. Nothing much touched him. Nothing physical ever really got through. Until Cassie, he'd never reveled in food, never lost himself in the pleasures of the flesh. She was his anchor, his tether, the string that kept him from floating away.

Which was odd. Externally, he appeared to be the calm, centered one, and she was the flighty butterfly. But while her mind was mercurial, her body was not. She lived her physicality. Embraced her essential humanness.

Harrison could not take his gaze from her. Never had he been so captivated by anyone's face. Her eyes had such clarity, such depth. Here she was, his destiny.

All those old misguided beliefs that had caused him so much pain disappeared in the light of her love. There was no curse. Her love for him transmuted it. He realized now the truth he'd been denying for so long.

He'd been running from the thing he most deeply wanted. Through her love, she'd helped him realize his true self. He recognized, without any more doubts or misconceptions, his real nature. The external was transient, but that essence of who he was would live forever.

Like Solen and Kiya, their spirits merged for eternity.

In that moment, in his heart, Harrison realized he had believed in love all along.

About the Author

New York Times and *USA Today* bestselling author Lori Wilde has written sixty novels. She holds a bachelor's degree in nursing from Texas Christian University and a certificate in forensics. She volunteers as a sexual assault first responder for Freedom House, a shelter for battered women. Lori is a past RITA finalist and has been nominated four times for the *Romantic Times* Reviewers' Choice Award. She's won the Colorado Award of Excellence, the Wisconsin Write Touch Award, the Lories, the More Than Maggie, the Golden Quill, the Laurel Wreath, and the Best Books of 2006 Book Award. Her books have been translated into twenty-five languages and featured in *Cosmopolitan*, *Redbook*, *Complete Woman*, *All You*, *TIME*, and *Quick and Simple* magazines. She lives in Texas with her husband, Bill.

You can learn more at:
LoriWilde.com
Twitter @LoriWilde
Facebook.com

Las Vegas private eye Charlee
Champagne is absolutely fearless.
But when handsome Mason Gentry
strides into her office, she can't
control the goose bumps...

Please see the next page for a preview of

License to Thrill

from the Lori Wilde collection

Mad About You.

Nothing but nothing scared Charlee Champagne except black widow spiders and wealthy, long-legged, brown-eyed, handsome men with matinee-idol smiles and a day's growth of beard stubble.

In her five years as a Las Vegas private investigator, Charlee had never once lost her cool. Being alley-cornered at midnight by a stiletto-wielding transvestite produced nary a wobbly knee. Getting dragged ten feet behind a robbery suspect's Nissan Pathfinder had created not a single spike in her pulse rate.

And just last week she'd averted disaster when she'd calmly faced down a halfdozen gangbangers and convinced them the banana in her jacket pocket was actually a forty-five-caliber Grizzly Magnum.

Cucumbers had nothing on Charlee.

But something about mean mama black widows and rich, long-legged, brown-eyed, handsome, matinee-idol-smiling, beard-stubble-sporting men slid right under her skin and wreaked havoc with her bravado.

She had earned both phobias legitimately. The spider heebie-jeebies dated back to an ugly outhouse incident in rural Wisconsin when she was twelve. She had never looked at a roll of toilet paper in quite the same way since.

Her second fear, however, was a bit more convoluted. At the same time George Clooneyesque men terrified her, she was wildly, madly, impossibly attracted to them.

And the scars from those mistakes, while less noticeable than the half-dollar-sized hole in her left butt cheek, were a sight more painful than any spider bite.

As a self-defense technique, she'd developed a highly honed sense of respect for her phobias. So when the hairs at the nape of her neck spiked that Wednesday afternoon in late March, she snapped to full alert.

She sat cocked back in front of the computer in her two-woman detective agency located in a downtown strip mall, her size ten, neon blue, Tony Lama boots propped up on one corner of the desk and her keyboard nestled in her lap. She was completing the final paperwork on a missing person's case where she had successfully located a six-year-old girl snatched by her father after a custody dispute didn't go in his favor.

Immediately, her gaze flew to the corners of the room. No sign of a black widow's unmistakably messy cobweb. Slowly, she released her drawn breath, but the prickly uproar on the back of her neck persisted.

From the corner of her eye she spied movement on the window ledge. Something small and black and spindly-legged scurried.

Her boots hit the cement floor and her hand grabbed for a makeshift weapon, coming up with a well-thumbed, trade paperback copy of *Find Out Anything About Anyone*.

Pulse pounding in her throat, she advanced upon the window.

The cool cobalt taste of fear spilled into her mouth. Her legs quivered like she had a neurological disorder. Instant sweat pearled into the delicate indentation between her nose and her upper lip.

She had to force each step, but finally she hovered within killing range. She raised the book over her head, sucked in her breath for added courage, and stared down at the intimidating creature.

No telltale red hourglass.

Hmm. Charlee narrowed her eyes.

Not a black widow after all. Closer scrutiny revealed the creature wasn't even black.

Just a fuzzy wolf spider.

Oh, thank heavens.

Relieved, she sank her forehead against the window-pane and let the book fall from her relaxed grasp.

And that's when she spotted him.

Zigzagging his way through the parking lot—looking utterly out of place in the Las Vegas desert in his rum-pled Armani suit, dusty Gucci loafers, and a red silk tie that appeared to cost more than Charlee's last tax refund check—meandered a fear far greater than a whole pack of poisonous arachnids.

Like a battalion of marines at roll call, her neck hairs marshaled to five-alarm status. She stumbled back to her desk, jerked open the bottom drawer, retrieved a pair of Nighthawk binoculars, fixed the scopes on him, and fid-dled with the focus.

Gotcha.

Hair the color of coal. Chocolate brown eyes. A five o'clock shadow ringing his craggy jawline. Handsome as the day was long.

Her heart tommy-gunned. Ratta-tatta-tat.

Charlee gulped. Please let him go to the Quickee-Lube-Express next door. Or better yet, the massage parlor on the corner.

No such luck. He headed straight for the Sikes Detective Agency, a determined look on his face. The one thing she still had going for her—he wasn't smiling. Charlee's hand trembled so hard that she fumbled with the binoculars.

Yipes.

She had to do something. Quick.

For some unfathomable reason, guys like him were often attracted to her and she never failed to fall for their smiles and swagger. Call it a genetic deficiency. Her mother, Bubbles, God rest her soul, had been the same way.

When Charlee was seven, Tommy Ledbetter, the devastatingly cute son of the man who owned the used car dealership where her grandmother Maybelline worked as a mechanic, had lured Charlee behind the garage for a rousing game of I'll-show-you-mine-if-you-show-me-yours.

She had obliged when he threw in a pack of Twizzlers as an added bribe, only to be caught red-hineyed by Mr. Ledbetter. Tommy, the wimp, had declared the whole thing Charlee's idea. Maybelline had gotten fired over that embarrassing incident.

Then when she was fourteen and Maybelline was tending bar at an exclusive country club in Estes Park, Colorado, Vincent Keneer, whose father owned part interest in the Denver Broncos, stole a kiss from her on the ninth green. She was in seventh heaven for a few hours only to later overhear him laughing with his friends. "Getting Charlee to kiss me was easier than turning on a light switch," he had bragged.

Charlee's temper had gotten the better of her and she'd shoved Vincent into the deep end of the pool with his cashmere vest on. Maybelline lost that job too for refusing to make Charlee apologize.

And then when she was nineteen...

She closed her eyes and swallowed hard. No, she refused to relive *that* excruciating memory. Some cuts sliced so deep they never healed.

What was it about her? She must secrete some kind of take-advantage-of-me-then-break-my-heart pheromone. Or maybe it was like how cats seemed to know when you were allergic to them and they singled you out in a crowd and insisted on crawling into your lap.

Why buck the odds? She needed all the help she could muster. Charlee snatched open the desk drawers in a desperate search for any kind of a disguise. Nabbing a pencil from the cup beside her printer, she harvested her hair off her shoulders, wound the thick mass into a twist, and anchored it to the top of her head.

Frumpy. Think frumpy.

If he so much as cracked a grin, even a little one, she was a goner.

Okay, librarian hair wasn't enough. She needed more. Charlee scuttled over to Maybelline's desk and rummaged through the contents.

Ah-ha! Her granny's spare pair of thick, black bifocals oughtta do the trick.

Charlee jammed the glasses on her face, grateful for the twofold shield. Now, not only would she look un-flirtworthy in the heavy frames, but also while peering through the blurry lenses she would be unable to fully ascertain his level of cuteness. She hazarded another quick peek out the window, but had to peer over the top of Maybelline's glasses in order to see him without getting dizzy.

Who was this guy?

He stopped when he passed her cherry red 1964 Corvette convertible in the parking lot and ran a lingering hand over the fender like he was caressing a woman's inner thigh. Charlee's stomach fluttered as if he'd stroked *her* and her muscles tightened a couple of notches below her turquoise belt buckle.

Repo man?

Nah. She was ninety-nine percent sure she'd mailed her car payment, even though she did have a tendency to get so wrapped up in a case she sometimes forgot to eat or sleep or post her bills. Besides, the dude looked nothing like a repo man. Actually, he resembled a refugee from an investment banker caucus.

Or an escapee from a corporate law office.

A lawyer?

Oh, no. Was Elwood in the pokey again and looking to her for bail money? Charlee shook her head. As if her no-account daddy could afford the services of a guy who dressed like a *GQ* cover model.

A lawsuit?

Her accountant Wilkie had warned her that being sued was an eventuality in her line of work and he'd encouraged her to take out more insurance. But between keeping the business afloat and bailing out her old man when he was in between his Elvis impersonating gigs and had succumbed to the lure of another get-rich-quick scheme, she didn't have a lot of spare cash left over for frivolous things like insurance.

The guy had almost reached her door and Charlee, roosting on the verge of hyperventilation, did not know which way to jump. She stepped right, then left, ended up doing a strange little mambo, and finally jammed the binoculars under a chair cushion. She even considered ducking into the closet until he went away.

But what if he wanted to hire her? Business was

business. She'd just completed her only pending case and she needed the money.

Yeah? So tell that to her stomach spinning like a whirligig in gale force winds. In the end, she leaped behind Maybelline's desk and feigned grave interest in her blank computer screen.

The silver cowbell over the door tinkled.

Be strong. Be brave. Be badass.

"Hello?"

Ah, damn. He possessed the deep, smoky voice of a late-night radio announcer. Charlee lifted her head and forced herself to look at the man standing in the doorway.

"Good afternoon," she replied, her tone a couple of degrees above frosty. No sense making the guy welcome. If she was rude enough, maybe he would take a hike.

The top of his head grazed the cowbell, causing it to peal again.

Dear God, he was at least six feet three, maybe even taller. And no wedding band graced the third finger of his left hand. Charlee tumbled as if she were on an Alpine ski run, a beginner who had taken a wrong turn and ended up on the black diamond expert slope with nowhere to go but down, down, down.

"Is there something you need?" she asked, making sure she sounded extra snippy and squinting disapprovingly at him through Maybelline's bifocals.

"Yes, ma'am," the paragon drawled in a smooth Texas accent.

In spite of his slightly blurry appearance, he was outrageously good-looking, right down to his straight white teeth. They had to be bonded. Nobody's natural teeth looked that perfect. His suit—while slightly wrinkled—fit like a dream, accentuating his broad shoulders and narrow hips.

He smelled like the wickedly wonderful blend of expensive cologne and the faint but manly musk of perspiration. His beautiful black hair was clipped short, making one statement while the dark stubble on his jaw made another.

Charlee wanted to rip off the borrowed glasses and feast on him like Thanksgiving turkey. The desire scared her to the very marrow of her bones.

Something sparked in his deep brown bedroom eyes and she caught a glimmer of sudden heat when their gazes met—or maybe it was just that Maybelline's glasses needed cleaning.

He sauntered toward her, oozing charisma from every pore.

Charlee forgot to breathe.

And then he committed the gravest sin of all, knocking her world helter-skelter.

The scoundrel smiled.

Mason Gentry gave the woman behind the desk his best public-relations grin. The grin—and the Gentry name— opened doors. Accustomed to getting what he wanted, Mason wanted one thing and one thing only.

To track down the floozy who'd lured his grandfather Nolan—along with a half-million dollars in family company funds—to sin city.

Mason's primary aim? Locate Gramps, drag him home to Houston (hopefully with the money still intact), and get back to the investment deal he'd been in the process of bringing in before his older brother, Hunter, had taken over and sent him after their grandfather. He was still seething about the injustice. Why did Hunter earn the plum jobs while he got scut work?

Oh, yes. One other thing. Nolan's unexpected and

larcenous departure had forced Mason to postpone his engagement party.

He'd planned to ask his girlfriend of three years, Daphne Maxwell, to marry him this weekend in exactly the same fashion his father had proposed to his mother. Over veal parmigiana at Delveccio's, with fifty of their closest friends joining the festivity.

At the thought of Daphne, Mason's spirits lifted. For once in his life, he would have one up on his brother. He would be married to the perfect high-society wife.

Everyone in his family loved Daphne. She was refined, cultured, and sophisticated, with a myriad of business contacts and a pedigree she could trace back to the *Mayflower*.

Daphne was everything he'd ever looked for in a wife. They had the same values, the same friends, and they wanted the same things from life. So what if there wasn't much sexual chemistry. A good marriage consisted of so much more than fireworks.

Right?

"What do you want?" the woman demanded, squinting up at him from behind an ugly pair of glasses, her long black hair spilling haphazardly from an awkward bun secured to her head with a pencil.

Could she be the woman he was searching for?

He remembered the paper in his pocket. He'd found Maybelline Sikes's name and this address scrawled on a notepad in Gramps's bedroom. The nameplate on the desk said Maybelline Sikes, but she didn't look like a Maybelline.

She looked like nothing but trouble with her determined little chin set and her smoldering emerald eyes flashing a challenge. Unlucky for her, Mason adored a challenge.

She wore an unflattering western-style shirt, faded jeans with a rip at the knee, and the most gawd-awful neon blue cowboy boots he had ever laid eyes upon. Not a shred of makeup graced her face. Granted, with her long, dark lashes and full raspberry-colored lips she didn't need cosmetics to look good, but she did not fit the image of the busty, brash, blond femme fatale in stilettos and pearls he'd concocted in his head.

Nor had he expected her to be a private detective. Really, she was way too young for Gramps. But then again, gold diggers came in all shapes, ages, and professions.

"I'm waiting." She arched an eyebrow and he noticed she clutched a pen so tight her knuckles were actually white. The lady was not nearly as composed as she appeared.

Mason draped one leg over the corner of her desk and leaned in close until they were almost nose-to-nose, his intent to intimidate.

"I want to know where my grandfather is," he said, continuing to smile but narrowing his eyes so she would understand he meant business. "And I want to know now."

She sank her top teeth into her bottom lip and unflinchingly returned his stare, but despite her bluster he could tell from the brief flicker of uneasiness flitting across her face she wanted to back away.

"You're gonna have to be more specific. I have no idea what you're talking about."

He shouldn't have noticed the long, smooth curve of her neck, but he found his gaze lingering on the pulse point jumping at her throat. She was nervous. Oh, yeah. But very adept at cloaking her uneasiness. He couldn't help but admire her grace under pressure. He had reduced many an inefficient employee to tongue-tied stammers with his silent stares. But she wasn't buying his bluster.

"Nolan Gentry. Where is he?"

She laid the pen down, steepled her fingertips, and

blinked owlishly at him from behind those hideous glasses. "Let me get this straight. Do you want to hire me to find your missing grandfather?"

"He came here to meet you. Are you telling me you haven't seen him?"

"I'm sorry, mister, I don't even know who he is. Or who you are for that matter."

"My name's Mason Gentry. I'm an investment banker from Houston and I've come to retrieve my grandfather."

"What does that have to do with me?"

She met his eyes. Their glares slammed into each other. Hot, hard, defiant.

She was a tough one all right, but he didn't miss her telltale gulp and the determined way she clenched her jaw. No matter how composed she might appear, the woman was afraid of him.

"Aren't you Maybelline Sikes?" He tapped the name-plate.

"No. I'm not. I'm her granddaughter."

Instant relief rolled over him. His grandfather had hightailed himself across the desert to see the woman's grandmother, not her. Why the knowledge lifted his spirits, he had no clue. What did it matter whether it was the granddaughter or the grandmother who was after Nolan's fortune? The results were the same.

"So what's your name?"

"Charlee Champagne."

"Beg your pardon?" he asked, not sure he'd heard correctly.

"Charlee Champagne," she repeated.

"Oh."

For no particular reason the phrase *Good Time Charlee* popped into his mind's eye along with a very provocative image of a tipsy Charlee boogieing with a lampshade on her head and wearing a very naughty black silk nightie. He could see the picture all too clearly. Perturbed, Mason shook his head to dispel the unwanted mental photograph.

Charlee sighed and then spoke as if she'd recited the details many times before. "My mother was a dancer at the Folies Bergère and had her name legally changed to Bubbles Champagne. She and my father were never married. What can I say? She was a bit frivolous. Any more questions?"

"Do you know where I can find Ms. Sikes?"

"She's incommunicado."

"Meaning?"

"She's gone on her annual fishing retreat and she can't be reached, but let me assure you she most certainly is not with your grandfather."

"How can you be so sure?"

"Maybelline hates men. Especially rich ones."

"Who said my grandfather is rich?" Mason didn't believe her for a second. No doubt she was covering for her grandmother.

Charlee waved a hand at his Rolex. "Like grandfather like grandson."

"So, you're claiming your grandmother can't be reached?"

"No claiming to it. It's the truth."

"No cell phone?"

"She can't stand 'em. Says they give you brain cancer."

"No beeper?"

"Nope. That's the whole point of the trip. Uninterrupted peace and quiet."

"I think you're lying."

Charlee shrugged. "Believe what you want."

"It's imperative I speak with Ms. Sikes," Mason said in a controlled, measured manner. He was through fooling around with Miss I'm-Going-To-Be-No-Help-Whatsoever

Champagne. He wanted his grandfather found. "If Ms. Sikes can't be reached by electronic means then I will go to her fishing cabin. Give me directions."

"No."

"What?" His glare intensified. Sweat pooled around his collar. In his mad, twenty-four-hour sprint from Houston to Vegas, he hadn't even bothered to change from his business suit and he was broiling like filet mignon at a backyard barbeque.

That's what happened when you allowed single-minded focus to overcome common sense. Stubborn persistence was his biggest flaw and his greatest strength. His father often joked Mason was like an obstinate snapping turtle, never knowing when to turn loose.

"You heard me." She raised her chin, daring him to call her bluff.

He stared openmouthed. He wasn't accustomed to being refused anything. Testiness was his first instinct but something told him venting his frustration would be the wrong tactic to take. She'd most likely dig into her view. He could see she had a bit of snapping turtle in her too.

Forcing a smile, he slipped an amiable tone into his voice. "I think maybe we got off on the wrong foot. Why don't we start over?"

"Okay."

"My grandfather Nolan disappeared out of the blue with a substantial amount of money. We found a note in his room indicating he was on his way to meet your grandmother here in Vegas. We're really concerned about him. He's been behaving a bit out of character lately. I need to speak with your grandmother to find out if she has heard from him."

"Sorry," she said. "Maybelline left strict orders not to be disturbed. I can't help you."

"Can't? Or won't?"

"Take your pick."

"So that's the way it's going to be."

"Maybelline will be home in a couple of days. You can speak to her then. In the meantime, relax. Have fun. See Vegas. Enjoy a holiday." Under her breath she muttered, "With that stick-up-your-butt attitude you certainly look as if you could use one."

Like hell.

No way was he waiting a couple of days. In a couple of days Nolan and Maybelline could run through the half million at the craps table. Besides, in a couple more days Hunter would have the Birkweilder deal—*his* deal—sewn up, and would be busily collecting accolades from their father without giving Mason credit.

He gritted his teeth and fell back on his third line of offense. When authority and charm fail, there's always money. He removed his wallet from his jacket pocket, unfolded the expensive leather case, and pulled out a crisp new Benjamin Franklin.

"How much is the information going to cost me?" He slapped a second hundred on the desk.

Charlee gasped. He could practically feel the anger emanating off of her.

What? Two C notes weren't enough. Obviously, she was as greedy as her grandmother.

"Three hundred?" Mason added another bill to the stack.

"Are you trying to buy me off?"

"Let's make it an even five."

"Buddy, you can just keep peeling until your wallet is empty, because I'll never tell you where Maybelline is. There isn't enough money in the world."

Fall in Love with Forever Romance

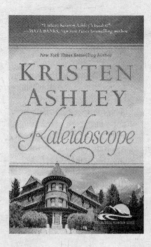

KALEIDOSCOPE
by Kristen Ashley

When old friends become new lovers, anything can happen. And now that Deck finally has a chance with Emme, he's not going to let her past get in the way of their future. Fans of Julie Ann Walker, Lauren Dane, and Julie James will love Kristen Ashley's *New York Times* bestselling Colorado Mountain series!

BOLD TRICKS
by Karina Halle

Ellie Watt has only one chance at saving the lives of her father and mother. But the only way to come out of this alive is to trust one of two very dangerous men who will stop at nothing to have her love in this riveting finale of Karina Halle's *USA Today* bestselling Artists Trilogy.

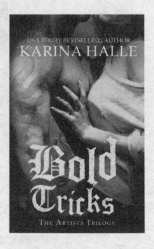

Fall in Love with Forever Romance

DECADENT
by Adrianne Lee

Fans of Robyn Carr and Sherryl Woods will enjoy the newest book set at Big Sky Pie! Fresh off a divorce, Roxy isn't looking for another relationship, but there's something about her buttoned-up contractor that she can't resist. What that man clearly needs is something decadent—like her...

THE LAST COWBOY IN TEXAS
by Katie Lane

Country music princess Starlet Brubaker has a sweet tooth for moon pies and cowboys: both are yummy—and you can never have just one. Beckett Cates may not be her usual type, but he may be the one to put Starlet's boy-crazy days behind her... Fans of Linda Lael Miller and Diana Palmer will love it, darlin'!

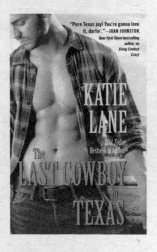

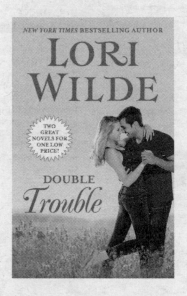